JUL - - 2021

GRACE AND GLORY

Books by Jennifer L. Armentrout
available from Inkyard Press

The Harbinger★
(in reading order)

Storm and Fury
Rage and Ruin
Grace and Glory

The Dark Elements
(in reading order)

Bitter Sweet Love★★
White Hot Kiss
Stone Cold Touch
Every Last Breath

Stand-alone titles

The Problem with Forever
If There's No Tomorrow

★Set in the world of The Dark Elements; can be read separately.
★★Ebook prequel companion novella; does not need to be read to
enjoy the full-length novels.

JENNIFER L. ARMENTROUT

GRACE AND GLORY

inkyard
PRESS

ISBN-13: 978-1-335-21278-8

Grace and Glory

This edition published by arrangement with Harlequin Books S.A.

For questions and comments about the quality of this book, please contact us at CustomerService@Harlequin.com.

Inkyard Press
22 Adelaide St. West, 40th Floor
Toronto, Ontario M5H 4E3, Canada
www.InkyardPress.com

Printed in U.S.A.

To all the health-care workers, first responders and essential workers who have worked tirelessly and endlessly to save lives and to keep stores open, at great risk to their own lives and the lives of their loved ones. Thank you.

1

Zayne stood only a few feet from me, the surprisingly cool July breeze lifting the edges of his blond hair off bare shoulders.

Or that was what I *believed* I was seeing.

I was slowly going blind. My line of sight was already severely restricted with little to no peripheral vision. Eventually, there'd be nothing but a pinprick of sight left. To make seeing things all the more iffy, cataracts had formed in both eyes, causing my central vision to be blurry and eyes even more sensitive to light. It was a genetic disease known as retinitis pigmentosa, and not even all the angelic blood pumping through my veins could prevent the disease from progressing. Bright light of any sort made it difficult for me to see and low light wasn't any better, making everything shadowy and hard to see at night.

So, with only the lampposts inside Rock Creek Park lighting the walking path behind me, it was more than possible that I wasn't seeing what I thought I was. I'd also gone through a hellish trauma mere days ago, handed a beatdown of epic proportions by the psychotic archangel Gabriel, also known as the Harbinger of Overlong Monologues, so God only knew what that had done to my eyes.

Or my brain.

Zayne could be a hallucination, one driven by brain damage or grief. Either of those two things actually made more sense. Because how was he standing in front of me? Zayne was...oh God, he had died, his body having turned to dust by now, as all Wardens' did upon death. The bond that had linked us together, made him my Protector, gave us both strength and speed, had turned on us the moment I truly acknowledged how much I was in love with him. He'd been physically weakened, and Gabriel had taken advantage of that. I'd heard Zayne say his last words. *It's okay.* I'd watched him take his last breath. I'd felt that cord that had connected us together as Protector and Trueborn snap inside me.

He'd died.

He was dead.

But he was right there, standing in front of me, and I smelled freshly fallen snow and mint—*wintermint.* It was stronger than before, as if the summer air was soaked in winter.

Because of that scent, for a moment, I wondered if he were a spirit—someone who'd died and crossed over. When souls who'd moved on to the great beyond came to check in on loved ones, people often smelled something that reminded them of the person who'd passed on. A perfume. Toothpaste. A cigar. Bonfire. It could be anything, because Heaven...Heaven had a certain scent; it smelled like whatever you desired most, and I wanted Zayne to be alive more than I wanted anything.

I smelled Heaven right now.

But even with my funky vision, I could see that Zayne wasn't a spirit. That he was flesh and blood—*glowing* flesh and blood. His skin held a faint luminous glow that hadn't been present before.

Dizziness swept through me as I stared into eyes that were no longer the palest blue. Now they were an intense, vibrant hue, reminding me of the brief moments at twilight when the sky was the deepest shade of sapphire. Wardens didn't even have eyes like that, nor did they glow like one of those old Glo Worm dolls Jada had once found in the attic when we were kids.

And Wardens sure as Hell didn't have the kind of wings spreading out from Zayne's broad shoulders. They weren't Warden wings, which often reminded me of smooth leather. Oh, no, these were feathered—white and thick with streaks of gold glowing with heavenly fire, with *grace*.

Only two things in this world and beyond, outside of God, carried the potent and all-powerful *grace* within them. I was one of those things.

But Zayne hadn't been a Trueborn like me, and neither had he been like the few humans who had an angel perched on their family tree, giving them a watered-down, way less powerful *grace* that either enabled them to see ghosts and spirits or caused them to display other psychic abilities. I'd been told my whole life that I was the only Trueborn, a first-generation child of an angel and a human, but that hadn't been exactly true. There had been Sulien, Gabriel's offspring, but Zayne had killed him, so I guessed I was back to being the unique person that I was. All of that was irrelevant, because Zayne had been a Warden.

The only other being with that kind of *grace* and wings was an angel, but Zayne hadn't been that, either.

But he totally had angel wings now—feathered angel wings that glowed with *grace*.

"Trin...?" he said, and I sucked in a sharp breath. Oh God, it was his voice, and my entire body seemed to shake. I would've given up just about anything to hear his voice again, and now I was.

I took a shaky step forward.

"I can...sense you." Confusion filled his voice as he stared at me.

Did he mean the Protector bond? I searched for the buzz of awareness, the hint of emotions that weren't mine. I found nothing. There was no cord. No bond.

He wasn't my Protector any longer.

"Trinity," he repeated softly, and I heard it then. The tone of his voice. It was off. More than just confusion. "The name...it means something."

My heart skipped a beat. "Because it's my name."

He tilted his head into the shadows, but I could still feel his stare. Did he...did he not remember me? Concern blossomed. I had no idea how he came back or why he resembled an angel, but if something had happened to him to affect his memory, I would help him. We'd figure it out together. All that mattered was that he was alive. I took another step, lifting my arm—

One moment he was standing several feet away, and then the next he was right in front of me, those incredible wings blocking out the world behind him. Zayne had moved faster than any Warden could—faster than even me.

I flinched in surprise, jerking my head away. In the back of my mind, I knew that Zayne, knowing how my vision worked and how hard it was for me to track movement, wouldn't have moved liked that. But something was clearly up with his memories and—

Zayne grabbed my hand as he dipped his chin, inhaling deeply. He shuddered, lifting his head. My eyes widened. As close as he was now, I could see the familiar lines and angles of his face, but I saw them...I saw them more clearly, and that didn't make sense, either. His wings blocked out the moonlight, and the glow of the nearby lampposts wasn't close enough to explain how I could see him so well. His features were too distinct, and there...there really was this glow under—

"Do you think you can take me on, little nephilim?" he demanded.

Wait. What?

All my senses went on high alert as I stared up at him. "Little—?"

Healing skin and muscles protested, flaring hotly as he pulled me against his chest. His arm clamped down on my waist like an arm of steel. The hold was crushing but the contact of his body against mine was still a shock to the system, scattering thoughts and silencing the warning bells that were starting to go off loudly. He lowered his head once more, and my entire body tensed in anticipation. There was a whole lot of weird going on, but he was going to kiss me, and I would never not want—

He buried his face in my hair, inhaling deeply once more. "Your scent… I know it. It calls to me. Why?"

"Because you, uh, know me?" I suggested.

"Maybe," Zayne murmured, and for a moment, he just held me, and I started to take that as a good sign. "But you… I recognize the *grace*. It's powerful. Like an *archangel*," he said, the last word spit out like he was talking about some kind of incurable disease.

What in the holy Hell?

I turned my head, unable to raise my arms from where they were trapped at my sides. "Zayne, it's me," I said, trying to make sense of what was happening. "Trinity."

He went incredibly still. "There is something important— your name, your smell," he interrupted, shuddering once more as his hold on me softened. "I feel too much. All the greed and gluttony, the loathing and hatred. It's *inside* me, filling me up."

That…that didn't sound good at all.

"But you smell amazing. Intoxicating. It's familiar," he repeated. He shifted his head, and I felt his mouth against my jaw.

I gasped, senses overwhelmed by the burst of warring sensations. My body was all on board with his closeness, but not my brain or my heart. "Let go of me, and we'll figure out what's going on."

Zayne didn't let go.

He *laughed*.

And that laugh…it was nothing like the sound I loved and cherished. Shivers crawled across my skin, and not in the fun, good way. His laugh was cold, cruel even, and there wasn't a single part of him that was cruel. "Put me down, Zayne."

"Stop calling me that."

My heart stuttered. "That's your name."

"I have no name."

"Yes, you do. It's Zayne—"

"And I'll put you down when I feel like it," he interrupted. "Guess what, little nephilim. I don't want to."

Okay. I loved him with my whole being—loved him more than anything. I was also superconcerned about his mental state at the moment. I wanted to help him, and I would, but he was really starting to tick me off.

"Stop calling me *little nephilim*," I warned.

"It's what you are."

"What I am is a Trueborn, but neither of those things are my name. It's Trinity or Trin." I squirmed, trying to wiggle free. A low, animalistic sound radiated from the back of his throat. "Put me down or I swear to God—"

"God? You swear to God?" He laughed again. "God has abandoned us all."

A shock went through me. A wild mixture of relief, confusion, irritation and something far stronger, and shattering. For the first time since I'd known Zayne, I felt fear in his arms.

My body went ice-cold, and my own personal alarm system reacted to the bolt of fear. Deep inside me, my *grace* sparked.

Zayne hissed—he actually *hissed*—like an angry, feral cat. An angry, very large feral cat the moment my *grace* pulsed inside me. That was beyond weird.

Instinct took over. Twisting my body, I ignored the pain from all the healing injuries and brought my knee up, slamming it into his groin.

Or at least, I tried to.

Zayne anticipated the move. My knee hit his thigh. A wave of anger and rapidly growing panic whipped through me as my *grace* pressed at me, demanding to be let out, but I fought it down. He was confused and he'd just come back from being dead with angel wings, so I didn't want to hurt him *too* badly. My *grace* would do more than that. It would kill him.

Managing to get an arm free, I punched him in the jaw, hard enough to send a flare of pain across my knuckles, and he smiled. He smiled like I hadn't even punched him, and the curve of his lips was all wrong. It was icy and inhuman.

"Ouch," he murmured. "You're going to have to do better than that."

I jabbed out with my palm, catching him under the chin. He grunted in pain as he pushed—no, *threw*—me aside. I hit the ground several feet back with a sharp yelp. Shock still had its tight grip on me, dampening the sting of a fresh new wave of pain as I looked up at him in realization.

This was Zayne but not.

He would never toss me like a Frisbee. Even if I deserved it, and God knows, I could be extremely obnoxious, but Zayne would never do that. I could kick him straight in the face, and he would never lift a finger against me in any way that would harm me.

Shaking off the pain and confusion, I climbed to my knees—

There was a blur of golden skin and wings, too fast for me to track, and then he had ahold of the scruff of my shirt. He lifted me off the ground and straight into the air. I dangled several *feet* from the ground.

Holy crap.

His wings rose and spread out. They were massive and beautiful. Also, really frightening at the moment. He held me there like I was nothing more than a toddler throwing a tantrum! A small one, at that.

And that really flipped my bitch switch.

I kicked out, catching him in the stomach. His grip on my shirt loosened, and then suddenly I was *flying*.

I landed on my stomach, slamming into the ground once more. Pain lanced my ribs as the air rushed out of my lungs. Okay. *That* was what being tossed like a Frisbee really felt like. Now I knew the difference. Good to know. Groaning, I flipped over and started to sit up. I didn't make it very far. He was there, above me, his face in mine. Those brilliant blue eyes were like shards of ice. His stare chilled my flesh, my soul.

"Zayne, please—"

He gripped my chin, fingers pressing into my skin. "Stop calling me that."

"It's your name—"

"It is not."

"Then what am I supposed to call you?" I shouted. "Jackass?"

One side of his lips kicked up. "You may call me death. How does that sound?"

A whole lot of fear blasted my system, but I hid it. "How does that sound? It sounds pretty stupid."

The smirk froze.

I swung my fist.

His hand snapped out, catching my wrist. He hadn't even

taken his eyes off mine—hadn't even let go of my chin. "This feels familiar."

"Me telling you something you've said sounds stupid? Because it should—"

"No." His eyes narrowed. "This. The fighting."

"That's because we've trained together! We've fought each other," I told him in a rush, trying to overcome my panic and anger. "Not to hurt each other. Never to hurt each other."

"Never to hurt each other," he repeated slowly, as if he couldn't comprehend how those words went together. His head twisted to the side as his eyes closed. "This isn't..." His fingers dug in, squeezing until I was sure that my jaw would splinter. "You know me. You're important."

I swallowed down the fear. "Because...because we do know each other. We're together. You wouldn't do this. You wouldn't hurt me."

"I wouldn't?" He sounded even more confused. "Why is that? You're a nephilim. You carry an archangel's *grace*."

"That doesn't matter. You wouldn't hurt me because you love me," I whispered, voice cracking. Tears filled my eyes. "That's why."

"Love?" He jolted as if burned, letting go of my chin. "I love you?"

"Yes. Yes! We love each other, Zayne, and whatever has happened to you, we can fix this. We can figure it out together and—"

"We?" His hand curled around my throat, the grip a fraction from being deadly. "There is no we. There is no Zayne," he spat. "I am *Fallen*."

There wasn't time for those words to do any damage or for them to make sense. His hand clamped down until only the thinnest amount of air could get through. I had no idea if he would squeeze or not. If so, had he come back to life just to kill me? Seemed fitting in an ironic way. If that turned out to be the case, obviously I was going to be superdead and superpissed, but I'd also be so heartbroken. Because when Zayne snapped out of whatever this was, the knowledge of what he'd done would kill him all over again.

I didn't deserve this.

Neither did he.

What I did next was hard to explain. My hands lifted without conscious thought. I placed my trembling fingers against his cheek and pressed my palm against his chest. Flesh against flesh.

Zayne blinked, releasing his hold as he jerked back. There was a brief glimpse of confusion clouding his bright eyes as I twisted to the side, sucking in glorious oxygen. I didn't know what made him let me go, what stopped him from applying just a little more pressure. Too happy to be breathing again, I really didn't care at the moment.

His hand closed over my shoulder, and I tensed, but all he did was roll me onto my back. It was *almost* tender.

"What…" He shook his head again, sending strands of blond hair swinging. "Why wouldn't you attack me? Why would you touch me? I can feel the power in you. You can fight me. You won't win, but it's better than just lying there."

Better than not killing him, I wanted to say, but even I could realize there was no point in doing so. Reasoning with him wasn't going to work. I could scream from the rooftops that I loved him, and it wasn't going to make a difference. I had to get out of here, get somewhere safe to figure out what the Hell was happening. I hated to do what I was about to do, but there was no other option.

Reaching to my thigh, I unsheathed the iron dagger that had remained hidden under the length of my shirt.

"Why won't you fight me?" he demanded. "You're the enemy. You should fight me."

I couldn't even process him calling me the enemy. "I won't fight you because I love you, you freaking idiot." My fingers wrapped around the handle of the dagger as his features settled into the look he always gave me when I did something he couldn't understand, which had been often. It tore at my heart.

"I'm sorry," I whispered.

Zayne tilted his head to the side again. "Sorry for—"

I reared off the dirt and grass, swiping my arm in a high arc. The sharp edge of the blade caught him under the chin. I kept the blow quick and shallow, just enough to stun him.

Zayne stumbled back, his beautiful face contorting in fury. He clasped his throat, letting out a roar that sent chills to my very soul. Springing to my feet, I didn't hesitate. I took off as if the very devil was after me.

I ran and ran, blindly cutting through traffic and nearly mowing down countless people as my sneakers pounded off pavement. How I didn't get flattened by a car was beyond me. Every part of my body hurt, but I didn't slow down. I didn't even know where I was going—

Follow me.

My feet stumbled as the voice that was so not mine echoed around me. Breathing heavy, I slowed. Harsh yellow street-lights cast ominous shadows along the sidewalks. Faces and bodies were nothing more than shapeless blurs as horns honked from the street and people shouted.

Follow me, Trueborn.

Either I was losing my mind, which in my humble, non-biased opinion would be completely understandable at this point, or I was actually hearing a voice in my head.

But didn't hearing voices in your head also mean you were losing your mind?

Follow me, child of Michael. It is your only hope to restore the one who Fell for you.

A sudden image of what had looked like a star plummeting to Earth formed. Zayne. That had been Zayne.

Fallen.

He said he was Fallen.

I knew what that meant, but it couldn't be.

Follow me.

The voice…it sounded like it bled power. It was no voice I could imagine. I swallowed dryly, my gaze darting around erratically and seeing nothing. Zayne had come back from the dead—he'd come back different in a very *Pet Sematary* way, and with wings, but he'd come back. That was him, and he was alive, so I could very well be hearing a real voice in my head.

Anything was possible at this point.

But if the voice was real, how in the world was I supposed to follow something I couldn't see?

No sooner had that thought finished, I heard, *Trust your* grace. *It knows where to go. You're already halfway to where you need to be.*

Trust my *grace*? I almost laughed, but I was too winded to

do so. I was already halfway to where I needed to be? All I
had been doing was running…

I'd been running blindly.

I'd run with no real conscious thought. Just like when I
touched Zayne. Instinct had taken over both times, and instinct and *grace* were one and the same.

I was willing to try anything that would help me figure
out what had happened to Zayne.

Picking up my pace, I started running and went straight
until I took a left. There was no reason. I just cut down a
street and then kept going. Then I took a right. It started
raining, coming down steadily. I had no idea where I was
going. Heart thumping against my ribs, I crossed a congested
corner. I hadn't heard the voice again, and just when I was
beginning to fear I had imagined it, I saw the…the church
across the street, slowly becoming more clear. Constructed
of stone and with many steeples and turrets, it looked like
something straight out of medieval times. Every part of me
knew that was where I'd been led to. How or why, I had
no idea.

I thought I recognized the church as I climbed the wide
steps, passing between two lit lampposts. Saint Patrick's or
something? Moonlight glinted off the cross above the doorway, and for a moment, it looked like it glowed with heavenly light.

Stepping under the alcove, I drew in a shallow breath.
Rain coursed down the side of my face and off my clothing. Blood caked under my mouth. Was it mine? Zayne's? I
wasn't sure. I had a sinking suspicion that I might've cracked
a rib that probably had just healed, but I felt no pain. Maybe

because I was feeling so much it didn't leave room for my body to beg for a time-out.

"Here goes nothing," I muttered, approaching the door, and halted.

Every hair on my body stood and the sense of unease grew until I found it difficult to swallow. Having no idea what to expect, I opened the heavy doors and stepped inside the building built over two centuries ago. An immediate fissure of electricity danced over my skin, like a warning that I was...that I was somewhere I didn't belong.

A child of any angel, let alone an archangel, was a big no-no even though I was basically created to fight for all the holy rollers. I shouldn't be all that surprised by how every instinct in me demanded that I turn and leave.

But I didn't.

My muscles locked as a small door to my right creaked open. A young priest swathed in white robes with red trim stepped out.

He nodded at me. "This way, please."

Unsure whether I should be grateful that I appeared to be expected or really freaked out, I got my feet moving. Quietly, I followed the priest down a narrow corridor. As we went, he stopped every few feet to light candles. If he hadn't, I probably would've walked into a wall.

Saint Brendan the Navigator's statue guarded the entrance to the nave of the church. He held a boat in one hand and a staff in the other. Saint Brigid stood opposite of him, a hand over her heart.

I had a creepy feeling that the statues were eyeing me as the priest led me toward the sanctuary. My steps faltered as my eyes slowly pieced together what I was seeing.

Four stone angels knelt on the floor, their wings tucked back. In their hands were basins of what I guessed was holy water, since I doubted they were collecting rainwater or something.

The priest stepped aside, motioning me forward. With my heart in my throat, I entered the sanctuary. Straight ahead, a thirteen-foot cross hung above the main altar, bearing both the crucified and risen Jesus.

A frigid breeze reached me, and the next breath I let out formed misty clouds. That was…odd. So was the rich scent of sandalwood accompanying the cold air. I turned and found the priest gone. Vanished.

Great.

Not to be sacrilegious or anything, but this wasn't a place I wanted to be left alone in. I started past the stone angels—

In unison, they lifted their bowed heads and held their basins out.

Oh my God, that was a whole bucketful of nightmares. My stomach dipped as I resisted the urge to run back through the hallway while stone ground against stone. One of the angels' arms broke away from the basin, moving slowly to point to the right of the altar. Chills ran over my skin as I slowly turned.

I gasped.

He stood before the altar, dressed in some sort of white tunic and pants that no one could buy off Amazon. The outline of his body seemed to shimmer as he took complete corporeal form. From the tips of the whitish blond curls down to his bare feet, he was the most beautiful thing I had ever seen.

I opened my mouth to speak, but then his wings unfolded

from his body, spanning at least eight feet in each direction. They were so luminous and white they glowed in the dim light. They moved noiselessly, but the power of those wings stirred the air, blowing back my hair even with several feet separating us. I squinted, leaning forward. What was on the tip of each wing? Something was...

Oh God.

There were eyes on the tips of his wings. Hundreds of them!

My skin crawled as my gaze went back to his face, but I had to look away quickly. It was painful—the purity to his beauty cut through my skin, shining a spotlight on every dark thought I'd ever had.

I knew what he was—what type of angel.

A Throne.

To look upon them was to expose every secret one ever held and be judged for each one. And I was being judged now. His whole demeanor, from the way he tilted his head to the side to the way his bright blue eyes seared through skin and muscle, told me that he was seeing *everything*.

And he wasn't impressed.

There was death in those crystal eyes. Not "moving on to the next stage in life" or "standing before the Pearly Gates" kind of death, but the vast emptiness of the final death— the death of a soul.

I took a deep breath and started to speak.

The angel opened his mouth.

An ear-piercing blare shook the stained-glass windows and the pews, hitting an octave that no human could make or stand. I doubled over, clutching my ears. It was like a thousand trumpets blaring at once, shaking me to the very core. The sound echoed through the sanctuary, bouncing around my skull until I was sure my head would explode. Wet warmth trickled out of my ears, down my hands.

When I didn't think I could take it anymore, the sound ceased.

Trembling, I lowered my bloodstained hands and lifted my head. The angel looked at me pitilessly as his wings continued their quiet movement.

"That was special," I croaked.

He didn't speak, and the silence that stretched out was unbearable.

"You summoned me here," I said, bracing myself for another unearthly wail. That didn't come. Neither did a response. "You said it was the only way to help Zayne."

Still, there was nothing.

And I just lost it. All the pain, the fear, the grief and even the joy of seeing Zayne again crashed through me. "You spoke in my head, didn't you? You told me to come to you."

Silence.

"Can you not hear me? Did your own scream burst your eardrums? Or is this amusing to you? Is that it? Is Gabriel trying to end this world and Heaven not enough entertainment for you? Damn you!" I yelled, scratching my throat raw. "Fine. You just want to stand here and stare at me? I can do the same thing. Better yet, how about I go outside and start telling every person I come across that angels are real. I can prove it. I'll just whip out my *grace*. Then I can introduce them to a few demons and when I'm done with—"

"That won't be necessary." He spoke in a voice that was richly musical, infinitely kind without a trace of humanity.

It was so at odds with itself that I winced. "You're here for him, the one who died protecting you."

I flinched then. "Yes. But he's alive."

"I know."

"He's not right."

"Of course not."

I shook—every part of me shook. "What happened to him? How is he here?"

The Throne tipped his head to the side. "He committed an act of selflessness and sacrifice by coming to your aid. He did so out of the purest love. He was restored to his Former Glory."

"Former Glory?" I had no idea what he was talking about.

The Throne nodded. "But he chose you. He chose to Fall."

2

The room seemed to spin as what the Throne was saying began to sink in. It didn't make sense, but I knew what the angel had meant by saying Zayne Fell. I knew what Zayne had meant when he said he was Fallen.

What I didn't understand was how it was possible.

I had to take several deep, calming breaths before I spoke again. "Zayne was a Warden and my Protector. How did he Fall when he was never an angel?"

His wings rose and then settled. "What do you think the Wardens were before they were cast unto stone? Did you believe the Creator snapped them into existence out of boredom?"

I started to frown. Yeah, that was exactly what I believed.

"No. God was not simply bored. What you call Wardens were once the guardians of man, great ones, but they failed. They caved to the lure of sin and vice. They Fell."

"I don't understand. I was told—"

"That the Fallen were wiped clean from this Earth by the Wardens?" He smiled faintly. "They rewrote their histories. Can you blame them for wanting to hide their shame?" He stepped down from the altar, causing me to tense. "They buried their deeds so deep that many generations have been born and gone to the Heavens, never knowing their true past. Some who Fell were stripped of their wings and their *grace* by the archangels and Alphas. Others escaped into Hell. But those who did not run, and recognized their sin, took their punishment. They were entombed in stone."

"Alive?" I whispered.

"They became the warning that evil was all around and no one, not even God's angels, were immune to it."

"They became the first stone gargoyles." I sucked in a small breath, horrified to think that anyone had been trapped in stone. "How long?"

"Centuries," the Throne answered with a shrug.

My mouth dropped open. Centuries trapped in stone? How did any of them come out of that with their minds intact?

"But with the demon populace increasing, God intervened, and the Alphas gave some of those entombed a choice—to be free to fight the demons and protect man or to remain entombed."

That didn't sound a whole lot like freedom or a choice to me, but what did I know?

"Those who accepted the choice became the first Wardens, their true stone form designed to serve as a reminder, and the human form given back so that they could blend in with humans. Their *grace* was still removed so that there was no risk of a rebellion and they were able to create a lineage who would continue to protect man and serve God's will," he explained. "That is who the Wardens truly are."

I suddenly thought of what the demon prince had said to me the day I'd gone to the coven to get Bambi, his familiar, back. *Good thing the Wardens wiped out the Fallen eons ago, eh?* Then Roth had chuckled as if he'd known something I hadn't. Roth knew! That was why he was constantly making snide comments about the Wardens.

"Wait. Those who didn't accept the choice? Or weren't given one?" I asked. "What happened to them?"

"You already know the answer to that."

I sucked in a sharp breath. I did. I just didn't want it to be true. "They're still entombed."

"They are."

Dear God.

The Throne watched me. "Then, when a Warden dies, he or she comes unto judgment. They will either be ushered into eternal peace or granted Glory. To be reborn as they once were."

Learning how the Wardens became who they were was mind-blowing, and I had questions. Like how in the world did the demons keep this a secret? If Roth knew the truth, which I was betting he did, then more had to. But at the moment only Zayne mattered. "So when you say he was restored, he was made an…an angel?"

He nodded.

"Zayne had wings—big, fluffy angel wings—and he had *grace*. A lot of it. I didn't think the Fallen had wings or *grace*." That was what I'd always been told, and even Roth had said so. Only Lucifer had retained his wings and *grace*, because he'd been kicked out before God realized that should be a thing to do.

"Not all are given redemption. Only those who are truly deserving or are found to be useful are restored to their Glory, given their *grace* and wings. He was chosen," the Throne repeated. "He was restored."

I opened my mouth, but there were no words as it finally, truly sunk in. Zayne had become an angel, an actual angel, and then he'd Fallen...

How could he have done that?

I wanted to go back out there, find him and smack him in the face. Not because I wasn't appreciative. I wanted Zayne back. I'd been prepared to go to the Grim Reaper to see what I could do, but he'd become a freaking angel in Heaven. Angels were often pretty much useless in the big scheme of things, but they were *angels*. I had no idea what that would feel like, to be a full-blooded one, but it had to be amazing. It had to be like...coming home.

I would've never taken him from this. Emotion choked me as tears burned my eyes. I looked away, pressing my lips together. How could there still be tears left when I'd cried so much? How could he do this? Seeing him tonight had been like a dream come true, but at what cost? He...he Fell for me, and he didn't seem to know who I was.

"You should want to weep," the angel said softly.

I jerked my heard toward the angel. There was a sadness in the angel's voice and in his smile that shocked me. I'd always believed angels were without emotion, but what I heard in his words was real.

"Zayne had accomplished what so very few have ever done on their own," he said. "If I had been him, I would've remained in the Heavens. I would've helped ensure that Heaven could no longer be accessed, sealing the gates before any corrupt soul could enter."

"Seal the gates?" I blinked the tears from my eyes.

The Throne nodded. "Many of us feel that this world," he said, spreading his arms wide, "has become a lost cause. That there will be no stopping Gabriel, and all that we can do is prevent his taint from reaching us."

Dumbfounded, I stared at him. "You basically want to quarantine Heaven from Earth?"

"But here I am instead," he said, as if that excused the fact that there were angels who basically wanted to wash their hands of their own freaking mess called Gabriel.

The only thing that could've distracted me from how utterly infuriating angels were was what he said next.

"Zayne was presented with many choices. He could go on to eternal peace. Reborn, he could remain in the Heavens to guard the gates. He could've chosen to train with our armies for the final battle that will come no matter what Gabriel accomplishes. He could've chosen to return to Earth at the right moment, the one where he would be needed most. But he chose to return to you, to fight beside you now and forever, even though we warned him that if he were to return now, he would Fall." There was a short laugh that sounded like wind on the mountains. "Even if he hadn't so vocally admitted what he wanted or if we hadn't presented him with such choices, we knew he would've found a way to return to you."

And wasn't that what he'd promised me? That no matter what, he'd find his way back to me.

"So, he Fell, and a Fallen can only be stripped of their

wings and *grace* once they are earthbound," the Throne explained. "No angel with the power to do so will attempt such a thing in these times." There was a pause. "Besides, we hoped that even as a Fallen, he would remain...useful to our cause. That he would retain who he was, in his heart, and be able to help defeat Gabriel. We warned him about the burn upon reentry."

"What does that mean exactly? The burn upon reentry?"

"When he Fell, he lost his Glory, and was exposed to the worst of the human soul. Greed. Lust. Gluttony. Sloth. Pride—"

"Wrath. Envy. I get it," I cut the Throne off, and if I hadn't already faced down Gabriel and if my father wasn't *the* archangel Michael, I might have been cowed by the look the Throne gave me. "He said something about feeling too much. It was like—I don't know. He seemed to find things about me familiar, but what he was feeling was blocking him or something. He seemed to be able to sense the *grace* in me. He attacked."

"That's because when he Fell, he was not only witness to the sin of humanity, he was exposed to the anger and bitterness of those who Fell before him."

I opened my mouth and then closed it. I...I couldn't even comprehend that, couldn't even begin to understand what Zayne must be feeling.

"We warned him that the Fall could overload his senses and infect him, potentially erasing who he was, but he was willing to risk becoming something as vile and evil as any demon, for you."

His words were a stab to the heart.

"When he saw you tonight, he sensed your *grace*. The

purity even in your muddied blood called to him," he said, and I couldn't even work up the energy to be offended by the muddied blood part. "In his conflicted state and with the anger and bitterness of all that Fell before him, he most likely viewed you as one of the brethren who'd cast him from the Heavens. He will see the Wardens the same way. The longer he remains in such a state, the more likely he is to act upon the violence that is seeping into every pore. He will become a danger to not just you or the Wardens, but to humans—to innocents." The Throne sighed. "A Fallen in possession of their *grace* is a very dangerous foe, no matter how clear their heart and mind is. We'd hoped he'd reenter unscathed. We were wrong. So here we are."

Those four words were so final.

An unbearable weight pressed down on my chest. Silly me for believing that my heart had taken all the pain it could. I'd been wrong. It was still in there, breaking all over again. He'd given up everything to be with me, and in a horrific twist of fate it sounded like he'd become something that he would've loathed.

"Is there no hope, then?" I asked, my voice sounding small and tired. "He won't become who he was before? Snap out of this?"

The Throne backed up, and the light around him slowly faded. "There is always hope if one has faith."

Faith. I almost laughed right then, but if I laughed, I'd probably never stop. The young priest would have to call someone.

If the young priest was still here. He seemed to have vanished into thin air.

The Throne started to flicker out but solidified. "You

have done well despite your shortcomings. Many did not believe you would survive your first battle with Gabriel."

Wow. That made me feel so much better about everything.

"Your father believed in you, though."

"He did?" Disbelief rang like a church bell in my voice.

I thought he smiled again, but with the fade of his glow, his features were blurry. "For that he has given you a gift."

"A gift?" I asked warily. I didn't want a gift. I wanted Zayne back—the Zayne I knew and loved. Not the deranged psycho who was out there doing God only knows what.

Doing things that would destroy every piece of Zayne, because he was good to the core.

"You've already been given the gift." The angel reached out, brushing his fingers over my cheek. A jolt of electricity went through me, causing my *grace* to spark and the corners of my vision to turn white. "What is inside you is the gift. It is both *grace* and Glory, a power that is beyond what your mind can comprehend and yet a power owned by you. Use it to strike through the heart encased in chaos."

I stared at him as understanding dawned. "The Sword of Michael."

He stepped back, those eyes on his wings blinking in unison.

"You're saying that I'm supposed to use the Sword of Michael against Zayne?" My voice pitched high. "Stab him in the heart with it? That would kill him!"

"Your *grace* can never harm what you cherish. It can only restore."

Now that sounded like some Jedi nonsense. "And I'm just supposed to take your word for that?" I demanded. Once the *grace* was summoned, it destroyed. Demon. Human. Warden. Even angels. He expected me to believe that because I loved Zayne, the Sword of Michael wouldn't harm him when it could slice through the skin of a Warden like it was nothing more than water? I'd cared about Misha, and my *grace* had ended his life.

"Do you not have any faith?"

I opened my mouth to respond.

"I already know this answer." His wings flared, and all those eyes stared straight into me. "It was a rhetorical question, Trueborn. You, a child of one of the most powerful archangels, have always lacked faith." The Throne smiled at me. "It is a good thing that neither God nor your father have ever lacked faith in you."

I jolted, struck speechless.

"Do not fail, Trueborn. You will need him to defeat Gabriel. You will need everything to defeat the Harbinger," the Throne said, and I wondered if he knew where Roth and Layla were currently. I wisely decided to not even address that as the intense golden glow rippled over him. My eyes watered and ached. "It may already be too late for him. Many who Fell were far too lost even after being entombed to be given the choice of redemption. I hope for your sake that is not the case. Gabriel will be the least of your concerns. Your Fallen, in his current state, can kill you. So be careful. It would be most displeasing for you to die by the hands of the one who Fell to be with you."

Displeasing?

I could think of a lot more descriptive words. Horrific. Heartbreaking. Messed up. Agonizing. Tragic.

I exhaled roughly. "And if it did work," I started, and

then corrected myself. "If I am successful, will Zayne return to being an angel?" I asked, my heart squeezing for a whole different reason.

Angels didn't have emotions. Or at least that's what I'd always believed, and Gabriel pretty much confirmed that. If Zayne was restored, I wouldn't get him back. Not like before. But he would be okay. He would be alive, and that... that had to be enough.

The Throne studied me silently for a couple of seconds. "Many believe that demons are incapable of love, do they not? As they do not have a human soul."

A shiver of unease drifted through me. Was he reading my mind?

God, I hoped not.

But demons could love. Roth loved Layla, and he was the Crown Prince of Hell.

The angel tilted his head. "Contrary to what is known and what some of our brethren will even claim, angels are not incapable of emotion, Trueborn. We just feel things... differently. For the oldest among us, it is difficult, but we are not incapable of love or lust or hate," he continued. "Those who Fell are proof. Gabriel is proof of that now."

As I stared at him, I realized that he was right. The angels who Fell did so because they caved to a whole slew of human emotions, and Gabriel...he had a mad case of jealousy and bitterness. Relief swept through me—

"But Zayne would not become an angel. He would not become a Warden. He would remain as he is," the Throne continued. "A Fallen who is earthbound, with one foot in Heaven and the other in Hell. There is only one other who was shunned by the Heavens and retained his *grace*."

My chest hollowed. "Lucifer."

"And you see how that turned out for him."

With that little piece of extremely distressing news and possibly the most demotivating pep talk, the Throne vanished, taking with him the frigid air and scent of sandalwood.

I had no idea how long I stood there, staring at the spot of the Blessed Sacrament, my mind alternating between being incapable of believing what the Throne had said I needed to do and inherently knowing there was no choice.

And the latter was true whether the Throne was right or wrong.

Slowly, I turned around. The stone angels were bowing over their basins once more. My gaze lifted to the pews. I couldn't let Zayne become something that he would've been horrified by, a monster that would eventually tarnish and destroy everything good about who he'd been. There was no way I could allow that, because for him, that would be a fate worse than death.

There really was no choice.

I sighed heavily, but with the next breath I took, steely determination filled me, dulling the pain and replacing the bone-deep exhaustion. There was a tiny spark of hope feeding the energy now buzzing through me, but I knew what I faced.

Either I saved Zayne or I killed him.

Or...he killed me.

3

There was a lot I needed to be focused on right now. During the upcoming Transfiguration, which was only weeks away, Gabriel planned on creating a rift between Earth and Heaven so that the demon Bael and souls that belonged to Hell could enter Heaven. I needed to find a way to stop him. That was my duty as the Trueborn—what I'd been waiting for—but I knew I wasn't enough to defeat Gabriel on my own. That was why Roth and Layla were trying to bring Lucifer topside. That was why the Throne had said I needed Zayne to defeat Gabriel. I should be working on a plan in case Roth and Layla failed, but Zayne…he was the priority now.

My duty would have to wait, and I didn't care if that ticked God off.

So the first thing I did when I walked outside the church was pull my phone out of my back pocket. Thankfully, the thing had survived me being thrown around like a rag doll.

Squinting at the light of the screen, I opened up my contacts. At some point, Zayne had added Nicolai's number in my phone. *In case of an emergency,* he'd said one night while we'd been hunting the Harbinger and the demon Bael.

If this wasn't an emergency, I didn't know what was.

I needed to give Nicolai and the clan a heads-up about Zayne just in case they came into contact with him. If he didn't remember me, I doubted he'd recognize them.

Heart heavy, my fingers tightened around the phone. Nicolai, the head of the DC clan of Wardens, answered on the second ring. "Hello?"

"Nicolai? It's Trinity," I said, keeping my eyes peeled wide, just in case Zayne decided that staying hidden from humans wasn't high on the priority list. "I need to see you. It's an emergency."

"Is everything okay?" he asked, concern evident in his voice. He'd visited more than once, along with Danika, while I'd been healing. He and Danika were...dating? Wardens didn't really date. They met and mated, but Nicolai and Danika were breaking with that tradition. "Hell," he said after a moment. "That's a stupid question. Are things as okay as they can be?"

"Well." I drew the word out, watching the blurred faces of people passing by, holding their umbrellas as if they had a hope of stopping the rain that was coming in sideways now. What I needed to tell him was not something to be done over the phone. "Kind of. And kind of not. I need to talk to you in person."

"You at the apartment? I can be there in twenty."

"I'm not at the apartment," I answered. "I think I'm at Saint Patrick's church?"

A moment of silence followed that statement. "Do I want to know what you're doing there?"

"Probably not, but I'll tell you all about it."

"Okay. Give me one second." There was a rustling of papers, and then he said, "Dez should be near there. I'll have him grab a car and pick you up." There was a pause while I wondered if he kept Warden schedules on paper. "You alone?"

"I'm demon free," I said, keeping my voice low.

"Wise of you to be out there alone?" he asked.

Mind way too occupied to be irritated by the question, I said, "Probably not. Tell Dez I'll be waiting for him."

Ending the call, I hung back under the alcove of the church, mulling over how I was going to tell Nicolai that Zayne was alive and all that was involved in that. I doubted he knew the truth about what he was, but the Throne hadn't said it was something that needed to remain a secret.

I leaned against the wall, an ache starting in my temples as I kept watch. My wary gaze darted over the steady stream of people and cars as I hoped Dez remembered I didn't have the greatest eyeballs. I really didn't want to end up getting into the wrong car.

About ten minutes later, a dark-colored SUV idled up to the curb and a moment later the passenger window rolled down. I couldn't see inside, but I recognized the voice.

"Trinity?" Dez called out.

Thank you baby Jesus, he remembered. I started to hurry forward but slowed since I could never judge the distance between steps in low light. I managed to get down the stairs without falling and breaking my face. There was one person I got all up close and personal with when I navigated the packed sidewalk. I'd gotten so used to walking the streets with Zayne, who cleared the sidewalk like some kind of hot Moses. Somehow, he'd lead the way even though he stayed beside me instead of walking ahead of me.

My heart squeezed as I opened the SUV door and climbed in. *I'll get him back. I will*, I promised myself as I squished into the leather seat. "Sorry." I winced, closing the door. "I'm soaked."

"No worries," he replied, and I glanced over at the Warden. He was young, a handful of years older than Zayne. He had the cutest twins I'd ever seen. One of them, Izzy, was just learning how to shift. She also had a habit of biting toes, which was weirdly adorable. "Nicolai said you needed to speak with him. That it was an emergency."

I nodded as I buckled myself in. "Thank you for picking me…" I trailed off as I looked out the passenger window.

An older man stood on the curb. At first glance, he looked normal. Dressed in dark trousers and a white button-down shirt, he could've been any number of the businessmen that stood around him, waiting to cross the street. Except he held no umbrella and the rain seemed to not touch him as he stood there, staring at me through the window. Half of his head looked…caved in, a bloody mess of bone and flesh as he stared back at me, a look of utter horror etched into the side of his face that wasn't ruined.

I recognized him.

It was Josh Fisher—the senator who'd been aiding Gabriel and Bael by buying Heights on the Hill under the guise that the school would be renovated into a facility that would service chronically ill children. In reality, the land that school sat on was basically a Hellmouth straight out of *Buffy*, situated smack-dab in the middle of a hub of spiritual power where several powerful ley lines crossed. Gabriel had needed access to the school, to get at what rested in the ground below it. There, he'd already created the portal that would eventually become the doorway into Heaven.

And Gabriel and Bael had found the perfect person to help them. Senator Fisher had signed right up, all out of a desperate attempt to be reunited with his deceased wife. A man I hadn't wanted to feel pity for, but now more than ever, I did. I understood how that kind of loss and grief would drive someone to do the unthinkable.

But he was dead now. Either by jumping out the window of his penthouse or by being thrown out of it.

"Shit," I whispered.

"What?" Dez pulled away from the curb. "What are you looking at?"

I cranked my neck, about to tell him to stop the vehicle, but in a blink of an eye, Senator Fisher was gone. Dammit. I sat back against the seat. He'd spilled the beans on the Harbinger and Bael after a few minutes of "talking" with Zayne, but he could've been holding back on information—information he might be more likely to share now that he was super-duper-dead.

"It was Senator Fisher," I told him.

Only a few Wardens knew what I was—Dez and Nicolai were two of them. Gideon, another Warden, only knew I could see ghosts, but since everything had gone down with Zayne, I was sure the Trueborn was out of the bag with the entire clan.

"Isn't he dead—wait." He glanced at me as we came to a stoplight. "You mean you saw his ghost?"

"Yeah, he...didn't look so great." Wondering if the senator had been looking for me, I kept my gaze glued to the windows for any sign of a possibly demented fallen angel. Not like I'd be able to see him coming until it was too late, but whatever.

"If someone is a ghost, that means they haven't moved on, right? And spirits are those who've crossed over." Dez had surmised correctly.

"Yep." I squeezed my knees with my icy fingers. "Can't say I'm surprised that Fisher hasn't moved on."

"Probably because he's afraid of where he's going to go."

"No doubt."

Silence fell between us as Dez drove, the twinkling city lights giving way to stretches of darkness as we crossed the Potomac. The silence didn't last long. "You hanging in there?" he asked.

I nodded.

"How are you healing?"

"Good," I said, my fingers tightening around my knees as I stamped down the burst of irritation. Dez wasn't just being nice. He *was* nice, like Zayne. I shouldn't be annoyed with his concern. "It looks worse than it feels."

"That's a relief, because I've got to be honest with you— it looks painful."

"It wasn't very...fun in the beginning." It actually had been Hell. Not just the torn skin healing or the shattered bones knitting together, but waking up and remembering that Zayne was really gone had been the worse part. I would gladly live through a thousand hours of my body healing over and over again to not experience the cold, heartbreaking reality of his death.

And there was a chance I'd have to go through that again.

I sucked in a sharp breath, loosening the grip on my knees.

"I know…I know Zayne meant a lot to you," Dez said after a moment, and I squeezed my eyes shut. The motion caused the tender, still healing skin to pull. "I know you meant a lot to him. He meant a lot to all of us." He inhaled a shaky breath, and it took everything in me not to tell him right then what was going on, but I only wanted to explain everything once. "He was…"

Zayne was everything.

Dez cleared his throat. "He was the best of us. I don't think he ever realized that, and I know for sure he didn't understand that all of us would've rallied behind him if he took over after his father. We didn't care about what happened in the past. He may have been missing a part of his soul, but he—he had more soul than most of us."

I looked over at him, wishing Zayne was here to hear that, but Dez would get the chance to tell him. I just had to…stab him in the heart with the Sword of Michael.

God.

Pulling my gaze away, I let out a ragged breath. "It bothered Zayne for a while—the whole not taking on the role as the clan leader thing—but he'd come to terms with it. He…he realized that who he was becoming didn't line up with a lot of what other Wardens believed. He was okay with it. Really."

"He told you this?"

"Yes."

"He was talking about the 'kill all demons on sight' stance most Wardens have?" he guessed. "Not all of us are that way. I'm not. Neither is Nicolai."

I'd already figured that, considering they had worked with Roth and Cayman in the past.

"But I get it," Dez went on. "Especially after what went down with Layla. There was no going back after that."

No, there wasn't. Not when Zayne's father and almost the entire clan had been ready to kill her after she'd accidentally taken a part of his soul. They'd raised her and should've known there had been no malicious intent behind her actions, just stupidity on both her side and Zayne's.

The jealousy over Zayne and Layla's previous relationship was long gone. So was the weird mixture of bitterness that surrounded the knowledge that it was supposed to have been me who'd been raised alongside Zayne.

None of that mattered now, and it annoyed me that I had wasted time on it.

"By the way," Dez said. "You're bleeding."

"What?" Lifting my hand, I touched my chin. My fingers came away smudged. So, it *was* my blood. I wiped my fingers on my jeans. "It's nothing."

"Uh-huh," he murmured.

Luckily, he didn't speak after that, but the trip to the Warden compound seemed to take forever. When he finally pulled up in front of the massive house, I nearly launched myself out of the SUV. Dez was right behind me. I started forward.

And promptly tripped over the first step, having not seen it.

Catching myself, I sighed and then carefully walked forward. Dez reached around me, opening the door, and we stepped inside. It took a couple of moments for my eyes to adjust to the bright light of the foyer as I followed Dez toward Nicolai's office. On the way we passed a few Wardens either off for the night or heading in. The wide berth they gave us told me they probably had learned the truth about me.

I should be worried. There were Wardens out there who weren't exactly comfortable with the idea of a Trueborn being around. A lot had to do with a history that was mostly forgotten, one that I hadn't even known about until Thierry, the head of the Potomac Highlands clan who was more of a father to me than Michael was, told me. Apparently it had to do with a bonding and it led to a rebellion. A whole lot of Wardens were killed, bonds to the Wardens were severed and the Trueborns died off.

Until me.

And until Sulien.

But he was dead, so whatever, until me.

Dez pushed open the door, and I saw Nicolai first. The youngest clan leader sat behind the kind of desk Thierry often sat behind. He had a pretty impressive scar along his face, which only added to his air of badassery. The dark, glossy-haired female Warden standing next to him also took him up a level. Danika was like no female Warden I knew. I couldn't even compare her to Jada, who was also bold. Danika simply didn't play by the archaic rules surrounding the females, and the fact that Nicolai didn't try to put her back in that gilded cage made me like him even more.

Gideon was also present, standing on the other side of Nicolai, his phone cradled in his palm. Zayne always referred to him as the resident tech expert while I thought of him as the resident hacker and jack-of-all-trades.

He eyed me as I walked forward, and I wondered if he

was thinking about the time he was in here with Nicolai and Zayne, when he learned I could see ghosts. He'd thought I had watered-down angel blood in me. Based on the tiny step back he took, I believed he now knew I had a whole lot in me.

Shoulder-length brown hair fell back as Nicolai lifted his head. He started to speak, but Danika beat him to it.

Concern filled her voice as she straightened. "Are you injured, Trinity?"

Wishing I'd stopped to wipe the blood from my face, I shook my head. "It's minor."

"I can get my sister," she offered, stepping away from the desk. "You have blood coming out of your ears. I'm no doctor, but that doesn't seem minor."

Crap.

I forgot about that, too.

"That's not necessary." I glanced at the chair and started to sit but remembered I was drenched. I'd already ruined enough upholstery today. "I'm fine."

Danika looked like she wanted to argue. "If you're sure." She glanced at Gideon. "We were just on our way out—"

"It's okay. You guys don't have to leave." I crossed my arms. "It's probably best if you all hear this firsthand."

"Does whatever you have to tell us explain why you look worse than the last time I saw you?" Nicolai asked.

My lips pursed. I thought I looked way improved from last time. Then again, I hadn't seen my reflection. "It does."

"Okay." He nodded at the chair. "At least sit down. I don't care if you get it wet."

Murmuring my thanks, I sat down. The immediate relief that shuttled through me was an indication that Nicolai's observation on my appearance probably wasn't far off from reality. "I don't know how to say this other than to just come out and say it," I said as Dez took a position against the wall. "Zayne is alive."

4

Everyone froze. I don't think they breathed, and no one said anything for so long I was about to say it again when Dez finally snapped out of it.

"Trinity, he can't be," he said, voice soft and too gentle.

"Trust me, I know how it sounds, but he's alive. I saw him. I talked to him. I *felt* him. He's flesh and bone and winged," I told them. "He's alive, but he's not exactly the same. He's a fallen angel, still in possession of his wings and a whole lot of heavenly fire. *Grace.*"

Nicolai and Danika stared blankly at me, and I assumed both Dez and Gideon were doing the same.

"And he's partly responsible for this." I gestured at myself. "And the Throne that I ended up talking to after seeing Zayne is responsible for the bleeding ears."

The phone slipped out of Gideon's palm and hit the floor with a heavy thud.

"You probably want to leave that there since I'm just getting started," I told him.

"Okay," Gideon whispered.

"Zayne found me in Rock Creek Park, and he didn't really recognize me. It was like he did and then he couldn't, and he went all *Fight Club* on me. I managed to get away—well, I sort of cut him and ran away, and while I was running, I heard this voice in my head telling me to go to the church."

Across from me, Nicolai blinked slowly.

Knowing how out there all of this sounded, I still forged forward. "That's where I saw the Throne, and a bunch of creepy stone angels, but they are kind of irrelevant even though the sight of them moving is going to haunt me for the rest of my life. The Throne told me what happened," I said, and then I told them everything that the Throne had shared with me up until what I had to do. How Zayne had been given a choice. The burn upon reentry. And how, in his current state, he viewed Wardens and anything with *grace* in them as the enemy. I told them that the Throne had warned that Zayne…that he could become a risk to innocent people. When I finished, all I wanted to do was get back out there and find him.

Find him before he became what the Throne warned— before he did something he could never forgive himself for.

"He…he earned back his Glory, which… I'm not quite sure what that means, and he Fell so that he could—" My voice cracked, and every part of me tensed. I exhaled slowly through my nose as my eyes burned. "He Fell to come back and fight beside me—for me."

"It's the soul," Gideon said hoarsely, drawing my attention. "Glory is basically the equivalent of a human soul, but for angels."

Oh.

That made sense.

And it also made it so much worse, because did that mean Zayne had lost his soul?

"The Glory is why we—why Wardens—have a pure soul," Gideon went on, and he looked like he needed to sit down. "Without it, he would be…"

I thought of what the Throne said, and I wanted to vomit. "He would be like a wraith?"

Gideon nodded, and if I hadn't been sitting, I probably would've fallen. Wraiths were humans who'd been stripped of their souls after death. Some demons were capable of doing it. Sometimes it happened when a ghost lingered too long and refused to move on. There was no time limit on what too long was. It was different for every ghost. It was something that could just happen. Either way, wraiths were incredibly dangerous, vindictive and spiteful. They were hatred and bitterness personified. Pure malevolence.

"But that can't be the only thing that happens to a Fallen," I argued. "The Throne said that they hoped Zayne would be unscathed during the Fall. They hoped he would be useful in the fight against Gabriel even after he chose to Fall. The lack of Glory or soul or whatever must not be the only thing that guides a Fallen's behavior." All of them were staring at me. "I really hope you guys believe me."

"What you're saying has to be true. It's the only way you'd know where we originated from." Gideon twisted to Nicolai. "It's the only way."

Nicolai nodded slowly and then sat back, dragging a hand

over his head and clasping the back of his neck. "He's really back."

"Yes. He really is." My brows pinched. "Did you two know that Wardens were originally fallen angels?"

"I learned when I took over this role. The Alphas told me," answered Nicolai, speaking of the class of angels who communicated with the Wardens.

"What?" Danika turned to Nicolai. "You knew?" She looked like she was a second away from hitting him. "And you didn't tell me?"

"There are a lot of things that I haven't told you." The look on Danika's face drove him to lean back. "That I can't tell you."

She folded her arms over her chest. "Really?"

"Why aren't you mad at him?" Nicolai pointed at Gideon.

"Because he's not sleeping in the same bed as me," she shot back.

Yikes-a-doodle.

Time to change the subject to a less awkward conversation.

"How did you know?" I asked Gideon. "I'm assuming this is something that clan leaders sort of take to their graves."

"It is, but I...I have access to a lot of old books—letters and journals from, well, a very long time ago. I stumbled across the journals of one of the second- or third-generation Wardens. That's where I read about it, and I had gone to Abbot about it," he explained, referencing Zayne's father. "He confirmed it."

"So, Zayne is..." Danika pressed her hand to her mouth, and that had to be the exact moment she truly realized that Zayne was alive. "How does he...how does he look?"

"Like Zayne—except for the wings. They're white and streaked with *grace*. His eyes are also a deep, deep blue. Like, the color is unreal." I looked down at my dirtied hands. "He looked good. Perfect actually." I swallowed hard. "He's very powerful—more so than even me."

"Because he's a fallen angel who still has his *grace*," Dez said, and his auburn curls looked like he been shoving his fingers through them the whole time we talked. "He's basically an angel."

"Not just any angel." Gideon was staring at me. "From what I could gather, most of those who Fell were from the second sphere. They were Powers—the first Order of Angels God created. They were like elite warriors, protecting the human and heavenly realms. That's what we descended from. He's a Power, and that's why the *grace* was visible in his wings. He has as much juice in him as an archangel."

Great.

Why couldn't they have originated from, I don't know, guardian angels, or like the ones who just sang about God or something? But no, it had to be *elite* warriors.

"A Fallen Power," Nicolai whispered, now dragging his hand down his face. "Jesus. He would be virtually unstoppable. The clan is already on high alert with the whole Harbinger-slash-Gabriel mess, but we need to make sure they're aware of Zayne and that he will be…unpredictable at the moment."

"I'll make sure everyone is aware," Gideon said.

It destroyed me to think of the Wardens having to be warned to stay away from Zayne. That was why I came here, but… "He's not completely bad yet. There was a part of him that did recognize me. That's not wishful thinking, because he could've done some serious damage to me. He could've killed me, but he didn't. He's still in there, and the Throne told me what I needed to do to bring him back before it becomes too late. I just…"

"What?" Dez asked.

"I just… I'm not sure how what I'm supposed to do won't actually kill him."

"I'm going to need details, Trinity," Nicolai said.

I rubbed my palms over my knees. "The Throne said that my *grace* would never harm someone I cared about. That I needed to use it to strike at a heart encased in chaos."

"The Sword of Michael." Nicolai's brows rose. "I'm guessing that means you're supposed to stab him in the heart with the Sword of Michael."

"Pretty much."

"How will that not kill him?" Danika's eyes went wide.

"That's what I'm wondering, but the Throne was all like, 'You got to have faith,'" I told them.

"I can't imagine the Throne lied to you," Gideon said.

"Really?" came Dez's response. "Angels don't often outright lie, but they sure as Hell leave a whole lot of truth out."

"Thrones are different, though. They are the speakers of truths and seers of lies," Gideon argued, and I thought of all those creepy eyes. "If the Throne told her this, then it has to be true."

"True or not, I have to do it." My hands stilled. "Zayne's out there right now, and I have no idea what he's doing. Hopefully he's napping or eating unhealthy food. That's probably not the case, and the Throne…he warned that it could already be too late. That all those things he felt when he Fell, what he's feeling now, could've already…infected him."

Danika turned her head away, and I knew she, like me, couldn't bear the thought of that.

I took a shaky breath. "If I don't try to bring him back and take that risk, he will become evil. He's going to do things that Zayne would never do."

"He already has, by the looks of it," Nicolai said softly, staring at me, and I knew what he saw. New bruises.

The truth in that burned. "I can't let him turn into a monster. I won't do that to him. I won't let that happen to him. I can't."

"Agreed," Dez said without a second of hesitation.

"Then what's the game plan?" Nicolai placed his hands on the desk. "What happens next?"

Shower? There was dirt and mud on me. And blood. I doubted that was what Nicolai meant. I also doubted there was time for that. "I'll head out there and look for Zayne. He found me once and I guess he'll find me again. The Throne made it sound like he would be drawn to my *grace*. Then I will…I will bring him back."

"Okay, then." He turned to Dez. "Let's roll out."

It took me a moment to realize what that meant. "You guys can't go out there looking for him. I told you that he's back so you all stay away from him."

Nicolai faced me. "We are in this with you. You head out there to find Zayne, we'll be there with you."

"Thanks, but I don't think that's wise. He's very—"

"Confused. Possibly even dangerous to us. Yes, I know. We all know, which is why you shouldn't be out there on your own."

"You're a Trueborn," Gideon said. "That's pretty cool. And it's also something I should've figured out, especially Zayne being your Protector. You're strong and deadly in your own right, but he's a fallen angel, Trinity. He may not be fully Fallen, as in the sense that he's completely lost to us, but you're going up against a very powerful class of angel that may not be able to stop himself from doing some major damage. You can't do this alone, and I doubt he's just going to allow you to walk right up to him and stab him. You're going to need us to distract him."

I tensed, humbled by their willingness to not stand by and also downright terrified. "Look, I appreciate the offer, but I didn't come here to ask for help—"

"I know. We all know that," Nicolai stated. "You came here to warn us off, and I appreciate the sentiment, but I'm not offering our help. You're getting it."

A knot formed in my chest as I tipped forward. "And what will happen if Zayne takes one of you out?"

"That is a risk we would take," Nicolai answered.

"Gladly," Dez tossed out, and when I looked over to him, I saw Gideon nod. "We would gladly risk our lives to help bring him back."

"That's great to hear. All of you are amazing. Really. But what if that does happen? And I succeed in bringing him back?" I asked, scanning the room. "What do you think that'll do to Zayne?"

Everyone in the room fell quiet.

"He's going to have to deal with enough crap as it is." I hoped said crap was minimal and limited to throwing me around, but knowing him, that would cut him deep. "We don't want to add to that."

"You're right," came Danika's voice. "We don't want to add to that, but we also aren't going to stand back and do nothing." She came forward, sitting beside me. "I think I know Zayne pretty well," she said, and that was true. They were friends, and at one point they could've become more. That was what Zayne's father had wanted. "If this was happening to any Warden, he wouldn't sit it out. You know that. He'd be right there, making damn sure that he came home and that he didn't add to the mess the other was in, and so would any of us."

"But you can't guarantee that. I can't even guarantee that," I argued.

"And you can't guarantee that this will even work," she countered. "That Zayne will even survive this."

Cold air filled my chest. "You're right. You all want to be there for that?"

"No," Nicolai answered. "We want to be there for you if this doesn't work."

5

There was no convincing Nicolai or the others that the smart and sane thing was to stay home. It wasn't like the city would descend into chaos if they did. Ever since the Harbinger had showed up, demon activity had gone way down. They could spend the next couple of days watching Netflix. There was some really interesting crap on that streaming service, according to Cayman, the demon who was sort of like middle management in the demonic world. When I left the apartment earlier that evening, he had passed out watching some kind of documentary about a guy with a mullet, big cats and murder.

But the Wardens weren't about that kind of life.

So after taking a moment to wash the blood off my chin and below my ears, I found myself walking aimlessly through Rock Creek Park with Dez at my side and several other Wardens nearby. Gideon had hung back at the compound, wiring into the police dispatch just in case any calls came in that would possibly give us a lead on Zayne's whereabouts. Nicolai was out here somewhere, but he'd left after Dez and I to "talk" things over with Danika. She wanted to help. Nicolai was dead set against that. I had no idea who won that battle, but I was betting on Danika.

Before we hit the park, we did swing by the apartment just in case Zayne somehow remembered the police and for me to let Cayman and my ghostly roommate, Peanut, know that I was alive.

The apartment was empty of all three of them.

Figuring Peanut was with his new friend who could see him—something I *still* needed to check on—or off doing whatever ghosts did in their spare, undead time, Dez and I had then headed to the park. Cayman had actually texted right before we got there. I had no idea how he'd gotten my phone number, but he'd sent a message that said, Are you still alive? I'd sent back a quick, Yes, and then received a response demanding proof that it was me and not an "asshole archangel" with my phone.

I'd texted back with, You're afraid of me.

Yep. It's you. Be safe. Roth would be mad if you got killed on my watch.

I really had no idea how to respond to that.

But all of that felt like an eternity ago.

Frustration burned its way through me as we passed by the bench I'd been sitting on when Zayne had arrived for what felt like the hundredth time. I stopped this time, scanning the dark tree line. At least it had stopped raining. The air was still weirdly cold for July.

Only a few steps ahead of me, Dez turned around. In his Warden form, his skin was a deep gray and as hard as granite, and the two thick horns that parted his hair could puncture through steel. He kept his large, leathery wings tucked back just in case I walked into one and lost an eyeball. Right now, most of him blended into the night. "Do you see anything?"

"Godzilla could be hiding among those trees and I wouldn't be able to see him."

"Sorry. I meant do you feel anything?"

"No." I placed my hands on my hips. "Either he's no longer in the park or he's staying back."

"Did he strike you as a type to stay back?" Dez asked, his voice raspier in his true form.

"Not particularly, but what do I know? It's not like I ever met a fallen angel before." I shook my head as my gaze fell to the outline of the bench. "I think we need to check someplace else." Or I needed to be out here without Warden babysitters, because there could be a sliver of a chance that Zayne wasn't coming close because of the Wardens. "Where? I have no idea."

"He could be anywhere in the city."

"That obvious piece of knowledge isn't exactly helpful," I replied.

Dez chuckled as he walked toward me. For someone so large, he moved as silently as a ghost. Zayne had been that way, too.

A sharp burst of agony pierced my heart.

He is that way, too.

"But we could try thinking like Zayne," he said, stopping close enough to me that he was no longer a blob of shadows.

Now he was a dark mass in the shape of a Warden. Improvement. "And I know—we have no idea what could be going through his mind, but we know what would go through his mind if there were some part of him still operating, and we know where evil tends to gather together."

I stared at the general direction of his face while I mulled that over. "That's smart." I blew out a breath. "All right. If there's a part of Zayne still operating, I think he would go... he would go to the apartment, but we were there and there was no sign of him. I think he'd go to..." I rubbed the heel of my palm over my aching hip. "The treehouse! The one at the compound. That was important to him."

"I'll have Gideon check there," he said, pulling the cell phone out of the back of his tactical pants that somehow didn't shred when he shifted. "Anyplace else?"

"A place that sells sandwiches without bread?" I said, and the tug on my heart threatened to pull me all the way to the ground. "The ice cream parlor! But that wouldn't be open. I guess he could break in, though." I racked my brain. "I think he used to like walking through the park area around the National Mall."

"I texted Gideon to check out the treehouse," he said. "We can canvass the other places."

"Don't you think we should check out the treehouse, too?"

"Gideon will be smart about checking out the area. He'll do it without being seen," Dez said. "And if Zayne is there, he'll let us know."

I guessed I was going to have to take his word on that. Another place popped into my head. "Crap. What about

Stacey? He's really close friends with her. Do you think he'd search her out?"

"If he didn't seem to really recognize you, I doubt he'd go for her," he said, and that was a relief. "But I'll get eyes on her place."

"What about the places where…where evil goes?" I asked as we started for the exit of the park. "Not that Zayne is evil," I added. "He just might be…unconsciously evil."

"I don't think Zayne is evil. If he was, I don't know if you'd be standing here."

I didn't have to concentrate to feel Zayne's hands around my throat, clamping down—hands that had been cold. I had no idea if he would've killed me if I hadn't touched him, but he had stopped. If he was truly lost already, my touch would've meant nothing.

"They'd go where the people are. At this time of night, they'd be around the bars and clubs," Dez continued. "There is a club where many of them hang out. Roth has or had a place above the club. He could take a look around, but I have no idea if a Fallen would go there—if demons can sense what he is or what he'd even do to them."

Considering that none of the Wardens had any idea where Roth and Layla were currently, I murmured something along the lines of getting Roth to check out this club.

Dez shifted back into his human form as we neared the parked SUV. He pulled on a plain, dark-colored shirt he'd snatched somewhere from the back seat area, and I wondered exactly how many of them he had stowed away.

Then we were off, and I told myself not to get hopeful. Which was pretty much like telling myself not to eat the whole bag of chips.

Even though it was well past most people's bedtime, there was still traffic, but we reached the ice cream parlor in record time, slowing down for Dez to check the building out. No lights on. No apparent signs of a break-in. My hope took a blow, but that had been a shot in the dark. Ten minutes later, we arrived at our second destination.

The National Mall.

There was a surprising amount of people about for the time of night. Dez remained in his human form as we started walking, and it didn't take very long before I felt the heavy tingle of awareness along the nape of my neck.

My senses sharpened as I eyed a group huddled under a tree. I couldn't make out any of their features, but I knew what I was feeling. "There are demons here."

Dez followed my gaze. "I see them."

They didn't seem to notice us as we passed them. "I think they're Fiends."

Fiends were lower level demons who were virtually the pranksters of the demon world, the living embodiment of Murphy's Law. They liked to mess with things, especially electronics. Though I supposed if someone was stuck in a traffic jam because one of them was bored and decided to brush up against several blocks' worth of streetlights, I guessed some wouldn't see them as harmless little pranksters.

"I'll keep an eye on them," Dez advised.

I glanced up at him. "You don't want to dispatch them to the fiery rings of Hell?"

He snorted as the wind lifted his hair from his forehead. "If they're not hurting anyone, I don't have a beef with them. You?"

I glanced back at them, barely able to distinguish them

from the shadows of the trees. "You know I grew up in the Potomac Highlands community. Obviously." He'd come with Zayne when Nicolai arrived before the Accolade, where Wardens in training became the warriors who protected the cities. "I was always raised to believe that all demons were bad, but Zayne…he kind of opened my eyes to the fact that wasn't always the case. Strange that a Warden was the source of that kind of enlightenment, but then I met Roth and Cayman, and…" How in the world did I describe the actual Crown Prince of Hell and a demon broker, who fulfilled humans' desires and wishes in return for pieces of the human's soul? Wasn't like they were upstanding citizens or anything. "They aren't good per se, but they are…carefully evil." Carefully evil? I rolled my own eyes at that. "That probably makes me a really bad Trueborn."

Dez laughed under his breath. "Never quite heard them described like that, but I get what you're saying. There's necessary evil in the world, right? A balance between good and bad that must be kept so that the agreement between God and Lucifer is honored. As long as everyone stays in their lane, it is what it is."

Dez was right. Demons were a necessity and they also served a purpose. They were the embodiment of the forbidden fruit. Their whispers, gifts and manipulations were all a test that every human faced. Demons caused humans to exercise free will. To do right or to do wrong. To make lemonade out of lemons or to raise holy Hell. To forgive or to seek vengeance. To be the one who lends a helping hand or to be the one who punches down. To educate or to misinform. To love or to hate. To be a part of the solution or part of the problem. To keep on the path to eternal righteousness or to be led astray, into eternal damnation.

There was a whole world of gray in between each of those things, and it was what people did in that gray area that determined where they ended up.

The problem was that many demons didn't stay in their lanes. There were the ones who were ordered to stay in Hell, but came topside, like Ravers, Nightcrawlers and others that couldn't possibly pass as human. Then there were the Upper Level demons, and they almost never paid any respect to that balance.

I also doubted Roth or Cayman stayed in their lane.

But whatever.

I wasn't here for them.

I was supposed to be here for the Harbinger. The archangel Gabriel, who dropped a nuclear bomb on that fragile balance. But right now? I was here for Zayne.

Dez and I traveled around the National Mall for quite some time, and it wasn't exactly a stroll in the park. It hurt to think that Zayne had planned on giving me a tour, taking me to the museums and such, but this was how I was being introduced to the Mall.

But it could still happen, and besides, it wasn't like I could see anything beyond a few feet in front of me and general shapes. I could always pretend I hadn't been here, because with each minute that turned into ten, it became clear that Zayne wasn't here.

Which left only the bars and clubs—where humans would be gathering. According to Dez, we had less than an hour before they closed.

I didn't even want to ask why Dez had thought a Fallen

would seek out humans, but I had to when we arrived at Dupont Circle, where the streets were lit by signs and the steady stream of headlights.

"Why do you think a Fallen would be drawn to the same area as a demon?" I kept close to Dez as we passed several packed bars, continuously scanning for doors randomly opening and stumbling drunks who would have more trouble than me when it came to navigating the sidewalk.

"There's not a lot of info out there about the Fallen," Dez said as I noticed a cluster of laughing girls headed down the sidewalk. "But I do remember what made God go after them."

"Besides producing nephilim offspring every five seconds, and I honestly don't see how that was such a big deal, because hello."

"Thought you didn't like that term."

"I don't."

I thought he grinned, because the giggling group of girls we passed went completely silent as they stared up at him. He didn't seem to notice. "That I can't answer, but the Fallen were drawn to humans in the same ways demons are. When they were still fully certified heavenly angels, they worked alongside man to achieve a better way of life, but once they Fell, they used their charisma and charm to... well, revel in sin."

My stomach soured. I didn't want to even think about Zayne reveling in sin. "Did fallen angels have the same kind of talents as some of the Upper Level demons?"

He hesitated, and I knew that was my answer. "I believe so."

Oh God.

Upper Level demons could sway people into doing all kinds of disturbing things with just their words alone.

My gaze crept toward an all-night coffee shop. There were a few people sitting at the bistro tables inside and a handful in line. Two young men headed for the door, Styrofoam cups in hand. Behind them, a child too young to be out at this time of night trailed after them. He was too far away for me to make out the little boy's features, but I knew he was a spirit. Perhaps their child? A younger brother? I wasn't sure, but I knew he'd crossed over and was now back.

I slowed down as the young men stepped out into the damp night air. The little spirit suddenly rushed forward, brushing past the one with rich brown skin. The guy stumbled, looking down as the spirit passed by and disappeared in a blink of an eye.

"You okay, Drew?" the other man asked, touching his arm.

"Yeah. I…" Drew stared at the spot where the child had disappeared. "Yeah, I am. Everything is good."

Watching them, I wondered just how much Drew had felt or was possibly aware of. People often could feel the presence of a ghost, especially if they did that creepy and annoying thing where they walked through a person. And depending on how active and strong the ghost was, they could even catch sight of one. Spirits were different, though. People often caught that familiar scent. Sometimes they would suddenly feel warm or inexplicably be reminded of the person who'd passed on. To feel one as intensely as the man called Drew just had made me think he had a little angelic blood in him.

Dez had stopped, and I got myself moving again. My empty stomach rumbled, and I realized I had no idea when I last ate. Normally on these patrols, I'd already eaten three days' worth of meals and half of whatever...whatever Zayne had picked up.

My appetite immediately vanished.

Foot traffic picked up once the bars started shutting down, making it a lot more difficult to walk the sidewalks, but I stuck close to the businesses. Roughly around the same time, I did feel the presence of demons. Nothing serious like an Upper Level demon, though, and the building frustration was quickly becoming desperation.

Where could he be? Lifting my gaze to the sky, I saw nothing but darkness. What was he doing? I trudged on, refusing to acknowledge the aches and pains I hadn't felt earlier but that were now rearing their ugly heads. What if he left the city? Panic blossomed, giving way to a sense of helplessness. God, I couldn't even consider that. I couldn't. I wouldn't.

Minutes turned into another hour. The streets quieted. The traffic slowed. Each step became more sluggish.

Dez finally stopped. "Trinity," he said, his voice weary and heavy. "It's time."

I knew what he meant, but I still asked, "For what?"

"To head home." He walked over, stopping to stand beside me. "We can pick this back up tomorrow, but if he's out here, he doesn't want to be found." There was a pause. "You need your rest, Trinity. Finding him while you're bone-dead tired isn't going to do any of us any favors."

Dez was right, but I wanted to argue. I wanted to stay out

here until I found Zayne, but I nodded and I followed Dez back to the car. I climbed into the passenger seat, closing my eyes and praying to whoever that was listening that Zayne was still in the city, that he was safe and that it wasn't too late.

6

It was close to dawn by the time I limped into the dimly lit apartment. I came to a stop as the elevator door slid closed behind me, unable to move as I looked around.

Everything I saw reminded me of Zayne. Not the Fallen Zayne, but *my* Zayne.

The exposed metal beams of the ceiling and the bare walls gave the apartment a very industrial vibe. Most of the living area was taken up by a large gray sectional couch wide enough for two Wardens to lay side by side. The simple chrome-finished end tables and coffee table were void of any personal touches. There was a punching bag hanging above rolled-up training mats, in the corner of a space I assumed was normally used for a dining area. Looking down, I saw a pair of Zayne's sneakers by the door, placed there in preparation for a run. No one had touched them in the days since his death. Not Roth or Layla. Not any number of the

Wardens who'd been in and out of the apartment. My heart ached as I lifted my gaze.

Well, *almost* everything reminded me of Zayne. The TV left on in the empty room wasn't something Zayne would do. That was courtesy of either Cayman, the demon broker, or Peanut, the ghostly roommate. The rolled-up bags of chips, the empty soda cans on the kitchen island and the dishes in the sink were most definitely not Zayne. The mess was the result of any number of the people who'd been here, but the package of Oreos ripped open down the middle was definitely me.

If Zayne was here to see this, he would...he would probably sigh and then get down to cleaning like the place needed to be decontaminated. That brought a smile to my lips.

And another pang to the chest.

Toeing my sneakers off, I dragged myself away from the door, shuffled over to the couch, and found the remote. I turned the TV off and, unable to deal with the silence, I turned the TV back on five seconds later.

I then headed into the narrow, short hall that led to two bedrooms. The one to the left was empty. Zayne had said that was his room for when I got annoyed with him. There was only one bed, and he'd put it in my room, but my room was really *our* room. I stared at the door left ajar. I stood there for what felt like an eternity before I pushed the door open.

I didn't dare look up. I couldn't do it—couldn't look directly at the stars Zayne had placed on the ceiling. I could barely deal with the faint, soft glow of them. Keeping my gaze lowered, I smacked around on the wall until I found the light switch, then walked past the unmade bed and rummaged around in the clothing spilling out of my suitcase until I found clean pajamas.

Walking into the bathroom, I turned the light on as I nudged the door shut behind me. In the mirror, I saw myself for the first time since I'd left the apartment.

The pajama bottoms slipped from my fingers, falling quietly to the floor. I left them there as I walked forward. My reflection shocked me.

My dark hair had dried in a ratty mess, but that was nothing new. Neither were the blue-tinted healing bruises along my cheeks, under my eyes. It was the new ones, the bruises that were more purplish along my chin. The new ones that had joined the healing ones around my throat.

I closed my eyes and clamped my jaw down, fighting the building scream. I wanted to scream until my throat hurt and my ears rang. I wanted to scream until I couldn't feel anything ever again, because this wasn't right. It wasn't fair. Not for me. Not for Zayne. If it wasn't too late, if I could bring him back and if he remembered this, he would...

It would kill a part of him.

God. I missed Zayne.

I missed Jada.

I missed Thierry and Matthew.

I missed Peanut's goofy ass.

But I knew if I talked to Jada or Thierry and Matthew, they would be worried about me—about all of this—and I didn't want to do that to them. Especially when there was nothing they could do. It wasn't like they could come here. With Gabriel lurking around, it was far too dangerous.

There was a small, childish part of me, though, that wanted to not only rewind time, but to also change the past to one where we were all at…like a barbecue or something. Even Cayman would be there, and Peanut would be doing something weird, like pretending to eat the hot dog someone was actually eating.

But I couldn't rewind time or change the past.

Heart and chest heavy, I moved away from the mirror and turned on the shower, cranking up the hot water. Stripping the soiled clothing off me, I stepped in. Air hissed through my clenched teeth as the hot spray hit old and new abrasions. I pushed through it, watching the pink and brown water circle the drain until it cleared. I washed my hair twice and overloaded the loofa with so much body wash the pineapple and mango scented gel oozed down my arm. By the time I was done, the bathroom was a steamy fruit basket.

Once dressed in the pajamas, I picked up Zayne's comb and worked out the tangles in my hair, hoping that there'd be a chance for him to get annoyed over that later. Leaving the bathroom, I grabbed the pillow and blanket, taking them out into the living room. I turned the corner of the couch into a bed and eased down, wrapping the blanket around me. The blanket smelled sweet, like chocolate and the sugary wine Matthew liked to drink. It smelled like Bambi—Roth's familiar. The six-foot snake had spent the last several days curled up beside me, resting with her head on my leg while I healed. I think she'd done that because I'd helped return her to Roth. The pillow, though…

I turned my head, pressing my cheek into the pillow. It smelled of wintermint. The backs of my eyes burned as I squeezed them shut.

There was still hope.

He was alive.

It wasn't too late.

That's what I kept telling myself until I began to drift off. It felt like minutes passed before I was jarred awake.

"Trinnie!" a voice shouted directly in my face.

I jerked upright, my heart launching itself somewhere into the vicinity of the ceiling as my eyes popped open. Hovering several feet off the floor was the ghostly form of Peanut.

"Jesus," I rasped, blinking several times. Muted daylight streamed in front of the windows. "I think you gave me a heart attack."

"You? I gave *you* a heart attack?" he screeched, and it was a good thing that 99.5 percent of the populace couldn't hear him. "Where have you been all night? I came home, and you were gone. I kept coming back and then *it* happened."

Shoving the hair out of my face, I waited until my vision cleared. Peanut's dark hair was messy, like he'd been inside a wind tunnel. The Whitesnake concert shirt was as vintage as his red Chuck Taylors, but when I focused on his feet, I realized from the knees down he was completely transparent.

My brows rose. "What time is it?"

"I don't know. I'm dead. Do I look like I have a watch or need one?"

"Well, you think you need your own bathroom so why wouldn't you think you need a watch?" I muttered.

"That's different," he argued, lowering. It looked like the coffee table ate half his body. "Just because I'm dead doesn't mean I don't need my privacy."

"As if you respect anyone else's privacy." I reached for my phone on the end table. I hit the screen, seeing only a handful of hours had passed since I'd fallen asleep. Not nearly enough to get any true rest.

But long enough for Zayne to get into any amount of trouble.

"Who cares about privacy right now? You've been gone all night and something...something happened." Not known for toning down the dramatics, he smacked his hands against his cheeks. "*It* happened."

"What happened?" I asked as I shoved the blanket off and rose. Knowing Peanut, whatever he was freaking out about was probably something normal. Like "it happening" was him hearing the refrigerator running.

"Something superweird, dudette."

Bones and muscles stiff, I shuffled toward the kitchen, feeling like a hundred years old. "What happened, Peanut?" I opened the fridge door and grabbed a Coke.

Peanut drifted out of the coffee table and turned toward the kitchen. His lower body became more solid. "I don't know what it was," he said as I snapped open the can and lifted it to my mouth. "But I was sucked into the nothing."

The bubbly carbonated goodness hit my throat, burning in the best way just as he spoke. I almost choked as I swallowed hard. "What? The nothing?"

He drew close enough for me to see how big his eyes were. "Yes. That is exactly what I said. I was chilling with Gena down below," he said, and I made a mental note that now I knew the girl lived on one of the lower floors—one of the many lower floors. For some concerning reason, Peanut was supervague when it came to this girl. "And then it felt like an invisible string had grabbed ahold of me and there was an intense flash of white light, but the light was, like, falling? I thought, no way, I'm going into the afterlife whether I want it or not."

I stared at him, taking another drink while wondering if it was possible for ghosts to do drugs. And if so, was I going to have to have a talk with him.

"But it wasn't the afterlife. No. I was suddenly in this place that was supergray and stagnant, with all these people that I'd never seen before. And I mean lots of people." He came through the kitchen island and to my side, so that he was two inches from me. "You see how close we are?"

"Uh. Yeah."

"This is how crowded the place was. We all were crammed into this nothing world, first to be all up in each other's personal space. I was so confused and freaked—totes freaked. Wherever I was, it wasn't dope or gnarly. Then a couple of moments later, I was thrust back to here. That place, though. It was…" He floated back, shaking out his shoulders. "It was empty, Trinnie. It was full of people but *empty*."

The fog of sleep and exhaustion cleared as I stared at him. This wasn't one of his normal overreactions to something extraordinarily common. He was being serious and—

I lowered the can of soda. "You said there was a pop of bright, falling light? Around what time?"

"I don't know. A few hours after the sunset? I wasn't really paying attention." Peanut started to rise. "I was watching *Poodle Exercise with Humans* on YouTube."

My brows knitted and I started to question that, but shook that idea out of my head. "And you don't know where you went to?"

"No, Trinnie. I mean, I don't know if it was *it*," he said, getting very close to one of the ceiling fans.

"What do you think *it* is?"

"You know, it." He reached the fan. The blades sliced

through the top of his head. "Purgatory. I was sucked into purgatory."

Okay. I hadn't expected him to say that. "Are you sure?"

"I've never been, so I could be wrong. The place doesn't sound rad at all," he said as the fan continued to churn through his head. It was a very disturbing thing to witness. "But that's how I imagine such a downer of a place to feel. Like there is no hope and there is just...nothing."

"That sounds...weird," I murmured, concerned. It was highly unlikely that what had happened to him had anything to do with Zayne, but a falling bright light that sucked him into what could possibly be purgatory around the same time Zayne arrived? Even if it didn't, could it happen again? Peanut could be superannoying, but I...well, I loved him like I imagined one grew to love an annoying sibling or something.

I guessed I'd add that to the ever-growing list of things to be stressed about.

"Anyhoo, so obviously I was super-freaked-out and I came to find you, but you weren't here." The ceiling fan was now cutting through his face. "What were you doing? It couldn't be hunting demons or the Harbinger of Doucheness?"

Harbinger of Doucheness? I almost laughed. "No, I wasn't hunting. I just needed to get out, clear my head and..." I frowned. "I know my vision is bad, but I can see you. Can you please get out of the fan. I don't think you understand how freaky that looks."

"Oh, my bad." He came back down, and even sat himself on the bar stool, hooking one leg over the other, sitting all prim and proper. "So, you needed some headspace? Did you find the space you were looking for?"

"Um. Yes and no." I came around the island and sat beside him. That was when I realized that he'd sunk into the seat, to his waist. Pulling my gaze from that, I placed the soda on the coaster and prepared myself for the one hundred and one questions that were, understandably, about to come my way. "I saw Zayne last night."

"Reaaaaally?" Peanut said, drawing the word out before I could continue.

"I know how it sounds, but it's true." I met his somewhat visible eyes. "He's alive, Peanut, and he's a fallen angel."

Now he was staring at me in a way I imagined I'd been staring at him moments before. I told him everything, and it took about an hour or so, because I had to keep repeating things. I started eating the Oreos that had been left out on the island around the whole Zayne didn't recognize me part and I'd nearly finished the entire package by the time I got to the I needed to stab him in the heart thing. Throughout the whole thing, Peanut pretty much freaked out, disappearing and coming back. He floated to the ceiling again and into the fan. Then he bounced around the apartment, but finally he'd returned to the island and seemed to have calmed down.

"So, that was what I was doing last night." I finished off my Coke. "I was with Dez and we were looking for him. We didn't find him obviously."

Peanut stared at me. "And here I thought Gabriel was the worst of your problems."

A strangled laugh left me. "You and me both." Stretching over, I grabbed the box of granola bars. I hadn't bought them, but I didn't think Zayne had, either, because these were of the unhealthy, chocolate chip variety. "I can't even

think about the Harbinger right now or how in the Hell I'm
supposed to stop him before the Transfiguration."

"Or stay alive until then," Peanut commented.

Biting down into the bar, I shot him a dark look.

"What?"

"That didn't help," I said around a mouthful of granola
and chocolate.

"I'm just donning my Captain Obvious hat, okay? I know
it's not helpful, but I don't even know how to be helpful.
Oh! Wait. Maybe I could ask the other ghosts if they've seen
him." He pitched forward, halfway into the island.

Sighing, I stared down at the crumbs and my darkest fears
sort of spilled out of me. "I have no idea where he is, if he's
even in the city still. What he's doing or if it's too late."

"He has to be in the city," Peanut stated. "And it can't be
too late. Don't even think that. It won't help you or him."

I didn't respond at first to the surprisingly calm and mea-
sured response from the ghost. Finally I nodded. "I know,
but it's kind of hard not to think like that. It's impossible to
not think about finding him and having to fight him for
real. Not because he's strong, but…"

"But because you love him," he said quietly.

I nodded. "I can't…" Inhaling sharply through my nose,
I tried again. "I can't even think about what it will be like
to use the Sword of Michael on him, even if it does work."

A couple of moments passed, and Peanut asked, "What
are you going to do? Don't answer that. You already know
what you have to do. You have to find him." He reached
out, placing his hand over mine, where it rested on the gray-
and-white marble. His hand went through mine, leaving a
wave of goose bumps behind.

"I know." And I did. "But if it doesn't work—if I do it and it kills him—"

"If that is what happens, you know, deep down, it will be the right thing. It will hurt like Hell. It will hurt worse than getting electrocuted, and I would know. But Zayne... he shouldn't be bad. That's not who he is. He's rare. He's a good guy. Like too good for you."

I laughed, because it was true.

"But you have to try, Trinnie."

I started to respond as I glanced down at where his hand was over mine. It was no longer sunken into the marble. It was above mine, like normal, and I must not have gotten enough sleep, because I swore I could... I could feel his hand. That was impossible, but there was a cool touch that really felt solid. Tangible. Slowly, I lifted my gaze to his.

"You need to find Zayne. You need to take care of him," he said, and for a moment, he was fully corporeal. It was almost like he was any living, breathing person sitting next to me, and he didn't look...like Peanut to me. His skin was almost...luminous, and his eyes were too bright, almost as if there was a white light behind them. "And then, after that, you need to stop the Harbinger. If not, none of this will matter. Not now and not even upon death."

7

Hours after my conversation with Peanut, I still had the jitters. Even as I hit the streets with Dez later that afternoon and well into the night, I couldn't shake the feeling. It wasn't that Peanut said anything I didn't already know, but there was just something about the way he said it.

Or about him that was just different.

But seconds later, he'd been back to his bizarre yet normal self.

Rubbing my right hand, I resisted the urge to kick a nearby trash can as Dez and I came to an intersection. At this point, it felt like we'd walked every block in the city. I also fought the urge to check my phone, which I had been doing every ten minutes it felt like.

I'd tried getting ahold of Cayman that afternoon, calling the number he'd texted from, more than once, but there'd been no answer. Based on how everyone first reacted to the news about Zayne, I figured that was not something I needed to text. But he hadn't called back. He hadn't even returned my text.

Of course, my mind immediately had gone to the worst-case scenario. Zayne had somehow found Cayman, did something fallen-angel terrible, and I was going to be sad, because I liked the dumb demon. Layla was going to be really sad, and then Roth was going to want to kill—

Dez's phone rang suddenly. "It's Gideon," he told me as he answered. "Talk to me."

Please. Please let there be some lead. Anything at this point, even if it was just some kind of rumor. There had been no sign of Zayne—not from us or any of the Wardens who were also combing the city for any sign of him—and not only that, I hadn't felt a single demon the whole time I'd been out here, not even a Fiend. There'd been less in the city since the arrival of Gabriel, but I at least always felt one.

"What? Yeah. That could be something," Dez was saying, turning around while I forced myself to remain silent. "We aren't too far actually. We'll check it out."

"What?" I demanded the moment he lowered his phone. "Has Gideon learned something?"

"I don't want us to get our hopes up, but he did hear a strange call go in to the police," he said.

"My hopes aren't up," I lied. They totally were. "What kind of call?"

"A man just called in, saying he saw a man getting beat up by an angel."

I blinked once and then twice. "That…that could definitely be Zayne." I paused. "With hopefully a really good reason to be beating someone up."

"Or it could be someone drunk or high," Dez replied.

"Gideon said he'd be surprised if the cops even do a drive-by of the park to check out the call."

"Where is the park? You said it's close?"

Dez turned to his left. "Just about two blocks down—"

I took off running in that direction, his curse blistering my ears. I didn't slow down. Dez was right behind me. We crossed the blissfully empty intersection, my heart jumping around as the brick walls of the park came into view. I kept running until I saw the entrance.

The entrance was closed—gated from the ground to the ceiling of the stone archway.

Swallowing a shriek of fury, I backed up toward the edge of the sidewalk just as Dez arrived. The wall was maybe nine or ten feet.

Doable with a bit more room. Glancing into the street behind me to make sure it was empty, I rushed out to the middle.

"Trinity—" Dez started.

Pushing off the ground, I ran hard toward the wall, arms and legs pumping. Muscles throughout my body tensed. About four feet out, I launched myself off the ground, rising into the air. There was a moment where I felt like I was flying. Weightless.

I'd judged the distance right.

Sort of.

I cleared the wall and went right over it.

Crap!

Preparing myself for a hard landing, I hit the ground below on both feet. The impact vibrated up my legs and throughout my hips, and along my spine. That kind of fall would've surely broken a bone or a spine in a human. If I was in tiptop shape, it wouldn't have even fazed me. I, however, was not in the best of shape, so the landing stung. A lot. But all the important bones were intact. I rose from the crouch just as Dez came over the wall, his landing way more graceful and light than mine. Without even looking, I knew that meant he'd shifted into his Warden form.

There was another curse from behind me as my sneakers pounded off the stone of the pathway. Following the solar-lit walkway, I raced past the kind of trees that reminded me of Christmas, bursting out into a brightly lit clearing. The sound of running water from a huge fountain seemed to move in the tune of my pulse. Beyond that was… I squinted.

You have to be kidding me.

There were like a million steps on the other side of the fountain, and even though I could make out the shape of them, they were nowhere near as lit as this area. Damn it all to—

"Stop!" Dez shouted.

Skidding to a stop, I looked down to see I had almost walked into a lumpy mass on the ground. A lumpy mass that was definitely a body.

"Damn," I whispered, jerking back a step.

It was a man on the ground. I couldn't make out what he was wearing, because of the…the blood that was coming from— I squinted. Oh. A whole lot of blood had poured out from where his eyes had been.

My stomach twisted. "Does, um, it look to you like his eyes were, like, burned out?"

"Yeah," came the curt response. Keeping his wings back, Dez knelt and checked the man's pulse. "He's dead."

I really didn't think that needed to be confirmed.

"This doesn't mean it was Zayne," Dez said before I could even voice my fear. He lifted his head toward me. "Some demons can change their appearance. You know this."

I did. "But why would a demon change their appearance and give themselves angel wings?"

"Because they're messed up like that? Fool someone into believing they're seeing an angel when in reality they're seeing a nightmare come to life," he answered. "Let me see if I can figure out who this poor soul is."

Looking around while Dez gently turned the guy on the side and went for a wallet, I took a deep breath and held it. My eyes burned. So did my nose and my throat. I wasn't going to cry. Nope. Crying solved nothing. Dez could be right. A demon could've done this. It didn't have to mean it was Zayne.

Because if it was, and Zayne had already taken a life, then was he already—

The air behind Dez rippled.

I cocked my head to the side. It could be my eyes. They were exhausted.

A moment later I knew it wasn't my eyes.

The sudden awareness of a demon—a very powerful demon—hit me as static charged the atmosphere.

"Dez! Incoming!" I shouted, already moving. I leaped over the body, putting myself between the portal and Dez. The air stirred around me as Dez rose, spinning around.

A hot, fetid wind blew my hair back from my face as a huge, hulking form took shape in the space in front of me. For a moment, I thought it was a Hellion or Nightcrawler, and while those two things wouldn't be something anyone should be glad to see, I was. I felt an answering pulse of *grace.* It tangled with all the anger and the desperation, and erupted into a need for violence.

But the second the demon took complete form, I knew it wasn't a Hellion or Nightcrawler. The demon was something I'd never seen before.

Its skin was milky white and the body hairless. The bullet-shaped head was...well, it consisted of one crimson red eye, two quarter-size holes I guessed were a nose and one giant, round mouth full of rows of tiny shark teeth.

It looked like a giant worm—a giant, muscular worm with two arms and two legs.

"What in the world is this?" I asked.

"A Ghoul," Dez snarled. "Flesh eaters. They also like to eat souls. Definitely forbidden to be topside. First one I've seen in real life."

My gaze dropped, and I wanted to bleach my eyeballs. "And why are demons *always* naked?"

The Ghoul opened its mouth and garbled grunts and high-pitched squeals came out.

"Sorry." Dez's wings unfurled. "I don't speak demon-worm."

The sounds rose and then...then became words—mushy-sounding words I heard perfectly clear. "We are here for the nephilim."

I rolled my eyes. They must've been sent by Gabriel. I guessed he wanted me under his tender, loving care until the Transfiguration. "Trueborn. The appropriate term is *Trueborn.*"

"We do not care," the Ghoul replied, and before I could question the "we" part, the entire left side of its body stretched and sort of plopped out another Ghoul.

"What in the actual wide world of fu—?" I snapped my mouth shut as another popped out of the right side of its body.

"I think they left the replicating thing out of the text-books," Dez commented.

"You think?"

The one to the right of the main Ghoul went right at Dez. He was fast, spinning out of its grip. The other two came toward me.

I had my iron daggers on me still, but my *grace* was push-ing at me. I wanted to use it. I'd moved past the idea of only using the *grace* in a worst-case scenario, having real-ized what I'd been taught and trained had been far more of a hindrance than my eyes.

But the problem with that was I didn't have a bonded Protector any longer. I couldn't pull strength to avoid the weakness that followed after using my *grace*. My nose would most likely bleed, possibly drawing more demons my direc-tion even though it hadn't the night before.

But not using my *grace* right now was okay.

I was more than happy to get stabby.

Pushing the *grace* down, I unsheathed my daggers. Adren-aline kicked my senses alive as the Ghouls charged me. An-ticipation licked through me, my muscles tensing. I knew to keep a distance between us so they didn't end up out-side my constricted line of vision, and I waited until the last possible moment and then spun around, kicking out. My sneaker caught the Ghoul in a very unmentionable place. It shrieked, doubling over as I popped back up.

The other Ghoul moved disturbingly fast, reaching for me with hands the size of my head. I dipped under its arm and whirled, slamming the dagger into the center of the Ghoul's back, right where the heart would be. Jerking the iron out, I waited for the burst of flames signaling its demise.

The Ghoul turned around and opened its mouth, roaring straight in my face.

"Whoa." My eyes watered. "Your breath…"

"The head!" Dez shouted, landing behind a Ghoul, and wrapped one arm around its neck. "You got to separate its head from the body."

My lip curled. "Ugh. Gross."

The Ghoul in front of me popped out another Ghoul, and I groaned. "Oh, come on."

As Dez jammed his clawed hands into the side of the Ghoul's throat, I looked around. Spotting the ledge of the fountain behind the Ghoul, I shot forward.

Ghoul Number 3 had recovered from my low blow—sort of—and shuffled at me. I hit the ground, kicking out and sweeping its legs out from underneath it. The Ghoul went down hard as I shot up and ran. Jumping on the four-foot ledge, I spun around.

"Oh my God!" I shouted, pointing toward the entrance. "Look! So much tasty flesh!"

The stupid Ghoul in front of me turned in the direction I pointed. Flames erupted from Dez's Ghoul and the smell of a busted sewer line hit me as I launched off the ledge. Landing on the back of the Ghoul, I wrapped my arm around its neck as its arms started pinwheeling. A meaty fist hit the side of my head, but I held on, shoving the dagger into the side of its throat, just under my arm.

Rotten blood gushed out as I pushed in, dragging the dagger across its neck while it thrashed. The dagger hit the spinal cord, and boy, did that take all the arm muscle I barely had. As it wheeled around, I saw Ghoul Number 4 rushing Dez like a linebacker.

The second I felt the head go loose, I used my knees and spring-boarded off the ghoul. I landed a few feet away as the body in front of me burst into flame—

"Eek!" The head I held caught fire. I tossed it away from me, shuddering.

A heavy hand landed on the scruff of my neck, and for the second time in two days, I was lifted into the air. The only difference this time was that I wasn't bedazzled by who was holding me.

Just really grossed out.

The air in front of me started to warp, and my heart dropped. Oh, Hell, no—it was not going to creepy magic pop me out of here.

Reaching back with one hand, I gripped the arm that held me, pulling my legs up toward my chest and then swinging them out and back. I slammed my feet into the midsection of the Ghoul, breaking its hold.

I fell, twisting at the last moment to land on my hip. That poor bone had just about had it. The pain in my hips slowed me down as I rolled onto my back, groaning.

When this was all over, I was going to be in the record books as one of the youngest people ever to need a hip replacement.

Before I could even get onto my feet, the Ghoul appeared in my line of vision. Pushing back on my elbows, I kicked out. The Ghoul caught my ankle.

"Dammit!" Sitting, I started to swing on the arm with the

dagger as he pulled me toward him. The air charged with electricity once more.

This Ghoul wasn't as dumb. He saw the move coming, and promptly lifted my entire body into the air. He shook me like a rattle. My *grace* sparked to life once more, and this time I didn't stop it. If I did, this punk was going to take me through some portal, and I was sure wherever it ended was where I didn't want to be. The corners of my vision turned white—

Without warning, the Ghoul let go and I dropped to the ground like a sack of lumpy potatoes. Landing first on my shoulder and then my ribs, I grunted. At least I hadn't dropped my daggers. So, win?

I was also going to need rib replacement if that existed. The *grace* retracted as I planted my hand in the grass and started to push up.

Something rolled past me. Something bullet-shaped and white. It smacked into the ledge of the fountain.

It was a Ghoul head.

Dumbly, I watched it catch fire as I let out of a tired breath.

"Thanks, Dez," I said, this close to lying down and taking a breather.

"That wasn't me," Dez replied, his voice barely above a whisper.

The corners of my lips turned down as I stared at the scorched cement of the ledge. The smell of an overused Porta-Potty receded, and a different scent washed over me—a fresher, crisp scent.

Wintermint.

My heart stuttered.

Slowly, I rolled to my back and onto my other side, looking up. The first thing I saw was bare feet. Somehow they were clean. I had no idea why I noticed that, but I had. How were his feet still clean? Had he just been flying around this whole time? My gaze lifted, and as close as he was now, I realized that the pants were the same kind of linen that the Throne had worn, a linen that looked incredibly well tailored. I kept looking up. The stomach and chest were still bare. Then I saw wings, gloriously white wings streaked with *grace*, spread wide and blocking out everything beyond them.

Zayne stood above, staring down at me with eyes that were too blue to be real, too cold to be his.

"Zayne," I whispered.

He didn't move. "That thing was going to kill you."

My heart started hammering. "Probably. Eventually."

Zayne tilted his head. "I couldn't allow that."

That was good. That was more than good actually. Relief started to creep into me—

"If you are to die," he continued, "then it seems only fitting that it should be by my hands."

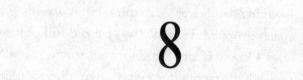

8

Well.

The relief and rising sense of hope was short-lived, crashing and burning rather spectacularly.

"How romantic," I muttered, ignoring the aching hollowness those words caused.

"You think?" he asked in a flatly apathetic way that was both unnerving and impressive. "After all, you said that I died because of you. Shouldn't you then die because of me?"

"I said you died *for* me, not because of me," I corrected.

"How is that any different?" He turned his head just slightly, and I could see that there was no wound under his chin. I hadn't cut him deep, but he'd already healed. "I wouldn't do that if I were you."

I couldn't see beyond his wings, but it didn't take a leap of logic to figure that Dez had been about to do something really brave and really stupid. And that he'd listened to Zayne's warning.

"Smart choice," Zayne said, his gaze settling back on me. There was a brief moment where I got to really look at that golden hue of his skin—at the luminosity that hadn't been there before Gabriel killed him. It was a subtle glow that probably wouldn't be noticeable to most, but it was his *grace*.

My stomach dropped. He truly was packed full of heavenly fire, and I knew if any Warden went toe to toe with him, to serve as a distraction for me to strike, they wouldn't survive. If Dez went after him…

I thought of Dez's wife, Jasmine, and how kind she'd been to me, and of his twin babies. He should be far, far from here.

But Zayne was in front of me, and I had to try, no matter the risk. No matter how selfish it was.

I managed to keep my voice level when I said, "We've been looking for you."

"I know."

"Is that so?" I worked hard to hide how his response unnerved me. "Why have you waited until now to make that known? Last time I saw you, you got up all in my face."

"I did," he replied without emotion. "But I've been busy."

My heart seized with dread. Were there more bodies, ones we just hadn't found? "With the dead guy behind us? That kind of busy?"

Zayne knelt, dropping down and tucking back his wings so quickly that I gasped. Our faces were only a few inches apart, and as close as we were, I could see that it wasn't just the color of his eyes that was different. The unearthly glow of *grace* was behind his pupils.

"Do you mourn his death?" he asked, the question startling me. The fact that he was kneeling with his back to

Dez told both of us he didn't remotely view the Warden as a threat. "Do you think he died an unjust death?"

"Why did you kill him?"

"Does it matter?"

"Yes," I said. "It does."

He eyed me coolly. "That man, if you could even call him that, was nothing more than the worst of predators. I sensed all his sin."

My heart tripped. "What…what do you mean?"

"I can sense the sin of man—their darkest, innermost thoughts," he repeated in a tone that suggested he didn't think I had two working brain cells to rub together. His gaze flicked up to the body behind me, and I mentally cursed the Throne for forgetting to fill me in on this new talent of his. "He didn't just have *thoughts* about children. He had *memories* of what he'd done."

I put two and two together and ended up with the taste of bile in my throat. I didn't know if it was right or wrong to feel a little bit of relief to know that the man had not been a good dude. Murder was bad and all, but if what Zayne claimed was true, I couldn't really feel all that bad for him. I just didn't know what that meant for Zayne.

Or for me.

But whatever.

"You're making a bad decision," Zayne said, jolting me out of my thoughts. He was watching me, but he wasn't speaking to me.

What was Dez doing?

"I'm feeling overly generous right now," Zayne said. "But take one more step and it will be the last step you take."

Did he have eyes in the back of his head? I had no idea,

but the cold threat carried the weight of truth. It was clear that it was his last warning.

Staring at him, I tried to reconcile the fact that even with the flatness of his tone and the predatory gleam in his eyes, it looked like Zayne. Yes, there were things that were different. The glow and the wings. But I couldn't process how changed he was. How could his Fall erase everything? Was the Glory—his soul—that powerful? Were there any memories of his life in him or just vague sensations associated with a consciousness he was no longer connected to? Was that why I felt familiar to him, but he didn't know why? Or care? Or was the reason why he killed the Ghoul, why he hadn't snapped my neck, because that consciousness still drove him on some primal, basic level he couldn't understand? Was it too late?

"Are you even still in there?" I whispered.

There was a flicker of emotion that tightened the skin around his eyes and mouth. Confusion? I thought so. It reminded me of how he'd stared at me when I'd touched his cheek instead of striking him.

If he was truly lost, he wouldn't feel confusion now. At least, that's what I thought—what I had to think. "Do you still feel too much?" I asked, remembering what he and the Throne had said about his Fall. "Do you know what you were before tonight? Who you were?"

He said nothing.

"You were a Warden, like him. You were my Protector, bonded to me. You died protecting me. Do you not remember that?"

Zayne's chest rose with a sharp breath.

"You did that because you love me and not because of any

bond or duty," I rushed on. "Do you not remember any-thing before Falling? Do you even remember your name?"

"I told you what you can call me," he snarled, sending a chill across my skin.

"What? Death? Fallen? That's not your name. It's Zayne," I stated, forcing everything I felt into the words. All of my love and fear for him, all my hope and my pain. "Do you remember his name? The Warden? He's like a brother to you—"

"Stop." He twisted his neck from side to side, eyes clos-ing briefly. "This is irrelevant. Who I was doesn't matter—"

"How can it not matter?" I argued. "You can't just be anger and hatred. That can't be all that you are. You didn't just start existing the moment you landed in the park. You had an entire life. You are kind and good and fair. You love. You grieve. You—"

"I am none of those things!" he roared, wings snapping out and spreading wide. The luminous glow intensified, pulsing so brightly that pain shot through my eyes. Golden-white light sparked from his arms, from *both* arms—

Several things happened at once.

I knew he was summoning his *grace*, and while I was cu-rious to see what kind of weapon it would produce, I wasn't stupid enough to find out. Dez shouted his name, shouted something else, and Zayne spun around. The edges of his wings glanced over my cheek in the softest caress as they rose high above me. I filed that away to obsess over later, surprised he hadn't whacked me over the head with them. Focused on Dez, his back was to me, and this was the mo-ment. He was distracted, and I couldn't let him reach Dez. This was my chance to either bring him back or...

Or give him peace.

He stepped away from me, and I called on my *grace*. Finally unleashed, it powered through me, turning the corners of my vision white. *Grace* powered down my right arm as I popped to my feet—

Zayne whirled so quickly it was almost unbelievable. He caught my right arm before my *grace* could even reach my wrist. Spinning me around, he clamped his other arm around my waist, drawing me back against him. The contact of his cold skin was a shock as he trapped my left arm to my side. "I don't think so."

The Sword of Michael flamed brightly, spitting and crackling heavenly fire, but his grip was like a vise. I could barely move my wrist. He'd known I was summoning the *grace*. I'd gone beyond stunned and straight into what the Hell territory. "How did you know?"

"I could feel it coming alive. I can feel it now, inside you. Calling to me," he answered, pressing his cool cheek to mine. "It's a fire in my blood and my bone. How could I not know?"

"That's a nifty and inconvenient ability," I snapped, barely resisting the urge to shriek. The Throne had insinuated such a thing, but he could've been way more clear about what he meant by Zayne being able to sense my *grace*.

"Isn't it?" His hand splayed across my hip. "You were going to attack me while my back was to you. Thought you loved me?"

Heart thumping against my ribs, I was acutely aware of how close his hand was to the hilt of my dagger and the grip he had on my wrist. It wasn't a painful hold. That seemed important to remember. "I do love you. I love you more than anything—"

"Doesn't seem like a very loving thing to do." His chin dragged along my cheek as his head shifted just the slightest. "Perhaps you don't value your life, because I would swear you just moved after I warned you not to. Maybe you value her life more? Keep moving, and I will kill her and then you."

The Warden froze, but a low, rumbling growl radiated from him.

Zayne chuckled, and the sound was so icy I shivered. "Is that supposed to scare me?"

"Yes." Dez clawed hands closed into fists. "It should."

"It doesn't."

I pulled at his grip, but I got nowhere with the sword. It jutted out into empty space. "You're not going to kill me."

"I'm not?"

"If you were, you would've done it already," I gritted out, still struggling.

"Perhaps I like playing with you." He moved his head again, gliding his cheek along mine in a way that was shockingly familiar and wholly different. "Maybe I will grow bored. Maybe I won't? But what I do know is you're going to burn yourself out the longer you pull on your *grace*, little nephilim."

"Of course you would remember *that* over everything else." Using everything in me, which was a lot, I pulled against his arm and his hold. A scream of frustration burst from me. I hadn't even moved an inch.

"You sound angry, *little nephilim*."

"It's not nephilim! It's Trueborn!"

Lifting my foot, I slammed it down on his bare one. Zayne yelped, more out of surprise than pain, but his hold on my waist loosened just enough. I ripped free, swinging my left arm down on the one that held mine. His fingers slipped an inch as I spun under his arm, twisting it. Edges of soft feathers tickled my cheek as a dark shape landed next to me. Dez reached for Zayne's arm, teeth bared.

One second I was so close to breaking Zayne's hold—so close to using the Sword of Michael—and the next I was swept off my feet and into the air. My *grace* sputtered out as I hit the grass. The impact was brutal, but it could've been worse. I could've been Dez.

He slammed into one of the fountain basins, cracking the stone. He dropped into the pool of water.

Zayne had flung both of us like we were paper planes, but somehow I ended up in a much softer, kinder to the body area. Dez was in his Warden form. He'd be fine, but if I had hit the basin at that kind of speed, I would be out like a light.

I started to pull on my *grace*. It flared weakly in my chest, just below my heart. I shouldn't be as tapped out as I was now. It had to be the fact my body was still healing itself from Gabriel's beatdown, because I shouldn't be *this* exhausted.

Wings stirred my hair, serving as a warning that Zayne was near. I flipped onto my side, tipping my head back. He stood above me, *grace* rippling through his widespread wings. Our gazes met and then held. He watched me, nostrils flared, as I struggled to my feet, not breaking eye contact. The opportunity to take me out was endless. At any point, he could end my life before I even realized what was happening. But he made no move against me. Maybe it was foolish naivety or desperation, but hope surged through me. If he was truly lost and saw me as nothing more than a threat and a challenge—and apparently a very poor one at the moment—he would take me out.

But he didn't.

He cocked his head as I stepped toward him, but he didn't move. Heart fluttering like a trapped bird, I took another step and then another, not stopping until there was only an inch or two separating us.

I had no idea what overtook me. Maybe I knocked a few important brain cells loose. Would make sense considering how many times I'd been thrown around in the last week. Or maybe I was too stupid to live. "Are you going to kill me now?"

A muscle ticked along his jaw.

Each breath I took was too shallow, too quick. "You could do it, right? Not even break a sweat. Why haven't you?"

His eyes widened slightly. "Do you want to die?"

I shook my head. "I want you. That's what I want. I want *you* back."

His brows knitted, and then I saw his gaze drop to my mouth. The predatory glint to his features changed, becoming intense in a wholly different way. Inherently, I recognized that look and the sudden tautness of need, of want. It was one of the first human things I'd seen from him since he returned. His lips parted, and I didn't know if he was about to say something or not. I moved faster than I realized I could right then. Reaching up, I clasped his chilled cheeks as I stretched onto the tips of my toes. I pulled his head down to mine, and I pressed my lips to his.

I kissed him.

The feel of him was the same in some ways. His skin was smooth under my palms. The shape and form of his lips were the same. He still tasted of fresh, morning air. But that was where the similarity ended. He didn't move. His lips were too cold. I wasn't sure if he breathed as I tilted my head, praying and begging for some reaction that proved Zayne was still in there, that he hadn't completely become this inhuman creature.

There was nothing.

Tears pricked at my eyes. I kissed him again and again, my cheeks becoming damp—

Then Zayne *changed*.

His mouth yielded under mine, softening and opening. He tilted his head, aligning his mouth with mine more fully, and I could've screamed hallelujah, but that would've been weird and counterproductive at the moment. That was the last thing I wanted to be. I felt the touch of his tongue, and that wasn't cold. My body flushed. It wasn't just me kissing him. He was kissing me back, and it didn't remain soft or questioning. It deepened, becoming hungry and wild, consuming and potent. A wave of shivers pimpled my skin. A deep rumbling sound came from the back of his throat, and the flush became even hotter. The tips of his fingers touched my cheek, my hair. His hand flattened, his skin cool but warming against mine—

Zayne jerked his head away so suddenly I almost toppled over. In a daze, I opened my eyes and saw that he was standing several feet away, under one of the bright park lights. Even I could see that his chest was rising and falling as sharply as mine.

"You're still in there," I whispered.

His head twisted to the left and then to the right, stretching the tendons of his neck as his eyes closed. "I don't know what you mean."

"That's okay," I said, wiping the tears from my face with shaking hands. "Because he does."

"Who?" he asked hoarsely.

"Zayne."

His eyes flew open. Those wings lifted, arcing high, and for a long moment, I thought I had it all wrong. He was going to use the *grace* burning through his wings against me, and that Throne was going to be real disappointed in me.

"I'm done playing with you," he warned. "The next time I see you, I will kill you."

And with that, he snapped those powerful wings down and lifted off. He rose so fast he was like a star ascending instead of falling. He shot into the night sky, rapidly becoming nothing more than memory.

Water sloshed as Dez climbed out of the fountain, grunting as he hit the ground. "Did you seriously just kiss him?"

"I did." I didn't take my eyes off the night sky. The darker shapes of the clouds that had lingered since yesterday's rainstorm were clearing. Wet warmth trickled out from my nose. I reached up, wiping the blood away before it could hit the ground.

"I honestly don't even know what to say about that."

"He's still in there." I squinted and then closed my right eye, the one with the thicker cataracts.

There was a pause of silence. "You sure about that, Trin-

ity? Because there was nothing about that thing that be-
haved like Zayne."

I saw them. Tiny specks of light. I saw *stars*. "Yes. I'm sure."

9

For the second night in a row, I limped back into the empty apartment in the dead of the night. Kicking off my shoes by the door, I dropped the key card on the counter and then headed straight for the shower. This time, there was only dirt and the pieces of grass that had somehow ended up in my hair circling the drain. No blood. I reckoned that was an improvement as I pulled on one of Zayne's clean shirts. It made for a pretty decent sleep shirt, and at the current moment, I doubted he cared.

Gathering up the blanket and pillow from where I left them on the couch, I brought them back into the bedroom— into the one that was supposed to be ours. Using an aching hip to close the door, I turned to the bed. The soft white glow from the ceiling wasn't nearly enough light, but I shuffled forward, squinting into the darkness—

My knee cracked off the frame of the bed. The sting of pain was deep and throbbing. "Crap."

Breathing through the obnoxiously intense pain, I dropped the blanket onto the bed and tossed the pillow to the head. Then I climbed in and, after taking a deep breath, I looked up at the ceiling. The pang to my heart felt like a stab wound as I tracked the faint light from each star randomly scattered across the ceiling.

Back in the Potomac Highlands, I had stars on my ceiling. Some may find them incredibly gaudy, but it was so difficult for me to see the real ones. Half of the time when I thought I saw a star, I was actually seeing lights from a plane or a cell phone tower. One day, a day I could tell was rapidly approaching, I would look up to the sky and no longer be able to see something as simple and stunning as a sky blanketed with stars.

Zayne had known how important being able to see stars, even fake, glow in the darkness was to me. What he'd done by placing them on the ceiling, during a time that I'd been convinced that he hated me and so regretted the Protector bond, was one of the most beautiful things anyone could ever have done for me. That was the Zayne I knew was still inside the fallen angel.

I had hope.

Not the wishful thinking kind of hope, but the real deal. I knew it wasn't too late. Zayne had endless opportunity to kill me. From the moment he arrived, right up until he took off like a rocket an hour or so ago, he could've done serious damage to me. And if he wanted me dead, taking out that Ghoul hadn't helped his cause.

Then again, the whole "I should be the one who kills you" thing didn't bring the warm and fuzzies, but maybe when he tossed Dez and I, it hadn't been a coincidence that

I ended up in a much softer area. Or that when he'd turned, he avoided knocking me out with those wings. It could've all been on an unconscious level, one he couldn't understand in his present state.

And the man that he'd killed? The jury was still technically out on that. Before we left the park, Dez had found the man's ID and had Gideon checking to see if he could dig up anything on the guy. If what Zayne had claimed was true, he hadn't taken an innocent's life. I could argue all day the semantics of whether any murder was justifiable, but it wasn't like Wardens hadn't taken out bad humans in the past who'd not only been assisting demons, but were actively committing horrendous deeds. So, No Regrets on that front for the time being.

What was important was that Zayne was still in there. I just needed to figure out how in the world I could pull this off.

I tugged the blanket up to my chin as I stared at the stars. Finding Zayne seemed damn near impossible. Was I going to need to put myself in harm's way with a demon for him to show up again? I didn't make a good damsel in distress, so I doubted that plan would work. Not only that, what if I ended up in Gabriel's hands? Even if I figured out a way to lure Zayne back out into the open, how would I be able to use the Sword of Michael? Since he could sense me calling on my *grace*, there would be no element of surprise. I was going to have to fight him, and somehow gain the upper hand. I was going to need everything in me to pull that off. It would be like fighting Gabriel all over again, and I knew how *that* had ended.

I wished I could find something that not only brought him to me but knocked him unconscious.

I sighed. I knew wishes on stars weren't answered, but I was willing to try—

My eyes widened. It was then, as I stared up at the softly glowing Constellation of Zayne, that my wish was granted in the form of an idea.

There was one person that I had a feeling could get Zayne to come to me, whether he wanted to or not. And if anyone knew how to incapacitate a fallen angel, it would have to be her.

The Crone.

There was no way I could sleep after discovering what I hoped was a way to get Zayne where I needed him.

Energized, I swung my legs off the bed and turned on the bedside lamp. The only problem was that I had no idea where that hotel had been that Roth had taken me to when we'd met the witches. It wasn't like I'd been able to see any of the street signs or had the foresight to ask directions. There was also a chance that the Crone had already left the city, like the rest of the coven had. Well, the ones who were still alive.

Wasn't like I could ask Roth or Layla since I figured Hell didn't have cell phone coverage. Gideon probably could find its location, but I wasn't sure I wanted to put what was left of the coven on the Wardens' radar. Sure, they had bigger problems right now. We all did, but witches were definitely on the to-kill Warden list. Some of them, namely Faye, had deserved it after providing a spell to the senator that basically turned humans into cannon fodder, but not all witches did.

Just ones who wanted to use parts of my body.

But there could be a chance that after everything, if there was an after, the Wardens could go after the witches. As bad as I needed to know that information, I couldn't do that.

However, I did know a certain demon who wasn't returning my calls who had showed up at the hotel to break the contract that freed Bambi.

Realizing I'd left my phone in the kitchen, I rose and went to the door, opening it.

The explosion of tingles along the base of my skull was sudden and sharp. My hand went to my thigh, only to discover that I didn't have my iron daggers with me. They were on the dresser? Nope. The bathroom counter. Dammit.

But I had my *grace*. It pulsed in my chest, not as intensely as usual. I needed rest and time, but neither thing was going to happen.

The open space in the narrow hallway warped. Really hoping this wasn't another creepy Ghoul and trying not to be freaked out by the implications that a demon was about to pop itself into the apartment, I tapped into the *grace*.

A second later, a dark-haired demon stood in front of me. Relief swept through me as I recognized Cayman.

I pulled the *grace* back in. "I was this close to killing you. How did you get in here?"

"Since I've been invited in, I can come here whenever I please." He dropped the bomb of information like it was nothing, knocking windswept hair back from his face. "And yes, before you ask, that's where the vampire mythos came from. Needing to be allowed in to enter. And no, vampires aren't real. Demons are."

I hadn't been planning to ask about the whole vampire thing, and I also didn't remember either Zayne or me in-

viting him in here at any point. I also superdoubted Zayne
would be pleased to learn this, but at the moment, it didn't
matter. "I've been trying to get ahold of you."

"Have you? Well, you see, I've been busy running around
the entire damn city, getting all the Fiends out while trying
to stay alive," he told me, and come to mention it, he did
look a little frazzled. He was normally quite polished, but
the black shirt featuring the band BTS was wrinkled and
torn at the collar, and I had no idea if the hole in the knee
of his jeans was a fashion statement or not.

"That's why I didn't sense any demons tonight. Why?" I
asked, wondering what else could possibly be going wrong.
"What's happening?"

"What's happening?" His dark brows climbed up his forehead. "Are you serious right now? As if you don't know?"
He stepped closer, and I caught the scent of…burned wood?
And his eyes, normally a golden hue, were now like heated
coal. "What did you do, Trinity?"

I frowned. "Uh, yeah, I have no idea what you're talking about. I didn't do anything, and yet, here you are, in
my personal space. Do I need to remind you that you're
afraid of me?"

"Yeah, you *were* one of the baddest creatures walking
these streets and I *was* afraid of you, but that was until I met
a certain freaking fallen angel rocking a Heaven ton worth
of *grace* who apparently has amnesia and a sudden, extreme
dislike of all demons."

"Oh," I whispered, tensing. "You're talking about Zayne."

"Oh? *Oh?* That's all you have to say? Yes! I'm talking
about Zayne, who just happens to be a very, very powerful

fallen freaking angel, in case you didn't hear me the first time around."

"I did hear you. That's why I've been trying to get ahold of you. I had no idea he was going to go after you or any demon, but I tried to give you a heads-up. You didn't answer."

His eyes narrowed. "I don't like to talk on phones."

"I texted you!" I shot back. "And I quote, 'I need to talk to you. It's important.'"

"And as I said, I was kind of busy trying to stay alive."

I crossed my arms. "And how was I supposed to know that?"

"Did it occur to you to leave a message that said, 'Hey, my favorite demon broker, Zayne is back. He's a Fallen, so you better run for the freaking hills'?"

"I didn't think that was something I should text or leave as a voice mail considering no one has believed me when I first told them that," I reasoned. "And I had no idea he would go after any demon."

"Of course he'll go after demons!" he said like it was something I should've already known. "He's obviously a recent Fallen. They go after any and everything that has an ounce of power in them, and they especially hate demons. It takes decades for them to get over the whole 'I'm still better than you lowly demons' attitude, which, hello, where do you think the Wardens got that from? Which is why not many of them joined Team Hell."

"Wait." I stared up at the demon. "You knew what the Wardens originally were?"

"Duh, Trinity. Duh." He turned and walked into the

kitchen. As he went, the lights turned on. "Running for your life works up an appetite, so I'm starving."

"How in the world did both you and Roth know this and manage to keep your mouths relatively shut?" I trailed after him. "How have demons not been shouting this from the rooftops?"

"Not every demon knows this." Cayman lifted his hand, and a box of Cheez-It Snack Mix flew across the room to his hand.

Man, I so wanted that talent.

"Only the oldest and the most connected with the Boss are aware of the true origins of the Warden. Shouting it from the rooftops would defeat that pesky blind faith thing, wouldn't it? That would tick off the One up there and the one down below. No one has time for that." He peeled open the box as he plopped down onto the couch. "And whatever Wardens have figured out their origins would go to their graves before admitting that they come from those who Fell," he said, repeating nearly the same thing the Throne had. "It was the Wardens who rewrote what became of the fallen angels. They killed their own dirty little secret."

"Okay. Great. You know all about the fallen angels, but you're still wrong." I dropped into the corner of the couch. "I didn't do anything. Zayne chose to Fall."

Cayman turned his head toward mine, and I wished I could tell if his eyes had lost the reddish black hue. "Do tell?"

I told.

I told Cayman all I knew, right up until moments earlier, when I realized that the Crone could be of help. "So, do you think what the Throne said was true? That my *grace* won't kill Zayne but bring him back?"

"Honest? I have no idea," he admitted, setting the empty box down on the counter. How he'd eaten the whole box of cheesy crackers was something I could relate to. "I've never known a Fallen to become anything other than a Warden or a really big player down below. And the ones who are on my team? Those who made it into Hell with their wings and *grace* still intact didn't keep them long. Our Boss is not dumb enough to allow something nearly as powerful as Him to be occupying the same 666 area code. He stripped their wings, therefore taking their *grace*. Even then, those Fallen are still hella powerful. Not even Roth wants to mess with one of them. Lucky for him and all of us, they take way too much pleasure in their jobs."

"Fallen angels in Hell have jobs?" I asked.

"Everyone has a job, Trin the Trueborn. We call them Judges. They spend their time making sure really bad people spend eternity wishing they had made better life choices," he said. "But the thing is, no angels have Fallen in a hella long time, like not since the Byzantine Empire kind of long time, and there's Layla. She's the closest thing to a Fallen, but not really."

"Huh? I thought she was part Warden and demon?"

"She is and she's not. Long story short, she was given the blood of one of the originals—you know, one of the very first of the angels to Fall. So was her mother, but again, she's not a true Fallen. Neither is Lilith."

I had not known that, and I felt like there was a whole lot of story there.

"Anyway, it's not like I'm an expert on what is possible for a recently Fallen who has their wings and *grace*, so I can't say if that Throne is telling the truth or not. I trust angels less than I do most demons, but I mean, it's sort of sweet."

My gaze flipped to him.

"That he Fell for you. That is…that is heavy, girl. The real deal kind of love. You know Roth went against the Boss's orders to be with Layla." He tipped forward. "That's like tantamount to angel falling, and that's real, deep love he has for you."

"I know," I whispered, sinking into the cushions of the couch.

"And call me a silly romantic demon, but I've got to believe anything is possible with that kind of love." Leaning back, he rested his ankle on his knee.

"I believe that, too." And I had to. I blew out a tired breath. "Did Zayne kill any demons?"

"Yeah. A couple. Okay, more than a couple. Took out a whole house of them to be honest," he answered.

"Oh, no." I rubbed my hand down my face.

Cayman chuckled. "Look at you, feeling bad for dead demons. You make a shit Trueborn, you know?"

"I know, but Zayne wasn't all about killing…well, not-really-evil demons."

"Yeah, I know. He's a progressive Warden," he said, and I dropped my hand. "Or was. Anyway, don't worry. They weren't 'not all that evil' demons. He got some who had it coming to them. Ones that were getting sloppy, blurring the rules. The ones in the house were nothing more than a pack of Ravers."

"You could've started with that, you know?" Ravers were like giant, walking-on-two-legs rat demons that ate everything, including people…and their bones.

"And you could've started with 'my boyfriend is now a fallen angel,'" he replied, and I thought I saw a smile on his face. "So, I guess we're even."

"I guess so. I'm sorry that he was chasing you," I offered. "I really do mean that."

"I know you do. And I don't take it personal." He paused. "And it was kind of hot."

My gaze shifted over to him as my brows lifted.

"What? Fallen angel Zayne tops the hotness meter. I can't help it." He shrugged. "I'm a demon."

"I'm sure Zayne would be happy to hear that he hasn't lost you as his number one fan," I said wryly.

"Oh, I'm not his number one fan. That's Bambi."

"What?" I held up my hand. "Wait. Don't answer that. I don't have the brain space to deal with hearing about that."

Cayman giggled, and it was as creepy as I imagined a demon giggling would be. "By the way, has he come here since he Fell? If so, I love chatting with you, but I'm going to have to bounce out of here like a rubber ball."

"He hasn't yet. I don't know if it's because he doesn't remember where he lives or if he's avoiding the apartment."

"Either way, I'm counting that as a bonus." He rested an arm on the back of the couch. "And you should, too."

I would, except Zayne coming here would make finding him a lot easier. Wouldn't help in the catching him off guard department, though. "So, do you know if the Crone is still at that hotel?" I got us back on track, and it was weird to be the person doing that when I was usually the one veering everyone off track. "And can you tell me where the hotel is?"

"I can take you to the hotel, but I have no idea if the Crone is still around and you're on your own once you get there," he added. "I think you're a cool little half angel, but I don't mess with the witches unless I'm summoned to broker a deal. I don't want to inadvertently tick one of them off and end with unmentionable parts of me that I'm fond of falling off or something equally terrible."

"Understandable."

"And before you demand that I take you there right now or when the sun comes up, you definitely won't find the Crone up at this time or anywhere but with her family on Sunday."

I hadn't even realized tomorrow was Sunday. Or today. Whatever. "Witches recognize Sunday as a day of rest?"

"That they do. So do some demons."

All righty, then.

"Your best bet is to try Monday afternoon." Kicking his feet up on the coffee table, he lifted his hand. The remote flung itself to him. "Get some rest. I'll hold down the fort."

Even though sleep seemed like the last thing I'd be able to do, I needed the rest, but Cayman couldn't stay here.

"You should leave," I told him.

Cayman arched a brow. "That's rude."

"It's not that I don't want you here. It's just not safe for you," I reasoned. "Zayne hasn't come here yet, but that doesn't mean he won't. Even you were worried about that, and if I'm asleep and he comes, you're dead."

"And if you're asleep and he comes, you're dead," he pointed out.

"He hasn't killed me yet and he's had plenty of opportunity. I don't think he's going to come here, but if you're here, I'm not going to get any rest worrying about you getting murdered while I'm getting my beauty sleep," I replied. "You do have someplace to go, right?"

He nodded. "I have places that Zayne hasn't been to."

"Then go there. I'll text you in the morning."

Cayman studied me for a moment. "Does this mean you like me? Care for me? Going to name any future babies after me?"

I rolled my eyes. "I wouldn't go that far."

"But you do like me." He pointed the remote at me and then him. "A wee little Trueborn cares about the safety of a demon. The world is surely going to end."

"Whatever." I grinned. "Get out of my house."

"It's an apartment."

"Shut up."

Cayman laughed as he rose from the couch. "I'm not going to lie. I'd rather be far away from wherever the Fallen-but-superhot Zayne will be, so try not to get killed between now and tomorrow."

"I'll try not to."

"See you later, home skillet." Cayman flashed the peace sign and then did the demon pop thing when he simply disappeared.

I really envied that.

Making sure the door was locked, I shuffled back to bed, and the moment my head hit the pillow I fell asleep.

I don't know what woke me, but something did. Disorientated, I sat up. It was still dark outside and the room was softly lit by the Constellation of Zayne. Wishing my eyes would get on board, I looked around the room.

A series of tingles erupted between my shoulder blades, erasing the lingering haze of sleep.

A demon was nearby.

Had Cayman returned? I doubted that as I shoved the blanket off and stood. The borrowed shirt slid past my hips and thighs as I reached for my daggers—

Dammit, they were still in the bathroom. I hurried in there, snatching them off the counter. I made my way into the living room. The overhead light in the kitchen had been left on, courtesy of Cayman, and I could see that no one was in the apartment. The feeling remained, though, buzzing between my shoulders. Was there a demon in a nearby apartment?

And where in the Hell was Peanut?

I started toward the door when I heard it—a clicking, scratching sound against glass. Slowly, I turned to the floor-to-ceiling windows. I could see nothing but darkness and distant, smudged light, but that didn't mean there wasn't something scratching at the windows.

"Oh, man," I muttered, creeping forward. Considering we were pretty high up in the apartment building, I knew there wasn't, like, a rather harmless, fluffy animal out there.

Grip tightening on the iron daggers, I passed the couch and my steps slowed. There was definitely something out there—the shadows were thicker. The eerie clicking came again, followed by the sound of something sharp digging against the thick glass.

I stopped in front of the window, squinting as I leaned forward, pressing my face against the cool—

Coal-red eyes set above flattened, fur-covered nostrils stared back at me.

I yelped, jumping back from the window. Suddenly I knew why it seemed like the shadows were moving. It was wings I'd been seeing, and there was definitely something furry outside the windows.

"Imps," I muttered, sighing heavily. The last time I'd seen them, they'd been sent by the Harbinger. Which meant if they were here now, Gabriel knew where I was.

Not exactly surprising, but scary.

And annoying.

Because I really just wanted to sleep, talk to the Crone and fix my slightly psychotic boyfriend. Was that too much to ask? Maybe if I just ignored the imp it would go away.

The imp slammed a clawed fist into the window, rattling the entire pane.

I guessed not.

The damn thing was going to crack the window, possibly even shatter it, and that was the last thing I wanted to deal with.

Sighing, I turned from the window. The imp hit the glass again. "Yeah, yeah. I hear you. You want to play. We'll play."

Barefoot, half-undressed and not even caring, I entered the elevator and hit the code for the rooftop. Hoping no one else was up there, I was relieved to find that it sounded empty as the doors quietly slid open.

I'd never been up here before, but I remembered Zayne saying once that it was designed as a green space for tenants. Solar string lights glimmered softly, strung from tall poles connected to white canopies stretched across large swaths of the rooftop. There was a pool somewhere if the scent of chlorine was any indication. Goose bumps pimpled my skin as I carefully navigated the deck chairs and round tables. Could be my eyes, but I sure didn't seen any "green" spaces as I prowled across the rooftop. A chilly breeze caught the canopies as I neared the glass plane that prevented people from toppling off the roof.

Tapping the iron dagger off the glass, I called out, "I'm up here waiting. Please hurry. I'm tired and cranky."

Silence, and then a low-pitched shriek reached my ears. Stepping back from the glass wall, I took a deep breath. There was barely enough light from the solar and moonlight for me to see, but it was manageable. I'd dealt with worse conditions before with far less training.

A second later, a dark shape swept up from the side of the building and over the glass wall. It landed on two clawed feet a foot or so from me, and for a moment, I really wished I hadn't been able to see the imp.

The thing must've fallen down a demon tree and hit every ugly branch on the way down. It looked like a giant, walking bat as it lifted nearly translucent wings and screeched.

I slammed the iron dagger deep into its chest. "Dumbass," I muttered as the demon went up in flames.

Imps were notoriously violent and their claws were quite toxic to humans and Wardens, but they weren't exactly known for their intelligence, as just proven.

Yawning, I pivoted and started back toward the door, dreams of the soft, Zayne-scented pillow occupying my thoughts. I made it two steps when a shadow dropped out of the sky, landing on the roof with a hard thump, and then another and another—

Seven imps stood in front of me, their bodies hunched. Maybe eight.

I skidded to a stop, my eyes widening as one of them hissed. Imps never traveled alone. I'd forgotten. "I'm the dumbass," I whispered, backing up as my *grace* throbbed inside me.

One of them lurched forward, and I hit the floor of the roof. Its outstretched arm swept over my head, and I popped up, shoving the dagger into its back. Heat blew back at me as I whirled, jabbing the dagger into the chest of another.

Flames erupted as a wing cut through the air, slamming into my side, and knocked me sideways. I tripped over a lounge chair that seriously came out of nowhere, landing in…plush grass.

Oh, hey, I found the green space.

I sprang up, scanning the shadowy rooftop, and spun around, heart thumping as I looked for any sign of the imps. There had to be five or six left. I wasn't sure. Counting was hard.

A blur of matted fur and red appeared in front of me. The imp was too close. I jumped back, grabbing the lounge chair that had just attacked me. Picking it up, I threw it at the imp.

The imp squeaked when the metal chair smacked it in the face. I stopped, never hearing a sound like that come from an imp before. "You sound like a dog toy. It's kind of cute."

Swiping the chair aside, it charged me.

I danced to the side, catching the demon in the throat with the dagger. The scent of sulfur choked me as I hobbled over the remains of the chair. "You don't smell cute, though." I gagged. "Or look cute at all—"

Talons gripped the back of my shirt, and a heartbeat later, I was in the air, high above the roof and rapidly climbing. The way-too-large shirt lifted as the imp flew over the roof. I began to slip out of the shirt. Panic exploded. What undies did I grab? Oh God, it was the pair that had Hump Day plastered across the ass. I was going to fall out of this damn shirt to my death and be found splattered on the sidewalk in undies that said Wednesday and it was *Sunday*.

People were gonna think I'd been wearing these for days. The medical examiner was going to be horrified.

I could not let that happen.

Still over the roof, I swept the daggers in a high, wide arc and sliced them through the imp's arms.

The imp shrieked as hot, wet blood sprayed the top of my head, and then I was falling, and fast. A wicked sense of déjà vu hit me, but this time there was no Protector to save me. This fall wouldn't kill me, but it was going to hurt bad, like a whole lot of broken bones kind of hurt, and I just got done healing.

At least, I didn't think this fall would kill me. My heart stuttered as I braced myself for pain—

An arm snagged me around the waist, stopping my free fall so suddenly the air was punched out of my lungs. I was a yo-yo, jerked up so fast that my entire body spasmed. My hands opened and the daggers slipped free, falling to the roof as my back connected with a hard chest that was colder than the air.

Wintermint surrounded me.

Heart thudding fast and heavily, I turned my head, catching the sight of plump white feathers streaked with gold cutting through the air.

Zayne had caught me.

Where he'd come from or why he was here didn't matter. He caught me, just like he had before, and that was further evidence he was still in there.

"You saved me," I gasped. "Again."

"Did I?"

"Obviously," I forced out, barely able to breathe through the gust of the cold wind as I looked over my shoulder.

Vivid blue eyes lit by *grace* met mine. "Huh."

I started to frown. "What does 'huh' mean?"

He veered to the left, out of the path of an imp. "It means this."

Zayne let go.

He dropped me.

10

Zayne actually dropped me.

I was too stunned to even scream as I plummeted. There was a shriek as the dark shape of an imp shot toward me, and wouldn't that be some shit if a damn imp saved my life.

Zayne caught the imp midair—

The shock of water seized my lungs as it reached up and swallowed me, dragging me down. Chlorine burned my eyes and nose.

I found the stupid pool.

Sinking to the floor of the pool like a bag of rocks, a red-hot fury whipped through me, igniting my *grace*. The corners of my vision turned white as I planted my feet on the bottom of the pool and kicked off. I swam upward, propelled by pure, unfettered rage. I broke the surface, dragging in mouthfuls of air as I shouted, "Asshole!"

The answering chuckle set me off further. I might have

had an anger-induced blackout, because I didn't even know how I made it to the deck of the pool. Water coursed off me as I *splashed* forward, the shirt clinging to some very unmentionable places. Heat rippled down my arm, followed by swirling white fire. *Grace* exploded from my hand, spitting flames as my fingers curled around the heated handle forming against my palm. The sword was heavy but inherently familiar.

An imp dropped out of the sky, landing in front of me. It opened its mouth.

"Shut up," I snarled as I sliced the Sword of Michael through the demon, my attention solely focused on the golden-white wings ahead.

Someone was about to lose some pretty feathers.

An imp erupted in flames as Zayne whirled toward me. His mouth opened as if he were about to say something. He snapped his jaw closed, his chin lowering along with his stare.

"That was not cool," I bit out.

"You stank of demon blood," he replied in that flat voice of his. His head tilted. "You're very wet, little nephilim."

Noting that his gaze was hung up on two very private areas that were clearly visible through the soaked shirt, I realized that I would have no problem stabbing him through the heart at the moment.

Not at all.

"I'm also very pissed." I joined my hands together on the hilt as I swung the sword forward. *Grace* spit and crackled, charging the air.

"I can tell." Zayne snapped forward, catching my wrists before the sword could reach him. "And I'm kind of turned on."

A scream of rage left me as I leaned back, bracing my weight on one foot. I kicked out, catching him in the stomach.

Zayne grunted, but didn't let go. "Ouch." He twisted his arm, spinning me around. He pulled me back against him and the chill of his skin seeped through the thin, wet shirt. "Didn't we just find ourselves in this very same predicament only a few hours ago?"

White fire crackled and throbbed as I pulled against his hold. "When you said you would kill me the next time you saw me?" I spat back. "Instead you saved me."

"But I'm still seeing you." His chin dipped, grazing my cheek. "Aren't I?"

"Yeah, and the night is still young." I threw my head back, but he avoided the blow. "Why are you even here?"

"I was watching your place."

I stiffened. Well, now I knew he remembered where we lived. "That's creepy."

"Is it?"

"Yes, and it's also wrong. It's *our* place."

His grip on my wrists tightened. "I don't know what you're talking about."

"Sure you don't. Keep telling yourself that you're going to kill me or that you didn't save me because you needed to do that. Whatever makes you feel good."

His other arm circled my waist. "You're making me feel good."

There was a rather shameful flash of heat in response to his words, to how his voice had finally changed, becoming rougher, deeper. I didn't know if I was more annoyed with myself or him at that moment.

"You're going to wear yourself out." His lips ghosted across the curve of my jaw, sending a fairly inappropriate shiver dancing over my skin. "And then what, little nephilim? No *grace*. No daggers. It'll just be me and you."

"It's always been just you and me, *Zayne*."

Whether it was my words or the use of his name that startled him, his hold loosened enough for me to slip my left wrist free. I twisted away from him, and for a second, the Sword of Michael throbbed intensely between us.

He smiled then, and my heart tripped over itself, because it was one of *his* smiles. Warm. Charming. Kind. Familiar.

"Maybe I'll keep you alive, then," he said. "Keep you in a cage, my pretty little nephilim. You can be my pet."

His pet? I blinked. He did not just suggest what I thought he did. "Maybe I'll cut off your—"

He yanked forward, and I tried to dig in, but my feet slipped over the wet deck. Tingles exploded along my shoulders.

He spun me out to the side. His wings snapped back as my gaze darted to the gathering shadows racing across the rooftop, toward us.

Chairs and tables lifted to the air, flying to the sides as two cyclones of red and black…smoke came at us.

I squinted. "What in the holy Hell?"

The smoke expanded and then scattered, revealing the demons' smooth, waxy skin and oval-shaped, pupilless eyes and holes for nostrils above wide, cruel mouths.

These weren't Ghouls. They were Seeker demons who were often sent to retrieve things of value for Hell.

How in the world did Gabriel get them on his side?

They skidded to a halt as they got an eyeful of…not me.

Of Zayne.

"Fallen," one of them whispered in a guttural voice.

Zayne lifted his wings. I didn't see it, but I felt them stir my hair as they rose above us.

The other Seeker demon cursed. "I didn't sign up for this." He turned on his heel and started to run, red and black smoke gathering around him.

Well, then.

Zayne lifted off the deck like a rocket. The Seeker demon didn't make it very far.

I glanced at the other demon. He started forward, clearly not as affected by me.

"You're coming with me, nephilim."

Now I was kind of offended.

"Don't make this hard," the demon ordered. "You'll just hurt yourself in the end."

"Really?" The Sword of Michael pulsed intensely. "God," I muttered, stepping to the side. "Tonight is the *worst*."

I swung the sword. The Seeker demon was fast, but I was faster. He jumped back, but I spun, slicing the sword high, catching him in the midsection. The fiery blade cut through him as if his bone and muscle were nothing more than tissue paper.

"Dammit," the Seeker demon muttered just before the flames rippled over his body...parts.

"Stimulating final words," I said, turning around.

The other Seeker demon met the same end. Sort of. There were sounds of a whole lot of...ripping and tearing that I didn't even want to think about.

My arms trembled as the *grace* throbbed in the center of my chest. I shouldn't be burned out yet, but I was getting close. Normally I could last longer, but again, wasn't like I was getting much rest. There was enough juice in me to do what needed to be done. My heart started racing again as wet warmth gathered under my nose. Zayne already felt my *grace*, so me pulling on it wouldn't alert him to what I was doing.

Now was a better time than any. That's what I told myself as I started across the roof to where Zayne stood. I wouldn't even need the Crone. Zayne was here, and even though I wanted to punch him really hard, he was in there. He had to be. Why else was he watching me? Why else had he showed not once but twice to back me up? He was in there, and I was going to free him, one way or the other.

Pressure clamped down on my chest as those magnificent wings soundlessly swept back. He looked over his shoulder at me. One side of his lips curled up as he dragged his lower lip between his teeth.

My stupid, *stupid* heart skipped, and my steps faltered for only a heartbeat.

And that was all it took.

He was just so fast, too fast, and even if I was in tiptop shape, it wouldn't have made a difference. He caught my arm before I could even lift the sword.

The glow under his skin increased as he lowered his head, coming within mere inches of the Sword of Michael. "You're bleeding."

I didn't get a chance to respond.

His other arm came around me, pulling me against him. I felt his muscles tense and bunch. For a moment, I thought he was going to lift in the air and take me away. Put me in a cage just like he said.

But he didn't fly in the air. He jumped sideways, and there was a second of realization. I lost my hold on the *grace*. The Sword of Michael collapsed just before we crashed through the water.

We went down together, a tangle of legs and churning bubbles. His gaze met mine through the rushing water as we sank and sank. His lips moved as he spoke, and Jesus, were angels part-fish or something? Were there gills in those feathers?

There was a better question to ask. Was he going to drown me? It was all too easy, with how tight he held me to him. There was no breaking his hold.

Before that question could give way to panic, he pushed off the bottom of the pool. We broke the surface moments later, and he let go. I didn't sink back, finding myself in a shallower end, where the water reached my waist.

Gasping for air, I backed up as I wiped under my nose. I glanced down, and in the faintest traces of the encroaching dawn, I could see the darker gleam of blood was absent on my fingers.

My heart stuttered again. Had he…had he known or remembered what my blood would do? Was that why he tossed us both in the pool?

I looked up, watching him…watch me. Neither of us spoke as I backed into the wall of the pool. He was close, his features clearer than they should've been to me. There was a tautness to the set of his lips, one I had only barely begun to understand but recognized nonetheless. My heart hammered now for a wholly different reason. He came closer, his wings slicing through the water behind him. I stiffened, but I didn't move.

He stopped in front of me, and I had to tilt my head back to meet his stare. "Why did you kiss me earlier?"

His question caught me off guard, and it took me a moment to answer. "Because I...I wanted to reach you."

Thick lashes I shouldn't be able to see lowered, shielding his gaze. "Did you?" he asked, his voice softer. More...more like Zayne than I'd ever heard.

A shivery wave of awareness skated through me. "You're here," I said thickly, lifting my hands from the water. I didn't even know what I was doing until I did it, placing my hands against his chest.

He seemed to suck in a deep breath at the contact, as I flattened my palms against his too-cold skin. I didn't push him away. I just...just touched him.

"You tell me if I reached you," I whispered as the edges of the shirt floated out from me, threatening to rise to the surface.

His gaze lifted to mine, and that glow...the radiance in his skin and his eyes burned brighter. He was almost painful to look at, but I didn't look away.

"I don't know why I'm here," he said.

I refused to believe that. "Yes, you do. On some level, you do."

His features tightened and then blurred as he lowered his head to mine. "Then tell me why."

11

How could I tell him in a way that he'd listen or understand, when I told him before? That it was because I loved him and he loved me, but words...words seemed to hold no meaning.

And I didn't know if that was why I did what I did next. If it was to reach him like I had before or if it was propelled by the ache that had settled low in me, or if it was just my reckless impulsivity that operated on the mantra of act first and think later.

The why didn't matter as I lifted my mouth to his. All that did was that it felt right even though he was either threatening to kill me or to put me in a cage, and I had really wanted to stab him in the heart earlier. For real. In no normal world would any of this be remotely okay. Certainly not what I was about to do. A whole lot of pearls would be clutched, but this...none of this was normal. We weren't normal, and the norms and rules and expectations were not black and white here. They were gray, and we were drowning in that, but I knew when he kissed me before, that there was still a part of Zayne in there that recognized me—recognized us, and everything we meant to one another. Reaching that part of Zayne was worth it all.

The moment my lips touched his, I shuddered—he shuddered. The kiss…it was nothing like in the park. There was no tentative prodding or hoping for a reaction in him. It was there, and his reaction was immediate.

"I… I need you," he said, voice thick.

"You always have me, Zayne."

His mouth pressed to mine, and the kiss tasted of water and wintermint, familiar yet unknown.

And that kiss, the touch of his lips, his tongue…it all quickly became something more, something deeper and harder. And it all quickly spun spectacularly out of control.

His arm swept around me and mine hooked around his neck. I pushed off the wall, pressing against him, and then he was pinning me back against the wall, the weight and feel of his body scattering any thoughts before they could form. My fingers sunk into the wet strands of his hair and his hand was under the water, gliding over my thigh and my hip, under the floating edges of the shirt and farther up, to exactly what had caught his attention earlier. My back arched as a strangled sort of sound left my lips.

It was captured in the maddening and dizzying kiss, and lost to all the soft sounds that followed. Heat burned me from the inside, warming his skin and setting fire to my blood. I lifted my legs and wrapped them around his waist, rocking against him as we kissed and kissed until I felt short of breath, and I didn't stop there. It was a primal sort of need that drove us, one that went beyond the physical, and it was like dancing precariously close to an edge—the way his tongue moved with mine, the way his hands explored and lingered on the swells and the dips of my body, moving over bare skin and then lower, slipping under the flimsy barriers of clothing. His hand opening and closing there, urging me to move, but I needed no urging. And it was a lot like tipping on that edge now—the way I grabbed at his skin, his shoulders, his arms, trying to bring him closer, and the way I moved and twisted, pressing against him until the throbbing ache became something so acute it was almost painful. It was in the way I pulled at the slippery, soaked waistband of his pants and in the way my hips jerked as he shredded the clothing.

Then we were toppling, tumbling and spinning over that edge.

And there was no coming back from this—from him—and no matter what the outcome was, I wouldn't want to. I wouldn't regret this, because this was him. It was Zayne who held and touched me, and it was he who created the tension deep inside me. That coil was already tightening and twisting when he lifted me away from the pool wall, when the immense pressure of him pushed in and in, until his hips met mine. There was a glance of discomfort, a shock of fullness that caused me to stiffen and gasp into his mouth, but it was Zayne who held himself still, and it was a ragged sound that came from his mouth. And then he moved. We moved, and there was nothing slow as we took each other.

And his mouth never left mine. I never stopped kissing him, not even when our bodies came together, not now when they rocked together, and when the coil unraveled, releasing a flood of rippling, intense pleasure, my cries fell on his lips as he shuddered all around me, in me.

It was only when the madness ebbed, long after the last of the tremors racking both of our bodies, that our lips finally parted. I didn't speak. Neither did he, but he still held me to him, his arms crossed over my back, and I still clutched his shoulders. He shifted, dragging his forehead across mine before he dropped it to my shoulder. His lips brushed the skin there and there was a soft nip.

Pulse slowing, I opened my eyes. The first thing I noticed was his wing. It was so close to my face that I could see that each panel of feathers was actually several smaller ones. I could see the fine network of veins glowing with *grace*.

I lifted a hand. The tips of my fingers brushed the downy softness—

His head snapped up and his hand was even faster. He caught my wrist, pulling my fingers back. "Don't," he warned, his other arm tensing around me. "They're..."

My heart was thumping again. "They're what?"

His eyes searched mine, but he didn't say anything for a long moment. He just held me there for what felt like a small eternity. "I know now," he said. "Why I come to you. It's this."

There was a spark of hope, but then my eyes narrowed. "It is not what we just did."

"It's not?" His arm tightened again, pulling me firmly against him and eliciting a gasp from me. "It's *this*." A look of arrogance settled into his features, but quickly vanished as his forehead returned to mine. "It's *more*."

The hope didn't just spark then. It roared like a bonfire. "It is more."

"I know." He let go of my hand and waist, clasping my hips. He lifted me away from him in a way that was surprisingly gentle, at least for this...version of Zayne. His hands remained there for a couple of moments and then slid away. He stepped back from me, the glow easing in his skin until it was faint. "That's why you need to stay away from me, because I will hurt you. Even if I don't want to or mean to, the thing that's taking up a part of me will hurt you. Stay away from me."

Then he was gone in a fine spray of water.

I sunk back against the wall of the pool as I stared at the spot Zayne had stood.

The thing that's taking up a part of me will hurt you.

Those words were important. There was a recognition there. There was more proof that on some functioning level, Zayne was in there. Not that I needed all that much more proof.

His words left a chill behind, but my heart... I pressed my fist against my chest. It wasn't hurting as bad as it had been.

I don't know how long I stayed in the pool, but the pearly gray of dawn had begun to track across the sky before I finally moved. There was no sign of my undies...or my critical-decision-making skills as I climbed out of the pool.

Did I regret what just happened? No. Should I? Some might think I should, and even I could recognize it wasn't the greatest life choice as I padded across the rooftop, finding my daggers by the stupid "green space" that was the size of a box. Had I missed an opportunity to use the Sword of Michael when he'd been...distracted? Probably not. Besides the fact that I had been equally distracted, I knew he still would have sensed me summoning my *grace*.

I entered in the code for the apartment as my mind turned over everything. Considering we hadn't…we hadn't used protection and we'd had no idea if making a baby was a thing that could occur between us before, let alone now, that hadn't exactly been the most intelligent of things. Hell, I didn't even know if it was possible for Trueborns to reproduce. What little I did know didn't include the birds and bees.

But it happened.

Nothing was going to change that.

And I would just have to add that to the ever-growing list of things to worry about, along with the fact that both Zayne the Fallen and Gabriel's minions knew exactly where to find me.

Man, I was actually grateful that Jada wasn't here, because I would blurt it out to her within five seconds, and she would…well, she would have a lot to say.

I didn't have the brain space for it right now, though. I couldn't even really think about what just happened. I changed into a dry shirt of Zayne's and climbed back into bed, falling asleep with the daggers on the pillow beside my head.

I slept through a good part of Sunday, waking only to answer texts and to use the bathroom. I didn't realize until then that I truly hadn't given my body all the time to heal that it needed. My body probably needed more time, but one of those texts I'd answered had been from Dez.

Something had happened at the world's worst high school. He'd planned on telling me more about it when he picked me up, but considering what was going on there, I doubted whatever happened was going to leave me feeling the warm and fuzzies afterward.

Luckily there were no additional demon or fallen angel visits while I was all but passed out, but I didn't know how long that reprieve would last. The apartment may be compromised, and even if I brought Zayne back to his senses, we may not be able to stay here.

But that was a problem for later. Just like what I'd done with Zayne in the early hours of the morning, and whether Peanut really was sucked momentarily into purgatory.

I saw Peanut after I pulled on a pair of jeans and a loose shirt long enough to hide my daggers. He'd asked about the scratches in the window, and when I told him it had been a demon trying to get in, he shrieked and disappeared.

I hadn't seen or heard him since.

After eating an entire box of microwave bacon—RIP, my arteries—I headed down to meet up with Dez.

Squinting in the overcast skies, I cautiously approached the black SUV idling at the curb. I hoped it was Dez, and I wasn't about to get kidnapped.

The passenger window rolled down, and Dez's blurry face came into view. "Hey," he called out. "Hop in."

Opening the door, I hoisted myself into the passenger seat. I glanced at him, and immediately thought of Zayne and that pool. Feeling my cheeks burn, I was grateful he was focused on pulling into the traffic. I really needed to not think about any of that at the moment.

"So, what's up with the school?" I asked as I leaned back and pulled a hair tie out of my pocket. I held the tie in my mouth and then gathered up my hair.

My hair smelled like chlorine.

Ugh.

"Other than something not good? Not exactly sure," he replied. "The police captain got in touch with us an hour or so ago on something she thinks is more up our alley of expertise."

The relationship between the Wardens and law enforcement was an odd one since ninety-nine percent of the world was oblivious to the truth because of stupid rules. As far as I knew, only those in the highest echelons of departments knew what Wardens really hunted. Most of them found out through some level of demon exposure. Exceptions to the rules had been made, and some were brought into the know after proving they could be trusted with the truth. How anyone could prove that they were that trustworthy was beyond me, but Thierry once told me that officials in every state and within every federal law enforcement agency, from the FBI to the Department of Defense, and every intelligence agency in between, were aware that demons were definitely among us. Matthew had hinted at a super-extra-secret department within one of the agencies that dealt with demon activity. I had no idea if that was true, but if it was, were they tapping out on the whole Gabriel issue?

Couldn't really blame them if they were.

"Apparently they received several missing-persons calls from families of construction workers who were working at the school on Saturday," Dez continued. "None of the workers returned home or are answering the phones."

"Oh, man," I muttered around the hair tie as I gathered my hair and quickly braided the mess. That school was packed with lost souls. Most of them had been ghosts who hadn't moved on and had become vengeful, angry wraiths. They posed a threat to anyone in that school, but they weren't the only ones there. The school was bursting at the seams with Shadow People—the essence left behind by a demon who died—and they were far more dangerous and terrifying than a wraith having a bad day on the Mondayest of Mondays. All of the ghosts, wraiths and Shadow People were basically trapped there, waiting for the portal to open so they could enter Heaven, infecting it like a really bad outbreak of chickenpox. How in the world anyone could actually work in that building was beyond me, but the facade of restoration was in full swing. Even humans who didn't believe in ghosts had to sense something off about the school.

"Yeah." Dez nodded as he slowed the SUV down at a crosswalk. "A unit went out to check on it and they lost contact with them after they entered the building."

Tying the end of the braid, I looked over at Dez. "That's not good."

"It's not."

"And let me guess, there's more not good news to be shared."

"Yep. Another unit went out to check on them. They went into the building and only one came out."

My brows lifted. "Did the school eat the partner?"

"According to the cop, his partner was sucked into the ceiling by a giant black mass."

My lips parted. "So, the school did eat their partner. Jesus." I shook my head. "That school needs to be shut down."

"Agreed, which is what I told the captain. Since it's probably going to be a crime scene of sorts, it'll stop people from going in for a short bit. She's looking into what she can do to get the construction stopped more long term." He turned right and we moved about a foot before stopping again.

I frowned as I stared out the window. Why in the world was there so much traffic on a Sunday evening?

Dez had a better question. "Did you happen to see a giant black mass the last time there?"

I snorted. "No, but I saw a crap ton of ghosts and Shadow People. I'm no expert on Shadow People, but that may be something they did—sucking someone through a ceiling."

"This should be fun," he commented. "I figured since you could see them and we can't, it was a good idea to bring you in."

I nodded. Made sense. "And something has to be happening there. As crazy as it seems, workers have been in there for how long without major problems. Before that, summer school? And the only thing I know that has happened has been a kid being pushed down the steps. So what could've possibly changed now?" I thought that over. "Then again, the spirit of Sam? He came back to warn Stacey to stay away from the school, because he sensed something bad was about to go down. I figured it was the portal he was sensing."

"Maybe they wanted to clear the school out in preparation for the Transfiguration?" Dez suggested. "But that doesn't make much sense." He dragged a hand through his hair. "That's at least two weeks from now."

Looking out the window, I wondered if something had triggered the ghosts and Shadow People to become more violent? Or if it was just nature taking its course? Any ghost or wraith would become more dangerous the longer it was trapped.

"You're awful quiet over there."

"Sorry. Just thinking."

"About Zayne?"

I shrugged. I hadn't told him about my plans to go to the Crone, but decided against it. That was something better left not being shared until tomorrow. I had a feeling he would either try to talk me out of it or invite himself along.

Dez was silent for a moment. "Nicolai didn't want me to call you in on this."

"What?" I looked over at him.

"With everything going on with Zayne, he's concerned you'll be distracted."

Me? Distracted? I almost laughed. "First off, I'm always distracted. I'm in a constant state of distraction." I held up two fingers. "Secondly, I'll admit it. Zayne is a priority. Right or wrong, I don't care. But dealing with the Harbinger is still my duty. This is what I've been...bred for." My lip curled. Bred? That sounded terrible. "This is what I've been *training* for. If something is going down with anything that has to do with the Harbinger, I need to be in on it. I can separate what's going on with Zayne and with the Harbinger, and finally..." I stared at my three raised fingers and then lowered my hand. "I don't have a finally. I just have one and two."

Dez grinned. "I know, but he's worried that this could be a trap. A way Gabriel is going to try to lure you out."

"It could be," I said, and Dez glanced over me. "I don't know if he believes that the Wardens would bring me in or not. Maybe he does, but it's not like he doesn't know where I live. Imps and another demon showed up last night."

"What? And you're just now bringing this up?"

My eyes widened as Dez hit the brakes. A smaller red car

had zipped out in front of him. "It's not a big deal. I took care of them."

"Not a big deal? You're not safe there if Gabriel knows where you're staying."

"Gabriel has probably always known where I've been staying, and for whatever reason he sent his minions after me last night," I pointed out.

"You can stay with us—"

"And put you in danger? Your wife and children? Is that what you're suggesting?" I watched his jaw harden. "Because what's stopping him from finding me there? I'm not willing to risk that. I don't think you are, either."

He was quiet as he guided the SUV down the tree-lined hill. "You shouldn't be there by yourself."

"I'm not. I have Peanut."

Dez looked over at me.

"He's a ghost," I stated with another shrug.

"I don't even know what to say to that."

"There's nothing to say." I tapped my foot on the floor of the car. "I appreciate your concern. Even Nicolai's. But I'm fine where I am and if that changes—" it quite possibly could "—I'll let you all know."

"I get why you don't want to leave the apartment."

"You do?" I arched a brow.

"You don't want to leave in case Zayne comes back. You want to be there."

I opened my mouth, but snapped it shut as I stared at the dark blue of the sky. Pressure clamped down on my chest. I didn't want to put anyone else at risk, and I knew there could come a time that I would have to leave the apartment, but Dez was also right. I wanted to be there in case Zayne somehow snapped out of this without my intervention. I wanted to be there in case he came looking for me.

Even if it wasn't to snuggle.

If Dez knew that Zayne had already been at the apartment—the roof of the apartment, to be exact—he'd probably hog-tie me and stash me away.

And I knew I was being irrational. I knew I should pack my ass up and hunker down, but when did I ever do the rational, sane thing? Never. I started nibbling on my thumbnail. But maybe by this time tomorrow night I'd have a way to neutralize Zayne so I could bring him back.

Or set him free.

"You need to be careful, Trinity," Dez started.

"I am." Kind of. Weight settled on my shoulders as the high school came into view. One marked police vehicle sat outside, beside another black, unmarked car.

Never did I think I'd be so happy to see a haunted high school.

Dez pulled in behind the unmarked vehicle. Killing the engine, he turned to me, and instinct told me he was gearing up for some kind of deep talk.

"Look! Cop lady!" I unhooked my seat belt and threw open the door. I all but fell out of the SUV.

Cop Lady was standing outside the unmarked sedan, speaking into her phone. Whether it was my shout or extraordinary exit/fall from the vehicle that gained her attention, the tall Black woman turned toward me.

I gave her a rather jaunty wave. "Did you call the Ghostbusters? If so, we're here."

She slowly lowered the phone and turned to Dez.

"Captain Washington, this is Trinity." Dez already sounded tired. "She's, uh, consulting with us."

"Really?" The police captain's tone was overflowing with doubt.

"She's an expert in these kinds of things," Dez insisted.

"'I see dead people.'"

The captain opened her mouth and it took a moment for her to say, "You know, that's just cool with me."

I grinned.

"So what's going on in there, Captain Washington?" Dez asked while shooting me a look I could read clearly.

Shut. Up.

"Hell if I know, Dez. I got three missing officers and one sitting in his cruiser," she said, and as she placed the phone into the front pocket of her dark slacks, the short-sleeved blazer was pushed back, revealing the gun holstered at her side. "All he's been doing is praying."

My brows lifted. "For real?"

She spared me a brief glance, nodding. "He hasn't said much. All I know is that they didn't make it past the main hall before Officer Lewis was grabbed."

"By a black mass in the ceiling?" Dez clarified.

"Yes, and let me tell you, Officer Lee has been on the force for thirty years. There is very little that freaks him out." Placing her hands on her hips, she looked up at the school. "I've never seen him like this. I believe he saw what he said he did. That's why I called you guys in, but like I told the other ones, I can't promise how long I can let you guys have first go at this. I have missing officers, and even though the second call wasn't over the radio, the first one was."

I frowned. "Others—?"

A shadow dropped from above, landing with a loud thump in front of me. I squeaked, jumping back. All I saw was the hard, gray skin of a Warden. "Good God."

"Sorry," came the gruff reply as smooth-skinned wings snapped back. The Warden put a good foot or three of personal space between us. The dark-haired head bowed. His horns were the color of polished obsidian. "I didn't mean to startle you."

"It's okay." I looked up at the roof, squinting. Another Warden was perched on the edge. He stepped off, joining the first Warden. This one had lighter brown hair, cropped close to the skull, and horns, like the one before. "It's raining gargoyles."

"We waited like you asked," the first Warden said, and as I recovered from my mini heart attack, I realized he was wearing a shirt. While he was in his Warden form with wings out.

Huh.

"We haven't heard anything coming from inside there," the other Warden said while I stepped sideways to get a better view.

The shirt the first Warden wore had two slits running up both sides of his spine. More than enough space for his wings to come out. That was ridiculously clever, and embarrassingly so, considering no one else seemed to have caught on to that method.

"Not a single sound," the first Warden confirmed, glancing at me.

I clasped my hands together and smiled. "I like your shirt."

He turned briefly to Dez and then swallowed. "Thanks?"

"She's a...consultant?" Captain Washington asked. "In what capacity other than seeing dead people?"

"*That* kind," I said, pointing to the darkening sky as I allowed the *grace* to pulse inside me.

People normally had no clue what I was. Not until I allowed a little of my *grace* through. I had no idea what they saw or if it was something they sensed—something that spoke to whatever survival instinct in them—but Captain Washington took a step back, bumping into the fender of the sedan.

And she didn't look like a lady that took a step back often.

"Cool. Cool," she whispered, clearing her throat. "You all should get in there."

"We'll find your officers," Dez promised, and I thought that probably wasn't the smartest thing to do.

Dez caught ahold of my shirt as he walked past, bringing me with him. "I thought you weren't supposed to reveal what you are," he stated in a low voice.

"She doesn't know what I am, and the Wardens already know, so whatever." Taking a deep breath, I finally lifted my gaze to the actual school.

Immediately, I wished I hadn't. Lights were on inside, a glare that was welcomed and yet grotesque. Hundreds of tiny bumps broke out over my skin. Like before, it felt like thousands of eyes were on me even though the lit windows of the first floor were empty.

They were still in there—the ghosts, wraiths and Shadow People. And they were waiting.

12

I climbed the wide steps carefully, not wanting to trip and break my neck in front of the captain. That would totally ruin my perceived badassery. My sedate pace had nothing to do with the creepy crawly sensation tap-dancing over my skin. Nope. Not at all.

Once we reached the covered entrance of the school, I drew in a shallow breath and looked to the two Wardens. The feeling of being watched increased tenfold. "I don't think I've met either of you."

"Only in passing," the one with the clever shirt replied. "My name is Jordan." He then nodded his head at the other Warden. "That's Teller."

The lighter-haired Warden nodded.

"It's nice to meet you guys." I refocused on the school. "I hope you all are smart and listen to me when I say you should stay out here."

"That's not going to happen," Dez stated in a gravelly voice, having shifted as we'd made our way up the steps.

"I already know you're not smart. I'm hoping they are." Tension settled on the nape of my neck. "You guys aren't going to be able to see what's in there unless they're really powerful. You might get lucky or unlucky, and be able to see the Shadow People if they want to be seen. Either way, there's probably not going to be much you can do."

"We know that," Teller answered as he scanned the windows. "But we're not letting you go in there by yourself. It's bad enough that you're even here. Nic's going to have our asses for that alone."

"You're not going to talk us out of this," Jordan confirmed. "We're going in there with you. Arguing will just delay this, and what good will that do?"

None. Because if anyone was still alive in there, they needed to be rescued. Worse yet, I had a feeling that the captain would have to make a move to get her officers out, which meant more people would be going in there, and that was the last thing I wanted.

"Okay. If you need years of therapy because of this, you can't say I didn't warn you," I said, starting forward.

My foot immediately snagged on the step I didn't see. I stumbled forward, catching myself as Dez took ahold of my arm.

"You okay?" Jordan asked.

"Yes." I sighed. "I'm basically legally blind—actually, I'm legally blind," I said, surprising myself with the truth.

"Damn," Jordan murmured. "I would've never noticed."

"Really?" I said doubtfully.

I thought I saw a half grin. "I just assumed you weren't very observant."

"Well, that's also true," Dez commented.

I rolled my eyes, but I… I couldn't believe I'd just admitted to virtual strangers that I couldn't see well. I always either kept my vision issues to myself or played it off like it wasn't that big of a deal, which usually ended with me walking into something sharp and painful or being unable to read instructions and winging it with disastrous results. It had taken eons for me to confide in Zayne, and I trusted him with my life, even now. I didn't even know why I was so reluctant to tell people.

Okay, that was a lie.

I knew exactly why.

I didn't want people to think my lack of vision made me weak or that I wasn't capable. I didn't want people's sympathy or pity. I wanted to be seen as me and not the girl who was going blind, but the thing was, I was me—a Trueborn who knew how to fight and was ready to throw down, who loved marathoning old '90s sitcoms and missed her mom, who knew what lost felt like and who was madly, deeply in love. I was also the girl who was going blind. What was happening to me wasn't the sum of who I was, but it was a part of who I was.

Why it took some nineteen years to realize that, I had no idea, but I felt way mature. I was smiling when I walked into the school.

The smile didn't last.

As soon as the door swung shut behind us, the air seemed to thicken and swirl around us. Continuously scanning the empty glass cases and closed locker doors, I walked forward.

The goose bumps returned with a vengeance as my ears pricked. My steps slowed as I strained to listen…

"Is it just me or does it feel as if it's damn near close to freezing in here?" Jordan asked.

I was half expecting to see my breath when I breathed, but that wasn't what I was focused on. Brows knitting, I tilted my head to the side, listening for a few more moments. "I'm guessing you guys don't hear that."

"I hear nothing other than the voice whispering in my head that this place gives me the creeps," Teller muttered. "And that's my own voice."

I cracked a grin. "I hear…chattering."

"You don't see anything?" Dez turned to me.

I shook my head. "Not yet." I glanced up at what appeared to be a normal ceiling. "The cop that got eaten by the ceiling? They didn't make it any farther than this, right?"

"Right," Jordan answered.

I turned to my right, entire body tensing. The doors to the gymnasium were closed and the lights were on inside, but I remembered what was beyond the doors last time. A gym full of dead people who weren't playing basketball.

"The portal is accessed through there, isn't it?" Jordan asked.

I nodded. "I'm sure you all are eager to see it, but I don't think it will be wise to go down there unless we have to. That's where a bulk of the Shadow People were last time. I killed a lot of them, but I bet they've been replaced."

"They're guarding the portal," Teller asserted.

"They're definitely—" A dark shape moved past the windows on the gym doors, and a second later, a face appeared in the window, gray and distorted as the mouth dropped open, letting out a silent scream.

Another ghost appeared, this one hanging upside down. Stringy, dark hair obscured the face. A hand clawed the glass, its skin patchy and an unnatural dark shade.

"Do I want to know what you're looking at?" Dez asked.

"A whole room full of nope." I exhaled noisily as I walked toward the gym. The hairs on my arms stood up as my *grace* pulsed and throbbed. I reached for the handle.

"Shouldn't we be looking upstairs since the officer was sucked through the ceiling?" Teller wondered.

We could, but I had a feeling we didn't need to. "Stay out here until I give you the all clear."

Hoping they listened to me, I opened the doors wide.

And ghosts spilled out into the hall, brushing past me and *through* me as I stared in. The last time I'd been here, the lights had been turned off. I hadn't been able to see what was in here, and I'd thought that had been a nightmare come to life.

I'd been wrong.

Seeing was so much worse.

The gym was packed with ghosts. Those milling about randomly looked the most…fresh. Some of them almost looked alive, having passed either naturally or from causes that weren't visible. They seemed unaware of the others around them, and they didn't even turn toward the open door. I had a sinking feeling they hadn't been here the last time. My heart ached upon the sight of them. Somehow they'd been led here and then trapped inside by the angelic wards. They were good people who would most likely never have a chance to move on.

A man in a white shirt with some kind of blue graphic on the chest and blue jeans paced, pulling at his brown hair. "I don't understand. I don't understand," he mumbled over and over.

I dragged my gaze from him. The others, though?

Ew.

They'd been dead awhile, and trapped here long enough that they were one step away from wraiths. Their skin was a ghoulish color, gray or waxy, and most had some really gross wounds. Holes in the head and chest. Bullet wounds. Throats cut. Faces bloated and bruised. Bodies swollen and misshapen.

They were well aware of our presence and they smiled, reeking of pure malevolency.

"What the…?" Jordan's wings fluttered as he looked around him. A man with a nasty, bloody hole in his head had just walked through him. The Warden's blue eyes went wide. "Did a—? You know what? Don't answer that. I don't want to know."

Swallowing roughly, I lifted my head and wished I hadn't. "God."

They swarmed the ceiling like a thousand cockroaches, crawling over the beams and each other. They smothered the walls and the stacked bleachers.

A ghost drifted past me and into the hall, coming into unfortunate detail. She was young—had been no older than me when she died. Her throat and chest were torn open, revealing thick, jellylike tissue. She looked like a Raver had gotten ahold of her, but blackened veins covered her shoulders and upper arms. Maybe a Nightcrawler? Their claws and teeth were poisonous, and there was definitely some-thing very wrong inside of her.

Her feet didn't touch the ground as she stopped in front of Dez. "Did you come to collect your dead?" she asked in a wispy, singsong voice. "Or did you come to die?"

"He can't see or hear you," I told her. "I can, so leave them alone."

Dez looked at me as the ghost's head swung jerkily in my direction. I waved at her. "Yeah. Hi. Where are the people?"

Teller and Jordan exchanged looks while another ghost shuffled out from the thickest crowd, dragging a mangled leg that was hanging on by a few stringy tendons. He was older, his plain shirt spotted with blood. "We're here," he whispered. "Right in front of you."

"Not you. The people who worked here. The cops?" I clarified. "The ones who are hopefully still alive and breath-ing?"

"This is really freaky," Teller murmured.

"There's no one alive here," the man growled. "Not even you. You're already dead and you—"

"Blabbity-blah-blah. Whatever, man. You weren't sup-posed to be here. You were probably a good person who should've moved on, but here we are. I'm not going to hold it against you unless you give me a reason to." The dead girl reached for my braid. I shot her a look of warning. "Don't even think about touching me," I warned, summoning my *grace* until the corners of my eyes turned white. "I won't just exorcise your ass from here, I will end you. Like perma-nently. So, back the Hell up."

Her lips peeled back as she gave a low whine the Wardens seemed to hear. They stopped, turning to us.

My brows lifted. "Oh, you're an old one, aren't you? Been dead awhile. Cool. I'm superimpressed. Why don't you tell me where the people are?"

She slunk back, her head hanging from an unnatural angle. "They're right behind you."

"I'm not talking about the people I'm with." My patience was wearing thin. "Obviously."

"I'm not, either," she sang.

The back of my neck tickled. I turned around, first seeing Dez and the others waiting in the hall. Teller wiped at his face like he was trying to get rid of a stray hair. There was no hair. One of the ghosts was trailing his fingers across his cheek.

Ghosts could be creepy like that.

Slowly, I lifted my gaze above the doors, to the large scoreboard—

Oh God.

They hung from the top of the scoreboard, heads bowed, their arms limp and legs swaying gently. There were a…a dozen of them. Nine dressed in jeans. Three wearing dark blue uniforms.

I stepped back, ignoring the coldness pressing against me. One of them had long brown hair. Wore a white shirt with something blue embossed across the front and jeans. Heart sinking, I looked behind me, finding the pacing man. I swallowed hard.

It was him. One of the missing workers.

"What's going on?" Dez lingered at the opening.

"I found the missing people." I cleared my throat. "I'm guessing all of them."

Dez strode forward, walking straight through an older

woman bloated with decay. "What...?" He trailed off, looking up. "Jesus."

A ghost laughed as another chanted, *"Jesus loves me, yes, he does..."*

Something fast and pitch-black darted out from the mass of ghosts. A Shadow Person. Dammit. Most ghosts couldn't do much damage. Wraiths could be a different story, but Shadow People? They could harm and they could kill.

"Watch out!" I shouted, spinning toward the hallway.

"What the—?" Teller's wings arced behind him as Jordan turned.

Holy crap, they could see the Shadow People, just like demons could.

Teller lifted off the ground, but he wasn't fast enough. The Shadow slammed into him, knocking him back as it went *through* him. The Warden fell backward. Lockers rattled as he slid down them, pink mottling his skin as he began to shift into his human form.

"You okay?" Dez shouted.

"Good God," he gasped, coughing as he maintained hold of his Warden form. "What in the Hell was that?"

"A Shadow Person," I said, scanning the hall. "It's gone." Behind me, one of the ghosts giggled. "I think."

"I'm fine." Teller rose to his feet, shaking out his wings. "That was like getting hit by a freight train." He straightened. "A freight train on fire."

"At least it didn't pick you up," I said, thinking of what one of them had done to Cayman.

"There's another!" Dez rose into the air. "Coming out the damn wall."

Spinning toward where he pointed, I caught sight of one peeling its way out of where the wall met the ceiling.

It darted down in a ball, unfurling to its full height halfway to the floor. It landed in the shape of a person, a combination of black smoke and shadow, eyes bloodred, like burning coals.

"I got it." I stalked forward, summoning my *grace*. The corners of my vision turned white as the whitish-gold fire spread down my arm, flowing to my hand. The weight of the handle formed against my palm as the blade erupted from sparks and flames.

"That's also something I've never seen before," Jordan commented from behind.

The SP rushed forward, leaving a stream of black smoke behind it. Stepping into the attack, I sliced through the midsection. The shadow folded into itself, shattering into wisps of smoke.

"They may be strong," I said, lowering the Sword of Michael. The ghosts gave me wide berth. "But they aren't the smartest." I turned back to the others. "There's got to be more here."

"You sure you're okay?" Jordan asked, and Teller nodded. He turned back to us. "They're dead, aren't they? The missing people?"

"Yeah," Dez grunted. "And the cops."

Pulling my gaze from Teller, I glanced up at the bodies. My stomach twisted. "Why?" My voice was hoarse as I looked at the dead girl.

"Because they hoped you'd come," she answered in a wispy voice.

Instinct flared to life at the same moment the door that

led to the basement and the portal flew open. I had a wicked sense of déjà vu and tensed for LUDs—little ugly demons that resembled foot-tall rats…if rats could run on their hind legs.

That wasn't what came through the door. In hindsight, I would've preferred LUDs.

A burst of bright white light exploded from the door, charging the air with power as it rippled over the ceiling and walls, pouring across the floor. I threw up a hand to shield my eyes, but the intensity was so sudden and extreme it still momentarily blinded me.

Something large crashed into the wall behind me as I lowered my hand. I really hoped it wasn't Dez. I blinked my vision clear enough to see that the ghosts had scattered to the sides. My *grace* throbbed in response to the…the heavenly glow.

A huge shape came through the door, and the first thing I saw was the wings—the massive white wings with inky veins streaked throughout.

My heart seized in my chest.

Gabriel.

13

Fear punched a hole through my chest as Gabriel entered the gymnasium, and every instinct demanded that I hightail my butt out of here, but I held my ground—I held on to my *grace*.

"Trinity," he spoke, and the sound of him was like rusty nails against my nerves. "I knew you would come."

Nicolai was going to be so mad when he learned he was right.

This had been a trap.

"Wow," I said, forcing my voice level. "That was a less than impressive entrance."

Gabriel stopped, cocking his head to the side. He was closer, his features were clearer to me, and I could also tell that the black in his veins was spreading across the ever-shifting shades of the skin of his neck.

That couldn't be good.

"What happened to the trumpets and earthquakes?

Couldn't perform?" I asked, tsking. "I hear they make a pill for that."

His head straightened. "I see you still have no control of your mouth."

"And I bet you have no idea what I was referencing, which makes my immature snarkiness less entertaining." The Sword of Michael spit fire as I took a careful step back. I heard no movement behind me, and I knew better than to take my gaze off the Harbinger. I just hoped the Wardens were down but not too badly injured.

"Don't worry, child of Michael. I always find you entertaining."

"Happy to hear that." I willed my heart to slow. I needed to conserve my energy. With no Protector, I would grow tired, slow to move and prone to errors. There was no set time limit to when that happened, but considering I was still healing, probably not that long.

"I'm sure you are." He lowered his wings. "I'll admit, I'm surprised to see you so belligerent. Maybe I just need to break some more of your bones and kill one of those Wardens behind you."

Potent rage swept through me, and the Sword of Michael flared intensely.

Gabriel laughed as his head fell back. "You're so angry. I can taste it. Do my words hurt? Is it because I took your Protector? You shouldn't be angry with me. If God cared, your losses wouldn't have piled up. You have to want revenge for the deaths of the ones you loved."

Gabriel had killed Zayne, and he'd been partly responsible for what had happened to Misha and even my mother, and he wanted me to blame God? He was out of his mind, but it also occurred to me that he might not be aware of Zayne's Fall and subsequent return. That could be beneficial.

If Zayne snapped out of it.

And if I even had a chance to try to bring him back.

"This is not a game, Trueborn. There is nothing you can win. It's already over. Why make this difficult? You couldn't save your Protector," he said, and I flinched. "And no one can save the human race, not when they're unwilling to save themselves. Their time has come to a close. There's no stopping it."

"This conversation again," I said.

"It's the truth. All you have to do is step outside to see it. They've allowed themselves to become consumed by hate, greed, pride and gluttony. They feed on others' pain. They're inherently self-centered. There's no fixing that, Trueborn. No saving them."

"You speak as if it's every person who's like that, and I'm not going to lie. There're a lot of crap human beings, but you know what?" I said. "Painting them all with the same brush would be like saying all angels are overgrown toddlers throwing a hissy fit because they're no longer BFFs with God."

"BFFs?" he repeated.

"Jesus," I muttered. "BFFs means best friends forever. Seriously, I ask yet again, how am I supposed to be afraid of you when you don't even know what that means?"

The tainted *grace* flared. "But you're already afraid—afraid of me, of the role you've played in the deaths of so many. Terrified because I'm right about *them*." He sneered. "The human race no longer deserves any more chances. They are without faith and damned, and God is just as lost as His creations are. Give in to your anger and join me." Gabriel lifted his hands, palms up. "I will be the father you never had, and with us together, you will have your ruin."

A laugh burst out of me—a loud, obnoxious and cackling laugh I couldn't hold back as I stared at him.

Gabriel started to frown.

"I'm sorry. I know you're trying to be all scary and threatening," I said. "But all you need to add to that is 'Luke, I am your father,' and it would just be perfect."

"I do not understand."

"Of course you don't." I shook my head. "Is that gross stuff in your wings infecting your brain or something? Because you're out of your mind." I clasped the handle of the sword with both hands. "You're right. I am angry, but I'm not irrational or stupid enough to blame anyone but you. You are the only thing I want revenge against. You may be the source of my rage, but you will not be my ruin."

His lip curled in a snarl. "That is incredibly disappointing to hear, especially when I'm being so generous by giving you not one but two chances to make this easy on you. I will give you no more."

Before I could formulate a less than wise response, Gabriel came at me. The only blessing was that he hadn't summoned his *grace*.

It was a small blessing.

I swung the Sword of Michael, but he caught both of my wrists in his hands.

"I know someone who is dying to spend time with you." Gabriel lifted me by the arms, clear off the ground. "Bael will be glad to hear that you've been less than willing. He has been so looking forward to getting to know you better."

Panic threatened to take hold as my feet dangled in the air. Sparks of heavenly fire spit harmlessly in the space between our faces.

"Demons do love to get their mouths and teeth on anything with angelic blood in them." Thin, inky black wisps seeped across his white eyes. "I only need you alive. I don't necessarily need you in one piece."

Pushing down the fear and panic, I tightened the muscles in my legs and stomach. "How would I still be alive if I'm not in one piece?"

"You'd be surprised by what a body will survive," he growled. "But you will discover such soon enough."

"Sounds like a great time, but I'm going to have to pass." I curled my legs up and then kicked out, slamming my feet into his chest.

The blow didn't hurt him, but it surprised him. He staggered back as I broke his hold. I twisted as I fell, hitting the floor on my poor left hip. Pain flared, but I didn't give my body a chance to really process it. I kicked out again, aiming for his feet, but he anticipated the move. In my blind spot, he grabbed ahold of my braid, jerking my head back.

"This seems familiar, doesn't it?" he cooed. "You have to know you can't beat me. That fighting back is pointless and painful. Why would you even try?"

"I don't know," I gasped as he strained the muscles of my neck. "I have a hard head."

"Thick skull or not, I can still shatter it with my hands alone."

"Congrats." I thrust the sword out.

Gabriel spun to the side, but the edge of the sword glided over his thigh, slicing open the white pants and the skin underneath. Black, oily liquid splattered his leg as he sucked in a sharp breath.

My heart lurched as my eyes widened in surprise. I cut him.

Holy shit, I cut him.

My wide gaze swung to his, and I saw the shock on his face. Gabriel was unbelievably fast, but I cut him. Did that mean he was weakening? Maybe there was something to that gunk in his wings and veins—

The blow alongside my cheek stunned me. I toppled over like a pile of bricks. Blood filled my mouth. The Sword of Michael fizzled out in a shower of golden white sparks as my *grace* retracted. Tiny bursts of black dotted my vision as I rolled onto my back.

"Ouch," I whispered, blinking away the spots from my vision.

A bare foot was inches from my face.

"Jesus," I stuttered, throwing myself onto my side.

The floor rattled with the impact of his stomp. I pushed up, unsheathing my daggers. His fingers clamped down on my throat, cutting off my breath as he lifted me off the floor once more. I swung my arms in a wide arc, thrusting both daggers down into Gabriel's shoulders. The blades cut through muscle and tissue, hitting bone.

He howled in pain. "You stupid—"

A series of pops interrupted him, reminding me of fireworks. Gabriel's entire body jerked and spasmed. He dropped me, tearing free of my daggers in the process. I landed on my feet, off balance, as Gabriel whirled around. His wings smacked into me, knocking me aside. I fell, gagging as the pops went off again in another rapid succession. I lifted my head.

Captain Washington stood in the doorway, gun leveled

on Gabriel. She fired without hesitation, striking the archangel repeatedly in the chest.

Gabriel's roar shook the floor as hands grabbed my shoulders. I started to swing, but caught sight of reddish-brown
hair and horns. *Dez.* Blood smeared his face. He dragged me
aside as I turned to find Gabriel. Bullets wouldn't take him
out, and probably would only irritate him more.

But Gabriel…he was up by the rafters of the gymnasium, where the ghosts were scrambling over one another
to get away from him. He flew back, in through the door
he'd come out.

He retreated.

I couldn't believe it as I dragged in deep, uneven breaths.

"Are you okay?" Dez lifted me to my feet, pulling me to
his chest. "Trinity?"

I nodded as I looked to where Captain Washington stood.
She still held the gun. Behind her, Teller and Jordan were
struggling to their feet.

"I think I just shot an actual angel. Multiple times," Captain Washington said hoarsely. "Does that mean I'm going
to Hell?"

"The opposite," I wheezed. "Believe it or not, it means
the opposite."

There had been no time to dwell on how close I'd come
to getting captured in the aftermath.

The poor captain seemed like she was in a state of shock
and finding her officers on the scoreboard didn't help. I had
no idea what Dez told her or how she was going to explain
any of this to her department, the public or the families of
the workers and officers. I didn't envy her.

Or Dez.

Nicolai had showed up shortly after we'd exited the school, and the moment he saw me, he looked like he wanted to murder the Warden.

The only good thing that came from the little adventure was the shutdown of any and all work on the renovations and the discovery of Gabriel's possible weakening. But those two things were overshadowed by the senseless loss of life. There was no reason for those workers or officers to be killed, and that was twelve sets of families and friends who would never be the same.

I'd crashed and burned the moment Dez had dropped me off back at the apartment. I knew the Wardens would be patrolling for Zayne, and would call if they spotted him, but instinct told me they wouldn't catch one glimpse of him. I slept through the night, slipping into the kind of deep sleep where the horrors of the gymnasium couldn't follow me. I'd slept well into early Monday afternoon, but I was still moving at the speed of a three-legged turtle when I finally dragged myself out of bed.

Getting ready took an extreme amount of time. My thoughts were consumed with everything from what happened the night before to my plan to see the Crone, and what I'd done with Zayne. Not only that, every muscle in my body was stiff as I pulled on a pair of black pants that were more leggings than they were actual pants, but came with handy back pockets. My back protested as I snatched up a sleeveless tunic that not only looked clean, but also hid the daggers strapped to my thighs. Forgoing the sneakers, I laced up a pair of thick-soled boots that had a lot of traction. I figured I was going to need it.

Then I pulled my hair back in a braid, using the time in front of the mirror to find some sort of center. Whatever progress I'd made in terms of bruises had been lost. I looked like I'd face-planted into a brick wall. A nice reddish-blue bruise covered my right cheek and the corner of my mouth. There was a small tear in my lip that hadn't appreciated the minty toothpaste, but I supposed that was by far an improvement from looking like I face-planted into said wall from twenty stories above.

I turned my head to the side, checking out the lovely imprint of Gabriel's fingers. Man, his last imprint had just healed—

It was then when I noticed the faint purplish bruise where my neck met my shoulder. Drawing the collar of the tunic aside, I leaned in closer to the mirror. My face flushed hot when I realized what it was.

A hickey.

"Oh, for the love of God," I muttered as my stomach curled. I tugged the collar back in place.

I returned to the bedroom and looked around. I half expected to find Peanut floating out from the walls, but there was no sign of him. Sighing, I picked up my phone. There was a message from Dez. As expected, there'd been no sign of Zayne, but Gideon had been able to track down the dead guy we'd found in the park the other night. The one Zayne had…dispatched. Apparently he was not a good dude. Multiple accusations ending in charges dropped in court, but plenty of evidence that suggested he'd needed to be imprisoned and on multiple advisory lists.

So Zayne hadn't lied, and as messed up as it still was, it was good news. Knowing I needed to give him a heads-up about what I planned to do tonight, I texted about how Cayman and I were going to check on a lead today.

My phone rang not even a minute after I sent the text.

He wasn't exactly thrilled about the lack of details, but I managed to convince him that I wasn't going out looking for Zayne alone.

It took a while.

"Did you really stay in last night? You didn't go back out there?" he asked. "Honestly?"

"You saw what kind of condition I was in. I was dragging. I slept all night," I told him as I picked up my dirty clothes, dropping them in a small hamper.

"Yeah, you definitely were dragging."

Wondering exactly how bad I looked to others and then remembering what I looked like in the mirror, I frowned.

Dez was quiet for a moment but then I heard his heavy sigh, and I knew something I probably didn't want to hear was coming. "I've been doing a lot of thinking about Zayne, Trinity. A lot of thinking I would rather not be doing but needed to. I think we need to prepare ourselves for the fact that he…that he may not return to us."

Stamping down the rush of anger, I placed the hamper by the stacked washer and dryer. "He's in there, Dez. I know he is."

"I want to believe that. More than you probably think I do, but who we saw in the park wasn't Zayne."

"He's still in there," I repeated, tossing a detergent pod in with the clothes as I thought about what Zayne said before he left. *The thing that's taking up a part of me will hurt you.*

"Trust me, I know he is. I'm going to get him back."

"We just need to be prepared," Dez replied. "That's all I'm saying."

"I know." I slammed the laundry door shut hard enough that it would've scared Peanut if he was nearby. *Peanut.* Something occurred to me. "Can you ask Gideon to check on something for me?"

"Sure. What you need?"

"I don't know if he can even help or not, but there's a girl that lives in this apartment complex. Her name is Gena," I told him. "I don't know her last name or who her parents are. All I know is that she's on a lower floor. I need to know what apartment she's in."

"That's going to be hard with just a kid's name, but some apartments require all occupants to be listed at the manager's office. I'll see if Gideon can crack into their systems."

"Perfect," I said, knowing it was a long shot.

"Do I want to know why you want this information?" he asked after a moment.

"It involves a ghost, so probably not."

"You're right. I don't."

As I walked over to the fridge, there was one other thing that randomly popped into my head. "There's something else I was wondering. Gideon seems to know a lot about the history of Wardens and even the Trueborns, right?"

"He knows more than any of us," Dez said.

I nibbled on my thumbnail as I stared at the fridge. "I was wondering if he could find out if…if it was documented that any Trueborns had ever, you know, given birth?" I cringed. "I mean, like any record of them ever getting pregnant or getting someone else pregnant."

It was so quiet on the other end I could probably hear a cricket sneeze.

Then Dez cleared his throat. "That was a very unexpected question, Trinity."

My entire face scrunched up. It was a random question, one I really didn't want to have to ask, but asking Dez was far better than calling up Thierry or Matthew and asking them. "I'm just curious."

"Or asking for a friend, right?" His tone was as dry as the desert.

"Yeah. Definitely asking for a friend." I turned and bent over, gently knocking my head off the cool granite of the counter. "So do you think Gideon would know or could find out?"

"I can ask," he said, and there was a pause and what sounded like a door closing on his end. "Look, um, I don't know how to say this without just coming out and saying it."

I stopped beating my head off the granite, leaving it resting there.

"But if Trueborns and Wardens are biologically compatible, I don't think after what you went through with Gabriel that any, uh, pregnancy would be…viable," he explained while sounding like he wanted to scrub his brain with a wire brush. "I'm just saying, you know, in case you're thinking that, but if you're worried, there's this thing called a pregnancy test, which can be picked up at just about—"

"Oh my God, I know that." I lifted my head. "And I know that after what happened with Gabriel, there'd be no chance of that being an issue."

"Then why would you even…?" His inhale was audible through the phone. "Trinity."

I cringed again. "Okay. Well, I need—"

"Don't you dare hang up that phone," he interrupted. "You saw Zayne again, didn't you? What in the Hell happened? What—?" He cut himself off with a curse, and when he spoke again, his voice was uncomfortably gentle. "Did something happen? Did he do something?"

Oh my God, I knew what he meant.

I returned to banging my head off the counter. "Nothing that I didn't actively and wholeheartedly partake in happened."

More silence greeted me.

"This is awkward," I said.

"No shit," he shot back.

"And I would like to pull a T. Swift, and remove myself from this narrative."

"This is your narrative, Trinity."

"I know," I muttered. "Can you just ask Gideon for me? Because honestly, I have no idea if it's even possible for Trueborns, and I would just like to know."

"For curiosity's sake."

"Sure."

His sigh was so heavy that I was surprised it didn't rattle my phone. "Yeah, I'll see if he knows."

"Thank you." At this point, I was half lying on the counter. "I'm going to get off here and drink some bleach. I'll let you know what happens with our lead."

"Trinity?"

"Yes?" I whined.

"Be careful," Dez said, his voice soft again. "Just be…just be damn careful, okay? Zayne means a lot to you. I know he does. He means a lot to us, too. But you mean the world to everyone else, and if something happens to you, there won't be a world."

★ ★ ★

Cayman showed up shortly after the most awkward conversation known to man. I didn't let myself think beyond the next minute as we left the apartment. Too much was up in the air and too much depended on what wasn't guaranteed. The Crone may have already left the city. She may still be at the hotel but ask for something I couldn't give in return for her aid; after all, I didn't expect her to just help me out of the kindness of her heart. She could possibly refuse. I kept my mind blank as Cayman and I rode the elevator down to ground level. He didn't have a car, but ordered Uber Black.

"It's the only way to Uber," he told me, straightening his sunglasses as a black town car pulled up to the curb.

My foot bounced the whole way to the hotel as nervous energy built and mingled with my *grace*. I felt like an exposed live wire when we arrived at the familiar hotel.

"I'll wait for you at the apartment," Cayman said. "Call me when you can."

"You'll answer this time?" I opened the door.

He nodded. "Thoughts and prayers."

I shot him a look from behind the sunglasses, and he was still chuckling when I closed the door on him. I turned around as the sleek car pulled away from the curb and walked across the sidewalk, out of the still oddly cool air and into the near frigid temps of the hotel lobby. I made a beeline for the elevator and, once inside, hit the button for the thirteenth floor.

Stepping back so I stood in front of the doors, I was motionless, sunglasses still shielding my eyes and hands at my sides. When the elevator came to a smooth stop, my racing heart finally calmed. I walked out and into the hallway, following it down to where it curved, and finally the restaurant came into view. I could see lights on behind the tinted windows.

Part of me couldn't believe I was here. After the last time, I really hadn't planned on coming back. Inside was nothing more than a cemetery in my opinion.

Pulling the sunglasses off, I tucked one of the arms into the collar of my top and then glanced up and to the left, where a camera Roth destroyed had been. It had been replaced. Another good sign. I opened the door. There was no breezy jazz music playing. No clinks and clangs of dishes and utensils. My eyes had a bit of trouble adjusting to the dimly lit interior, but I recognized the woman behind the hostess table, and based on the way the dark-haired woman muttered an impressive stream of curses under her breath, she recognized me.

"Rowena—"

"Just so you know," she cut in. "I am not cleaning up any messes this time. I was finding ash in places ash should never be for days."

Considering that the ash she referenced was human remains of her fellow coven, I was thinking there really was no place that stuff should've been, but whatever. "Hopefully there'll be no reason to leave a mess behind this time. Is the Crone here?"

Rowena didn't answer for a long moment, but then she nodded curtly. She motioned for me to follow her.

Thank you baby alpacas everywhere.

We walked past the wall that blocked the dining area, and I tried to see everything that I could as quickly as possible. The restaurant looked a lot different from before. All the booths had been stripped out, along with all of the tables and chairs, all except one round table. It sat under a glittering chandelier, and there were three chairs. One was occupied.

"There you go," Rowena said, and she pivoted, stalking back to the front of the restaurant.

"Don't just stand there, girl," the Crone, whose back was to me, called out. "I'm not getting any younger. You can have the seat to the left."

Goose bumps prickled my skin as I walked forward. Obviously my appearance wasn't a surprise. I swallowed and went to the chair she indicated, then sat down, able to see her more clearly. The Crone was old, like had seen the turn of the last century kind of old. Hair the color of snow, and her rich brown skin was heavily lined and creased, but her eyes were as sharp and as shrewd as ever. My gaze dipped to the front of her purple and pink shimmery shirt. It read DAYS THAT END IN AY ARE WINE DAYS.

I met her stare. "You were expecting me?"

"Of course I was." The Crone smiled, and the creases deepened. "Don't you remember? I told you the last time I saw you that you'd bring me something I'd never seen before. A real prize."

Another wave of shivers broke out over my skin. "You did say that, but I... I haven't brought you anything."

"Not yet," she replied, picking up what I suspected to be, well, a glass of wine. "But you will when you bring me the Fallen."

14

Disbelief thundered through me as I stared at the Crone. She'd known. I didn't know if I should be mad that she hadn't given me just the tiniest heads-up or if I should be freaked out.

Probably freaked out.

"I know what you're thinking," she said, reaching over and patting my hand as I blanched. "Not literally. Mind reading has never been a skill I wanted to learn, but I knew the moment I saw you that you'd bring me something very special."

I started to respond, but became aware of a presence—a warmth against my skin in the cool air. I turned to look to my left and squinted, unsure if I was seeing what I thought I was.

It appeared to be a small…boy coming our way. A kid with a pile of golden curls on his head. As he drew closer, I saw that he couldn't be older than ten or eleven. I watched him take the seat opposite of me, wondering if he was lost and if we needed to find his parents, call the cops or whatever it was that you did when you found a random child somewhere no kid should be.

Then I saw his eyes.

I jerked back with a gasp of surprise, my hand slipping out from underneath the Crone's. His eyes were a vibrant blue, like a Warden's, but the pupils were all white.

His little face broke out into a smile. "Hello, Trinity." He extended a small hand, his arm barely reaching the middle of the table. "I'm Tony. It's good to finally meet another like me."

My gaze dropped to his hand and then rose to his face. "You're a…"

"I'm not a Trueborn, but I do have a whole lot of angel blood kicking around in me, more than most," he said, and I blinked. He looked like a kid, sounded like one, but he spoke like an adult. "My grandfather was an angel. A Throne."

A Throne.

Oh. My. God.

Was it the one who—

"Visited you in the church?" he finished my thought. "And gave you the lowdown on how you can help Zayne?"

I blinked again. "Can you read thoughts?"

"No." Tony giggled, and he sounded very much like a small child then. "But I've seen this already."

He was prophetic. A seer. A real one, and not one of the 1-800-Hotline-Psychics. It made sense that he had a Throne in his family tree, with the whole seeing the future thing, but a grandfather?

"Yeah, angels tend to bend the rules when the sin benefits

the greater good," he answered the question I didn't speak. "Just like your father did. Just like many more have done."

He wiggled his fingers then.

Slowly, I reached across the table and took his small hand in mine. The moment our skin touched, there was a jolt that traveled up my arm, raising the hair.

Tony grinned, squeezing my hand before letting go. I watched him pick up a glass. "Apple juice. It's amazing."

"Yeah," I whispered.

The Crone chuckled, drawing my gaze. "You came here for a reason, didn't you, Trueborn?"

"Yeah," I repeated, sitting back. It took a moment, but I pulled myself together. "Yes, I am. You know what has happened to Zayne?"

"I know that he was given his Glory and that he Fell." The Crone sipped her wine.

"I told her that," Tony announced.

"He did," the Crone confirmed as my gaze darted between them. "Of course, he did so in the vaguest possible way."

"Hey." Tony lifted his empty hand. "I can only help so much. Them's the rules. I didn't make them, but I personally think that's what I said, which was, and I quote, 'One born of the blood of the holy sword will hold in her hand the heart of one born after a second Fall.'" He snapped his fingers. "Pretty obvious, right?"

I opened my mouth and then closed it.

One side of the Crone's mouth curled upward. "Ah, yes, so very obvious."

All of that sounded somewhat obvious now, but... Shaking my head, I refocused on the Crone. "I came to see if there was any way that you could help me. I need to lure Zayne to me and somehow..." God, I hated even saying this. "I need to incapacitate him without hurting him so that I can try...try to bring him back to the way he was. He can sense when I'm about to use my *grace*, and he's very powerful and...well, he's unpredictable. I need to gain the upper hand."

"And what if you cannot bring him back to the way he was?" the Crone asked. "What if he is lost to you?"

My breath caught as my chest seized with pain. For a moment, I couldn't vocalize what I'd already acknowledged I had to do. "I will do what is necessary to make sure Zayne doesn't become a monster he would've hunted, but I don't believe he's lost to me. I know he's not. I *know.*"

"So, you have faith?" Toby asked.

I looked at him. "I have..." I trailed off. Why was it so hard to say? Faith was...it was a slippery thing, staying with you and then slipping through your fingers before you knew it. If I had time to psychoanalyze myself, I was sure it would have something to do with my absentee father, the loss I had experienced throughout the years and the general unfairness of life, but I didn't have time for all of that. The important part was that I did. I knew that as I stared at the kid. There were moments when I didn't. Hell, there were entire days when I didn't, but even when I had doubts, and Lord, did I have a lot of them, I had faith that there was a purpose.

I drew in a deep breath. "I have faith. Maybe not always. Maybe tomorrow I won't, but I...I refuse to believe that I would be put in this position with everything else going on, only to lose him all over again. I have faith in our love. He had enough faith in our love that he Fell for me. I have faith that what I feel for him will be enough to bring him back."

Tony stared at me through eyes that seemed decades, if not more, older. He nodded, and I wanted to ask if the honest answer had been the right one.

"I can help you," the Crone announced.

My head snapped back in her direction, and I almost couldn't breathe. "You can?"

She nodded as she took another sip of the pink, fruity-scented wine. "You need a spell that brings him to you and also traps him."

Traps him? Suddenly an image of Dean and Sam Winchester formed in my heads. "Like an Angel Trap? That sounds like some *Supernatural*-esque stuff."

"Heh," giggled Tony. "I'm a Castiel fan. You?"

I almost pointed out he seemed too young to be watching that show but refrained. He'd probably seen some crazy stuff. "I'm a Dean fan."

"Of course you are." His eyes rolled.

"I have no idea what you two are talking about," the Crone said. "But yes, like an Angel Trap, I suppose. Well, more like a person trap, but that's neither here nor there."

My brows lifted as I saw an encircled pentagram in my head. I really needed to stop watching TV. "How do I create this spell—trap, whatever?"

"You will need a few things." She lifted a hand, motioning with her fingers.

From wherever Tony had roamed out from, a male came forward, looking more like an accountant than an actual witch. He was fair-skinned and middle-aged, dressed in a black suit. He carried something in his hand. He placed it on the table beside the Crone, bowing in her direction before turning and heading back to wherever he came from.

The Crone picked up what I now realized was a small glass decanter, no bigger than the length of her hand. "I had this cooked up for you today, you know, just in case today was the day," she said with a wink, and I shivered. "So, it's still fresh, but it must be used tonight." She handed it to me.

I carefully took it, turning the narrow, oval-shaped glass in my hand. There was deep gold liquid inside and...and smoke? Golden smoke? "What is in this?"

"This and that and probably a whole lot of what you wouldn't want to know," she answered, and the look she gave me warned I would be wise to not pursue her comment. "All you need to know is that it won't harm him. You need to take that to where you first saw him as a Fallen."

"Rock Creek Park," I told her, and of course it would have to be somewhere superpublic.

She nodded. "You will open it tonight, when the sun retires."

"That would be approximately 8:32 p.m., just in case you are wondering," Tony supplied.

"You must bring with you a personal item of his and place it on the earth. The item must be freshly marked with your blood," she instructed, and I couldn't help but hope all nearby demons were nicely hidden so they didn't catch the scent of my blood.

Apparently Tony was thinking the same, because his head swiveled toward the Crone.

"Then you will need to open the vial, emptying all the contents onto the item you have brought with you. You will briefly see a circle form," she went on. "Once he is inside the circle, his *grace* will be cut off to him and he will be brought to his knees. Make sure you step out of it before it disappears, or you, too, will be trapped inside without your *grace* or strength. You do not want that."

No. I did not.

"This will only hold for a few minutes," she continued. "Angels, Fallen or not, Trueborn or not, are too powerful to contain for any lengthy period of time. You must act fast and you must not hesitate."

"I won't." Closing my fingers around the vial, I inhaled deeply. The vial warmed to my touch. Some of the panic and hopelessness that had been weighing on me since I woke up to find that Zayne was gone abated. "Thank you."

She nodded.

I lifted my gaze to hers. "And what do you want in exchange?"

The Crone's answering smile was tight-lipped. "Do you not think that I give you this out of the kindness of my old heart?"

Holding her stare, I smiled in return. "I don't know a whole lot about witches, but I know enough about humans in general to know that nearly nothing of importance is given without strings attached. What are those strings?"

"Smart girl," murmured Tony.

One white, caterpillar-like brow rose. "What I want, if you succeed, is for you to bring the Fallen to me."

My grip on the vial tightened. "What do you want from him?"

Her dark eyes sharpened into shards of obsidian. "I want just one feather."

"Just one feather?" Unease festered. "What can you do with just one feather from a Fallen?"

"Endless things, child." A smile came to her then, a dreamy, wistful one as her eyes closed. "Great and impossible things."

"Terrible things?" I asked, hating how my conscience was tapping itself on my shoulder.

"All magic can be used for the great and for the terrible." The Crone opened her eyes. "The outcome is always in the hands of those who wield it, and I have never used it in the way you fear on anyone who wasn't deserving of it."

I stared at her, knowing that wasn't an exact confirmation that Zayne's feather wouldn't be used for something incredibly evil, but I either had to take her word on it or hand the vial back to her, find another way to even the playing field with Zayne. The latter could take too long. I may never find it.

"Okay," I said. This was probably something I was going to have to account for once I received judgment, but I would do anything for Zayne. Just like he'd done anything for me. "I will bring Zayne to you."

"Good." She reached for the wineglass.

"But just so you know," I said, waiting until her attention returned to me. "If you harm him in any way, I will kill you. You won't even have a chance to use your magic against me. It will happen before you even realize it."

The Crone took a slow drink. "I wouldn't expect anything less."

"Glad we're on the same page."

"So am I," Tony said. "Because this was getting super-awkward."

"As most adult conversations do," the Crone replied. "One day you will understand that."

"Seriously?" The tiny seer looked offended.

The Crone laughed softly. "Don't you still have a bed-time?"

The child's eyes narrowed.

"He does," the Crone told me, and I really had no idea what to say to that. "One last thing before we part ways, which we must do very shortly. I have to get this one back to his mother before she thinks I stole him."

"Oh my God," Tony muttered under his breath. "The things I could tell you…"

"But you won't." She leaned over, and for a moment, I feared she might topple right out of her chair and, like, break a hip. She kissed the seer on the cheek.

Tony rolled his eyes and wrinkled his nose in a way I imagined a normal kid of his age would. There was a smudge of bright pink lipstick on his cheek.

Sitting upright once more, the Crone refocused on me. "You must do this alone tonight. No friends, demonic or Warden. Their energies will interfere with the spell."

I guessed I better hope this worked, because if it didn't keep Zayne contained long enough, he was going to be very angry.

Rising from my chair, I hesitated as I looked over at the kid. "Will I see you again?"

Those eerie eyes lifted to mine. "I can't answer that."

The why occurred to me. Because if he did, it would tell me too much. It could possibly tell me that there was an after to all of this. Or that there wasn't. A chill skated down my spine as I nodded and turned.

"Tell Roth I said hi," Tony added, and my gaze swept back to him. He smiled, and my heart rate kicked up. "Tell him that my mom would love one of those chickens he brought me. He'll understand."

"Okay," I heard myself say, and then I left, a small smile tugging at my lips.

Tony had just shared that I would see Roth again, and unless Roth returned from Hell between now and tonight, which was unlikely, it meant I survived tonight.

So at least there was that.

Updating Dez on everything that had gone down went just as I had expected it to.

Dez wasn't remotely on board with the idea of me using something a witch had given me to draw Zayne out, nor was he happy that I was doing this alone. It took a while to convince him that this was something I had to try, and finally he relented after I told him he could help by making sure the park was cleared of all people by seven. I promised that I would let him know what happened as soon as I could.

At least that conversation was far less awkward than the one before.

Cayman, on the other hand, was just not about that kind of life, anyway. He promised to remain back at the apartment.

"Call me if the spell somehow doesn't contain him and you need to run for your life," he'd told me. "I'll run with you."

That wasn't the most inspiring of all comments, but he did tell me that I probably didn't need to worry about drawing any demons to me. He had a feeling that after Zayne's show-and-tell from Saturday night, most had hightailed their butts back to Hell or out of the city, but that didn't include the demons who were working with Gabriel, obviously.

So, yeah, thoughts and prayers on that front.

Finding a personal item of Zayne's wasn't exactly easy since he didn't have a lot of personal items outside of the bare necessities. I didn't want to take his toothbrush or comb since I had to bleed all over it and dump only God knew what on top of it, so I opted for one of his unwashed gray shirts I'd been planning to sleep in again. It still smelled like him, and I stood there holding it to my face for a probably disturbing amount of time.

The hours dragged by and by, and I couldn't wait around any longer. Cayman had ordered up a car for me, and I headed to Rock Creek Park. That was where I spent the last hour or so, claiming ownership of the bench, his shirt and the vial close to my thudding heart.

It will be okay.

It will be okay.

I kept repeating that, over and over, while I stared at the empty walking path. I had no idea what kind of strings the Wardens had pulled, but the last person I'd seen had been at least forty-some minutes ago. I guessed it was a small blessing that I had this to stress over so I wasn't obsessing over, well, everything else. I looked up at the gradually darkening sky, and my chest tightened.

The reminder I set on my phone dinged, letting me know it was one minute till sunset.

Jumping from the bench, I hurried to the grassy area behind it. Carefully, I placed Zayne's shirt on the ground beside the vial. I knelt, unsheathing the dagger. With my hand above his shirt, I placed the dagger against my palm. My heart was pounding. Both my hands were shaking.

This will work.

This will work.

This will work.

The second reminder went off from my phone. There wasn't a moment of hesitation as the sky above me turned to the deepest, darkest blue. I sliced the blade along my palm. A hiss of pain escaped me as bright red blood bubbled and welled. Squeezing my hand into a fist as I sheathed my dagger, I lowered my palm and opened my hand. I dragged it across his shirt, smearing the cotton with blood.

Snatching up the vial, I popped the lid off and tilted the bottle over the same spot my blood marked Zayne's shirt as I prayed Zayne wasn't playing creeping stalker and watching me.

Which was something I hadn't even considered until now.

Too late to worry about that, I supposed.

The golden liquid poured over the shirt. It wasn't a lot, and the smoke leaked out next, glittering like dozens of fireflies as it drifted slowly to the shirt.

A bolt of light flashed from the shirt, whipping out faster than I could track. Dropping the vial, I rose as the gold light raced to form a circle.

Spinning around, I pushed—pushed hard with my legs as the circle completed. The light pulsed, streaming upward as I jumped through it, hitting the ground on my hands and knees just outside the circle as the light collapsed.

"God," I whispered, pushing my braid back over my shoulder. That was...that was too close of a call.

I stood, turning back. I couldn't see any signs of the light. I could barely make out the lump of his shirt in the encroaching shadows, but it was done.

The park lights flicked on as I stood there, chest rising and falling rapidly. My *grace* hummed in me, ramped up by my anxiety.

Please.

Please.

Please.

Lifting my gaze to the now dark sky, I strained to see anything. There was nothing. Not even a hint of a star. What if this didn't work? What if I did something wrong? Was I supposed to dump the contents out first and then cut myself? I should've written the instructions down, because my memory—

I saw him only for a second before he dropped out of the sky, landing in a crouch mere feet from where I thought the circle started.

My heart stammered as he rose, his wings emanating a soft white glow as he spread them wide. Show-off. He'd changed into a faded pair of jeans. Where he got them, or better yet, who he *borrowed* them from, I decided I didn't want to know.

At least right now.

From opposite sides of what I hoped was a functional trap, we stared at one another. Too many seconds ticked by unused. I needed to get him in the trap.

I stepped forward, only about a foot. "Miss me?"

His head tilted. "You did something. I know you did. I felt this uncontrollable urge to come here."

"You weren't watching me?"

He shook his head. "I can no longer watch you."

Because he could no longer trust himself? There wasn't time to figure that out. "Well, I didn't want to walk the streets looking for you."

"I told you to stay away from me. That I would hurt you," he said, voice a low rumble. "And yet, you did something to bring me to you. I'm beginning to believe you have a death wish."

"You think you can kill me?" I summoned my *grace*, and it responded in a rush. The corners of my eyes turned white as whitish-gold light spilled out from my shoulder, swirling down my arm. The hilt of the Sword of Michael formed against my palm, warm and welcomed. The flaming blade erupted, crackling and hissing. "Then come and get me, Fallen."

For a heart-stopping moment, I didn't think he would rise to the challenge. That he'd refuse, and while that could be further proof that he was still in there, I didn't need Zayne rearing his head right now. I needed the Fallen.

"I don't think it's a fight you want." A cruel smile twisted his lips. "It's me."

My skin flushed but I lifted my chin. "Maybe it is you I want. Maybe not."

His head twisted from side to side and then his jaw hardened. "Can't say I didn't try to warn you," he growled, and he moved so fast that he was nothing but a blur of gold and white.

But I saw the moment he entered the trap.

Golden, shimmery light pulsed low to the ground, in the shape of a circle. Zayne skidded to a stop, his chin dipping as he stared at the fading light—at his shirt.

He lifted his head. "What did you do?"

"Leveled the playing field."

His lips pulled back, and the *sound* that came from him sent a bolt of fear through me. It was inhuman. Terrible. He charged forward, and I braced for the trap to fail—

He jerked to a stop, hands balling to his fists, and he was close enough I could see the fury etched into his features. His upper body tipped forward. Tendons stood out from his neck. Muscles flexed along his shoulders as he fought, but he went down on his knees, just like the Crone promised.

Vivid, burning eyes lifted to mine. From his heaving chest, his voice rumbled, "You cheated."

"I did." I brought the sword forward, wrapping my other hand around the hilt.

His eyes narrowed. "You going to use that? On me? Thought you loved me, little nephilim?"

"I do," I whispered, throat and eyes burning.

"Love," he spat as his wings lowered and his chest rose, as if he were daring me to do it. "Do your worst, nephilim, but strike true. If you don't, I will get out of this. Then I will destroy you and I won't care."

"But I think you would," I told him as tears blurred his features. I stepped forward. "I love you. I love you now and I'll love you forever."

I moved before he had a chance to respond to my words, unable to truly allow myself to consider what I was doing. I drew the Sword of Michael back.

I love you.

My heart stuttered and then cracked. The next breath I took went nowhere as a violent storm of emotions erupted out of me in a scream.

I love you.

Thrusting the flaming, golden sword forward, I shoved it deep into Zayne's chest, into his heart.

15

Time slowed and then seemed to stop as his gaze met mine and held. His were wide with what looked like shock, and in the mess of tumbling thoughts, one became clear. I didn't think he believed I would do this. Did the shock filling those stunning blue eyes come from the part of him that had been lost when he Fell or from the part of Zayne that remained inside him?

I didn't know, but I felt that fiery blade as if it had been shoved deep in my own chest, piercing through my heart and my soul. Panic fluttered through me, mixing with soul-deep grief. I wanted to rewind time. I wanted to go back and to have never done this, because if it didn't work, I wasn't sure…I wasn't sure I could survive this even if it was the right thing to do. I'd been foolish to think I could weather this— that I was strong enough, brave enough. I wasn't. I wasn't inhuman, and I was sure my father would be disappointed to realize that, but it was true. If this didn't work, the look in his eyes, the shock and disbelief, would haunt me long after my body was nothing more than dust. It would kill me. Maybe not in the physical sense, but it would devastate every part of me that made me who I was. I wouldn't be the same, and in a moment of startling certainty, I realized that this was what Gabriel had meant by my rage being my ruin. I would become something as cold and terrible as Sulien.

And then...then time was no longer frozen.

Zayne's eyes closed as he threw his arms back, a terrible scream splitting the night air. His wings lifted, each beautiful, lush wing spreading wide. His head kicked back, causing those tendons in his neck to stand out even further.

From the center of his chest, where the sword was buried deep, a pulse of energy rippled out, washing over his shoulders and arms in streaks of rolling, golden light. There was a brief second where he was awash in the heavenly fire, his body and features completely lost in the blaze. I could no longer see him.

Terror seized me as a tremor coursed through my body. Fearing the fire would swallow him whole, I tried to pull the sword free. It wouldn't budge, and the sound—oh God, the sound that was coming from Zayne... It was animalistic and raw, shredding through me. My heart lurched as I stepped back with my right leg, bracing myself and tugging. There was no give. The sword seemed lodged, as if it were now a part of his body as it was an extension of mine, and nothing like that had ever happened before.

The whirling, whipping fire suddenly retracted, sucking back to where the blade was embedded deep.

Silence.

No screams.

No calls from nearby birds or insects.

Nothing.

Where the sword met his chest, divine energy built and throbbed. Zayne's arms fell to his sides, his wings lowered and the mass of golden-white light stretched out, wrapping itself around the length of the blade, churning and twisting its way back to me. Instinct screamed that I let go of the sword, but I couldn't, because the *grace* was mine—a part of me—and it wouldn't allow it. But there was something else in there that didn't belong to me. The first tendrils reached the hilt and then whatever it was licked over my fingers, obliterating every thought on contact.

The heavenly power hit the center of my chest, and it was like a bomb detonating. It washed over my entire body, drenching my skin and soaking into my muscles, entrenching itself deep in my bones and entwining itself around my organs. The divine energy stole my breath, curling itself around my heart and then settling in my back, rooting in my shoulders. There was no ability to process if what I was feeling was pain, a pleasure so acute that it became pain or both as it swept me off my feet. I was falling before I could even realize what was happening.

I didn't feel the impact with the ground. I didn't see when the Sword of Michael collapsed or feel the exact moment my *grace* retracted. I didn't even realize that my eyes were closed or that there was a high likelihood that I'd been knocked unconscious, and that had to have happened, because when I managed to open my eyes, there was a sense that time had passed and an immeasurable confusion, loss.

Drawing in each short, shallow breath as my senses slowly, painstakingly pieced themselves back together, I stared up at a dark sea full…full of dazzling, twinkling lights. And there were so many of them. Thousands. Millions. Numerous and countless constellations of luminous, celestial bodies, and I could *see* them. All of them. I saw them in a way I had long since forgotten, with a clarity that proved my memories of them hadn't done them justice. They were so beautiful, so endless. Tears filled my eyes as I lay there, overcome by the simple splendor of a night sky full of stars, each one representing infinite wishes and boundless dreams. I didn't dare blink, not even as each and every one of the lights dimmed until they were nothing but blurred specks of distant light, until that, too, faded beyond my sight. I closed my eyes then, instinctually knowing that I'd been given a gift greater than I could probably ever realize. One last clear memory that would never fade, and I suspected I would never see the stars again.

Zayne.

That was the first rational, coherent thought that took form and made sense to me.

Opening my eyes, I didn't look at the sky as I forced my sore body to move, to respond to the commands my brain was firing off. My muscles and nerves were slow to act, but once they seemed to get with the program, I clambered to my knees and hands. Every fiber of my being focused on the shadowy shape several feet from me.

Zayne.

He was on his hands and knees, like me, his head bowed. I could still make out the shape of wings draped along his shoulders, resting against the ground.

He was alive.

Trembling, I almost broke down right there, but somehow I managed to keep it together. He was still alive and breathing, but I had no idea what kind of state he was in.

I inched forward, squinting. His hair had fallen forward, shielding his face. I opened my mouth to say his name, but a childish sort of fear silenced my tongue.

What if it didn't work? What if it somehow did something worse?

He moved then, his large body shuddering. Slowly, he lifted his head. Strands of hair slid back from his face. His eyes were closed, and his features still seemed clearer to me, even with the limited light, but this time I knew it was the luminous glow to his skin, the *grace* that hummed under the surface. Those wings twitched and heaved, lifting. *Grace* still streaked the feathers like currents of electricity. His eyes opened, hazy and unfocused, but they were still that unreal shade of blue as they focused on me. Cleared. I couldn't breathe as I tensed, desperately trying to prepare myself for…for anything.

"Trin?" he whispered hoarsely, and a ragged breath punched out of me. *"Trin."*

I started to move, to crawl forward, but somehow I ended up scuttling back a foot or more. "Are you…?" I cleared my throat. "Are you Zayne?"

Those beautiful wings rose slightly and then lowered, and his eyes closed briefly. "It's me."

Pressure clamped down on my chest, twisting and squeezing as a hundred different emotions erupted inside me, flooding me. Hope and yearning crashed into uncertainty and even fear. What if this was some kind of trick? He hadn't sounded like that when he said my name before. In the back of my mind, I recognized that, but I realized then

I hadn't really prepared myself for this actually working. I was afraid that this wasn't real. Sorrow tangled with joy, and my body felt weak.

"I'm—" He straightened as if to rise.

I jerked back, falling onto my butt. It seemed like I had no control over my movements. A conflicting mess of emotions ruled me, and I was too afraid of the crushing disappointment if I allowed hope to seize me.

Zayne had halted, and in the chaos of my mind, I knew that meant something. "I'm not going to hurt you. I could never hurt you—" He cut himself off, his shoulders tensing. "But I did. I hurt you. I had…" He rocked back, still on his knees as he looked down at his hands. "I hurt you—"

"No. You didn't hurt me," I whispered, thinking that it actually sounded like him. There was inflection in his tone. Warmth.

"I didn't?" His hands closed. "I *remember.*" Those wings lifted again, startling me as they stretched high and away. He tore his gaze from his hands then and looked over his shoulder. There was a curse under his breath as the breeze ruffled some of the smaller feathers, exposing the streaks of *grace.* "I…I keep forgetting that they're there. They don't feel like my old ones. Neither does shifting. Most things don't feel the same."

He looked at me again, and the glow of his skin pulsed intently, causing me to flinch. His feathered wings folded back, tucking inward, and then they were…they were simply gone, as if they'd seeped into his skin—into his back—or vanished. The luminous golden shine faded, and he looked more like…well, more like Zayne and not the psychotic Fallen.

"Is this real?" I heard myself ask. The disappearing wings sort of made me think that I was still lying on my back with a head injury. "Did it really work? This is you, really you? You remember me? And you aren't about to…well, call me 'little nephilim'?"

"This is real. I'm real." His voice was rough. "I hate that you have to ask that. I'm sorry. I'm so damn sorry, Trin. I couldn't stop myself…" His gaze dropped to his hands again, to where they hung by his thighs, palms up. "That's not true. I could stop myself. I did, but it was…it was too late." He shook his head as he continued to stare at his hands. "It was like something was missing in me. Memories. Access to them—to what they felt like and meant. They warned me, and I thought I could handle it." His gaze returned to mine. "But it's me. I promise you, Trin. It's really me. Ask me something only I would remember."

I stared blankly at him. "I can't think of anything right now. My brain is too full and too empty."

He smiled then, and my heart jumped. It was *his* smile, one that was warm and open, and I never thought I'd see that smile again. "Okay. Let me think of something." He sucked his lower lip in between his teeth, and if I had been standing, I knew my legs would've given out on me. Zayne… he did that all the time, but he'd only done that once after the Fall. "I got it. You have a constellation on your ceiling."

I truly stopped breathing then. Honest to God, my lungs seized right up as I stumbled to my feet.

"I put it there," he continued, slowly standing. "I called it the Constellation of Zayne, and what happened after I showed you that ceiling has to be one of my fondest memories of all time." His voice deepened as he bit down on that lip again. "You showed me just how much you loved me. You gave me everything—your body, your heart, your *trust*."

For the second time, the world slammed to another halt. I wasn't aware of moving. The achy protest of muscles and bones didn't stop me as I threw myself at him. Or attempted to. My balance was off, my movements too jerky and stiff, and it was more like falling at him—

He was a blur of speed as he snapped forward, moving so fast that I didn't even have a chance to be startled. He caught me, his arms sweeping around me, and the moment my hands connected with the bare skin of his chest, I knew.

This was *him*. It was *his* skin against my palms, and it was warm, no longer cool to the touch, *his* breath coasting over my cheek. It was *him* holding me.

It was Zayne.

16

Somehow, we ended up on the ground again, but this time with Zayne sitting upright and me in his lap. I turned into a total octopus, wrapping my legs around his hips and clamping my arms around his shoulders.

"You really remember," I whispered, burying my face in his neck. Each breath I took was full of him.

"I remember the first time I saw you," he said, and I shuddered as I felt his hand curl around the back of my head. "You were hiding behind a curtain, where you weren't supposed to be. You were eavesdropping."

"I wasn't eavesdropping," I denied, my words mostly muffled by his skin.

He chuckled, and even though it sounded hoarse and shaky, it did strange and wonderful things to my heart. It wasn't that cold, apathetic laugh of a Fallen. "You were totally eavesdropping."

I totally had been.

"I also remember that you took a swing at me when I tried to introduce myself."

I frowned against his neck. "That's because you snuck up on me at night, in the middle of the woods."

"You meant to say that you weren't being very observant, and correct me if I'm wrong, I wasn't the one sneaking around," he teased.

"You're wrong." I squeezed him tighter.

He responded by dropping a kiss to the crown of my head. "I remember the first time you revealed yourself. We were in Thierry's office, and I think Nicolai might've choked on his own breath. I remember the first time you gave me a heart attack. It was after you told me about your vision."

The corners of my lips turned up. Not wanting him to think that I wasn't, well, capable after dropping the whole going blind bomb, I'd taken off and jumped from one rooftop to the next. He'd acted as if he hadn't been all that happy with it, but I knew he'd been secretly pleased—excited and challenged.

"And I remember the night you helped get the imp's claw out of me." His voice deepened, and this time, my shiver had everything to do with the memory of him and I, in his bathroom and in his bed. "I remember it all now—those feelings and memories are a part of me."

I couldn't speak as I squeezed my eyes shut against the flood of emotion. All my senses concentrated on the feel of his skin under my fingers. His body temperature was as warm as before, running hotter than a normal human's. Hands shaking, I drew them down, over his chest, stopping over his heart.

His heart beat strongly against my palm.

It really did work.

The Throne hadn't been lying. The Crone hadn't given me some kind of bunk spell. I hadn't messed up. It really worked.

Tears slipped free, and there was no stopping them. I broke wide open, and all the hopelessness and despair, the sorrow and grief, crashed into the relief and pounding joy spilling out of me. I tried to rein it all back in. This was a happy moment, a good one, and I didn't need to spend it drowning Zayne in my tears, but I couldn't stop myself.

Zayne pressed his cheek to the side of my head. He spoke as my body shook, releasing all the pent-up emotion that I'd barely been able to keep leashed from the moment I'd lost him. I had no idea what he said. He could've been telling me that he was part-platypus at this point, and I wouldn't have cared. I lifted my hands, sinking my fingers into the soft strands of his hair.

"Your tears are killing me," he said, and that I understood fully. "Killing me."

It was Zayne.

It was Zayne.

It was Zayne.

That was all I could think as I soaked in the feel of him. Zayne was alive, he was back and it was really him. I don't know how much time passed while Zayne continued to whisper to me, gently rocking us while I cried enough to sink the entire city of Washington, DC. Eventually, after what felt like an absurd amount of time, the tears lessened, and the tremors that coursed through me every couple of seconds ceased. I could breathe. I could finally breathe.

Zayne carefully guided my face out of his neck. Blinking until his features cleared, I shuddered as I reached up, wrapping my fingers around his wrists. "I'm sorry. I just— you're alive and it's you, and I'm so happy, and I can't stop crying, because what if this is some kind of superdetailed dream? That seems more plausible. I lost you, and when you came back, I thought—" As close as we were, I could see his eyes—really see them since I didn't have to worry about him throwing me somewhere. "Your eyes." I leaned in until our noses almost touched. I squinted. "Wow."

His hands dropped to my hips. "What? I haven't seen them."

Did Heaven not have mirrors? Better yet, had he not looked in the mirror since he...since he Fell? I touched his cheek. "They're really blue. Like very, very blue," I told him, at an utter loss when it came to using descriptive words. "But there's a...white-gold behind your pupils. I can see just the edges of it. It's *grace*. I noticed it before, but to really see it like this? I've just never seen anything like that."

Thick lashes swept down, shielding his eyes as he turned his head, pressing his cheek into my palm. "How notice-able is it?"

"Have you really not looked at yourself recently?"

"No. I..."

"What?" When he didn't answer, I guided his face toward mine. "What, Zayne?"

"I think I was avoiding my reflection." His eyes opened, but his gaze was focused beyond me. "I don't know why. I don't even know if it was a conscious choice or if it was me, but what I became...even then I didn't want to see myself. That probably doesn't make sense."

"It does." A pang tore at my heart as I smoothed my

thumb along his jaw. "Do you remember what the last couple of days were like?"

Zayne didn't answer for a long moment. "There was a lot of confusion. A lot of feelings and thoughts I didn't understand, but it was all very consuming. That's the only way I can describe it, and what I felt..." His jaw tensed against my palm. "It was so much anger and arrogance and this, I don't know...sense of twisted righteousness? Like I suddenly had all this hate toward angels and anything with *grace* in it, but I also hated demons—all demons. I believed I was better than demons and more... I don't know. More aware than those who hadn't Fallen? I just hated everything and everyone, and it was like...like being aware of what I was doing and saying, and either not connecting with it or not understanding it."

Zayne's entire body had tensed against mine as he continued. "They warned me it could happen, but I thought I could handle it. I guess I already had a healthy dose of arrogance going into it, but I can't even describe what it was like being bombarded with all these...powerful, violent emotions that suddenly felt right, like they had always been a part of me. This belief that I was judge and jury, and could do whatever I wanted, whenever I wanted."

"You sound like a lot of humans," I said.

His laugh was dry and short. "But I... I remember what I've done," he said, and guilt threaded his voice. "When I saw you after I Fell?" His eyes closed again. "I knew you. When I saw you, I knew you and your name, and then I just lost those memories. The reason why you were important to me. You were an enemy I had to..." Lines of tension bracketed the skin around his mouth. "I had to dominate.

That's all I knew until you kissed me in the park, and I don't know how to explain it, but it was like being electrocuted. All of the sudden, I was hit with all these other emotions that weren't hate, and when I saw you again—in that pool? I still didn't understand what I was feeling, but all I knew in that moment, was you. All I knew was that I wanted you. That I had wanted you and that was me. Zayne." His eyes opened then, meeting mine. "I'm just so damn sorry, Trinity. I know what I did. I know how you tried to reach me, and I—"

"Stop." I cupped his face with my hands. "Don't do this to yourself. That wasn't you."

"But it was," he said quietly, dragging his hands up my arms. "That was me, Trin. I was in there—"

"And that's why you never really hurt me."

"Never hurt you?" Disbelief joined the guilt. "I threw you around like a rag doll."

"Well, I wouldn't go that far," I muttered even though it was true.

He ignored that. "I threatened you—I threatened you more than once." His gaze lowered, and when he spoke, his voice cracked. "I had my hands around your neck. I can't unsee that."

My heart wept as I leaned in, pressing my forehead to his. "You are not at fault, Zayne. You have to understand that, and you have to realize what you did do. You could've hurt me bad. You could've killed me at any point, and you didn't. That's because you were in there, right? It was *you* who stopped. It was *you* who showed up and killed that Ghoul and it was *you* who came to the rooftop."

"I dropped you in a pool."

"I'll probably punch you for that when you least expect it, but it was you in that *pool* with me. It was you and whatever you'd become after Falling, and I was there, too. You didn't do those things to me. We did those things together because I knew you were in there," I told him. "You might not have known why at the time, but you made sure neither you nor anything else hurt me. You even warned me to stay away from you. You said that—"

"What was in me would hurt you. It would've. Eventually I wouldn't have been able to stop myself. Hell, when you trapped me, I wanted at you." His eyes searched mine. "And that part of me was growing stronger every hour."

"And it was that part that wanted to throw me around?" I slipped my fingers into his hair. "I mean, I can get pretty annoying, so that's probably not the first time."

"It was." He shuddered. "Even when you are being especially annoying."

"I know." Of course I did. I could probably kick Zayne in the face, and he would sigh with disappointment. Why? Because he was good to the core. I leaned back so that I could see his face. "But that part of you that was still in there stopped it from happening. That is all that matters. That is all that can matter. Do you know why?"

"Why?"

"Because you were given back your Glory—an angelic soul—and you Fell for me. I don't know if I should punch you or kiss you. You gave up being an actual angel to be with me. You Fell, taking a huge risk, to be with me, and you're here. You came back to me."

"Because of you. You brought me back." He slid his hands back up my arms, leaving a trail of shivers in their wake. "What did you do? I was out there, contemplating another round of arson on another demon hole," he said, and I blinked. "And then there was this uncontrollable urge to come here. How did you know what to do?"

"After you first showed up here, I was led to this church by a voice in my head, and yes, that was as creepy as it sounds. I thought I was losing my mind, but I wasn't. A Throne met me at the church. He told me what I needed to do." I let his hair sift through my fingers as I soaked in every line of his face. "He said my *grace* would never harm what I cherished, but I was scared. I wanted to believe it would work. I needed to believe that, and there were moments that I did, but…" A bit of the panic crept back in. "But I had to try. I kept telling myself that if it didn't work, it was still the right thing. That you…"

"Wouldn't want to be left in that state?" he finished for me. "You're right. I wouldn't have."

His agreement should've made me feel better, but it didn't. The idea that I could've killed him made me want to vomit. "I knew I needed to lure you out and somehow trap you, and I finally thought of the Crone. She gave it to me—actually, she had it ready for me. She knew. Well, there was this kid with her. He's a seer. He knew, and told her, and anyway, she gave me a spell, and it worked."

His brows lifted. "She just gave it to you? Don't get me wrong. I'm appreciative. More than I can put into words. But a witch never just gives anything away for free."

"They don't." I dropped my hands to his shoulders. "She did it in exchange for one of your feathers."

He stared at me.

"She gave me the impression that she wasn't going to use

it for something bad, and I believe her." I paused. "Kind of. Truth is, I would've made the deal as long as she promised it wouldn't hurt you, and she did. And I know you probably don't agree with that and I get it. I do, but—"

"It's okay." He lifted his hand slowly, making sure I saw him before he touched my cheek, and I almost started crying again. That was further proof that this was *my* Zayne. "I would've done the same thing—would've agreed to anything." He gently traced the line of my cheek. "What I was like is going to get to me and it's going to sit in the back of my mind. I'm sure some moments are going to be worse than others, but I'm going to deal with it. I'll make sure of it, because enough has already gotten between us."

"That is so true," I whispered. We had so many hurdles between us, and I wanted our very own happily-ever-after, like the ones in the romance books my mom had loved. We didn't need to be our own obstacles.

His fingers stilled near where my jaw was still slightly swollen and bruised. "Is my touching you causing you any pain?"

"No. I don't feel anything bad right now."

"You look...more banged up than the last time I saw you."

"Well." I drew the word out. "I sort of had a run-in with Gabriel."

Every part of him seemed to grow impossibly still. "When?"

"Last night." I quickly told him what happened. "Good news, no one is going to be allowed in that school for a while, and I think he's weakened somehow."

"I should've been there."

"You're here now. That's all that matters," I told him. "I'm not hurt. Seriously."

He gave a small shake of his head as his gaze continued to trek over my features. "I can't believe that. Not when you…" He looked up briefly, his chest rising with a deep breath, and when his gaze met mine again, I would swear the glow behind his eyes was brighter. "How are you up, walking around so quickly?" His gaze traveled the length of my arm, to the numerous bruises that were now barely visible. Then his eyes narrowed. "Better yet, what in the Hell were you even doing here by yourself the night I came back? Even right now?"

I recognized that tone. He sounded just like he had the night I leaped from rooftop to rooftop without warning.

"You really shouldn't be out here alone. Not with Gabriel still out there," he continued. "He sent those demons after you. Shit. They were at the apartment."

He had that same tone when I roamed off ahead of him in an unfamiliar area.

"At least the other night Dez was with you." A slight frown pulled at his lips. "Is Dez okay? I think I—"

"Threw him into a fountain? Yes. He's fine."

Zayne sighed. "Good, but where in the Hell is Roth? Layla? You shouldn't be out here, Trin. Not alone when you're not fully healed, and I know you're not fully healed. I can tell. I can feel that your *grace* has been weakened."

Okay, his ability to sense that was annoying, because it was true, but Zayne sounded like he was gearing up for a lecture of epic proportions, and I couldn't even be mad. The corners of my lips curled, and it felt weird and right and wonderful all at the same time.

"And why are you smiling?" he demanded, disbelief filling his tone once more.

A shaky laugh left me. "I just never thought I'd hear you lecture me again and enjoy it."

"Try to remember that the next time I do."

I probably wouldn't.

"I..." I drew in shallow breath. "When you died, I thought I would never see you again."

Every line of his face softened. "What did I promise you? If something happened, I would find my way back to you."

His face blurred again, and had everything to do with the tears filling them. "I still can't believe you Fell for me."

"The Glory was nothing compared to your love." He leaned in, resting his forehead with the barest weight against mine. His breath coasted over my lips as he tucked strands of hair that had escaped my braid back from my face. "I did everything that I could. You did everything that you could. I love you, Trinity, and not even death can break that kind of bond."

The bond.

I pulled back a little. "I don't feel you," I said, and his brows lowered. "I mean, I haven't felt the Protector bond. I haven't felt the little, fuzzy ball of warmth in my chest since you came back."

"Little, *fuzzy* ball of warmth?" he repeated quietly.

"And I... I haven't felt any of your emotions." It wasn't like I was just realizing that. There just hadn't been any time to really think about it. "We're not bonded anymore."

"No, we're not."

I stared at him, at the unearthly glow of light behind his

pupils. "That's good news. I can't weaken you again and we can be together."

"Me being your Protector hadn't really stopped us from being together in the first place," he replied dryly, and he was sort of right. It had only delayed the inevitable, but it hadn't been wise. He'd become virtually human. "But there are no rules. Definitely none of the angelic variety. I'm still a… I'm still a Fallen. Just not…"

"Psychotic?"

"Yeah, just not that." He ran the length of my braid through his hand. "Is a Trueborn going to want a Fallen?"

"I always want you, no matter what you are," I said earnestly, and his answering smile filled my chest with a sweet, sweeping motion. "But I do kind of miss that little, fuzzy ball of—"

Zayne reclaimed the distance between us, and in one stuttered heartbeat, his lips met mine. He kissed me, and it never ceased to amaze me, the riot of sensations that one single touch could drum up. The taste of him on my lips, on my tongue, was a balm for all the rough, ragged patches scarring my soul, and an awakening. The press of his mouth to mine was gentle, but there was an edge to it, a restraint that was so close to breaking. I knew he was trying to be careful even though he hadn't thought to be that way in the pool, but that hadn't been just him. This was only Zayne. I didn't want him to be restrained. I wanted him, all he had to offer—

Zayne pulled back suddenly, stiffening at the same second an explosion of tingles erupted along the nape of my neck. I stared at him, still a little dazed from his kiss. "You…you feel it, don't you?"

His gaze moved beyond me. "A demon is near."

I opened my mouth, and out of all the stuff I could've said, the stupidest thing spilled out of my mouth. "Demons don't come to the park because of the zoo. Roth said so."

"Roth doesn't know everything." Zayne rose swiftly, bringing me with him. He gently sat me on my feet behind him. I blinked, wondering how he'd managed that maneuver and sort of jealous that he'd been able to when he said, "Stay put."

I turned around. "But—"

"You're hurt. I'm not."

"I'm not hurt. I'm the Trueborn—oh God," I groaned, nose scrunching as the scent of sulfur and decay reached us.

"The smell," Zayne confirmed.

I squinted as a dark shape appeared from out of the tree line across from the path. Whatever it was, the thing was at least seven feet tall, and smelled like the bowels of Hell on a bad day. *Grace* sparked inside me. The only demons I knew who were that tall and smelled that bad were the kind not allowed topside for obvious reasons. I really hoped it wasn't another Ghoul.

The thing crossed under the lamppost, and I sighed, recognizing its moonstone-colored skin.

Nightcrawler.

Which was worse than a Ghoul.

That was the kind of demon one didn't want to tangle with. They were extraordinarily strong and they carried a toxic venom in their mouth and claws that could render a person paralyzed, but this one was…chained? The metal circled its neck and clanged against the ground, and at the end of the chain…

The pressure at the nape of my neck intensified, and within a heartbeat I could make out the shape of another form. This one wasn't as tall or broad, but instinct told me it was far more dangerous than the Nightcrawler.

As if it were out for an evening stroll, it slowly crested the embankment and passed through the lamplight. His features were blurry, but I knew he had to be painfully beautiful.

All Upper Level demons were.

I frowned as I realized he held the end of the chain.

"Are you actually walking a Nightcrawler?" Zayne asked, and my brows lifted. I was seriously wondering the same thing, and I was glad he'd asked.

The Upper Level demon laughed, but the Nightcrawler didn't find the comment amusing. A low, rumbling growl radiated from the rabid creature, raising the tiny hairs all over my body.

"My name is Purson," the Upper Level demon announced in a voice full of brimstone and smoke. "I'm the Great King of Hell, commander of twenty-two legions of *pet* Night-crawlers, and I'm here for the nephilim."

17

I inhaled deeply and then slowly exhaled. "No one uses *nephilim* anymore," I said for what had to be the millionth time in my life. "It's offensive and outdated."

"Do I look like someone who cares if you find it offensive or outdated?" Purson said, and I was going to go out on a limb and say no. "I'm not."

"Shocker," I muttered.

He ignored that. "I want to make it very clear who I am so there is no unnecessary drama."

Him talking sure felt like a whole lot of unnecessary drama.

"I'm the finder of hidden treasures and knower of secrets. There is nowhere you can hide that I won't discover."

"So, you're the Indiana Jones of demons?" I asked. "Cool."

"Indiana Jones?" the demon repeated. "I don't who that is."

My brows lifted. "You don't know who Indiana Jones is,

and I'm supposed to believe that you're the knower of secrets and finder of things?"

"I don't care what you believe. If you run from me, you
won't make it far," Purson warned. "You'll just irritate me,
and you don't—"

"Shut up." Zayne cut him off. "I don't have the time for
this. I was just reunited with my girl, and you're really ru-
ining the moment."

Slowly, I looked at Zayne—

Oh.

Oh, wow.

I saw his back sans wings for the first time. With just the
moonlight, I could make out an odd pattern along his back
that hadn't been there before. It looked sort of like a tattoo
with ink only a degree or so darker than his skin, but it…it
appeared raised, like a scar.

"I don't know who you are." Purson sounded curious, and
that was interesting. He couldn't tell what Zayne was, but
the Seeker demon had. It had run, but Zayne had the wings
out then. "You feel…different and yet familiar. It would be
very intriguing to explore, but you're standing between me
and what I need. Therefore, you're nothing but his personal
chew toy."

The Nightcrawler let out a chuffing laugh. "I like to gnaw
on things I'm not supposed to."

"Sorry," Zayne replied. "I'm a one-person, personal chew
toy, and I belong to her, so I'm going to have to pass on the
offer. Appreciated, though."

"I didn't say you had a choice," Purson snapped.

I needed to be paying attention, but the pattern along
Zayne's back fascinated me. Because I had absolutely no con-

trol over myself or the common sense that dictated that now wasn't the time for such nonsense, I reached out to touch—

"I got this," Zayne said to me.

A golden fire lit the veins under his skin, racing across his back. I jerked my hand back in surprise, my mouth falling open as the *grace* rushed down his right and left arms, flowing under the skin and then firing into the air.

Heavenly fire spilled from his hands, churning and spiraling, taking shape and solidifying rapidly. Two burning handles. Two four-foot flaming blades shaped in a semicircle.

The Nightcrawler jerked back a step.

So did I.

Holy crap, he had *that* inside him this whole time? Even when he was a Fallen determined to dominate me, he hadn't whipped his *grace* out like that.

"What was it that you said?" Zayne asked casually. "I don't have a choice? We all have choices. Well, except for you. You definitely don't have one when it comes to living or dying. You're going to die."

It happened so quickly.

Purson let go of the chain, and the Nightcrawler rushed forward, but Zayne was…he was like a bolt of lightning, and I didn't think that even with 20/20 vision I would've tracked his movements. He was in front of me and then he was dipping under the Nightcrawler's outstretched arm and popping up behind it—

Something fell off the Nightcrawler, hitting the ground with a fleshy plop.

It was an arm, an actual whole arm.

Okay.

Zayne got this.

He *so* got this.

Throwing his head back, the Nightcrawler howled in pain, the sound a cross between a fox and bobcat. Zayne spun, arcing one crescent-shaped blade through the air and straight through the neck of the Nightcrawler.

Falling forward, the creature burst into flames, disintegrating into a shower of ash before hitting the ground as Purson slipped into what he really looked like. His skin thinned and turned a shade of sand. Fur sprouted all over his face, joining with the mane of blond hair. Leathery, coarse wings sprouted from his back. His nostrils elongated and flattened as his mouth stretched grotesquely wide. Sharp canines sprouted as the demon's eyes glowed iridescent, pupils stretching vertically.

Purson had the head of…the head of a lion.

I would never unsee this.

Snapping out of my stupor, I started to summon my own *grace*—

Zayne spun toward the Upper Level demon and he *changed*, but it was nothing like when he was a Warden. The luminous glow pulsed over his body as the raised markings stretched and lifted off his back, becoming solid.

Wings. The markings on his back were where his wings had gone, and how freaking crazy was that?

Now they spilled outward, unfolding and rising high on either side of Zayne. Golden streaks of light pulsed throughout the snow-white feathers.

"Oh, shit," Purson uttered in a garbled voice, and I think that was the exact moment he realized what Zayne was. He lifted his hands. There were no nasty balls of energy that

Upper Level demons could often summon and control. He held his hands in surrender.

"You can have whatever you want. Anything. My legions, my loyalty. My fidelity," the Upper Level demon pleaded as he summoned the chain to his hands. "Anything. I swear to you. Anything."

"Your silence would be nice," Zayne told him, and then he struck.

It was a graceful move, a spin of golden skin and fire. His wings lifted him in the air and then brought him down, tucking back as the flaming curved blade sliced cleanly through the air.

Purson didn't even have a chance to do whatever he planned to with that chain. Zayne's blade caught him at the shoulders, cleaving straight through him.

"Dammit," Purson muttered, and then burst into flames, incinerated on the spot.

That seemed to be a favorite of last words among demons.

Straightening, Zayne shook his wings out before folding them back. They settled against his back and then...they seemed to seep into his skin, leaving behind the raised pattern of what I now knew were wings.

The sickle blades collapsed, shattering into golden dust that glimmered against the dark ground only for a few seconds before disappearing. The network of lit veins faded as Zayne turned back to where I was standing, having done absolutely nothing other than try to touch him.

Finally, I found my voice. "You could do that? Like from the moment you Fell, you could do all of that?"

"Yeah," he answered.

"I don't care what you think, a huge part of you had to

still be in there when you were all Mr. Fallen, because you could've done that at any time and you didn't."

"I could. I did. There were demons I took out that way." He looked down at his hands while I thought of that garbage human he'd killed. Had there been other humans? "But you're right, because I didn't want to when it came to you."

"Thank God," I said. "You're...you're badass, Zayne."

His lifted his head. "I thought I was badass before."

"You were. Like you were badass, but now you're bad-period-ass-period," I told him. "I'm kind of having sword envy right now."

"It doesn't really bother you, does it?"

"Does what?"

"What I am now. What I'm capable of. Because this is me." He placed his hand over his heart as he walked forward, stopping in front of me. "But I'm different now. I can feel that. There's this... I don't know how to explain it, but there's this coldness in me, and that need...that need to dominate is still there. It's not directed at you. It will never be again, but I don't know if there's more about me that has changed."

Staring up at him, I knew what he was saying wasn't a case of him being overdramatic. He *was* different. How he spoke to the demon wasn't like Zayne—like the old Zayne. There'd been a taunting quality to his words that said he was going to enjoy what he was about to do. The way he took out the Nightcrawler was another example. Old Zayne wouldn't have chopped off an arm. He would've gone straight for the kill, and the old Zayne would've taken out Purson no matter what the demon claimed or tried to barter. There were differences and there could be more, but I also knew that I would always be safe with him. Hell, I was beginning to think that I'd actually been more safe with him when he was Scary Fallen than I even realized before.

And that coldness he felt? I wondered if it was the loss of his Glory he was feeling, which was sort of equivalent to a human soul. I had no idea what that meant for him long term, and that worried me, but I knew that no matter what, I would still love him and his lack of Glory didn't stop him from loving me. We'd figure out whatever else may have changed together.

I met his gaze. "The only thing that bothers me is how unfair it is that you have two swords and I have one. That's BS."

A wide, beautiful smile broke out across Zayne's face. He laughed, the sound deep and familiar and warm like sunshine, stealing my breath. That was another thing I didn't know if I'd ever hear again. *His* laugh, and it was beautiful.

My lips twitched. "I have a feeling you're laughing at me."

"I just told you that I know that I've changed and I don't know exactly how much, and all you can think about is that I have two swords and you only have one."

"Well, yeah. That's a big deal. I'm an envious kind of person."

He laughed again, the sound lighting my whole chest. "Only you would respond that way."

That could be true.

A warm breeze caught the strands of his hair, lifting them from his bare shoulders as he looked around. Come to think of it, the abnormal chill was gone from the air. It wasn't unbearably hot or muggy, but it was far more seasonable.

I watched him, wondering if he had something to do with

the weather. How strange would that be? But it couldn't have been a coincidence that it had been twenty or more degrees cooler than normal up until he'd been restored—well, mostly restored—to who he'd been before.

"This is the...what—third demon that's come for you? Have there been more?"

"It's only been the Ghouls, the ones from the other night and this dork," I told him, thinking it was probably best not to mention that two out of three times I left the house I'd had a run-in with a demon looking for me.

"Why isn't Dez with you?"

"The Crone told me that a Warden or demon's energy could mess with the spell." I started to reach for my phone. "I should call him. Share the good news."

"We can do that later. Right now I want to get you home."

Home.

The new apartment that Zayne had barely spent any time in, where he'd placed glow-in-the-dark stars on the ceiling for me. *Home.* My chest squeezed. Before it was just walls and a roof with my clothing still half-packed away in luggage. The stars had made it feel more, but it wasn't until now that it felt like a home.

Before I turned into a weepy mess all over again, I got my mind back on track. "Gabriel obviously knows where I am. He'll come again."

"But you won't be alone then," he said, and my heart turned into a gooey mess. "We may have to figure out somewhere else to stay if it becomes too much of a problem."

I nodded. "The Transfiguration—wait, you weren't there

for that part of his extremely long-winded speech on how he plans to end everything."

"I know about it." He took my hand, and the feel of his palm firmly against mine was a wonderful feeling. "I've been filled in on a few things, the Transfiguration being one of them. He plans to open a rift between Earth and Heaven so that the demon Bael along with souls that belong to Hell can enter Heaven."

My brows rose. "You really have been updated. Was it the Alphas? God. I still can't believe you were actually in Heaven—*the* Heaven." My eyes got wide, and I stopped walking. "What was it like? Is it just fluffy white clouds and angels chilling and doing nothing? Souls roaming around, having everything they could ever want? Or does it look like this place? But with angels and souls? I've asked so many spirits, but none of them will tell me—" My heart skipped a beat. "Oh my God, did you see your father?"

A grin played across his lips as he stared down at me and I…

I didn't even realize what I was doing until I was jumping on him.

Zayne caught me as I wrapped my arms around his neck, and this time, he kept his footing. My legs clamped down on his hips, and there was no way he was shaking me off. Not that he tried. His arms immediately swept over me, and he held me just as tight as I clung to him.

Raw emotion crashed through me as it hit me once more that Zayne was alive and it was him, a little bit different but *him*. Tears pricked at my eyes. "I'm sorry. Okay, I'm not sorry. I just needed a hug."

His chin grazed the top of my head. "This has to be my favorite kind of hug."

"Mine, too," I said, voice muffled. "I just… I can't believe you're really here." My heart pounded and my stomach got into the mix, jumping all over the place. I wanted to laugh and cry, be silent and contemplative and yet scream as loud as I could. I felt like I was coming out of my skin.

"If you need to remind yourself that I'm really here, please feel free to jump on me. I won't mind," he said. "I'll catch you."

I squeezed my eyes shut. "Why do you always have to say such perfect things?"

"I don't always say the right things," he denied. "You know that more than anyone else."

"I do," I told him. "That's why I know what you say is usually just perfect. I'm an expert in these things."

"I probably shouldn't argue with you, then," he said, his voice thicker, rougher with what he'd lacked before. Emotion.

"Yep." I squeezed him with my arms and legs, and for just a few moments, I let reality soak its way in. I'd helped him find his way back to me, just as he promised, and even though he came back…different, it was *him*. There was a whole lot of bad stuff we still needed to face, but with him by my side, there was more than just a chance that we'd defeat Gabriel. There was hope. There was a light at the end of the tunnel. He was the silver lining, and this moment was proof that miracles were possible. There was a future beyond all of this.

Pulling myself together, I slowly disentangled myself. Once I was on my two feet and ninety-nine percent confident that I wasn't going to launch myself at him again, I said, "Okay. I need to focus. I *am* focused. You can answer all of the questions about Heaven later, but back to what's important. What did the angels tell you——?" I started walking again, pulling Zayne along with me until I stopped. "Where am I walking to, by the way?"

"I figured we'd catch a ride, since I'd rather speak to Nic before I take to the air," he reasoned, and I wholeheartedly agreed with that. "I can get high enough that humans can't tell my wings aren't like a Warden's, but I want to make sure none of the Wardens think I'm going to kill them."

The Wardens.

He'd said that like he was no longer one of them, and he wasn't. Obviously. I already knew that, but it was still a shock to the system.

"Good call," I murmured, and then got back on track as we started walking down the path. "Is it possible? What Gabriel claimed? That Bael and the souls would infect Heaven and that God would close the gates?"

"Yes, which basically means any human that dies would no longer be able to enter Heaven. All the souls would be trapped on Earth, either becoming wraiths or tortured by demons," Zayne finished with a sigh. "With the spheres of Heaven closed off, demons would have no reason to stay hidden. Earth would become Hell, and parts of Heaven would be lost. What Gabriel plans is possible."

"I was kind of hoping he was just delusional."

"Unfortunately not," he said. "Some of the Alphas and other angels already want to close up shop."

"The Throne said as much." I wondered if my father was one of them as my gaze swept over the dense, shapeless tree line. Anger flashed through me. What had become of Gabriel couldn't have been such a complete shock to the other archangels. He had to have showed signs of being out of control, with homicidal, world-destroying tendencies. That kind of stuff didn't just appear out of the blue. None of them had done anything. My own father hadn't even told me that Gabriel was the Harbinger, let alone remotely prepared me to come face-to-face with an archangel.

Angels were virtually useless.

Well, except that Throne. He'd been helpful. I peeked over at Zayne, who was technically an angel but not. He wasn't useless, but any number of the angels, from the lowest class all the way up to the archangels, could've done something other than standing by, playing *Animal Crossing* or whatever it was that angels did in all their spare time.

"You have your phone on you, right?" he asked as we reached the mouth of the park. I nodded, pulling it out of my back pocket. "Want me to order a pickup?"

"Yep." The entrance spotlights weren't nearly bright enough to minimize the glare of the phone, so I eagerly handed it over.

As he opened up the app, I let my gaze drift over him. I wondered what the driver was going to think when he climbed into the car shirtless. My gaze got a little hung up on the breadth of his shoulders, the clearly delineated lines of his chest, and lower, to the hint of tight, coiled muscles mostly hidden by the night. Zayne had always been in the kind of shape that made me feel like I needed to add cardio or sit-ups to my nonexistent workout routine. I trained to fight. That was enough exercise for me, but his body was proof that it could cash whatever check his mouth was writing.

And I knew I was definitely staring at Zayne a little too intensely, but I wasn't ogling him because he was pretty to look at. That was something I'd done a time or a hundred in the past, but I was staring at him now because he was here and he was okay. The disbelief wasn't going to go away any time soon.

Dragging my gaze back to his face, I thought about how his features still were far clearer than they had been before. In this kind of light, I would've never been able to make out the slash of his brow or the set of his lips. That hadn't been my imagination. It had to be because of what he was, of the *grace* inside him. Nothing else around me seemed more clear. I couldn't remember what it was like when I saw my father. Those rare visits were all too brief, and I'd had other concerns when I'd been with Gabriel, like staying alive for example, and when I met the Throne. But when I thought about it, I had seen those creepy eyes in the Throne's wings. I didn't think I would've been able to see something that small at that distance.

Halfway through ordering an Uber, Zayne's fingers stilled and he looked over at me.

"Sorry." I flushed. "I was staring at you like a total creeper."

"You should know by now that I have no problem with you staring at me." He handed my phone over, and after I slid it into my back pocket, he caught my hand and tugged me against his chest, and I burrowed in like a barnacle. "I'm sorry."

"For what?" I started to lift my head.

"For what?" he repeated with a low laugh as he cupped

the back of my head, keeping me there, with my cheek above his heart. "For leaving you."

"That wasn't your fault, Zayne. It's not like you chose to."

"I know, but that doesn't make it easier knowing that you've been through Hell, physically and mentally, and I couldn't be there for you." His next breath was ragged. "I wanted to go to you as soon as I realized I could, but when I did, well, that sure as Hell didn't help."

I had questions about exactly what happened to him, but they'd have to wait. "You're here now. That's all that matters."

"Agreed." His fingers curled through my hair. "And I'm not going to leave you. Never again, Trin. Never."

18

The ride to the apartment was...interesting.

The driver, an older man, kept glancing in the back seat, and I didn't think it had much to do with Zayne being shirtless or the fact I was attached to his side like we were pieces of Velcro. There was a nervousness in the older man's movements and chatter that ended as abruptly as it started.

When the man's eyes weren't on the road or darting to the back seat, they were on the gently swinging cross hanging from his rearview mirror.

I wondered if the man sensed something...otherworldly about Zayne. I knew it wasn't me. I had no impact on humans. People also never seemed to realize when they were with Wardens in their human form, but there was definitely an...energy around Zayne that hadn't been there before.

It was hard to explain, but it reminded me of how the air charged and became eerily still right before a terrible storm or in the eye of a hurricane. That's what it felt like. There was a stillness to Zayne even as he continuously ran his fingertips up and down my arm, one that made the air around him feel as if it was seconds away from exploding into violent energy. As if the very atmosphere itself was holding its breath, waiting to see what he was going to do.

It was kind of cool.

And a little scary.

On the way, I did send Dez a quick text letting him know that Zayne was all right, and that we'd call him in a bit. My phone immediately lit up with a dozen or so silent texts I didn't get a chance to respond to because Zayne had dipped his head and pressed his lips to my temple, and the sweet kiss nearly sent me into a complete breakdown.

I think the driver took his first real breath when we pulled up to the apartment building and Zayne opened the door. As I climbed out, I saw the driver's gaze follow Zayne as he stepped under a streetlamp. The imprint of Zayne's wings was faint but visible to me, so I had no doubt the older man saw it.

I shut the door as the driver unhooked the cross and brought it to his lips.

"We definitely need to make sure you have a shirt on when out in public," I said, joining him on the sidewalk.

A wry grin appeared as we entered the lobby. "You think?" He glanced over his shoulder. "How visible is it?"

"Well, I can see it, so…" I said as we stepped into the lobby. Luckily, it was empty, and with it being brightly lit, I was able to get a better look at it. "Sort of looks like a white ink tattoo of angel wings. It covers your entire back, and it looks like it's slightly raised." Each curved feather looked as if it had been painstakingly etched onto his skin, no detail missed. The slightly raised quality to it gave it the shaded appearance of a normal tattoo. The urge to touch it hit me hard again as we made our way to the elevator. But remembering how he reacted in the pool, I resisted. "It's really beautiful, Zayne."

"You're beautiful."

My head jerked up, and I found him staring down at me with a soft, tender pull to his lips. I could feel warmth hitting my cheeks even as I snorted in the most unattractive manner possible. "I've seen what I look like right now, and—"

"And you're even more beautiful than before." He lifted his hand slowly to my face. His thumb brushed over the curve of my chin. "Each and every bruise is a badge of your strength."

"There you go again, saying all the right things," I murmured.

"How is this for not being the right thing to say?" He traced a finger along the line of my cheek, stopping where I knew the skin was still a lovely shade of bluish-purple. "I'm going to hurt Gabriel. Every bruise he left behind, every hurt he inflicted, I will repay tenfold. I want him to be alive and breathing when I strip his flesh from his bones and tear his organs from his body, and then, before he takes his last breath, I want the last thing he sees to be you before you kill him."

Oh.

Wow.

My heart skipped a beat. Not at the cold promise in his voice that assured he planned to do exactly that or at the violence he wanted to reap, but because he would face Gabriel again. We both would face the archangel, and what if something happened to him? Again? My insides turned cold and panic started to take root. Could I convince Zayne to take a vacay? To sit this out—?

I stopped myself right there as I stared up into his eyes. Every day carried the risk of one of us meeting an untimely demise. That hadn't changed. If anything, now Zayne would be less easy to kill. That was good news, something I needed to remember, but Zayne hadn't asked me to sit this out.

Inherently, I knew *he* wouldn't.

I also knew I needed Zayne at my side when I faced off with Gabriel, even if Roth and Layla were successful in recruiting Lucifer. And it wasn't like Zayne would listen to such a request. He hadn't when I asked him to before, and maybe him charging in when he did, drawn by the pain the bond was feeding him, had played a role that had ultimately led to his death.

I couldn't ask that Zayne not let guilt get in the way of us living. And I couldn't let fear do the same.

I wouldn't.

I took a small breath. "That was also the right thing to say."

Zayne raised one eyebrow.

I shrugged. "I mean, probably not to most, but I have absolutely no problem with you doing exactly that."

A faint grin appeared. "I shouldn't be surprised that you'd say that. You've always been bloodthirsty."

"True," I said, stepping into the elevator. Though I had to admit that I wouldn't have thought the Zayne from before would've said all of that. Yeah, he would've wanted to hurt and kill Gabriel, but the whole stripping the skin and tearing out organs thing? That was different.

As the elevator took us up, I stared at him. With the better lighting, I could see he looked the same.

But not.

"You know, your features are sharper to me, more defined. Like a picture coming into focus in high-res," I explained. "It's been like that since you came back."

He started to respond when I felt the awareness swirl along the nape of my neck. His gaze swung toward the elevator doors as he stepped forward, somewhat blocking me. "There's a demon near."

"It's probably Cayman. He was going to hang out here until he heard from me," I told him. "You're bright."

"What?" Zayne glanced at me as the elevator slowed to a halt.

"Your skin is brighter." I poked his arm. "It's like there's a faint light under your skin, and I think that's why I can see you better than before."

His brows rose. "I look like a walking light bulb?"

I grinned. "I don't think it's all that noticeable. I mean, if I can see it, I'm sure others can, but I don't think they'll be able to put their finger on what it is. They'll probably think you have a nice, healthy glow."

He opened his mouth as he turned back to the front of the elevator, his attention focused on the inside of the room as the door opened. Whatever he was about to say was forgotten as the dark-haired demon *shimmied* into our line of sight. Cayman's back was to us as his head bopped and his hips swayed. In one hand was a bag of chips and in the other was a can of soda. Music thumped from his earphones in a familiar beat.

Was that... *Hey Mama*?

Suddenly Cayman bent at the waist. His ass went up in the air and he shook that thing like...like he was getting paid. Good money, too.

My lips parted.

"This was not what I expected," Zayne murmured.

"I don't think anyone would expect this."

Cayman whipped upright, the movement smooth and sinuous, popping a chip into his mouth.

The demon could dance.

I stepped out of the elevator, unsure if we should interrupt him or not. He seemed to be having so much fun as he danced backward—

He spun toward us. A high-pitched shriek erupted from him, causing me to jump. The bag of chips slipped from his fingers and slices of deep-fried potatoes scattered across the floor.

"I wish we'd had the foresight to record this," Zayne commented.

I smirked.

"Oh, man." Cayman reached into his pocket and the sound of music ceased. Slowly, he tugged his earbuds out as he stared at Zayne. "Should I be running for my life right now?"

"Instead of dancing for your life?" I asked.

"This is not the time for jokes," the demon replied.

"But I've got jokes for days."

Cayman ignored me and lowered his voice as if Zayne couldn't hear him. "I really do not want to have a repeat of Saturday night."

"Yeah, I'm sorry about that," Zayne offered. "I wasn't quite myself."

"No shit," Cayman whispered. "You don't feel the un-controllable urge to hunt me down and make me scream like a small child?"

Zayne bent down, picking up the fallen chips. "I don't feel like doing that or hearing you scream again." Glancing at the kitchen, he did a double take as he got a load of the mess. "On second thought..."

I bit down on the inside of my cheek.

"I'll clean it all up." Cayman lifted his hands. "Even the mess Trinity left out."

My eyes narrowed on the demon.

He winked at me before turning his attention back to Zayne. "Damn, angel boy, look at how far you've fallen. Literally." He sounded like he'd just paid Zayne one of the biggest compliments. "Glad you're back."

"Thanks," Zayne replied. "I think."

"I was afraid I was going to have to move in with Trinity if this didn't work out. You know, keep her sane." He paused. "Sedated."

My eyes narrowed. "Do you want to scream like a small child again?"

"Maybe later. I'll let you know." Cayman took a drink of his soda.

Zayne tossed the bag of chips onto the counter. "Do I look like a walking light bulb to you?"

Rolling my eyes, I turned to him. "I said you didn't look like that."

"Just making sure." He shot me a grin that shouldn't have caused my heart to do a pitter-patter, but did.

Cayman shook his head. "No, but you do have a luminous... undertone now that you mention it."

"See?"

Zayne's grin kicked up a notch. "Got a question for you, Cayman. Do you feel anything when you're around me?"

Cayman lowered his can of soda. "Depends on what you mean."

Remembering how Purson had reacted to Zayne, I followed where he was leading with that question. "I think he's talking about if you can sense what he is?"

"Other than the wings being a dead giveaway?" Cayman's dark brows knitted. "Where are they, anyway?"

"I have them." Zayne turned, giving Cayman a view of his back.

The demon let out a low whistle as he saw the markings. "Incognito. Nice. I haven't seen that since angels worked side by side with man."

My brows climbed up my forehead. "How old are you?"

"Old enough that I've seen entire civilizations fall only to be reborn," Cayman replied.

"All righty, then," I murmured.

"But to answer your question, you definitely don't feel like a Warden." His forehead creased as he studied Zayne. "You feel different." His head tilted, sending a sheet of black hair over his shoulder. "But if I hadn't seen the wings, I wouldn't have known what you are."

"How is that?" I asked, shifting from one foot to the next. Weariness was creeping into my muscles. It had been a long couple of days, and a day's worth of sleep hadn't gone as far as I thought it would.

"I guess it's the same thing that prevents most demons from sensing that you're a Trueborn. Some kind of heavenly shield attached to the *grace*, I suppose."

"Could you sense a normal Fallen—one without its *grace*?" I asked, wondering if I could sense one myself.

Cayman nodded. "They feel like...like a very powerful demon. Not exactly but similar." He leaned against the back of the couch. "Any demon worth its name will be able to pick up the aura of power around you, but their minds would never put holy and crap together and end up with a Fallen as the reason why. There just hasn't been one roaming around for, well, since the Wardens came out of their shells. Obviously."

"Interesting." Zayne glanced over at me. "That is something that could be of benefit."

"Yeah, except your little Targaryen burn-them-all moment Saturday night made it clear there was a Fallen on the scene—one with his wings and *grace*. I'm sure that's spread farther and wider than obvious fake news on social media," Cayman said. I guessed Purson wasn't included in the DC Demons Facebook group or something. "Especially considering the way you feel reminds me of only one other being."

My stomach tumbled. I knew who he was referencing. Lucifer.

"How does it feel, though?" Cayman asked. "Knowing where you really come from?"

"Honestly? Doesn't feel good or bad. It just...makes sense." Zayne briefly glanced at the demon. "Who I am or even who I was has nothing to do with ancestors who lived some thousands of years ago."

"You're such a disappointment," Cayman muttered.

"Really?" Zayne replied.

"Yeah, because you're so damn well adapted." Cayman

pouted. "It's no fun to mess with you about your less than holy origins if it doesn't bother you."

"Sorry." Zayne strode toward me. He took my hand, pulling me toward the couch. "Sit with me?"

"Of course," I murmured, grateful to not be standing the moment my butt hit the cushion.

"But now I understand why Roth said some of the things he said," Zayne added as he sat beside me. "And also surprised he's managed to keep that to himself."

"You and me both."

"Even Roth follows some rules," Cayman said.

Something occurred to me then. "You know what I don't understand?"

"How humans still think climate change is junk science?" Cayman suggested.

"Yeah, that also, but—"

"Bitcoins?" he offered up next. "Because even I don't understand Bitcoins and I've seen all manner of money."

I frowned. "No. I'm not talking about Bitcoins. How did the future Wardens end up getting created? There weren't any female Fallen, right? There's no female angels."

"Who says there aren't any female angels?" Cayman asked, turning around so he was facing us.

I blinked rapidly. "I've never seen nor heard of one."

"There are female angels," Zayne confirmed. "I saw a few."

"Wait. For real? What did they look like?"

"They looked like...female angels," he said.

"That's real helpful." I turned to Cayman. "Why is this the first time I'm hearing about this? Why is there no mention of a female angel in any—wait." I held up my hand. "I honestly don't even need that answered. The patriarchy."

"Yep." Cayman nodded. "And that's a human construct. Can't even blame us demons for that."

"Okay. So there were female angels who Fell?"

"I bet you won't be surprised to hear that no female angels have ever gotten themselves kicked out of Heaven," Cayman said. "Not because they never questioned anything. It's just that they actually questioned things in a logical, thoughtful manner instead of acting like general fools."

"No," I muttered. "Not surprised at all to hear that."

"Anyway, remember the thing where God flooded the Earth to rid the world of the nephilim offspring that resulted from naughty-fun times before the Fallen were cast to stone? Well, God didn't get all of them."

Zayne draped my braid over my shoulder. "There were only a few human women whose genetics matched up with Wardens', allowing them to become pregnant with a Warden. Come to find out, those women were all descendants of the children of those who Fell."

"Watered-down nephilim," Cayman said.

"Watered-down Trueborns," I muttered, thinking all of that sounded potentially incestuous. I was just going to hope that the first generation of Wardens had hooked up with women who weren't their offspring, and leave it at that.

Besides, I needed to be more worried about the functionality of my own womb.

"So what was it like?" Cayman asked, picking up a small box of animal crackers before all but rolling over the back of the couch and into a corner of the sectional. "The whole dying thing? I'm curious. You know—'cuz I've never died."

"That's kind of a rude question to ask," I pointed out.

Cayman shrugged.

The corners of Zayne's lips tipped up. "As if you don't want to know."

I opened my mouth to deny that, but then sighed. "Yeah, I can't even lie. I am curious."

"Knew it." He ran a hand over his head, dragging his hair back from his face. "I remember dying. Kind of."

"Kind of?" Cayman asked around a mouthful of crackers.

He nodded. "I remember being under the school, in that cavern, and knowing I was dying and being...scared out of my mind for you—for what would happen once I was gone. I could feel your pain, and all I wanted was to make sure you knew it would be okay."

God.

It took everything in me not to launch myself at Zayne again.

"And then there was a loud snapping sound, almost like thunder, and this flash of intense light. Never seen something so bright before." A far-off look crept into his expression, but he didn't take his gaze off me. Actually, he hadn't for more than a few moments, and I wondered if it was because he was feeling the same as me. Like, deep down, he couldn't believe we were here. Together. "The light receded pretty quickly, and when it did, I was in some kind of building."

"A building? Instead of clouds?" I sighed. "I am so disappointed."

A grin appeared. "I eventually saw clouds."

I clasped my hands under my chin. "With angels resting on them?"

Cayman snorted.

Zayne laughed. "You're going to be really disappointed, but just normal clouds in the sky."

He was right, but I was still curious. "Heaven has a sky with clouds in it?" When he nodded, my nose wrinkled. "Are you sure you really were in Heaven?"

"I'm really curious as to what you think Heaven looks like," Cayman admitted.

Before I could launch into my vivid and overly detailed description of cloud cities, Zayne cut in. "I was definitely in Heaven."

I eyed him. "How can you be sure?"

"This is going to sound crazy, but it was how the air felt—like the perfect temperature. Not hot. Not cold. The right amount of humidity. It was how the place sounded, like a spring morning. It was the smell. The whole place smelled like…"

Wondering what Heaven smelled like to him, I leaned forward.

Zayne cleared his throat as his lashes lowered. "It smelled amazing," he said, and I sat back, bummed he hadn't shared. "And the building I was in was like a coliseum, and I'm pretty sure it was constructed of gold."

"Like the whole thing?"

"Yep."

"Damn," Cayman murmured, shoving another handful of carb-rich goodness into his mouth. "God spares no expense."

I wondered if a demon should learn any details about Heaven, but I figured if there was an issue, Zayne wouldn't be talking so openly about it.

"I could see the clouds through the opening in the roof, by the way," Zayne added. "If it makes you feel better, the sky was an incredible shade of blue and the clouds appeared fluffy."

"Like your eyes," I said. "The color of the sky, that is."

The grin reappeared. "At first I was confused. I knew I was in Heaven. I knew that in my bones, but I was...surprised to find myself there."

Obviously Zayne thought that because he was missing a part of his soul, thanks to Layla. That was water under a bridge that had been burned down, but there was no stopping the spike of anger that followed any thoughts of how badly Zayne had been wounded by Layla, even though it was before we'd even met. It wasn't like I held that against her or anything.

Okay. I kind of did, but I was working on getting over that and being an overall better person.

I just needed a whole lot of improvement on both of those fronts.

"I wasn't alone. Took me a couple of moments to realize that someone was there with me—behind me." Zayne leaned back, his head tilted toward me. "It was your father."

19

I didn't think I heard him right at first. "Really? *My* father?"
"Yes."

I was stuck in disbelief for several moments before acknowledging that it had been my father who had finally corrected a destiny that had gone off the rails, not only for Zayne and I, but also for Misha. That thought of my old Protector, my friend, still brought a wealth of pain. I would never completely get over his betrayal or how I'd been so wrapped up in myself that I'd missed how unhappy Misha had been.

But it made sense that Michael, my father, would be there. Zayne had been my Protector when he…when he died. My initial shock showed I wasn't thinking about his presence correctly. I was attributing it to some kind of fatherly obligation—something that he knew nothing about, even if the Throne claimed that my father had faith in me.

I made sure my voice was level when I asked, "Was it him who told you about who the Wardens were originally?"

"Basically, and yeah, that was a shock, but first he made sure I knew how incredibly disappointed he was that I'd already, as he put it, 'gotten myself killed.'"

"What an asshole!" I exclaimed, wishing my father was in front of me so I could punt-kick him in the freaking face.

"Have you met an archangel that wasn't one?" Cayman asked.

"Since I've only met two, no." I folded my arms over my chest. "You didn't get yourself killed, Zayne."

"Well, I guess that is debatable."

I opened my mouth to give a highly detailed thesis on how wrong he was.

"I knew I was weakened and that I needed to stay back, but when I felt your pain and fear, I had to do something. I don't regret that," Zayne said before I could launch into all the reasons why my father had no idea what he was talking about. "No matter what the outcome could've been, I don't regret coming to your aid. I told your father that after he finally shut up, which felt like hours later and probably was."

Despite the seriousness of the conversation, a smile tugged at my lips. "And how did he react to that?" In my mind, I pictured the archangel being coolly displeased and disgusted by Zayne taking action based on his emotions.

"Surprisingly well," he said, and I blinked as the image of my father poofed into smoke. "I think he respected what I did, maybe even hoped that was what I would say. I don't know. He's hard to read. Sort of has the same expression on his face no matter what is happening."

That coolly displeased image took form once more.

"He then asked if I loved you."

My heart gave a little jump. I knew the answer, but for my...father to ask that?

His gaze held mine. "I told him that I was willing to die a thousand deaths for you. That I loved you that much. Then he asked what I would do to be reunited with you. I told him I'd do anything."

Tears filled my eyes as Cayman whispered from his side of the couch, "I wish I had chocolate."

Ignoring that, Zayne swallowed thickly. "He didn't seem surprised to hear that, but he told me that many of his brethren believe that kind of love to be a weakness."

"His brethren are stupid," I muttered.

"I think Michael thinks so, too. He seems to believe that kind of love is a strength if...used right."

Instinct sparked, and I remembered how the Throne had said they believed that Zayne could be useful. My eyes narrowed. "What did he mean by that?"

"Well, he feels that love can be the proper motivator to not fail in the upcoming battle," he explained. "Then he asked if I would be willing to be reborn again, even if that process was...less than pleasant. Honestly, I didn't understand what that meant. At first, I thought he was talking about being reincarnated, and that just confused the Hell out of me. That was roughly when he told me about the origins of the Wardens."

"Sounds like Michael expected you to Fall," Cayman pointed out.

"You know, I was thinking that myself. It was the others who explained that once I had my Glory, I could stay. Protect Heaven. Or return to Earth when the time was right to aid you. Your father stood back and said nothing while they sort of pitched their side, but it wasn't even a choice. I told them that I wanted to return to you and that would be the only way I would help fight Gabriel or protect Heaven."

"You negotiated with angels before you were given your Glory and reborn?" I asked, a little dumbfounded.

"I did."

"Surprised they didn't just kick you out and send you way downtown at that point," Cayman said.

I nodded. "Agreed."

Zayne seemed generally unaffected by the shock both Cayman and I were feeling. "I knew I would find my way back to you, one way or the other. They needed me more than I needed them."

"You are…" At a loss for words, I shook my head.

"Amazing?" he suggested, eyes glimmering.

"And so humble." That earned me another laugh, and each of his laughs had a healing quality to it. One less ache became apparent. "How bad was it? Being reborn and getting your Glory back?"

"It was nothing." He looked away then.

"Liar," I said. "It hurt. Didn't it?"

"Kind of a silly question." Cayman shook a few animal crackers into his palm. "Besides the fact he had to get outfitted with superspecial wings, he got pumped full of *grace*. I doubt it felt like a massage."

I shot him a look, and Cayman responded by tossing the handful of crackers into his mouth. "I need to know," I told Zayne. "I need to know what you went through."

His gaze coasted over my face. "Do you?"

"You would need to know if our situation was reversed."

His chest rose with a deep breath, and I knew then he

realized I was right. "It was like being on fire. Not just my skin, but my veins, my bones—every part of me. I thought I was dying all over again, and when I thought I couldn't take it anymore, that was when my wings changed. It felt like my skin was being carved open and new bone was being grown. It wasn't exactly a quick process."

"God." I tipped over, plopping my forehead on his shoulder. "I'm—"

"Do not say you're sorry. You have nothing to apologize for." He cupped the back of my head. "I survived it. I'm here. I'd go through that a thousand times if necessary."

"You guys are too cute," Cayman commented. "I think I'm getting a toothache from all the sweetness."

"Shut up." I lifted my head.

Zayne's hand slid to the nape of my neck as his gaze flicked over my shoulder. "You're more than welcome to leave."

"Hell, no. This is better than watching old episodes of *The Bachelor*."

As close as our faces were, I saw Zayne roll his eyes before he slid his hand to my cheek, where he gently splayed his fingers. "What I felt was nothing compared to what I feared was happening to you," he said, voice low. "It was temporary and worth it. Now I'm here, and nowhere near as easy to kill as before." Sliding his hand away, Zayne sat back. "Michael already told me what Gabriel planned to do and what would happen if he succeeded. He told me you..." He trailed off, shaking his head. "It doesn't matter."

"What did he tell you?" I persisted when he didn't answer. "What? Did he tell you I would die? That Gabriel planned to use my blood to basically create the back door into Heaven?"

A muscle flexed along Zayne's jaw. "That was all he needed to tell me." The glow in his eyes brightened. "It's not going to happen."

"You're right. It won't," I agreed even as unease blossomed in the pit of my stomach. Something about this wasn't adding up. Zayne had been given unimaginable power even though my father and the Throne had suspected that he would Fall. They allowed it so he could come back to me. Sure, he'd have to deal with Gabriel, but would the angels be that accepting of Zayne's choice, that generous afterward? Nothing I knew about them would suggest so. Then what was the catch? The sacrifice? The cost?

Fear punched through me. What if after we defeated Gabriel, they'd come after Zayne? Hunt him to either strip him of his *grace* or entomb him? What if Zayne's return was temporary?

Unaware of my complete panic spiral, Zayne said, "It took me a bit to get used to the *grace*, how to control it and deal with it." He moved, placing his hand on his chest. "I'm still not quite used to it. Sort of feels like a—"

"A constant low-level buzz of energy?" I finished for him, pushing the panic back. Now, while we had an audience, wasn't the time to ask what the cost was. I really didn't need to have a complete breakdown in front of Cayman.

Zayne smiled that beautiful smile then, and I felt the catch in my chest. "Now I know why you have such a hard time sitting still."

"That's it?" Cayman asked, and I looked over at him. He'd set the box on the coffee table. "They gave you a superdose of *grace* and allowed you to Fall. Let's be real. They didn't do that so you could be with Trinity. Most of them don't care about all your warm fuzzies for one another."

Cayman was obviously thinking the same thing I was but with far less panic.

"You're right. Most of the angels don't care about Trin's and my feelings for each other," Zayne responded, and my whole brain zeroed in on the "most of the angels" part. "They let me Fall and remain as a new and improved version to fight Gabriel."

"The Throne did tell me that none of the angels that could strip him of his wings and *grace* would come down here while Gabriel was here," I said even though that didn't answer what they'd do once Gabriel wasn't a problem.

"You're giving them way too much credit." Cayman snorted. "Angels are self-righteous enough to try such a thing, no matter the risks. They're not showing up to take his *grace* because he has all the power of an angel, but he's not bound to angelic law."

"Angelic law?" I twisted toward Zayne. "Like what kind of law?"

Zayne glanced at Cayman, his brow furrowing. "I think he's talking about their law of combat. Apparently it's forbidden for an angel to attack another."

"Even in this kind of situation?" I asked, thinking that couldn't be right. "Like even when one of their own is trying to end Heaven?"

"Yep," Zayne confirmed.

"You've got to be kidding me." Disbelief flooded me. "That has got to be the stupidest thing I've ever heard."

"They believe that to take up arms against another is lifting a sword against God," Zayne said. "It didn't make sense to me, either, but he said it was a pledge they all took after the war. Obviously they didn't put a whole lot of thought into the pledge."

By war, I was guessing he was referencing when Lucifer was booted. I processed all of that and suddenly a lot of things made sense. Big things.

Like why I was here.

"That's why I was… I was born," I announced, and yeah, it sounded way overdramatic to me, but it *was* dramatic. "There's no way that a single angel didn't see what Gabriel was becoming. They just couldn't stop him, because of the pledge. They must've realized this was as good a time as any to bring back the Trueborn and I guess they just rolled the dice to find out who would be the baby daddy."

"Rolled the dice to see who would…" Zayne shook his head as he processed what I said.

"Okay. Maybe not rolled the dice, but you get what I'm saying." I swallowed hard as I sat back against the cushion. I really was created to be a weapon. That wasn't breaking news or anything, but I guessed there had been this tiny, childish part of me that had hoped my father had seen my mother and fallen for her. That there had been some emotion behind my creation. But there really wasn't. "I was a loophole. With my father's *grace*, I could fight Gabriel. And Gabriel knew about me, and he tried to do the same with Sulien."

"That didn't end well for him." Zayne smirked.

No, it hadn't. "While I was waiting in the Potomac Highlands to be summoned, I always thought it was for the battle that ended all battles, but my father was just waiting for Gabriel to make his move." Thoughts whirling, I rubbed my hands over my thighs. "It makes you wonder if there were more... Trueborns? I mean, after they all died off. If my father had...made one each generation or if others—"

"I don't think there were more," Zayne interrupted. "At least not from Michael. He strikes me as the type that would bring up other Trueborns as a way to either compliment or insult you."

Pursing my lips, I nodded. "You have a point there."

"Look at you all, putting two and two together," Cayman said.

"Like you knew any of that," I scoffed.

"I didn't," he replied. "But what I do know is that Gabriel can most likely rip the head off a Fallen."

I slowly turned to the demon.

"What?" He lifted his hands. "I'm just being honest."

"Yeah, they told me that I'd probably still die," Zayne answered. "They're real motivators. That's why some of them want to close Heaven now, but we stand a better chance together in defeating Gabriel. Even Michael believes so."

"You all stand a better chance if Roth's mission is a success," Cayman tossed out. "That's about the only chance you stand."

"What?" Zayne glanced between us. "What mission?"

My eyes widened. "Uh..."

"He doesn't know yet?" The demon's yellow eyes grew as big as saucers.

"Know what?" Zayne demanded.

"I haven't had a chance to tell him," I said. "We've all been a little busy."

"I don't think I've ever been more happy in my life to be the bearer of news." Cayman scooted across the couch, stopping once he was mere inches from us. A slow, wicked grin spread across his face, and he did look beyond thrilled. "Roth and Layla are trying to recruit reinforcements. Well, one reinforcement in particular."

Zayne's brows furrowed even further. "Why do I have a feeling this is something that's going to disturb me?"

"Weeelll." I drew the word out.

"Roth is trying to convince the one thing that can go toe to toe with an archangel to get involved," Cayman said, and even I could see that his eyes were glittering with glee. "Who would have no problem breaking any celestial rule. One who actually has a lot of experience in doing just that."

Zayne didn't speak for a moment. "Please tell me that what I'm thinking is wrong."

The demon clapped his hands against his cheeks. "Depends on what you're thinking."

"There's no way Roth is planning to get Lucifer topside. That would make no sense, right?" Zayne looked at me, and I shrunk as far as I could into the cushion. "Because wouldn't that jump-start the biblical apocalypse and cause us to have even more problems to deal with?"

"Weeelll," I repeated. "We're sort of hoping that God will overlook his presence since we're trying to save mankind and Heaven, and you know."

"No. I do not know." Zayne stared at me.

"What?" I threw up my hands. "We decided this when you were kind of dead."

He blinked slowly.

"And even with you being a badass fallen angel and me being a badass Trueborn, we still need help," I reasoned. "Look, Roth didn't sound like he was going to be able to pull it off, anyway. So, we'll probably have to find a different way."

"I don't know." Cayman sat back, grinning. "Lucifer has one big bone to pick with Gabriel, and if he succeeds? Saves mankind and Heaven? What do you think that will do for his ego? He'll never let it go. Pride is, after all, his favorite of all sins."

I could think of a lot more fun sins, but whatever.

"Lucifer?" Zayne spoke his name like he'd never said it before. "What in the Hell are we supposed to do with him if he does come topside?"

"I don't know, but he's not staying with us," Cayman said.

"He's not staying with us." I glared at him. "And you guys live in a huge mansion. You have room and you all are demons." I paused. "Well, Layla is a half demon or whatever, but we are not demons and we live in an apartment."

"A state isn't enough room if you have to be sharing it with Lucifer." Cayman rested his arm on the back of the couch. "Well, you'll know if they're successful. You'll feel it."

"What does that mean?" I asked.

Cayman shrugged. "Lucifer loves to make an entrance."

That...sounded concerning.

"You know, this also reminds me of something I need to ask." Zayne's ultrabright eyes focused on the demon. "What in the Hell were you thinking letting her go out there by herself? An Upper Level demon came for her tonight. Imps and Seeker demons came for her here just two days ago. Earlier that same day? Ghouls were after her."

"Excuse me?" My head snapped toward Zayne. "I could've completely handled Nightcrawler and Purson, and I would've gotten control of the Ghouls and imps."

"Maybe. Maybe not. You're still recovering, and I can tell your *grace* isn't up to normal," he reminded me, and I really, really did not like this new talent of his. "The last thing you need to do is injure yourself further."

"She needed fresh air and time alone. Everyone was crawling all over her, and in case you forgot, I was kind of running for my life. From you," Cayman defended. "I know she can take care of herself, and I didn't—*wait*. Did you say Purson?" Cayman pitched forward. "Purson came for you? And Ghouls and Seeker demons?"

I nodded. "Yeah, and Purson was walking a Nightcrawler. On a leash. It was all very odd."

"Gabriel must have demons out looking for her," Zayne said.

"No." Cayman rose. "There is no way Purson's working with Gabriel."

"*Was*," Zayne corrected. "He's dead."

Cayman's jaw locked down. "Purson has always been loyal to Lucifer. And Ghouls? There is no way Gabriel would have the kind of reach to sway them to his cause. Ghouls only exist in the lowest circles of Hell."

"If it wasn't Gabriel, then who?" I demanded.

The demon looked a bit ill. "Lucifer."

20

Cayman bounced out of the apartment shortly after dropping that bomb.

I'd assumed that he was going to try to reach Roth and Layla, but apparently they were most likely in an area of Hell that Cayman wouldn't even venture into. After telling us he wanted to see if anyone knew for sure that it was Lucifer who put a hit out on me, he'd blinked out of existence.

That was another cool demon talent I wished I had.

"Lucifer," Zayne said once Cayman was gone. "Really?"

"It was Roth's idea."

"Shocker."

"But I agreed to it. We need to bring out the big guns to defeat Gabriel, and it seemed like a rational decision at the time." I stretched my tired legs out, letting them dangle over the edge. "It still does. Hopefully Cayman's wrong and those demons weren't sent by Lucifer. That would be a complication we don't need."

"You think?"

It was a complication that I could add to the ever-growing list of very real and possible complications. I just hoped that if Lucifer was behind this, Roth and Layla would be able to sway him to our side and out of wanting to do who knew what to me. "I know you don't think bringing him into this is a wise idea, but we will…just need to control him somehow."

"Control Lucifer?" Zayne laughed under his breath as he scrunched a hand through his hair. "That should be easy. He seems like the kind of guy who'd be easily manageable."

I grinned. "Maybe he just has a bad rap?"

"Or he's learned to be a calmer, nicer ruler of Hell through yoga and meditation?" He picked up my braid, gently tugging the band free.

"Hey, stranger things have happened."

He snorted. "I have a feeling he's going to be just like Roth but worse."

Another grin tugged at my lips, and for a couple of moments, I got a little lost in watching him. He was slowly unthreading the braid. There was a lot we needed to talk about, but I started with what felt like the most important. "Did you get to see your father?"

His fingers stilled around my hair. "There wasn't a lot of time for visitations. It took every moment there for me to get control of the *grace*." He returned to undoing my braid. "The first time I summoned it, I blew a hole through one of the buildings. Was it like that for you?"

"I never blew a hole through a building, but I would have a hard time keeping it under control when I got angry or upset." I touched his arm. "That means you didn't get to see your father?"

Zayne shook his head. "I didn't see anyone other than Michael, a few other angels and the Alphas."

"I'm sorry." I curled my fingers around his wrist. "They could've made sure you had a chance to see him—to see anyone you wanted."

Letting go of my hair, he threaded his fingers around mine. "I would've loved to see my father. To see Sam," he said, referencing the spirit who'd come back to warn us about what was happening at the high school. "But I needed to make sure I could handle what was given to me." Thick lashes lifted. "I needed to get back to you. That was the most important thing."

My heart gave a happy little dance in my chest, and for a moment, there was nothing but warmth and joy. It didn't last long.

Because what was the cost?

Air snagged in my chest as the razor-edged panic resurfaced. I pulled back, slipping my hand free.

"What?" His eyes searched mine.

Suddenly needing to move, I rose, and the dull flare of pain in my shoulders and spine was nothing compared to the deeper pain of fear. "I need to ask you something and you have to be honest."

"I'm always honest with you." Zayne stared up at me as a half grin formed. "Well, mostly. There were a few times in the past I wasn't completely honest."

I almost started to ask which times he was referencing in case there was more than I knew, but stopped myself. "I need you to be completely honest now, no matter what the answer is."

"Of course."

Skin prickling, I started to pace in front of the TV. "I need to know the truth, Zayne."

He moved to the edge of the couch. "Yeah, I've gotten that. What do you need to know?"

Swallowing the rise of fear-induced nausea, I forced the question out. "You came back to me without me having to barter or plead. You came back more powerful than even me, and yes, I had to do the thing with the Sword of Michael, and that was stressful and all, but you are alive after dying."

His head tilted. "Yes." A pause. "I am."

"They wanted you here to help stop Gabriel, but them letting you Fall? Having no problem with you being with me? All of it seems too good to be true. There has to have been a cost to this. A catch." I crossed my arms, still pacing in front of the TV. "I need to know if this is temporary? You being here with me? Are you going to be taken away from me once we defeat Gabriel? Are the Alphas and other angels going to come for you? Try to take your *grace* or entomb you?"

"No." There was no hesitation there. "I feared that myself, and knowing what I do about angels, I didn't trust that there was no catch. Them making this something temporary sounds like something they'd enjoy. I expected that to be the case, but this isn't temporary, Trin."

"How can you be sure?" I asked.

"Because your father told me it wasn't."

I stopped moving. My heart might've stopped moving.

"He said you get to stay with me? He said those exact words and didn't leave it up to interpretation?"

"Michael said I would remain by your side as long as you would have me." Never taking his gaze off me, he bent to swipe a chip off the floor and tossed it onto the coffee table. "And then he thoughtfully tacked on that I would remain by your side as long as I stayed alive."

"Really?" I whispered, too afraid to relax. "The 'as long as you stayed alive' part sounds like something he'd say."

Zayne nodded. "This isn't temporary, Trin."

"But why?" I asked, walking forward and stopping in front of him. "Why would they do something so…so nice?" I knew how bad that sounded, but people thought angels were pillars of virtue and generosity. They were more of the teach people a lesson through loss and grief type, and yeah, I was sure there were fluffy and loving ones out there. We just never dealt with that kind. "It just doesn't sound like them."

"It's not, but I think…your father had a lot to do with them allowing this. Actually, I know your father did."

"Really?" I wanted to believe that but his history proved that he wasn't the type of dad to get heavily involved.

Or to care.

"You know how I thought that Michael expected me to Fall? Even Cayman thought that." Zayne's hands reached out and settled on my hips. He pulled me into the vee of his legs. "Could it be because he realized I wouldn't be bound to their rules of combat between angels? Sure. I bet that was what he used to convince the other angels. But I know it was more than that." He stared up at me, the striking lines of his face more clear to me than they'd ever been. "The night he made me your Protector, he whispered something to me. I thought I understood what it meant, but I think he was telling me more than I realized."

I remembered seeing my father whisper to him. When I asked Zayne about it, he'd said it hadn't been about the Harbinger. Then I got, well, distracted as per usual. "What did he say?"

"He said, 'My daughter will one day give you *grace* and restore you to your Glory.' Then he said he hoped I'd learned to know when to follow the rules and when not to," he told me. "I really didn't get that whole *grace* and Glory thing, but I knew what he meant by following the rules. He was talking about us—about the rules that governed a Trueborn and Protector, and I know he was telling me to not follow them."

A shaky breath left me. Zayne had followed the rules his entire life, and what had that gotten him? He'd lost Layla before he even had her, and it didn't matter that if they had gotten together he would've realized how strong his feelings were or weren't. He followed the rules, and grew farther apart from his clan. And I remembered when he told me he was tired of following the rules. That was the first night we'd been together.

"But you were weakened because we didn't follow the rules," I reasoned. "You died because—"

"And my Glory was restored because of you—because I loved you. I was given *grace* because I love you," he said. "Not following the rules led me to this very moment, and yeah, I lost my Glory in the Fall, but I'm here. I'm with you, and sure, we could think that he gave me that heads-up so I was more likely to be here with you to fight Gabriel, but I think it was more than that. I know it was. He wants you to be happy, and he knew that allowing me to return to you would do that."

Never in a million years would I have considered that was what my father had whispered to him. Nor would I have ever considered that he even spared a moment to think of my happiness. Ever.

"There isn't a lot he can do for you, being what he is or being what I imagine is expected of him." He stared up at me, eyes a stunning clear blue. "And I don't say that as a way to excuse his general lack of paternal abilities, but this was something he could do for you."

"If you're right, I…I don't even know what to say," I admitted, squeezing my eyes shut. When they reopened, there were tiny bursts of light. "I think it's easier for me to think he's not capable of doing something like that."

"Why?" Zayne asked.

It was hard to put what I felt into words. "Because it… makes me think about what it's like to have a father, a real one who is involved and cares. It makes me want that."

"There's nothing wrong with wanting that."

"I know, but it makes me sad and angry to know that I have one who can't be that," I admitted. "So it's easier just to think of him as what he is—an archangel who is capable of only feeling cool displeasure."

His gaze searched my face. "I understand," he said, and I believed that he did even though he had a father who had been a daily part of his life. Who he loved and had been loved by, even when they had disagreed fiercely with one another.

"Just so you know," I said, letting out a breath and letting hope in as I shoved thoughts of my father aside and focused on Zayne and I. "You don't have to worry about how I feel. I will always have you. *Always*."

"I know." That was said without an ounce of arrogance as he tugged me down to his lap. When he lifted his hands, he did so slowly, making sure he didn't startle me as he gently clasped my cheeks. "It's been six days, four hours and roughly twenty minutes since I've been able to really talk to you and to see you through *my* eyes. Others have gone longer. Weeks. Months. Years. But those days and hours and minutes have felt like an eternity. I can't even imagine what it's been like for you."

I placed my hands against the warm skin of his chest. "I always thought losing my vision was the scariest thing that could happen to me, but then I...I lost my mother, and that was worse. I dealt with it, but then I lost Misha, and I thought everything he'd done was the worst thing I could possibly experience. I was wrong. Each of those things has been terrible or hard or life-changing in its own way, but losing you felt like every breath I needed to take was stolen away before I could inhale." The back of my throat burned again. "It was worse than Hell, and it wasn't even the healing part. That sucked, but being awake was worse. Being aware that you...you were gone was the worst part, and you know, I didn't know how I could go on, and I was planning to..."

"Planning what?" He carefully smoothed his thumbs under my eyes, and it was then that I realized I was crying. Again. I really needed to stop doing that. Jesus.

I stitched myself together. Sort of. "I was planning to go to Grim—to the Angel of Death—and force him to bring you back."

"You were going to do what?"

"Go to Grim and force him to bring you back. I didn't know how I would do it, but then I...I didn't know if that was the right thing, you know? Like what if you were at peace and I was pulling you away from that? Bringing you back to life and for what? To fight Gabriel. To possibly die again?" Those feelings—that confusion—still pooled in the back of my throat like battery acid. "But I knew that if I survived Gabriel, I don't think...I don't think I would've survived losing you. A part of me would be forever gone—the part that belongs to you. And that night you came back? I was in that park trying to figure out what would be the right thing to do and if I could live with myself no matter what I decided."

Whispering my name, he lowered his head and kissed my forehead and then the tip of my nose. "I'm glad you didn't have to make that choice." He pulled me against his chest, folding his arms around me. "I wouldn't have found peace, Trin. You would've known. You would've seen me as a ghost or spirit. I would've come back to you."

I looped my arms around his waist, knowing he was right. I should've known when I woke up, and in the days that passed, that something was happening, because I hadn't seen him as a ghost or spirit. "I think I was afraid that Gabriel had managed to do something to your soul," I admitted, and Zayne tensed against me. "I know that probably sounds bizarre, but I was just so afraid."

"It's not bizarre." Zayne guided my head back as he pulled away just enough that he could see me. "You know I'm always going to be here. Remember? I'll always be here to make sure you can see the stars. I'm just your Guide...Fallen Angel."

A shaky laugh left me as I leaned in. Zayne met me halfway, and the moment our lips touched, I let myself finally find a measure of relief. His wintermint scent surrounded me. I could kiss him for an eternity—

Jerking back, my eyes popped open as it hit me. My chest hollowed as I stared at the striking planes and angles of his face, and I thought about my father and all the other angels I'd ever seen. None of them looked older than midtwenties. Hell, most demons didn't look all that much older. I didn't know if they just aged incredibly slowly or if they reached a certain maturity and stopped aging. With a sinking sort of feeling, I inherently knew that the Fallen were the same.

I would age each year.

Zayne would not.

21

"Are you okay?" Zayne asked while I continued to stare at him, on the brink of yet another panic spiral.

"Are you, like, immortal now?" I asked. "Like you won't age?"

There was a soft, heavy-lidded look that settled into his features. "I was wondering if you were going to ask about that."

"Oh, no. You're not going to age, are you?" Groaning, I let my head fall back. "Here I thought going blind and you having to, I don't know, pick out my clothes for me would eventually strain our relationship—"

"Why in the Hell would you think that would strain our relationship?"

"Well, maybe not the clothing thing, but you know."

"No. I don't." He tipped my head forward so we were eye to eye again. "Explain."

"If I get lucky, I'll have enough vision left to see like this much." I held up my thumb and forefinger, keeping them about an inch apart. "As much as I hate to admit it, I'm going to need help with a lot of things."

A big, bright smile broke out across his face, surprising me. I rocked back a little. "Why are you smiling?"

"Because you admitted that you're going to need help and that's huge. I figured I was just going to have to sit back and watch you walk into walls for months before you asked for help."

I stared at him.

"But back to the not smiling part?" he went on. "I'm sort of offended that you think your vision is going to somehow affect the way I feel about you and strain our relationship. Actually, I *am* offended."

"I'm not trying to offend you, and it's not like I think you don't love me enough to deal with it, but I can't help worrying about that," I admitted, feeling like I was naked even though I was completely clothed. "And considering what we faced—what we will face—it feels stupid to even be talking about this right now."

"It's not stupid," Zayne argued. "It's important. Continue."

I took a deep breath. "I don't even know how bad it's going to get for me. So how can you know that it won't get annoying? And if it did, I wouldn't blame you. I get annoyed with myself when I walk into whatever stupid thing that's been in the same place since the beginning of time. I get annoyed even now when I try to read the instructions or expiration dates on something and I have to guess what I'm reading. So, I just… I don't want to feel…" Trailing off,

I lifted my shoulders in a shrug. "How did we even end up talking about this?"

"You brought it up," he reminded me, brushing my hair back from my cheek. "I know what you were going to say."

"Do you know, all-knowing one?"

One side of his lips tipped up. It was a brief grin. "You don't want to feel like a burden. That's what you were going to say, but, Trin, nothing about you will ever be a burden. Everything about you is a goddamn privilege."

My chest.

Ugh.

It swelled like there was a balloon inside it. "Why?" I toppled forward, dropping my head on his shoulder. "Why do you have to always say the right stuff, Zayne? I'm trying to freak out over here and you're getting in the way of that."

"Sorry?" He sounded like he was trying not to laugh.

"And look, my crappy vision isn't even an issue right now. You're going to stay perpetually young and buff, and I'm going to get old and my hips are going to break. Then I'll have to become this better person who discovers if you love someone you set them free. And I'll have to tell you to go and live your life, find someone young—"

"Stop." Zayne did laugh then, catching my arms and lifting me off his shoulder. His eyes met mine—eyes that would never dull or become rheumy with age. "That's not what's going to happen."

"You're right." I glared at him. "I am so not going to be that person. I think 'if you love someone, set them free' is one of the stupidest sayings out there. I'm way too jealous and selfish. I don't care if I'm ninety, I will still cut a—"

"I don't want you to be a better person. I like you being

jealous and selfish." He grinned at me like I was being silly, and of course he could think that since he was a freaking fallen angel. "There won't be another person for me. Not now. Not even when you're ninety."

"Easy for you to say when you'll look like this forever." Eventually people would think I was a cougar when they saw me with Zayne, and there would be a future where that happened, because I refused to believe that we wouldn't defeat Gabriel.

"It's easy for me to say that because I love you, and that runs deeper than skin or broken hips," he said, and without any warning, he moved. He lifted me out of his lap and onto my back, slipping my body under his. He held his weight off me, bracing one arm by my head. "That's not something that goes away with age. It'll strengthen and become unbreakable. That I know for a fact. I wouldn't have Fallen if what I felt for you was that weak. You wouldn't have fought for me, refusing to give up, if your love for me was that easy to break."

I pressed my lips together in a mulish line. "You're doing it again."

"Doing what?"

"Saying the right stuff."

He arched an eyebrow. "Do you want me to stop doing that?"

"Yes." I sighed. "No."

Zayne's smile wrapped its way around my heart. "I get why this would freak you out, I do, but that's borrowing tomorrow's problems. We got enough for today, don't we?"

"We do." Lifting a hand, I touched his chin. His skin was so warm. "But that's a lot like crossing that bridge when we get there, and we will get there, Zayne. That bridge is going to come."

"And we'll cross it together." He dipped his chin, pressing a quick kiss to the tips of my fingers. "We'll figure it out together. That's all we can do, because you just got me back. I just got you back. We have what so many people never have—a second chance. We deserve that, and we're still going to have to fight for it. What could happen years from now is not going to steal every day between now and then from us. That's what it will do if we stress over it now."

He was right. There was already enough threatening to take away that second chance. It would be hard not to worry about it, just like it was hard not to stress over my vision, but I'd learned to not let what would eventually happen get in the way of living. Just like he couldn't let what he'd done when he first Fell change who he was now.

Zayne's lips brushed over mine in a sweet, soft kiss, and I opened up, letting him in. All the many concerns fell to the wayside. That was how powerful his kisses were. Or maybe that was just how powerful my love for him was.

And God, I would never get tired of how his lips felt against mine. I would never not be awed by how the gentle and questioning press of his mouth to mine could elicit such a maddening rush of sensations from me.

Slipping my hands up to his shoulders, I tugged on him until I felt the warmth of his skin through my shirt. The edges of his hair tickled my cheeks as I nipped on his lower lip.

There was an answering rumble from deep inside his throat that curled my toes. The kiss deepened, and the air around us seemed to crackle. There was a razor-sharp, almost desperate edge to the way our mouths met, and I imagined it was hitting us right then how incredibly lucky we were that we got to experience this again. It wasn't that what we'd done in the pool hadn't counted. It had, and it, too, had been powerful. Those early-morning hours had been proof that Zayne had still been in there, that his love for me was still guiding his actions. This was different, though, because it was *us*.

We got a little lost in just…in just kissing. There were soft and achingly sweet ones. Kisses that were teasing and playful. Then there were the ones that left me aching and breathless. All of them were my favorite, because it was Zayne who I was kissing.

More than anything I wanted to lose myself in him, to forget about everything. And I think he did, too, but he lifted his head after one last drugging kiss.

"I've missed you," he said, his voice as unsteady as the breaths he took.

"Same," I whispered, dragging my fingers along his cheek. The glow behind his pupils appeared muted.

He shifted his weight onto one arm, and slowly, he lifted his hand and tucked the strands of my hair back from my face. "When we were together early Sunday morning?" He swallowed as he drew the tip of his finger along the curve of my cheek. "I…I don't know how to feel about that."

"What do you mean?"

"That was me and it wasn't me. I knew what was happening. That was something that I was controlling, but I just think what if you did that because you felt like you had to? If I could go back, I wouldn't have done that," he admitted. "Not that I didn't enjoy it—"

"I know. I enjoyed it." I cupped his cheeks. "You didn't force me. I initiated it. I knew what I was doing and I didn't feel like I had to."

"I know I didn't do that, but it just doesn't...it doesn't sit well with me. You had no idea if the Crone would be able to help you at that point." His finger ghosted over my lower lip. "I'd just dropped you in a pool, and earlier that night, I fought you. I threatened you, and then I was inside you. I could've hurt you during it. I could've hurt you afterward."

"I understand why you feel this way. I do," I said softly, and I did. Zayne was *good* to the core, even when he was missing a part of his soul, and even now, when he was a Fallen and technically had no soul. It really made me question the whole soul thing and how much it played a role in people's feelings and actions, but now wasn't the time for that. "You didn't hurt me, Zayne. You had control, and what we did gave me hope. I know how crazy that sounds, but it was further proof that you were still in there, and I needed that." I lifted my head, kissing him softly. "You don't have to like what happened. I can understand why you couldn't. I just don't want it to hurt you."

He slid a hand down my arm, curling his fingers around my wrist. Pulling the hand away from his cheek, he kissed the center of my palm again. When his eyes met mine again, he let out a ragged breath and his shoulders seemed to loosen. "We didn't use protection."

There was a trip in my heart. "I know," I whispered.

He kissed my palm again. "Fallen are able to reproduce with humans."

"I know," I repeated. "But I don't know if I can. I started

thinking about it afterward, because…well, for obvious reasons, and don't know if any Trueborn has ever reproduced."

"You don't know a lot about Trueborns," he pointed out.

"And that's why I asked Dez to see if Gideon could find anything that would indicate either way."

Zayne blinked. "You asked Dez to ask Gideon?"

"Who else was I supposed to ask? I don't think Thierry or Matthew would know—and that is a conversation I so do not want to have with them—and I thought of Gideon. He knows a lot and has access to a bunch of dusty books that no one reads," I told him. "Unless an angel is going to pop up and answer the question, he was the best idea I could come up with."

"I can't even imagine what that conversation with Dez went like."

"Oh, trust me, you don't want to. I would like to pretend it never happened, but hopefully he finds something out so we…"

Those ultrabright eyes met mine. "So we know."

Stomach flip-flopping all over the place, I nodded and then I started to speak but stopped.

Always observant, he caught it. "What? What were you about to say?"

Warmth crept into my cheeks as I untangled my tongue. "What would we do if I… God," I groaned. "I can barely say it, which I know is stupid. But saying it makes it a more real possibility, and that reality is superscary now or ten years from now."

"Agreed." He nodded.

"But we're adults, right? Basically. You more so than me, but it's not like we're not old enough—" I stopped myself with a shaky laugh. "Who am I kidding? If I was thirty, I wouldn't feel old enough. What are we going to do if what you've got going on works with what I've got going on?"

One of his brows rose. "You mean, what if I got you pregnant?"

"What if we got ourselves pregnant," I corrected.

"I don't know," he said with a soft, somewhat uncertain laugh. "We would—"

"Have to figure it out?"

"Together. Yes."

"I can't... I can't even think about it," I admitted. "That's possibly the most immature response, which is a key sign that I'll make a terrible parent, but I can't even wrap my head around that possibility."

"I can't, either. And it's not that I wouldn't be okay with the idea—if that's what you decided," he said, and the next breath I took lodged somewhere in the swelling in my chest. "It's just not something I've prepared myself for, but I will get prepared no matter what happens or is decided."

Some of the unacknowledged tension loosened. It wasn't that the possibility of being pregnant didn't still freak me the Hell out. It did and then some, but it wouldn't be something I faced alone. There was nothing I would face alone now.

"So, we've covered my dad, what it was like to get pumped full of *grace*, Lucifer, my crap vision, the fact I will grow old and you won't, your dismay over what happened between us in the pool and the possibility of me being pregnant." I grinned. "What a reunion, huh?"

Zayne laughed. "It's perfect."

"Whatever."

"It is." Dipping his head, he kissed me. "I need a shower. Want to join me?"

My heart skipped a beat and muscles low in my stomach tightened even as tiny beads of uncertainty pilled up in my stomach. I'd never showered with someone before. Obviously. Zayne was the first guy I'd ever been completely naked with, so my mind immediately showed me, in detail, all the ways I'd end up looking and behaving like a total goober, but my heart and my body was screaming, *Shower? With Zayne? Yes and yes, please.*

Those tiny beads in my stomach started bouncing with nervous energy, but now more than ever, I couldn't let fear and self-consciousness drive my decisions. Not after learning the hard way that tomorrow wasn't promised.

"Okay," I said, hoping my voice didn't sound as squeaky to him as it did to me. "I mean, yes. Sure." Heat crept into my cheeks. "I'd like that."

"You sure?" A softness had settled into his features. "We don't have—"

"I'm sure," I interrupted. "Hundred percent sure."

"Good." Zayne smiled then, and a whooshing motion swept through my chest. "Because I really don't want to let you out of my sight for more than a few minutes. That probably sounds needy as Hell, but I just…" Lashes swept down, hiding his eyes. "I don't know. I'm not expecting anything beyond you being there with me. I just need to be able to see you."

"I get it." And Lord, did I ever completely understand. "I feel the same way."

He dipped his head, kissing me. "Why don't you go ahead

and get the shower started? I'm going to de-Cayman-ize the kitchen first."

Since part of that mess was mine, I started to tell him he didn't have to do that, but then it struck me. He was giving me time, making this less awkward, and yeah, getting undressed and stepping into the shower with him probably would have me giggling like there was something wrong with me.

Whatever it was that made Zayne so incredibly thoughtful and considerate was still there. It was the part of him that set him apart from so many and it made it all too easy to fall in love with him despite the risks.

Heart squeezing, I stretched up and kissed him. What was supposed to be a thank-you turned into something a little more, and it was several moments before Zayne rolled off me. I got a little hung up in staring at the markings on his back, but finally got my body moving.

I hurried to the bathroom, my heart beating way too fast as I brushed my teeth and cranked on the water. There was a dizzying rush of anticipation and nervousness, and an acute sense of surreality as I stripped off my clothes, toeing them into a corner and then picking them up, actually making use of the empty laundry hamper. Quickly grabbing the other small piles of clothing scattered about, I tossed them where they belonged and, before I started giggling like I'd been afraid of or passed out, I stepped under the hot spray.

My senses were so hyperaware that my hands were trembling as I turned slowly. It wasn't that I was scared. It wasn't like I wasn't ready. It wasn't anything like that. It was just that everything felt like...like it was a first. The showering together thing definitely was, but even though we'd experienced all manner of kisses and so much more, everything felt different and new now.

Water plastered my hair to my back and streamed over my body as I looked down at the numerous fading cuts and bruises. My body was a patchwork of old scars and new ones, and I knew that each one of those flaws was exactly as Zayne had said earlier—a badge of strength. I wasn't embarrassed by them. I was proud.

The corners of my lips tipped down as water sluiced between my breasts. The skin in between was pinker than normal, and it almost looked like a...scratch in a straight line. I touched the skin. It was tender, but not exactly painful. Having no idea where that came from, I closed my eyes and lifted my chin, letting the showerhead wash more than just the last twenty-four hours away. Soon, Zayne and I were going to have to talk to the clan and let them know more than that he was okay. We'd have to start working on a plan B just in case Lucifer wasn't interested in stroking his ego and saving the world. Even with his help, we still needed to discover where Gabriel and Bael were holed up. There was the school and the damn portal underneath that needed to be dealt with. I could call Jada now and not freak her out...too much, and I needed to figure out what in the heck was going on with this Gena person Peanut appeared to be spending more and more time with. I also needed to carve out some time to truly freak out over the fact that Zayne wasn't going to age, and continue to worry about the big what-if. What if I ended up pregnant? What would that really mean?

Looking down once more, I wiggled my toes as I placed the tips of my fingers against my stomach. No amount of chasing demons and leaping from building to building would ever result in a flat stomach. The junk food probably had a lot to do with that, but if I had to choose between a flat stomach and French fries, I was always going to choose the fries. But if I was pregnant, wouldn't I have to eat healthier food? I shuddered and then flattened my hands against my lower belly, pressing—

What in the Hell was I doing? I yanked my hands away, making a face. Rolling my eyes, I turned back into the spray of water. What would we do? What *could* we do? Being pregnant couldn't change anything. I would still be a Trueborn. I would still need to find Gabriel and whatever came after that.

All of this was just banana pants to me, because I couldn't even say if I wanted to be a mother, but I knew Zayne—he would make an amazing father to our…

What in the holy handbasket would a child of a Trueborn and a Fallen even be? Would the human part of me even be passed on? Would the genetic flaw I carried that had caused retinitis pigmentosa rear its head? My stomach dipped with the possibilities.

I needed to stop, because now wasn't the time for any of that, especially things that may never come to fruition.

Hearing the bathroom door snick shut, my pulse skyrocketed into uncharted territories. I kept my eyes forward as I focused on breathing, which was strangely requiring a lot of effort.

The slightest movement behind me threw that hard work with the breathing out the window. Skin brushed against skin, sending a tight, intense shiver down my spine.

A moment passed and I felt the light touch of Zayne's fingers on my shoulders, sweeping my hair to one side. His lips then pressed against the skin below the nape of my neck, and my toes curled against the floor of the stall.

Unable to keep silent in the highly charged silence, I said, "The de-Cayman-izing didn't take very long."

"I only got through the first layer before I grew too impatient," he said, and I grinned. "It's going to require another round later. Maybe a third by the looks of it."

"I'll do both rounds," I offered. "Do you want the stuff for your hair?" When he said yes, I grabbed the bottle he used, the one that was both a shampoo and conditioner. If I used that stuff on my hair, it would be as dry as a bird's nest afterward, and I had no idea how his wasn't.

A companionable silence descended in the bathroom as we got down to using the shower for what it was designed for. The awkwardness faded even though I was overly aware of every moment his skin touched mine, when he reached around me to place a bottle on the shelf and his arm grazed mine. Or when I washed the shampoo and then the conditioner out of my hair, having to turn around to do so. My hip had brushed against his thighs, and he'd gone as still as a statue again. I'd kept my eyes closed through all of that, and when he reached for the body wash, I wished I had the courage to offer my assistance, but I was too afraid of sounding like a dork, so I kept quiet as the steamy air filled with the minty scent of whatever wash he used and the lusher tones of jasmine that came from the body wash I always used.

When he rinsed off and moved behind me again, I expected him to step out, but he didn't. My breath caught as his hands glided down the slick, still soapy skin of my arms, over my elbows and then to my wrists. I hadn't even realized until then that I'd folded my arms over my waist. With impossible gentleness, he eased my arms to my sides.

The edges of his wet hair brushed my cheek as he lowered his head, this time pressing a kiss to the spot between my neck and shoulder, where he'd nipped the skin and left a mark. "Sorry about that," he offered. "I've never done that before."

"It's okay," I told him. "It's not like it's noticeable."

He kissed the spot again. Legs trembling, I opened my eyes as his thumbs moved in slow, idle circles along the insides of my wrists. I watched his hands slide from my wrists to my stomach. His deep golden skin was such a contrast against the more yellow, olive tones of mine. He didn't press his hands against my belly like I had done earlier. Obviously he wasn't as much of a mess as I was, but I wondered if he was trying to imagine the same thing I had—a stomach far more swollen than the typical carb bloat I was normally rocking.

A heartbeat later he confirmed as much. "If it turns out that you're pregnant and if you decide that's what you want, it'll be okay," he said, his voice rough with emotion. "But you did say something wrong earlier."

"Only one thing?"

"You wouldn't make a terrible mother," Zayne said.

I choked out a laugh. "I wasn't wrong."

"You don't give yourself enough credit, Trin. You'd be one of the fiercest mothers there is, and you would stop at nothing to give them the best possible life," he told me. "I don't doubt that for a second."

A ragged breath left me. "We." I turned my head toward his. "If *we* decide if that's what we want, it'll be okay."

"Right," he said thickly. His lips found my cheek. "We got this, no matter what."

"We do." And I believed that. I really did.

A flutter started in my chest and moved lower as I felt his gaze on me from behind. There was a tightening all over.

Zayne's head dipped once more, his chin grazing the side of my head as his mouth found its way to my ear. "I am not worthy of you."

"That's the farthest thing from the truth."

"It's not. You're brave and strong. Fearless. You're intelligent, kind and loyal." His large hands slid to my hips. "You're breathtaking." He kissed my neck, and I shuddered. "I want you, now and always."

Heart thumping as instinct guided me, I took a step back, allowing our bodies to come into full contact. He made a raw sound, and heat lit up my veins.

His hands spasmed against my hips. "I already wanted you badly, but now I feel like I'm coming out of my skin," he said, and I could feel him, all of him, and there was no doubting the truth behind his words. "But I know things are probably weird for you right now, so that is why I'm going to wait until you leave and then turn this water ice cold."

A heady riot of sensations skated over my skin as I turned in his arms. I didn't let myself overthink what I was doing. I looked up, blinking the wetness off my lashes. He stared down at me, his jaw clenched and his gaze filled with stark need. The glow behind his pupils was more vibrant. I placed my hands on his chest. "Kiss me?"

"Trin," he rasped, the word more of a growl than anything I'd ever heard from him. I shivered as his hands tensed around my hips. "I want to do that more than anything I've ever wanted in my life, but I'm quickly learning that I feel things a bit more intensely than before. I'm trying to do the right thing. You need time, and if I kiss you, I…I don't think my restraint is what it used to be. I don't want to—" He groaned, body shuddering as I slid my hands down his stomach. "I don't want to be that kind of person who loses control."

My gaze drifted over the harsher lines of his features. "You could never be that person. Right now is proof of that."

"The pool was proof of exactly the opposite."

"Not true," I insisted. "I know even then, if I hadn't wanted to do anything, you would've stopped. I *know*."

His lips thinned as he stared down at me. "You think too highly of me."

"I think just right about you," I corrected, and his eyes became liquid, heated sapphire. "The bruises and stuff barely hurt now. I don't need time. Nothing is weird for me. Is anything weird for you?"

He shook his head no.

"Good, because what I do want is you, Zayne, now and always." I felt my cheeks warm. "Key emphasis on the now part."

For a moment, I thought he was going to refuse, and at that point, I planned on just jumping on him. I hoped he kept his footing on the slippery tile, but then he did move.

He lowered his head, and when his mouth touched mine, I realized that I had in no way experienced all his kisses, because this one was *everything*. Both infinitely tender and wholly demanding, he kissed with a sense of urgency and yet in a way that made me feel like we had all the time in the world.

And this kiss…it flipped and twisted my insides into a heady mess. Sensations raced over my skin and through me. My heart surged and the feeling unfurling in my chest was just as intense as the throb of *grace*. He kissed me as if he sought to erase the endless hours and days we'd been apart.

Under my hands, I could feel his muscles flex as he lifted me in his arms. I wrapped my legs around him as the arm around my waist kept me tight against him. His mouth never left mine as he turned us. I had no idea how he managed to shut the water off, and I didn't even know exactly when we'd left the shower. There were moments in the bathroom when he stopped, and I was pressed between him and the wall. Then we were moving again, and it wasn't long before my back hit the rumpled blankets on the bed. We were together, our bodies slippery, our wet hair soaking the sheets we quickly became tangled in, and then we were wrapped up in one another. His hands were everywhere, the heat of his mouth following as I traced the lines of his chest and stomach, reveling in the feel of him. His mouth was wicked, dragging breathy sounds from me, lingering on my breasts, and then he was moving lower, below my navel and even lower still. When his mouth closed over that sensitive part, he devoured me, and I was left mindless and throbbing from those drugging kisses.

This time, there was a brief pause for protection. We weren't going to keep testing fate there. Then he was settling over me, his warmth and weight welcomed and so desperately missed.

"I love you," I whispered against his mouth as I urged him closer with my hands and my kisses.

I moved against him and then he moved inside me. There

were no more words from there. None were necessary as we fell headfirst into the desire and passion, but those weren't the only things between us. In each kiss and touch were relief, acceptance and a need and want that went beyond the physical. And there was so much love building between us, we were happily drowning in it.

There had been no real semblance of control before that, but things got…they became frantic. I lifted my hips to meet his thrusts, and he worked both arms under me, lifting me against him. We both were like ropes stretched too far, and when we snapped, we did so together, tumbling over the edge. As tight, rolling shocks came in endless waves, I felt the stir of air against my cheek and the feel of something soft lying against my arm. My eyes fluttered.

It was Zayne's wings.

They had come off his back and now draped over the both of us, the feathers. My gaze lifted, and I saw the stars on the ceiling, glowing as softly as Zayne's wings.

22

Sometime later, we lay facing each other. A sheet was tucked under my arms, and he was, well, gloriously naked and completely at ease with all of that. Probably because the bedside lamp he'd turned on left all those interesting bits of his in the shadows. His hand was wrapped around mine—the one I had sliced open during the spell. I was bone-deep tired and I had no idea what time it was, but his wings were still out, one resting on his side and the other behind him, and I wanted...I wanted to touch one so badly.

But I was being an adult and operating by the no-touch-without-asking rule. Warden wings could sometimes be sensitive, and you didn't just go around willy-nilly touching them. I imagined these must be the same, since he reacted so strongly when I did try to touch them before.

God, Zayne actually was an angel. Well, a fallen angel, to be exact. It was weird how every so often the reality seemed to smack me straight in the face.

"The wings," I said, smothering a yawn. "That was different."

"I didn't know that would happen." He started to tuck his one wing back.

"No. Don't put them away. The wings don't bother me. It was just something new."

Turning my hand over, he kissed the healing cut. The glow behind his pupils was once more muted. "And it's different."

"Yes, but I like them." I wiggled closer. "They're beautiful, Zayne."

"Thank you." He kissed the tip of a finger. "Let me guess, you're jealous of them?"

I grinned. "Maybe."

His deep chuckle caused my grin to grow. "I guess I'm still getting used to them," he said.

"It feels different than being a Warden?"

"It does. All of it does actually." Another kiss was pressed to the next finger. "Being in my human and Warden states felt natural unless I was wounded and needed to go into a deep healing state," he explained, referencing when they took stone form to slumber. I hadn't seen him do that. "Keeping my wings hidden doesn't feel natural. It makes my back feel itchy. That's the best way I can describe it."

"Then don't keep them hidden when you don't have to, especially when you're with me." I glanced at them, my fingers tingling. "They're amazing. I would love to have wings and to be able to fly."

"I'll make sure you fly whenever you want." He kissed my ring finger. "You want to touch them, don't you?"

I gave him a sheepish grin as I curled my toes. "Yes. I do. Really badly."

"Then why haven't you?"

"I've been working really hard on the whole not touching without permission thing, and it's been killing me." I squirmed another inch closer. "They look so soft and fluffy."

He chuckled, lowering my hand and tipping his head down to mine. The kiss sent a pulse of warmth through me. "Since you've worked so hard, I think you deserve a reward."

My mind immediately jumped in the gutter and happily splashed around, but then I noticed movement. He lifted his wing, letting it lie over us and against my hip. The wing was so long that it reached behind me, and the weight of it reminded me of a thick, lush blanket. The top was so close I could practically kiss one of the feathers. I sucked in a breath, eyes going wide.

"You don't mind?" I asked, five seconds from squealing with excitement.

"No." He let go of my hand. "It's not too heavy?"

"Not at all." Biting down on my lip, I reached out and ran my fingers over the curve of the nearest feather.

It was as soft as I imagined, like chenille, but under the downy feathers was thick muscle. The entire wing of a Warden was muscle and tendon, but an angel had...God, they had to have hundreds of muscles hidden under the gorgeous fluff. I skimmed my fingers down, and my breath caught. That wasn't the only thing hidden within the feathers.

So was the *grace*.

It pulsed along the center of each feather, sparking out in a network of delicate veins. It seemed to follow my touch as my fingers drifted, flaring and then subsiding.

I glanced up at his face. The glow behind his pupils was brighter. I pulled my hand away. "Does touching your wings bother you? If so, be honest. It won't hurt my feelings."

"No. Quite the opposite." Catching my hand, he placed my fingers against the underside of his wing once more. "I like it."

"Is it relaxing?" I asked. "Sort of like when a dog is petted?"

"If anyone else made that comparison, I might be offended."

I smiled.

"In a way, it's relaxing," he said, reaching between us and placing his hand on the curve of my waist. "They are really sensitive."

"More so than Warden's wings?"

His hand slid under his wing to my hip. "Way more. I can feel each touch along my back…and in other places."

"Other places?" I sent him a grin, wondering if that was what had caused his reaction in the pool. "Interesting."

He let out a throaty hum as he squeezed my hip. Filing away that piece of knowledge, I kept petting his wing. I wasn't sure how much time passed as my mind wandered. Somehow I ended up on what I'd seen earlier that night.

"I saw the stars tonight," I announced as randomly as humanly possible. "I mean, I really saw them."

His hand had been moving idly, sweeping up and down my waist and hip, but it stilled then. "What do you mean?"

"It happened right after I…well, after I stabbed you in the heart and this burst of light knocked me over. I think it was your *grace*." I looked over at him. His gaze was zeroed in on me, and it was always like that whenever I spoke, even before. It was like I was the only person in his world. "When I opened my eyes, I could see all of them, Zayne. There were so many and they were really clear, like I imagine they must be for people with good eyesight. I could've been imagining things, but even if it was, they were beautiful."

"I don't know why you would've imagined something like that. Not sure what could've happened to cause that, though," he said.

"Me, neither. Your wings kind of remind me of it. How the *grace* winks between layers of feathers. It's like stars peeking out behind clouds." I ran my fingers farther along his wings, toward his back. The feathers were thinner there, the muscles underneath more prominent. "My vision went back to normal after a few moments, but I'm glad I got to see it."

"I'm happy for you—that you got to see them," he said, his voice rougher.

I glanced back at him again, and that glow in his eyes was once again vibrant. "You're more sensitive the closer it gets to your back, aren't you?"

"Yes." That one word sounded as if it had to fight its way out between clenched teeth.

The warmth in my stomach coiled tight. I rose onto my elbow so I could reach around his shoulders. The sheet slipped a little as my fingers neared the smooth skin of the anchor, and Zayne's entire body jerked. "Interesting," I murmured.

"Very," he rasped, head kicking back as I ran my fingers along the muscle. "I think you're teasing me."

"Maybe." I started to pull my hand back, but Zayne was as fast as he was strong. He moved before I even realized what he was doing, shifting onto his back and pulling me on top of him. Somehow he'd gotten rid of the sheet. When the bare skin of his chest made contact with mine, I shivered from the pleasure of it. "You have amazing multitasking skills."

"I do." A hint of arrogance hardened his tone. He curled his hand around the back of my head, drawing my mouth to his. "Just remember, you started this."

"I'm not going to complain," I told him.

And I didn't.

His hunger was evident in the way he kissed me, in how his hand skimmed the side of my body, of my breast. Zayne sat up, bringing me with him. Our bodies were lined up in all sorts of fun ways. My head fell back as his lips trailed a path of kisses down my throat. His hands went to my waist and he lifted me a few inches, and his lips were moving lower still. I gasped, jerking. He held me steady as he pulled me closer to him. Reaching behind him, I slid my hand over the base of his wing.

Zayne dragged me back down, against his chest. "You're probably going to do that as much as possible, aren't you?"

"Probably," I admitted.

"Good."

Then I felt the stir of air as he folded his wings around me, and the feel of the soft strength against my back and the hard heat of his chest pressed to mine had to be an aphrodisiac all by itself. We kissed again, and the only sounds in the room were that of us coming together, moving together. It was no less intense than before. Every breath and thought left me, and there was only him, how he felt and the maddening, tightening rush.

When our bodies finally settled and our breathing calmed, we were on our sides again. This time, there was no space between us. Exhaustion dogged me now, and I imagined it did so for Zayne. Just before sleep claimed me, I felt the soft weight of one of his wings settling over me, easing me into a blissful, dreamless slumber.

A distant thumping sound that steadily seemed to grow louder and closer wasn't what woke me. It was the loss of all the wonderful heat of Zayne's body.

I stirred, blinking open my eyes to see Zayne making for the door. He'd already put a pair of sweats on and was in the process of pulling on a shirt. The wings were concealed and the markings along his back were nothing but a blur to me.

"What is that?" I asked as the pounding continued.

Zayne glanced over his shoulder. "Someone's at the door."

"Sounds like we're about to be raided by a drug task force or something," I muttered, pushing the hair out of my face.

He chuckled. "How would you know what that sounds like?"

"TV."

I thought he might've shook his head at me. "Go back to sleep. I'll be right back. We're not doing anything today other than sleep."

"Witches," I reminded him as I rolled onto my back. "We have to go see the Crone and give her one of your feathers."

"Later," he replied, and before I could respond, he was slipping out of the bedroom. The banging got louder, and then quieted when he closed the door behind him.

I wondered how were we supposed to get a feather? Pluck it from his...wings? That sounded painful.

My gaze slid to the floor-to-ceiling window. I could tell by the bright sunlight seeping under the blinds that it at least had to be late morning or afternoon.

While sleeping the day away sounded marvelous, I needed to get up. There was a lot of stuff to do, starting with the Crone and ending with Gabriel.

Yawning, I stretched and my cheeks flushed in response to the dull twinge in certain areas. Last night had been beautiful and perfect and—

A scream from the living room jarred me out of the pleasant, sleepy haze. I jerked upright and twisted at the waist, blurry eyes searching for my daggers as my *grace* pulsed in my chest.

"Oh my God!" came a high-pitched, feminine shriek.

Recognizing the sound of Danika's voice, my heart slowed. Crap. We'd forgotten to call and give them more details. Guilt surfaced. They were very much Zayne's family and time should've been made. We'd just been so caught up in one another and in the joy of being reunited, we hadn't thought about anyone else.

Well, that wasn't exactly true. We'd discussed Gabriel and Lucifer briefly.

Shifting toward the side of the bed, I happened to glance down. The sheet had slipped, baring my chest. I froze on the edge of the bed, feet settling against the cool hardwood.

"What in the world?" I whispered.

The mark I'd seen on my chest when I'd showered had darkened to a dusty pink. I gently touched the straight line between my breasts, just above my stomach. It was slightly raised, like a welt. At the ends of the line, where it had looked like blemishes the night before, there was now a clear, shaded circle at one end and another at the other end that wasn't filled in.

I had no idea what could've caused that, but the skin didn't hurt. It had to be some kind of scratch.

There was a burst of laughter from the living room, drawing my attention. Pushing aside the strange mark, I scrambled from the bed before someone opened the door. Though I doubted Zayne would allow that. Snatching another long, dark tunic tank top, clean leggings and underclothing, I hurried into the bathroom. I didn't bother with a shower, just brushed my teeth, scrubbed my face until it was pink and, after a quick comb, tucked my hair into a bun that was sure to unravel within the hour.

Feet bare, I opened the bedroom door and padded out in the hallway. Bright sunlight poured into the living area, and although my eyes needed a minute to adjust, I saw that Danika was there, her long dark hair glossy in the sunlight, and...who I was guessing was Dez, based on the reddish glint of hair, standing beside Zayne. I wished I could see his expression, because he had a fist planted on the island, as if he needed to brace himself.

Nicolai was also there, one hand on Zayne's shoulder and the other on his jaw. He was speaking too low for me to hear, but the sight of them standing there caught me in the heart. They were more than friends. In a way, they were brothers, and I could tell Nicolai seeing him after fearing he was forever lost was a powerful moment, thickening the air.

Feeling a little like I was intruding, I crept silently out into the living room. I made it about two steps. Almost as if Zayne could sense me, he turned from Nicolai. It struck me again how much more clearly I could see him compared to others. Granted, his features were like looking through a steamed window, but I could see his lips curling into a smile. I could see the way his lashes lowered halfway and feel the weight of his gaze.

It had to be the *grace* in him. That was—

A blur of movement startled me, and I turned just as Danika rushed me. There was no chance to prepare myself. A second later, I was enveloped in a warm, tight hug that smelled like roses. Danika lifted me clear off my feet.

Girl was strong.

"You did it," she said, voice choked. "You brought him back to us. You did it."

I didn't know what to say. *You're welcome* seemed a weird way to respond, so all I could do was hug her back, and that…that felt good.

"I think you might be squishing her," Nicolai said, voice close.

"Am I squishing you?" Danika asked.

"No." A laugh made its way around the surprising knot in my throat.

"Good." She squeezed me tighter and then let go.

I caught a brief glimpse of her wiping at her cheeks before a slight touch on my arm caused me to look up at Nicolai.

Only a few inches from me, I could see the glassiness to his Warden-blue eyes and the emotion building in them.

"Thank you," he said, voice hoarse.

Oh God, the knot in my throat expanded as I nodded. He hugged me, too, not nearly as tight as Danika, and when he stepped back, Dez was there. As he folded his arms around me, I felt him tremor.

"I was afraid, girl." His voice was thick, too, and my eyes and throat burned. Ugh. Emotions sucked. I did not want to cry *again*. "When we didn't hear from you, I thought…"

"I'm sorry," I whispered. "We just—"

"No. You don't need to apologize. I get it. If this was Jasmine and me, calling anyone would be the last thing we'd be doing," he said with a hoarse laugh, and I flushed. "I don't know what we expected when we came here, but I couldn't be more glad to see both of you."

"Same," I murmured, cringing the moment that left my mouth, because that made no sense.

"I think Trin's all hugged out." Zayne was there suddenly, easing me out from Dez's embrace. He pulled me to his side, curling his arm around me. "We should've called. Sorry about that," he said, and I detected a small hint of insincerity that was so not like Zayne and yet still made me turn and hide my grin. "We were a little busy."

"No doubt," remarked Nicolai.

Oh, dear.

Now my face was on fire as Zayne glanced down at me. "You want something to drink?" he asked. "I think I actually spied some OJ and water amid the cartons and cartons of soda."

I pulled back. "You're still hung up on the water thing?"

He dragged his teeth over his lower lip as he stared down at me. "You can always drink more water."

I rolled my eyes. "You're a fallen angel now. Drink some carbonated, tasty goodness. Live a little."

Zayne dipped his head, brushing his lips over mine. He then took my hand, squeezing it as he guided me toward the kitchen. "Grab a seat."

I was still stuck on the kiss, so I grabbed a bar stool and sat. The old Zayne could be touchy and sometimes flirtatious in front of others. He'd even gotten caught up in the building tension between us before, seeming to forget when we weren't alone, but to be that bold? That was a new side of him.

I liked that side.

He met my gaze, and there was no mistaking the heat in his eyes. I had to wonder if he knew what I was thinking as he dragged his damn lip between his teeth and then turned to the fridge. "You guys need anything?"

There were a chorus of noes as I toyed with a coaster, knowing my face was a thousand shades of red at that moment.

And I couldn't seriously care less.

"Fallen angel." Danika and the others joined us at the island. "I still can't believe you're here. I saw your..." She trailed off, and I knew where her mind had gone. She and others had witnessed his body turning to nothing more than dust, just like all Wardens did upon death. Her inhale was ragged. "I was so mad at you even though I knew it wasn't your fault."

"It is...different seeing you standing there." Dez folded his arms against the island and leaned in. "So, if I'm staring at you a little too long, that's why."

"You sure it's not my amazing hair?" Zayne asked, closing the fridge door. Of course he'd gone for the OJ and not the soda. "I know you've always been jealous of my luscious locks."

"Yeah." Dez drew the word out. "That's exactly it."

Chuckling, Zayne managed to find two clean glasses and poured us a drink. "You all think it's weird seeing me? Imagine what it feels like to die, but then to wake up."

Even though the whole topic of Zayne dying wigged me

out, it appeared to utterly fascinate the Wardens. Zayne answered all their questions, but it was in the vaguest means possible. What he had shared with me and even with Cayman he wasn't willing to go into a lot of detail about now. As I drank my OJ, I had a feeling he didn't want to relive everything for a third time and it had little to do with trust. These Wardens that were standing in the kitchen were like family to him. So was Gideon, even though he wasn't here.

"Based on what Dez said about you, I got to admit, now that I see you," Nicolai said, "I'm kind of disappointed."

"Wow." Danika turned to look at Nicolai.

"Sorry," he replied, and I squinted, thinking he smiled. "But where are these wings Dez kept talking about every five seconds."

I grinned around my glass.

"It wasn't every five seconds," Dez muttered. "More like every twenty seconds or so."

"I still have them." Zayne turned, scanning the counter behind him. He picked something up.

"Are they...invisible?" Danika asked.

"Only when they need to be." Zayne leaned across the island, and I looked down, seeing my glasses. I had no idea that I'd left them in the kitchen.

I smiled, taking them. "Thank you."

He nodded as I slipped them on. The Wardens' faces became a little more clear, but not by much. Glasses only went so far with cataracts and RP.

"So is it magic?" Danika asked.

"Kind of. Apparently it's some kind of old-school angelic magic that was used back when angels worked alongside man. They remain hidden until I need them."

"They look like a tattoo on his back," I said, finishing off my OJ. "It's really cool, and yes, the wings are as amazing as Dez has surely told you."

"Not quite sure I used the word *amazing*," Dez muttered.

"Maybe not those exact words." Nicolai leaned a hip against the counter. "Pretty sure you said something like you were so distracted by his huge-ass wings that you didn't even realize he'd thrown you into the fountain until you sank under the water."

Dez's exhale could've been heard next door.

"Sorry about that," Zayne said as he walked around the island, coming to stand behind me. "I wasn't in the right frame of mind."

"Never would've guessed that," Dez stated dryly. "But there's no need to apologize. I needed the bath, anyway."

I laughed as Zayne placed his hands on my shoulders. "To be honest, he held back."

"Oh, I know. He could've done some real damage," Dez agreed.

"The fact that Dez walked away from that little meet-and-greet is proof that you were still in there," Nicolai said.

"I was." *Barely* hung unspoken in the space between all of us. Zayne dipped his head, kissing my temple, just above the arm of my glasses.

"I had doubts," Dez admitted, surprising me. "I hated that I did, but I was trying to prepare myself in case…in case you didn't come back to us."

"I don't hold that against you," Zayne said, and I knew he didn't.

"Good." Dez appeared to have smiled. "Next time try to give me a warning before throwing me into a fountain."

Zayne laughed. "That I can do."

They went back and forth, ribbing each other until Nicolai cut in. "We're also here on some official Harbinger business."

That perked my little ears. "Did something happen?" I really hoped not, but I wouldn't have known since I'd been superfocused on Zayne, which probably made me a very bad Trueborn.

Oh, well.

"Not that we know of, but we did discover something," Nicolai told me.

"It was actually my idea," Danika chimed in with a grin. "So, I got to thinking about this whole ley-line thing, and how Gabriel is using them to open this portal. They're basically energy lines, right, and energy can be disrupted. Anything can."

"I like where you're going with this," Zayne said, gently squeezing my shoulders. "Sounds like someone else should've been in the running to lead the clan."

A half smile formed on Nicolai's face. "I would've voted 'Hell, yeah' to that."

Danika snorted. "As if that would even be an option. Half of the clan—no, half of the damn population of Wardens—would crap themselves at the mere idea of a female running a clan."

That was sad.

And true.

Part of their mentality toward the females could land at the feet of their archaic social structure. The other half was because too many demons weren't stupid.

Unfortunately.

Demons knew that the one surefire way to cut the Wardens off at the knees was to go after the next generation. Females and young Wardens were targeted. The locations of the communities they lived in were well-protected secrets. That was why the fact Danika was often out and about was surprising.

But also, again, they were superarchaic in their beliefs. Yes, it was more dangerous for the females and the wee baby Wardens, but if they were trained to fight and defend themselves, like Danika and Jada were, they wouldn't be such easy targets.

One day and one day soon, they were going to have to change.

"I don't know why we're all standing here pretending like Danika doesn't already run the show," Dez commented from where he stood.

That got another big smile from Danika and a rather muted nod of agreement from Nicolai. I liked them together. A lot.

"Anyway, I started doing some research on ley lines and what could possibly disrupt them since we can't very well go in and just blow the school and portal up," Danika continued, and she was right. So charged with celestial energy, it would take out half, if not all, of the city if we attempted something like that, which would result in a whole lot of loss of human life.

And possible exposure.

"I couldn't find anything on the internet other than some really weird stuff that made no sense," Danika was saying, drawing my attention back to her. "So I went to our very own personal internet service."

"Gideon?" Zayne surmised.

She nodded. "I asked if he knew anything, and at first, he wasn't sure of anything, but he went and locked himself in the library for a couple of hours, emerging with an answer."

While I wondered if he had found an answer to my oh-so-personal question about reproduction, hope sparked in my chest. I tried not to let it ignite. "Did he find anything?"

"He did." Danika's gaze bounced between Zayne and I. "Black tourmaline, hematite and black onyx."

"Huh?" I murmured.

"Gemstones." Zayne's hands slid off my shoulders. "You're talking about *gemstones*?"

"Yeah. I know, sounds like some hocus-pocus crap," Dez said, looking at me. "But we know hocus-pocus crap is some legit stuff, don't we?"

Yeah.

Yeah, we did.

Nicolai nudged Danika. "Tell them the rest."

"Those gemstones can block energy—all kinds—and Gideon theorizes that enough of it could very well disrupt the energy of the ley lines," she explained. "Not only allowing us to possibly destroy it without blowing up the nation's capital, but if not, definitely rendering the portal useless to the Harbinger."

23

"That's huge," I whispered, placing my hands on the cool granite. "Like really freaking huge."

Danika's smile was big enough for me to see as she lifted her shoulder in a shrug. "I don't know if it's huge or not since it doesn't completely eradicate the whole Gabriel issue, but it could at least prevent him from carrying through with his plans."

"Being able to shut down his plans is huge," I told her, nodding empathetically just in case she needed the extra reinforcement. "You're brilliant."

"That's what I tell her." Warmth filled Nicolai's voice. "At least twice a day, and three times on Wednesdays."

I thought Danika might've blushed. "You need to make that four times on Wednesdays."

"That I can do," Nicolai murmured.

Energy buzzed through my veins, mingling with my *grace*. I slid from the stool and started pacing. "How much of it would we need? Those gemstones?" I asked, already for-getting two of the names. "Onyx and what were the other two?"

"Black tourmaline and hematite," Zayne answered, be-cause of course he remembered.

"A lot." Danika twisted at the waist. "Like either several tons of tiny pieces or a really large chunk of the stuff."

Several tons? I folded an arm across my stomach.

"Where would we even find it?" Zayne asked.

"I doubt the answer is going to be Amazon," I muttered.

"Not if we want to make sure we have the real deal," Dez answered with a grin. "Black tourmaline is mined in Bra-zil and some other places in the world, but most of it comes out of Africa. And no, I didn't know that until yesterday."

"Africa?" I stopped for a second. "Brazil? How are we supposed to get our hands on that?"

"I've reached out to a few of the clans in those regions to see what they can get their hands on and how long it would take to get it to us," Nicolai said.

"How would they get several tons or a large chunk to us?" I started pacing again. "I doubt that would be something you can put on a plane."

"I imagine they'd ship it." Zayne looked over at Nico-lai. "Right?" When the clan leader nodded, Zayne sent me a quick grin.

I rolled my eyes. "What about the others? The onyx and..." Crap, I forgot the other one again.

"Hematite." Zayne reached out, snagging my arm. He pulled my hand and therefore my poor thumbnail away from my mouth.

"Better news on that front. Hematite can be found in

the States. Yellowstone, to be exact," Danika leaned against the island. "We should be able to get our hands on that and black onyx since it can also be found in various states. How much is available is what's up in the air. Hopefully we hear something shortly."

"Gideon has been on the phone with anyone and everyone who has access to any of the gemstones in the States while we wait to hear back about the tourmaline," Nicolai said. "That's what he's doing now. The phone is practically attached to his ear."

"Do you think we can get enough?" Keeping my hand away from my mouth, I got back to wearing a path in the floor.

"Gideon thinks it's possible." Dez tipped his head back against the wall. "The question is going to be, can we get what we need in the time we need it."

"The Transfiguration is in a few weeks. The sixth." I started to chew on my thumbnail again, but stopped. "A Friday."

"What's today's date?" Zayne asked.

"The twentieth," Danika answered.

Zayne frowned as his gaze returned to me. "So, we have a little over two weeks. Your idea of a few weeks differs from mine."

"A few is at least two," I reasoned. "We have at least two weeks and some change."

"And that's going to be cutting it close." Nicolai crossed his arms. "Doable. But down to the wire kind of doable."

Doable was better than *LOL, yeah, right.*

"If we are able to get enough of these gemstones in time, what do we need to do with them?"

"That's the simple part," Danika told us. "Since the portal is smack-dab in the middle of the hub of ley lines, we just need to place them around the portal, cutting over the lines."

"The simple part?" I stopped, facing her. "I'm assuming you mean around the portal and not just the school?"

She nodded.

"There's going to be nothing simple about that." Lifting a hand, I straightened my glasses as they started to slip down my nose. "Besides the fact that our friendly neighborhood homicidal archangel has to have eyes on that school, the place is like a nightmare sandwich of very angry ghosts and wraiths as the bread and Shadow People as the rancid meat."

"Besides the really strange description, Trin is right," Zayne said.

"We know," Nicolai replied. "And that's where we come in to help. There's no way just you two are going to be able to move that kind of weight in there."

He was right, and there was no point in arguing against it. We needed all the help we could get.

"But it will still be doable," Zayne added.

I nodded. "Yes. Totally doable as in you'll probably need some intensive therapy afterward, because even though you won't be able to see most of what's in there, they're going to make their presence known and then some."

"Can't wait," Dez said without an ounce of enthusiasm. "So if we're successful in shutting down the portal—"

"We will be," Danika interrupted.

"Okay. When we're successful and we shut down the portal," Dez began again. "That leaves Gabriel to be dealt with."

"That's me." I raised a hand. "And Zayne," I tacked on before he could say it. "You guys can't be anywhere near him. Not to be a downer, but he would kill any Warden in a heartbeat."

"She's right again." Zayne caught my arm again, but this time stopping me. He guided me over to a bar stool. "You're wearing me out, and I'm just watching you."

"Not to doubt the awesomeness of a Trueborn and Fallen combined," Nicolai said as I sat in the bar stool. "But are you two going to be enough?"

"Apparently it won't be just…" Zayne's hands landed on my shoulders. "Wait. They don't know, do they?"

I pursed my lips as I tipped my head back.

"Know about what?" Dez asked.

Zayne met my gaze as he stared down at me. "You didn't tell them?"

"Didn't exactly seem like a wise thing to do." My eyes narrowed. "And it's probably still not the greatest idea to share, *Zayne*."

"Tell us what?" Nicolai demanded.

One side of Zayne's lips curved up, and he had the same air of wicked anticipation as Cayman had when the demon told him about our plans. He drew his lower lip between his teeth.

"Zayne," I warned.

"Too late." He dropped a quick kiss on my lips before I could say another word. "Trin, along with Roth and Layla, came up with the spectacular idea to get backup."

"Backup doesn't sound bad." Dez sounded confused.

"Oh, wait until you hear who it is," Zayne replied. "And just so you know, I had nothing to do with it. This was when I was presumed dead."

I shoved my elbow back, but Zayne easily avoided the

blow with a laugh. "I don't know what you think is so funny."

"I'm starting to get concerned," Nicolai remarked.

Zayne squeezed my shoulders. "Tell them."

"I'm going to punch you," I warned. "Later, when we're not in front of people, so they don't think I have an anger problem."

"Looking forward to it," he replied, thick lashes lowering halfway. "Later, when we're alone, so no one thinks I'm perverse when I get turned on by you attempting to kick my ass."

My eyes widened as a sweet hot flush moved through me—*wait*. Attempting to kick his ass?

"Just FYI," Nicolai interrupted. "You're not alone right now, so..."

Dragging my gaze from Zayne's, I exhaled loudly. "Roth and Layla are currently trying to recruit Lucifer to help us fight Gabriel."

The three Wardens stared at us in blank silence...or abject horror. One or the other.

Then Dez pushed off the wall. "You don't mean *the* Lucifer. Right?"

"Is there another Lucifer I'm unaware of?" I asked, looking around the room. "Yes, *the* Lucifer."

"You can't be serious," Danika whispered.

Dez stopped moving. "You're totally serious."

"She is," Zayne confirmed.

"In my defense, Roth came up with this idea during the Zayne is dead phase of my life. Now whether or not that had anything to do with me agreeing with this potentially very bad idea is totally up for debate." I lifted a hand when

Nicolai lowered his head from the other side of the island. "And look, there is no way that Zayne and I can defeat an archangel—"

"Well, we don't know that for sure," Zayne cut in. "Since there's never been a Fallen and a Trueborn teamed up against an archangel. But YOLO, right?"

My lips thinned.

"I am...actually speechless," Dez said, shaking his head. "I honestly don't know what to say. Roth and Layla are seriously trying to recruit Lucifer? The only thing in this entire world that I can think of that is worse than an archangel hell-bent on destroying mankind."

For someone who didn't know what to say, he sure had a lot to say.

Danika appeared to blink slowly. "I think I need to sit down."

"You are sitting down."

"Oh." She swallowed thickly. "All right, then."

Frowning slightly, I wondered if she was okay.

Nicolai finally found his voice, which led to the same questions Zayne had when he first learned of the plan to bring Lucifer into the mix. Were we out of our minds? Would this kick off the biblical end times? How could we control him? All valid questions.

"What will we even do with him once he's topside?" Nicolai demanded.

"Ehh," I said. "Haven't gotten to that point yet."

He stared at me.

"Mainly because we're not even sure if he's going to be game to play," I reasoned. "And because I've been kind of busy with this one." I jabbed a finger in Zayne's direction.

"So, I haven't had a lot of time to really think the whole thing through."

Zayne snorted from behind me. "Thinking things through would've come in handy, especially since Lucifer is also out looking for Trin. He sent Ghouls and an Upper Level demon after her."

Dez came forward. "That's who sent the Ghouls?"

I nodded. "What can I say? I'm popular."

Zayne tugged gently on the bun. "That you are."

"Why is Lucifer looking for you?" Nicolai demanded.

"Not sure," I said. "Maybe he's just looking to expand his friend circle?"

"I know I don't have a whole lot of experience with demons," Danika said. "But I cannot imagine having Lucifer looking for you is something good."

I sighed. "Probably not, and I don't know if those orders are recent, like coming after Roth and Layla had spoken to him, or if they were issued before. I'm hoping they came before."

"But even if they came before Roth and Layla met with him, it's still an issue." Zayne's hands returned to my shoulders. "That needs to be dealt with."

"It's been added to the ever-growing list," I murmured.

Zayne squeezed my shoulders again. "I'm guessing we don't know where Gabriel is hiding?"

Nicolai shook his head. "We've been keeping an eye out for Bael or any sign of Gabriel, but there's been nothing since the night at the school."

"There's been no more Warden deaths?" Zayne asked.

"No," answered Dez. "There's also been very little demon activity."

As they talked, my mind wandered as it often did, skipping from one thought to the next, starting with the horrible final moments under the school, when Zayne showed up and killed Sulien. My mind snagged on the other Trueborn. Had it been him who left the angelic weapon behind? Or Gabriel, since only archangels carried them? Either way, it was incredibly reckless of either of them, to the point it seemed impossible for either of them to have been responsible. The golden, luminous spikes were angel blades, capable of killing anything, including angels—

Holy crap.

I'd totally forgotten about the damn angel blades and the fact we had in our grasp a plan A and B this whole time.

And that was one of the strange, marvelous mysteries of a random brain. No joke. Sometimes all the random thoughts served a purpose and were connected. Sometimes they didn't and just led me to do things that were quite impulsive or nonsensical to most.

"We need the angel blades," I blurted out.

Nicolai's head inclined. "Angel blades?"

"That's what those golden spikes were." I looked back at Zayne. "Remember when Roth saw the writing in the tunnels?"

Understanding washed across his expression and his gaze snapped to Nicolai's. "They're angelic weapons used by archangels, and they can kill anything with angelic blood, including an angel. We need them."

Dez let out a low whistle as Nicolai nodded. "We'll get them to you ASAP."

"Why would Gabriel leave them behind if they can kill

him?" Danika wondered the same thing I had. "Or anyone working with him?"

"They were found on Morgan," Zayne said, referencing one of the Wardens who'd been killed. "Gabriel was the one killing Wardens, and I seriously doubt he would've left them behind."

"Unless he's that arrogant," Dez mused. "And thought we wouldn't figure out what they were."

"Possible." Zayne's thumbs pressed into the tight muscles at the base of my neck.

Arrogance could lead to some pretty stupefying decisions, but that? "Could it be possible that someone else did? Archangels are fast, and that camera feed was messed with."

"You're suggesting that another archangel could've left the blades there?" Danika tipped forward. "Impaled them in the Warden after Gabriel killed him?"

"That sounds really disturbing when you put it that way." I wrinkled my nose. "But maybe it was the only way it could be done without anyone knowing who did it?"

"Why would they be worried about anyone knowing they did it?" Dez asked.

"Probably due to some stupid heavenly rule," I muttered.

"Actually, it would be against a rule," Zayne said. "The agreement angels made to not raise arms against one another. You were that loophole," he reminded me. "I'm a loophole. An archangel *leaving* those weapons behind could technically be considered another loophole."

"With those blades, do we even need Lucifer's help?" Danika asked.

"I think we'll need all the help we can get," I told them.

"To use those blades, we have to get close to him, and he's... he's strong and fast."

"But Lucifer?" Dez repeated.

"With or without Lucifer, we need to be able to actually find Gabriel—"

"I know how we can find Gabriel," I announced, the idea taking shape. "All we need is me."

"Going to need more detail there," Zayne said.

"Gabriel has sent demons for me. The imps? He sent them before, and I bet he sent the Seeker demons," I said. "He's not going to let me sit and chill between now and the Transfiguration. So, we set a trap—"

"I know where you're going with this," Zayne interrupted. "And no."

The corners of my lips turned down. "Excuse me?"

"You're going to suggest using yourself as bait and I cannot get behind that."

"I didn't know I needed you to get behind—" I squeaked as Zayne spun me and the bar stool around. I stared up at him, eyes wide. "That was like one of those carnival rides. The kind with those little teacups that spin and—"

"You're not using yourself as bait, Trin." He glared down at me, the glow behind his eyes intensifying. "No way. That's too dangerous."

"Anything we are about to do is too dangerous," I argued. "We need to be able to find Gabriel, and as far as I know, there's no archangel private investigator we can hire."

"You're right that everything we *have* to do is dangerous, so we don't need to go out there with the mentality on how we can make this even more so."

"He's not going to kill me, Zayne. Spoiler alert, he needs me alive until the Transfiguration."

The white light flared behind his pupils. "Death isn't the only thing I'm worried about. Bael is most likely with him, and that is one demented, pain-loving demon."

"It's not like I don't know how to defend myself. I have *grace* and those angel blades." I struggled not to get too angry since I knew his refusal to hear this out was coming from a place of love and fear. "I could easily be tagged with a tracer or something, and you can follow me to where he is—"

"And what if something goes wrong? The tracer doesn't work or they find it on you?" he shot back. With his hands still on the sides of the bar stool, he lowered his head so we were almost eye level. "What if I don't get to you in time?"

I took a deep breath and released it slowly. "Just a reminder—he needs me alive."

"And just a reminder, he can hurt you. Bad. He could hurt our—" He cut himself off with a sharp breath. "Death isn't the only thing we have to worry about."

But he didn't need to finish what he was going to say, because I knew what he was thinking of. Our child. Our *possible* child. My stomach dipped sharply. I hadn't even thought of that.

Which was yet another indication that child-rearing was not going to be something I excelled at.

Like at all.

God, I didn't even know if I wanted a child, sooner *or* later. I didn't even know if Zayne was really okay with the possibility of one or he was just being a good...fallen angel, but I didn't want to hurt...*it* until I knew.

Referring to a child as "it" was probably another good indication that I should not even be considering a child.

"He's right," Dez chimed in with that voice—that too-gentle one. My back stiffened, and I immediately regretted going to Dez about the whole baby thing, because I now recognized that voice. "It's too dangerous, Trinity."

I opened my mouth, but snapped it shut as my stomach decided to take another dip all the way to the floor. Was Dez weighing in because he'd discovered something? Panic blossomed in my chest, but I shut that down before it could take root. Even if Trueborns could reproduce, that didn't mean I was automatically pregnant after having unprotected sex one time. My reproductive system wasn't a bad Sex Ed video. I needed to calm down.

Because pregnant or not, I still had a duty, a dangerous one, and Zayne needed to understand that.

"I know what the risks are. All of them." I placed my hands over his. "And you know what the risks are if we fail. Even if we managed to disrupt the ley lines, we still have to deal with Gabriel. He has to be stopped, because he won't. He'll keep killing and he'll keep plotting. You know that."

His jaw hardened. "I do."

"We just need to be careful."

"That's what I'm saying." His gaze searched mine. "Getting yourself caught isn't being careful."

"It's better than getting captured unprepared," I pointed out.

"He's not going to capture you," he swore.

I leaned in so our faces were only inches apart. "We need all the upper hands we can get, Zayne. Setting a trap is one way."

"She's right," Danika said.

I sent her a quick smile. "Thank—"

"And kind of not," she added, and my eyes narrowed. "We can set a trap, not for him to take her, but to lure him out."

Zayne held my gaze for a moment longer and then straightened, glancing at Danika. "I like the sound of this better, but how can we lure him? I doubt he'll come for her himself again. He'll send demons."

"You say he's really arrogant, right?"

"And slightly unhinged," I said, and Zayne arched a brow. "Okay. He's a lot unhinged."

"I know a lot of arrogant males." She paused. "Obviously. You can get them to do just about anything simply by goading them. I doubt Gabriel will be much better. Kill the demons that come for you and then send one back with a message that he'd be a coward to refuse. We can still put a tracer on her in case things go south."

"I don't know if I should be worried about being included in that generalization," Nicolai said. "But do we really think he's that foolish?"

I toed myself around, toward Danika. "We are talking about the archangel who referred to Instagram as Picture Book, so yeah, I think he's that foolish."

But it was the kind of plan that would possibly take multiple attempts. One that hinged on keeping a demon alive, which wasn't exactly easy when you wanted to kill them.

They stayed for a bit after that, discussing how to move the gemstones into the school, and of course, the idea of Lucifer coming topside. None of them seemed to know how to process that, and I couldn't blame them. After Zayne promising he would swing by the compound for dinner, which seemed really out of place with the rest of our topics, they started for the door.

Dez hung back, though. "I'll meet you guys in the garage in a few minutes."

A curious look settled over Danika's face as Nicolai guided her out the door. I was still sitting on the bar stool when the elevator doors slid shut behind them. Honestly, I was frozen there, because I knew why he was staying behind.

"So." Dez dragged the word out as he shoved his hands in his pockets.

"I know." Zayne stood behind me as he curled his arm loosely around my shoulders. "What you were supposed to ask Gideon about."

Dez nodded as he moved closer. His features became clearer. "Gideon has been so wrapped up in disrupting the ley lines that he didn't ask too many questions when I went to him about a Trueborn's ability to reproduce."

It was the strangest thing as I sat there. My heart wasn't pounding. My stomach was settled. I was just prepared, at least on a surface level, to hear whatever it was he was going to say. "Was he able to find anything?"

"He pulled out some dusty old books he knew referenced Trueborns. Took him a couple of hours to go through what he has on hand," Dez explained. "But I have either an answer or no answer, depending on the way you look at it. He could find nothing referencing any Trueborn having a child."

There was no loosening of the tension nor any tightening. "That could mean that no Trueborn has ever had a child or none was ever recorded."

"Yes, but it would seem strange for there to be no mention at all," Dez said. "I think you're going to have to find out the old-fashioned way. They make tests now that can tell you yes or no within a day or so of conception."

I nodded slowly.

"Thank you for looking into it," Zayne said, the warmth of him pressing against my back.

"No problem. I just wish I had more of a clear answer," he said, and I could see a faint curve of his lips. "And that this was happening during easier times."

"I think we can all agree on that," Zayne replied.

"Depending on what you all find out, let me know? When you're ready? And if it's a yes, call me when you flip out, Zayne. Trust me when I say that's definitely going to happen."

Zayne must've nodded behind me, because Dez started to turn to the door but then stopped. "Oh, and, Trin, he checked out that name you were asking about."

I blinked, seeming to come out of a stupor. "Any more information on that front?"

"Actually, yeah, there is," Dez said. "Luckily this apartment requires names of all occupants to be listed on file, including children. He looked at current and the last decade or so. There's no Gena or any variation of that name that Gideon could find on any records listed here."

24

"What is the Gena thing about?" Zayne asked after Dez left.

"The girl that Peanut has supposedly been hanging out with." I turned to where Zayne leaned against the back of the couch. "He told me her name is Gena, and other than things being weird with her parents, he's been really vague about her. I wanted to check in on her to see if everything is on the up-and-up, but apparently she's not real?"

"Or he gave you a fake name." He crossed his legs at the ankles. "But why would he do that?"

"I have no idea." I shook my head. "Usually he's into oversharing about everything, but he's been acting weird since we came here. He's been disappearing for longer and longer times."

"He didn't come and go when he was with you in the Potomac Highlands?"

"He did, but he was around more." I thought about what

Peanut told me when I saw him last. "He did say something weird happened to him, roughly around the time I think you Fell. He said he was sucked into what he thinks was purgatory for a few moments."

"Okay. I wasn't expecting that."

"Neither was I." I rose from the bar stool. "And I have no idea if what happened to him was somehow related to your Fall."

"I don't, either." Zayne brushed his hair behind his ear. "But maybe my Fall created some kind of momentary pull?"

"Maybe," I murmured, lifting my gaze to his. He watched me closely, and I exhaled loudly. "We need to talk, don't we?"

He nodded. "Yep."

"Do I get to pretend that I have no idea what you want to talk about?"

One side of his lips curved up. "I'm surprised you're not already yelling at me for not backing you up on your poorly thought through plan."

I stared at him blandly. "I wasn't going to yell at you, but now I'm rethinking that."

"It's too much of a risk, Trin. Even if there was no chance of you being pregnant."

There was a whooshing motion in my stomach. "And like I said before, everything we do is a risk. Using myself as bait is the quickest way to get to Gabriel."

"And stupidest—"

"Do you want me to yell at you? Because I'm getting pretty close to that happening."

"Sorry." He didn't sound sorry at all. "But too many things could go wrong with that."

"And too many things could go wrong with Danika's idea, starting with it not working at all."

His brows lowered. "You sounded like you were on board with her idea when she talked about it."

"I'm not against it. I just don't think that's the fastest way to get to Gabriel. How many demons will we have to kill to find the one who will carry the message back?" I folded my arms across my chest. "And while I do think Gabriel is arrogant enough to rise to the challenge, I don't know if any demon we leave alive will actually risk Gabriel killing them to deliver the message. They'll probably run for the hills."

"That might happen, but Gabriel has to come for you before the Transfiguration. If we end up killing every demon or they end up running, he will get desperate enough to come for you himself," Zayne reasoned.

"And you're not worried that will be cutting it real close to the Transfiguration? All he needs is my blood, Zayne. He manages to get me near that portal and draws my blood? Then what?" I lifted a shoulder. "We need to take him out before the Transfiguration."

"I agree with the latter, but I can't get behind letting you get captured." Uncrossing his ankles, he pushed off the back of the couch. "And it doesn't have anything to do with you possibly being pregnant."

"It really doesn't?" I lifted my chin as he stopped in front of me. "Are you sure you'd be this against it if there was no chance of me being pregnant?"

"Yes." There wasn't an ounce of hesitation there. "The mere idea of you being in Gabriel's hands or anywhere near Bael makes me want to destroy something—something very large." Slowly, so that I saw him, he lifted his hand and fixed my cockeyed glasses. "And if you think it's because I believe you can't handle yourself, you're wrong. I know you can, but—"

"You do realize that anything that comes before the word *but* is basically nullified, right?"

"But," he repeated, lowering his hand to the nape of my neck, "Gabriel knows that, too. He knows you can fight. He'll be prepared for that."

"Will he be prepared for it being a trap? Doubtful."

"Would you be okay with me being used as bait?" he asked instead. "If it were me who was being tagged with a tracer that can fail and being taken only God knows where?"

I opened my mouth, but I couldn't get the word *yes* out of my mouth.

Zayne's eyes searched mine. "You wouldn't be. Not because you think I can't defend myself, but for the same reasons as me. You couldn't bear the idea of me being in the hands of a being that could kill me, because you love me, and because of that, you would want to try every other avenue first before you put my life in jeopardy."

Pressing my lips together, I shook my head. "You're right, and that annoys me greatly."

"I know it does." A grin appeared.

"Smiling doesn't help." I moved in closer, resting my cheek against his chest. The placement caused my glasses to go askew once more, but I didn't care. "Okay. We'll try the other avenues first, but if they don't work, then we have to do it this way."

"Even though I don't like it, I can agree with that." He folded his arms around me, resting his chin on the top of my head. "Sometimes I wish you weren't so damn brave."

I smiled at that. "The feeling is mutual."

His arms tightened around me. "What do you think about what Dez had to say about Gideon not being able to find anything on Trueborns reproducing?" he asked after a few moments.

"I don't know what I think or what to think," I admitted, closing my eyes. "What about you?"

"The same." He dragged a hand up my back. "I think we need to get one of those tests."

"Yeah, I think we do, too." I pulled back, smiling a little when he fixed my glasses yet again. "But there's something else we need to do first. We have to go see the Crone."

Zayne used my phone to call Stacey—who he'd grown close to after his father's death and the fallout with Layla. When I thought about how jealous I'd been when I'd discovered them in the ice cream shop, I sort of wanted to punch myself in the actual face. I tried to give him a little space because I was sure it would be an emotional call, but he tugged me down to where he sat on the couch, holding me close. The whole time he spoke with her, he smoothed his hand through my hair and down my back. Every so often, he would stop and drop a kiss on my temple or my forehead, and I... I soaked up the affection like a happy little sponge. He seemed to need to be as close to me as I needed the same from him, and I imagined the trauma of the last several days drove the desire. Stacey wanted to see Zayne, and I couldn't blame her for that. I could tell just from what he was saying that she was shocked, but Zayne felt it was too risky. He was right. Gabriel might not know Zayne was back yet, but he would, and I wouldn't put it past the archangel to go after anyone close to either of us.

After the call, we'd decided it was best if we went ahead and removed one of his feathers while in the apartment. That prevented Zayne from having to do the show-and-tell with his wings with the Crone and any other witch present. It wasn't that we didn't trust her...

Okay, we didn't trust her.

It wasn't anything personal. We just didn't trust any witch.

Of course, when he tugged his shirt off and his wings unfurled, I got a little distracted staring at them. Dragging my gaze from one graceful arch, I got down to business. "So how do we do this?"

"You can just grab one," he offered.

"Wait. What? You want me to do what?" My brows flew up. "Just yank one out?"

He shrugged. "Or I can do it."

"Yeah, you should do it." I wrinkled my nose. "Because nope, I can't."

"It's not like I'm suggesting that you pull off a toenail."

"Ew," I muttered as he swept a wing forward.

Laughing softly, he ran his fingers through the underside of his wing. "Just one?"

I nodded. "Make it a small one."

He shot me a grin as he curled a finger around a feather. "You may want to look away."

Not even bothering to pretend like I could stomach it, I focused on the somewhat decluttered kitchen counter. "You know when we were in the pool and I went to touch your wings? You didn't seem to like it then."

"That's a random question."

"Yeah, well, I'm trying to not focus—" There was a soft snapping sound and I flinched. "On *that*."

"Barely even hurt," he replied. "You can look now."

Peeking over at him, I saw that his wings were folded back. He held a feather the size of his palm in his hand. Could've just been my eyes, but the feather appeared to glow faintly.

"The reason why I stopped you in the pool had nothing to do with my feathers," he told me, drawing my gaze to his. "Grab a ziplock baggie for the feather."

"There's something extremely wrong with putting a feather in a ziplock baggie." Pivoting, I walked over to the small pantry built into the cabinets. "So why did you stop me, then?"

"When I was with you, in the pool? For a few minutes, I didn't feel…exposed to all that hate and bitterness. All I felt were my own emotions. I was quiet. Calm," he explained. "But then I started to feel those things again. It was insidious, like a snake slithering through my veins, and I didn't want to hurt you."

My heart twisted as I opened the pantry door and grabbed a baggie out of the box. I turned to him. "Do you feel that now? The hate and bitterness?"

"Not like that since I came to after you used the Sword of Michael. But I can still feel others'…intent. Their darkest secrets. But it's controllable."

"What do you mean?" I walked the baggie over to him.

"It's hard to explain." He took it from me. "But it kind of reminds me of what Layla can do with seeing auras—the color of people's souls. It's like that, but I just feel their intent if I want to."

My brows lifted. "Like how? You just look at them, and bam, you know if they're good or bad or something in between?"

"I just have to focus on them—I have to want to know." He slipped the luminous feather into the baggie, then sealed the top. "One of the angels explained that I would be able to feel the true intentions of mortals. That all angels can. I guess that is a part of the reason that when an angel Falls, that sense is overwhelmed. It wasn't until we were in the Uber with the driver that I even remembered. And that was because I realized I wasn't feeling his intentions when before I felt everything without even trying."

"That had to be…God, that had to be overwhelming."

"It was, but with the driver, I wasn't being bombarded, and that's when I remembered what the angel told me," he explained. "So I tried it out and he was right. I just had to want to know and focus."

"So, what did you find out?" Curiosity got the best of me.

"The driver was a good man."

"Happy to hear that since he was all about clutching the cross when we left the car." I glanced at his wings, but resisted the urge to reach out and stroke one. "So, what you really mean when you say you feel their intentions is that you're feeling their souls."

His wings tucked back and then disappeared as he handed the baggie to me. "It just…feels weird to say that."

I took the bag, trying not to cringe. "You have two swords and can tell if a person is a good or bad dude. Why do you have to be so special?"

That got a smile out of him before he turned to pick up the shirt he'd draped over the couch. My gaze fixed on the raised imprint of his wings, and I thought about what Layla had said when she saw my aura. It was both pure white and pure black.

Good and…what? Bad? Layla had said that the darker the shade of the aura meant more sin, but she'd never seen a human with a black aura.

Holding the bagged feather, which felt like I was holding a finger or something, I watched him pull the shirt on and tug it into place. When he faced me, I opened my mouth and the question sort of spewed out of me. "What do you feel when you focus on me? What is my *intention*?"

"Other than to drive me crazy?" he asked, tucking the sides of his hair back.

I nodded. "Other than that."

"I don't know. I haven't tried to find out. Not on you or the others when they were here. It doesn't seem right to do so for no reason."

I stared at him and then sighed.

"What?"

"Why do you have to be so good? I would be peeking at everyone's soul every chance I got."

He chuckled as he dipped his head and kissed me. "Let's head out and take care of this feather thing."

Lips tingling from the brief contact, I trailed after him. He picked up his keys from the island, where he'd last dropped them, and stopped. No one had touched them since then. Holding them in his palm, he stared down at them.

"Are you okay?" I touched his arm.

Clearing his throat, he glanced over at me. "Yeah. I am." His fingers curled around the keys. "Have you seen my phone, by the way?"

I shook my head. "It was…it was on you that night. I haven't seen it since."

"I bet Nic or Dez has it, then. They would've been the ones to gather up my…personal belongings. I guess they didn't think of bringing it with them when they came by. Probably because they…"

I knew where he was going with that. They probably feared Zayne hadn't returned to them and bringing his belongings would somehow jinx everything. Clutching the baggie to my chest, I asked, "Does it feel weird? Thinking about having died? Okay. That's a lame question. Obviously it has to feel weird."

"It does." He took my hand in his. "Especially when I think about the fact my body would've done the whole dust thing and yet I'm here."

I shivered. "Same. That messes with my head and it's not even my body."

"So, let's not dwell on that, okay?"

"I can do that." I squeezed his hand as we stepped into the elevator.

We reached the garage in record time, and when he saw his Impala, he looked like me when I saw a cheeseburger.

He placed his palm on the trunk, sliding it across the smooth metal as he walked us to the passenger door. I could make out a grin in the dim, yellowing light of the garage, something I knew I wouldn't have been able to see before.

"Do you want some time alone?" I offered as his hand glided over the back door. "You know, in case you want to make out with your car in private."

Zayne laughed as he opened the passenger door. "Get in."

"Bossy." I glanced down at where he held my hand. "You're going to have to let go."

"I know."

My brows lifted. "Before we can get into the car."

"I know," he repeated, but this time, he lowered his mouth to mine as his other hand curled around the nape of my neck. It was a deep and fierce kiss, sending a rolling wave of heat through me. I wondered if he could devour me with just one kiss. I was so willing to engage in a little public indecency and find out, right here, in the parking garage. But he lifted his head, nipping at my lower lip in a way that sent a curling motion through my stomach.

"Goodness," I whispered as he let go of my hand. "You're really happy to see your car, aren't you?"

"After we deal with the Crone, how about we find out?" he suggested.

A flutter moved from my chest to my stomach and then lower. "I am so okay with that."

"Then let's get this over with as quick as possible."

I all but threw myself into the passenger seat. Letting the bagged feather rest in my lap, I buckled myself up as Zayne climbed in behind the wheel. He took a moment, checking the rearview mirror, gripping the steering wheel and straightening the visor before turning the key. The engine purred to life, and the smile that broke out across his face caused my heart to squeeze.

Shifting the gears into Reverse, he looked over at me. "Where's your sunglasses?"

"Lost them."

"Again?"

"Again."

"Man, we're going to have to start ordering them in bulk."

"So I can start losing them in bulk?"

"Maybe we need to get a sunglasses subscription service for you, then." He reached over, opening the glove department. He pulled out a pair of silver aviator-style sunglasses. "These aren't that dark, but they'll work until we can get you another pair."

"Thank you." I took the sunglasses and slipped them on. "How do I look? Badass?"

"Beautiful." He backed the Impala out. "And badass."

My smile was so big I was sure I looked like the biggest dweeb known to man, and the smile pretty much remained there as we drove to the Hotel Witchy. We chatted about Peanut and made plans to stop by the Warden compound to retrieve his phone after we made a pit stop at a drugstore... to purchase a pregnancy test for the first time in my life.

Fun times.

We arrived at the hotel, parking in the nearby garage. When we entered the hotel and I went to push up the sunglasses, Zayne took them from me.

"I think I'll have better luck with them," he said, hooking an arm of the sunglasses around the collar of his shirt.

"Probably."

As we rode the elevator up to the thirteenth floor and walked the hall to the restaurant, I wasn't at all worried about whether the Crone would be here. I had a feeling she knew exactly what day we'd return.

And wouldn't you know, Rowena was behind the hostess's table, and before either of us could speak, she stepped out behind it and said in the most annoyed voice possible, "This way, please."

I raised a brow as my gaze swept the dimly lit interior. "You really love these little visits, don't you?"

"I await them with bated breath," she responded.

I smirked as Zayne's brows lifted. "That's right. You've never had the pleasure of being greeted by Rowena. She's always so eager to see me here."

"I can tell," Zayne replied flatly.

Rowena said nothing as she led us past the partition wall. Like before, everything but the round table in the middle of the room had been removed. Only three chairs were positioned at the table, and the Crone sat this time facing us. The table was bare of plates and glasses, and I had a sudden feeling that after this meeting, the table and chairs would disappear.

And so would the Crone.

Her shirt was the brightest pink I'd ever seen, and something...glittered across the front of it.

"How old is she?" Zayne whispered to me.

"Older than you think I look," the Crone answered. Apparently her hearing wasn't affected by age. "Come. Sit with me," she called, her head tilted toward Zayne.

As we got closer, there was no mistaking the look of awe that settled into the lined, deep brown skin as she stared up at Zayne.

And there was also no mistaking what was bedazzled across her shirt in purple crystals. DON'T FLIP MY WITCH SWITCH.

Nice.

Zayne pulled out the chair to the Crone's left for me to sit. I murmured my thanks.

The Crone chuckled as she watched Zayne take the seat

to her right. "A Fallen with manners?" The skin at the corners of her eyes creased even further. "Or a Fallen who is in love?"

"The latter would probably be a more accurate observation," Zayne answered, and my heart did a little jig in my chest.

Her lips turned up in a smile as she leaned toward Zayne. "You are something I'd never seen before, unique before even now. A Warden who befriended demons, something that has always set you above others. You achieved restoration of your Glory, a nearly impossible feat, and you gave away heavenly acceptance for love. Now, a Fallen with heavenly fire coursing through your veins. I've waited a very long time to say this. You have always been undervalued and underrated, but that has changed." Her gaze roamed over Zayne. "You're magnificent."

"I really like her," Zayne said to me. "Should've come here sooner."

The Crone batted her white-tipped eyelashes—actually fluttered them at Zayne. "You are always welcome." She lifted a small hand, stopping short before touching his arm. "May I?"

Muscles tensed as Zayne nodded for her to continue. I didn't think she would be stupid enough to try something, but then again, people were generally stupid.

The Crone placed her hand on his arm. Her eyes drifted shut for a moment. "Yes," she said softly. "You are utterly unique."

I rolled my eyes. "He's going to end up with a huge ego if you keep this up."

"But it is an ego well deserved," the Crone replied, slipping her hand from Zayne's skin. "Do you not agree?"

"I agree," I muttered.

Zayne shot me a half grin. "We owe you a thank-you, Crone."

"Is that so?" Bushy white brows lifted.

Zayne nodded. "You gave her the means to help me."

"But those means did not come without strings," the Crone reminded us.

"I know." I lifted the baggie. "We have your feather."

Her smile grew as she eyed the bag. "I knew you would not fail." Those eyes, as sharp as anyone half her age—whatever that age was—rose to mine. "You feared that you would. No one would blame you for that. Either you restored him or ended him, and that is no action taken lightly."

"No." I placed the baggie on the table. "It wasn't."

"I like you," the Crone said.

"As much as you like him?" I countered.

Her laugh was raspy. "I like both of you. Together. You're two halves meant to be one. Always have been. Always will be."

There was a skipping motion in my chest as she looked down at the feather. "It's sad, is it not? What Gabriel plots to do to this world and to Heaven."

I stilled. I'd never shared with her what Gabriel planned... or that he was the Harbinger, but I wasn't exactly surprised that she knew. "I could think of a stronger adjective to describe what he plans, but yes."

She nodded slowly. "I've lived a long time, but I never thought I'd live to see the end of days."

My breath caught.

"We won't allow that to happen," Zayne spoke up.

"No, I do not think you two will," she said, and confusion rose as she curled gnarled fingers around the top of the baggie. "Not now at least."

I glanced at Zayne and saw that his perplexed expression most likely matched mine. "I'm not really tracking what you're saying."

"I don't suspect you will. Not for a very long time."

Well, that statement sure didn't clear anything up.

The Crone lifted the bag, holding it in one hand as she ran her fingers along the outline of the feather.

"You going to tell us what you plan to do with that feather?" I asked.

She looked over at me as she opened the baggie. "Nothing as dangerous as what you plan."

"And what do you think I plan?" I countered.

"She has a long list of dangerous things," Zayne tacked on, helpful as always.

The Crone only smiled. "Sometimes you got to raise a little Hell to get things done."

25

I stared at her as tiny goose bumps broke out over my skin.
"Thank you for this," she said, nodding at me and then
Zayne as the man from the last time I'd been here appeared,
still wearing a suit. He carried a champagne glass to the table
and placed it front of the Crone. The liquid was a frothy
pink.

"I told you that there are all manner of things that can
be accomplished with a feather from one who has Fallen."
The Crone slipped said item from the bag. "Especially one
who still carries *grace* within them. There is only one other
in this world and beyond, but his...well, I'm not quite sure
any beauty can be accomplished with his feather."

"You talking about Lucifer?" I watched her curl the
feather in her hand.

"Who else?" She held her hand over the opening of the
glass. Her lips moved, her voice too fast and low for me to
understand, but whatever she said sounded like a prayer to me.

Zayne shifted across from me, his brows knitted as he watched the Crone.

"I'm leaving the city today," she continued, opening her hand. Flecks of crumbled feather dusted in golden light fell into the glass. "Heading south to visit my grandbabies."

"Sounds like as good a time as any to get out of the city," I commented as she dropped what was left of the poor feather onto the table.

The Crone picked up the champagne glass. "But I doubt they will recognize me."

My heart thumped against my chest as she lifted the glass to her lips. I started to move forward—

"It's okay," Zayne said, voice low. "Whatever she is doing, it's okay."

He was sensing her intentions—her soul—and whatever he was feeling didn't concern him. I guessed that was good since she took a drink of whatever the hell she'd concocted… and kept drinking.

And drinking.

My eyes widened as she downed the entire glass in one gulp like she was a pro at doing shots.

"Goodness," she whispered hoarsely, pressing the back of her hand against her mouth as she let out a little belch. "Woo, that has a bite. Tangy."

Slowly, I looked over at Zayne. He blinked, his head jerking back. "Holy…"

My gaze snapped back to the Crone and my jaw hit the floor. "Shit…"

I don't know what I was expecting when I looked at her, but what I saw wasn't anything on the potential WTF list.

It was like watching someone age…in reverse.

Her snowy white hair thickened and darkened to the shade of midnight, lengthening as the springy curls became defined. The skin of her forehead smoothed and the heavy lines by her eyes and bracketing her mouth disappeared. Her cheeks and lips plumped as her jawline became defined. Her body shuddered, her back straightening and her shoulders lifting. The chest of the bright pink shirt lifted and the dark spots along the hand still holding the champagne flute vanished as if someone had taken an eraser to them.

My jaw was still on the floor when she tipped her head back and the lines around her throat faded. She swallowed, lowering her head.

Her eyebrows were the last to change. They thinned and darkened, following the graceful curve of her brow bone, and now I was staring at someone who appeared to be no older than her late twenties or early thirties.

Someone who was stunningly gorgeous.

The Crone placed the empty glass on the table. "Why age gracefully when you can erase the years with a drink and a spell?"

I closed my mouth, having literally nothing to say in response to what I just witnessed.

She smiled, her gaze flicking between the two of us as she rose from the chair with the fluidity of someone who didn't look like they'd break a hip. "It's time for me to leave."

"Okay," I mumbled.

"I wish you both blessings in the battles to come," she said.

I found myself standing beside Zayne. Battles? As in plural? Zayne steered me around, his hand on my lower back.

"Trueborn?" she called, and I stopped, looking over my

shoulder. "He may not be your Protector, but he is still a source of your strength. Remember that when the snow falls."

"Well, that was interesting," Zayne said once we returned to the Impala. "And not at all expected."

I let out a shaky laugh. "Yeah. Wow. Your feathers are like a...a mommy makeover."

"I don't think that was just my feather," he pointed out, looking over at me. The lines of his face were barely visible in the shadowy interior. "I'm just glad that's what she used my feather for."

"Same," I agreed. "I still can't believe I just saw that. At first, I thought it was my eyes."

"You and me both." He reached over, fixing the twisted hem of my shirt. "I felt like she was telling us something important, but I'm too stupid to figure out what it was."

"She makes being vague an art form. The battles to come? As in more than one? I really hope that was just for dramatic effect because I really want to take a vacay after we defeat Gabriel."

"Where would you like to go?"

"I don't know."

"Come on." He tugged lightly on my shirt. "I'm sure there are people and places you want to see."

"I..." My lips pursed. "I would like to go visit Jada and Thierry."

"We can do that. What else? Someplace you've never been."

I tipped my head back against the seat. "Maybe go to a... beach? Like not a superbusy one. I've never stepped into the sea and I'd like to see the ocean before, you know, so

I would like to do that. And I've always wanted to see the Hollywood sign. I know that sounds cheesy."

"It doesn't," he said. "Where else?"

"Like anywhere?"

"Anywhere."

A grin pulled at my lips. "I'd love to see Edinburgh and Rome with my own eyes and touch the buildings. Oh—and Sicily. I would like to visit where my family comes from— well, where my mother's side of the family comes from. What about you?"

"Anyplace you want to go, I'm down with."

I looked over at him. "But there has to be a place you'd prefer."

"Where you are is where I prefer." He lifted a hand, making sure I saw it first before he cupped my cheek. "Seriously. You want to go visit the community, we can do that. You want to find a distant private beach, we can do that. You want to rent a cabin in the mountains, it'll be my new favorite place. Rome? Sicily? I'd love to see them with you." He smoothed his thumb along my lower lip. "Better yet, we should keep adding to the list of the places you want to see and we'll do it. We'll see all of the places. It doesn't matter if it takes months or an entire year. We'll do it and make enough memories."

My throat constricted with emotion. I knew what he was up to. Make enough memories so that when my vision went, I still had those to look back on instead of canvases empty of color and shape. "You're doing it again."

"Doing what?"

"Being perfect." I leaned over, missing his mouth on the first go but finding his lips quickly after. I kissed him. "I love you."

He kissed me back, the touch of his lips sweet and gentle. "I love you, Trinity."

Squeezing my eyes shut to stop the rush of silly tears, I pressed my forehead against his. "I like this plan."

"So do I." He kissed the corner of my lips. "But first..."

"But first we need to go to the drugstore," I told him, stomach taking a leap.

"We do."

"And then swing by the compound to get your phone."

"Maybe we can talk them into making us dinner," he suggested.

I smiled against his lips. "Then see if we can draw out any demons."

"Don't forget to pencil time in there for me to show you how happy I was to see my car."

I laughed as I slipped a hand around the back of his neck, threading my fingers through his hair. "I have not forgotten that. We can make time for that at any point." I kissed him quickly. "And then we need to shut down the portals and kill Gabriel."

"I want to get back to making time for that at any point." His hand slid from my cheek, all the way down my side. "How about now?"

My pulse immediately skyrocketed into uncharted territories. "Anytime," I whispered.

"Then get over here," he said, his voice coming out deep and rough as he curled his arm around my waist.

And I got over there.

Well, Zayne got me over there, because there was a whole lot of maneuvering that was beyond me in the dark interior, but he had me in his lap in a nanosecond and our bodies lined up in all the fun and very inappropriate ways. My hands moved from his shoulders toward the center of his chest.

"Careful." His mouth hovered against mine. "You're going to break those sunglasses."

I pulled them free from the collar of his shirt and tossed them onto the back seat. "They're safe now."

Zayne laughed as he steeled his hands on my hips. "We're going to have to see about that."

"Later," I insisted, brushing my nose along his.

"Yes." His lips glided over mine. "Later."

The pressure of his mouth increased against mine as I leaned into him, reveling in the feel of him. I would never grow tired—

My phone rang, rattling from the cupholder I'd stashed it in. "We can ignore it."

His hand drifted up, over the swell of my breast. His touch scorched me through the thin shirt. "We should."

I don't know who kissed who then. It didn't matter. The rawness of the kiss left me breathless as need and love and a thousand other crazy, wonderful sensations pounded through me. My skin burned as his thumb swept over the center of my breast, creating a fire in me.

My phone alerted to a text. Then another, and I pressed more fully against him, willing the phone to shut up. I wanted to be irresponsible—

"We should see who it is." Zayne turned his head, and I groaned as I pressed my forehead to his cheek. He fished my phone out of the cupholder.

I kissed the underside of his jaw. "Who is it?"

"Well, the text says, 'Answer the phone, you trifling Trueborn.'" He paused. "Am I going to need to kill someone for sending a text like that to you?"

I pulled back. "No. That has to be Cayman. Gimmie." I wiggled my fingers, squinting at the brightness on my phone as he handed it over. I went to hit the option to call the demon back as I looked at Zayne. "And if it weren't Cayman, would you really kill someone for calling me a trifling Trueborn?"

His head cocked to the side. "Honest?"

I nodded.

"Probably."

"Um." Pressing my lips together, I popped out my cheeks. "That may be an excessive reaction."

"I know." His hand returned to my hip and was on the move.

"And I am sensing that you don't care."

"Correct."

I shook my head as I hit the number. "We're going to need to talk about that later."

As close as we were, I saw his smile and my eyes narrowed. I put the phone on speaker.

It rang twice, and Cayman answered. "I cannot believe you didn't pick up—"

"Careful. Zayne wanted to kill you because you called me a trifling Trueborn."

"Zayne sounds like he has anger management issues," Cayman responded. "But we don't have time for that. Roth and Layla are coming back, and they need you guys to meet them."

My gaze shot to Zayne's as Cayman continued. "Well, they think they're just meeting with you, Trinity. I didn't exactly have a chance to tell them about you, angel boy. Cell reception in Hell is terrible."

I was honestly just stuck on the fact that Hell had cell phone reception at all when the corner of the bathroom in the apartment didn't.

"Where are we meeting them?" Zayne asked, showing off his multitasking skills as he slid his hand down my outer thigh.

"Head to their place, but instead of stopping there, keep going down the road. You'll come to a stop. That's where they'll meet you. Call me when you get there."

"And where are you going to be?" I asked.

"You know, doing things," he replied. "And stuff."

I frowned at the phone.

"Call me," he repeated, and then the phone went dead.

"I wonder if he even found out if Lucifer really has people looking for me," I said, wiggling out of Zayne's lap and into the passenger seat.

I might've pulled a butt muscle doing that.

"I wonder if Roth and Layla were successful in getting Lucifer to come topside."

"I guess we'll find out." I then realized the sunglasses were on the back seat. Groaning, I half climbed between the seats and grabbed them.

"You ready over there?" Zayne asked as the engine rumbled.

"Yeah." I put the glasses on. "How far are we from their place? I don't remember."

"About thirty minutes once we cross the bridge," he said, one hand resting on my knee while he used the other to steer. "More than enough time."

"More than enough time for what?"

He squeezed my knee gently. "You'll see."

My gaze lowered to where his hand rested. I liked that, how he liked physical contact between us. He was like that before.

Killing someone for calling me trifling was new.

At least, I thought it was as I placed my hand over his, and looked out the window. When we pulled out of the garage, I realized it was near dusk.

Staring at the blurred shapes of people and storefronts while Zayne's thumb moved in slow circles, I tried not to get too worried about whether or not Roth and Layla were successful. I didn't even know if I should be worried or grateful if they were.

Thoughts of Lucifer slipped from my mind as I focused on Zayne—on his hand and his fingers. It had moved farther up my leg, and even though his fingers were just moving in slow circles along my inner thigh, every part of my being became hyperaware. I flushed hot as my chest rose with a deep breath, and I looked down. My hand still rested lightly on his. He wasn't doing anything. Not really. I needed to get my hormones under control—

I bit down on the inside of my lip as his fingers slowly crept upward, reaching the very center of me. My gaze shot to him as my mouth dried, my body sizzled.

He spared a quick glance in my direction, a faint curve to his lips. "More than enough time," he repeated.

"For what?" My breath caught as his fingers continued to move in those slow, tight circles.

"To show you how happy I was." He focused on the road. "You want to find out?"

"Oh," I whispered, my heart beating so fast I thought I was going to have a heart attack. "I do."

I should've said no. I had no idea if any of the cars we passed could see inside, but I didn't as my gaze bounced from the windshield to the passenger window as we crossed the bridge and Zayne...

He drove me mad.

That was how it felt with each circle and the featherlight touches and the harder ones. The leggings and the undies underneath really weren't much of a barrier, but then his hand was slipping out from underneath mine and working its way under the band of the leggings. He stopped there, waiting for...for permission, and as I stared rather blindly out the window, I curled my hand around his forearm, urging him to continue.

And he did.

I don't know what it was. If it was the touch of his fingers against my bare skin or if it was what we were doing and how delightfully wicked it felt. If it was how he was so into it or if it was all of those things, but I closed my eyes and just existed, there in the moment, with him and what he was doing with those strokes of his finger, teasing and shallow, and then relentless and deep. My head fell back and my eyes closed as my hips moved, chasing his hand. I felt out of control, pressing my thighs against his wrist as I dug my fingers into the skin of his forearm. My entire body arched as he delved deep.

"Zayne," I whispered, barely recognizing my voice as every part of me tensed, coiling tighter and tighter. From the muscles in my fingers, all the way down to my toes, it was like the moments before making a dangerous jump, when my feet left the ground and there was that weightless moment where the heart skipped—the very second when I felt like I was flying. I cried out, lost as my body spun and spun before liquefying. I couldn't catch my breath as release powered through me, throbbing and pulsing. My entire body trembled as I held on to his hand, feeling the tendons moving under my fingers. The echo of soft sounds coming from me heated my cheeks as the darts of sensation slowed.

Vaguely aware of him easing his hand away, I opened my eyes and looked down. Slowly I lifted my fingers. His skin was pinker from where I'd gripped him, but not broken. I shuddered.

"You..." It took me a moment to remember how to speak. "You really were happy."

He chuckled. "Not about the car. Though it was nice being reunited with it," he said, and I looked over at him. "You're beautiful, Trin." He glanced at me. "God, you're beautiful."

I blushed. "Thank you. For the compliment." The flush deepened. "And for what came before that."

"It was my pleasure. My honor." He sucked his lower lip between his teeth. "We're almost there."

Lazily, I turned my head just in time to see us pass the road I believed led to Roth and Layla's house, which was a legit mansion.

I was still holding on to Zayne's arm as the trees around us thickened and the road came to a dead end.

"I guess this is it," Zayne said, turning off the car as I looked around and saw...trees. "You ready to check this out?"

"Uh-huh." I took the sunglasses off and placed them on the dashboard. "Can you get my phone?"

"Already got it."

"Great."

"You got to let go of my arm, though."

"Oh." I let go. Feeling a little loosey-goosey, I opened up the door and climbed out. Gravel crunched under my boots as I walked to the front of the Impala. "I could use a nap."

"I think you're going to have wait on that." Zayne joined me, dipping his head and kissing me softly.

"Boo." I snuggled against him for a few seconds, inhaling the winter, minty scent of his, and then pulled away. It was time to be mature and responsible or whatever. "I guess we should call Cayman."

The screen of my phone flared to life as Zayne called the demon. I looked out into the rapidly darkening field. It was pretty open minus a few giant oaks. The only sound other than the ringing phone was the hum of katydids or locusts or cicadas. They all were *holy crap, huge flying bug* to me, so I could never tell them apart.

"We're here," Zayne said when Cayman answered the phone.

"Took you guys long enough," came the response through the speakerphone.

Flushing, I glanced at Zayne. With nothing but the encroaching moonlight, his features were barely visible to me, but I detected a hint of a grin. "I took the scenic route," he said, and my face burned even hotter. "We're here, and unless they're suddenly invisible, I don't see Roth or Layla."

"They should be here any minute now. They'll come through a portal somewhere in the field."

I arched a brow as I carefully stepped off the asphalt and walked through the calf-high grass. "I hope they don't take long, because I'm pretty sure I'll be covered with ticks by the end of this night."

"I'll help you check later," Zayne offered from a few steps behind me.

I grinned as Cayman said, "I'm sure that's exactly what you'll be helping her do later."

"You sound jealous," Zayne said as he caught up to me, finding my hand and threading his fingers through mine. My grin increased exponentially.

"I kinda am," Cayman replied, and I could practically see his pout.

"Does anyone own this land?" I asked, scanning the shadowy field and surrounding trees. "If so, just give us a warning in case someone comes out with a shotgun."

"Roth owns it since he didn't want neighbors," Cayman explained. "So he bought about a hundred acres surrounding the house."

I blinked. "Being a demon must pay well."

"Being a demon prince sure does," Cayman said. "But in other words, there's no one around to hear you scream."

Frowning, I stopped and looked at the phone Zayne held in his palm. "Well, that's creepy."

"I know." Cayman giggled, and that was even more creepy.

Zayne shook his head as he slipped his hand free from mine, and walked a few steps ahead. "Do you know if they're bringing back an extraspecial friend with them?"

"No idea," he told us. "Like I said, reception was terrible."

I folded my arms. "And did you happen to find out anything about Lucifer potentially sending demons after me?"

"Since none of those who'd be in the know have been

easy to find, the answer is no," Cayman said. "And I know, I'm oh so very helpful these days."

"That you are." Zayne turned his face as the sound of… running water came through the phone. "What are you doing?"

"Taking a bath."

"You're taking a bath right now?" I asked. "While you're on the phone with us? When Roth and Layla may or may not be showing up with Lucifer?"

"Hey, it's not often I get some me time," he countered. "So when I find that time, I seize it. Also, it's a bubble bath."

"You're a mess," I told him.

"I know—oh, I have a text coming through. Let me check this out." There were several moments of what sounded like…splashing and then Cayman said, "Captain? On your left."

Zayne glanced at me. "Did he just quote Falcon from *Endgame*?"

"Kind of." Squinting, I looked over Zayne's shoulder. The world was stuck in those minutes where everything was sort of gray, and it wasn't the greatest time for my eyeballs, but the space behind Zayne appeared to ripple. "It could just be my eyes, but there might be a portal opening behind you."

Zayne turned. "Definitely a portal, but I doubt the King of Wakanda is about to show."

"That would be cool, though," I murmured.

Red sparked in the rippling air as the scent of sulfur reached us. My *grace* pulsed in response, and my muscles tensed. A moment later, a series of tingles erupted along the nape of my neck.

The Crown Prince of Hell and the daughter of *the* Lilith stepped out of the portal.

As always, I was a bit dumbstruck by their contrasting appearances. Roth with his dark, messy hair and penchant for black and Layla with hers long, platinum blond and love of pastel colors, they were a striking contradiction to one another and yet they seemed to fit together perfectly, like day and night.

Roth was inhumanly beautiful, like he'd been molded from clay by a skilled artist, but there was a trace of coldness there that made his beauty almost brutal. His attractiveness was no surprise. Upper Level demons were universally attractive, no matter their gender or the viewer's sexuality. They were the embodiment of temptation, and Layla was just as gorgeous, but in an ethereal way. She looked more angelic than me, and she didn't have angel blood in her... Well, except for the Fallen blood she apparently drank.

They stepped forward, hands joined. I wasn't sure which one saw Zayne first, but they both stopped at the same time. They were too far away for me to make out their expressions, but I was betting shock and awe were etched into their features as they stared at Zayne.

Neither of them moved as I looked for the very scary third arrival, but they were alone as the portal closed behind them. Did that mean they failed?

"Holy shit," Roth whispered, his attention fixed on Zayne.

Layla stepped forward, her hand falling free of Roth's. "Zayne?" she whispered, not making it very far. Roth captured her hand, holding her back as he stared at Zayne. "Is that—?" Her voice cracked. "Is that really you? How?" She jerked her head toward me. "Did Grim help you?"

"It wasn't Grim," Zayne answered, his voice thicker. "But it's me, Layla-bug."

"Layla-bug?" she whispered as I repeated the rather cute nickname in my mind, and then it appeared as if her face crumpled. A knot of emotion swelled in my throat as she pulled against Roth's hold, reaching for Zayne.

"He doesn't feel right." Roth stopped her. "What do you see around him, Layla?"

"I…" White-blond hair swayed as she shook her head. Her gasp reached my ears. "I don't see *anything*."

"You wouldn't, because I'm not a Warden any longer," Zayne said, standing still. "Roth knows what I am. Apparently he's always known what we once were."

Layla's head jerked back to Roth and then swung back to Zayne. "Wardens were once angels who Fell, but you're not an angel. You don't have an aura—"

"That's because he's a goddamn Fallen." Roth yanked Layla back then as he stepped in front of her. "With his *grace*."

"What?" Layla demanded, sidestepping Roth.

"Yes, he's a Fallen," I chimed in. "And yes, he still has a whole lot of heavenly fire in him, but he's still Zayne."

"Impossible," Roth bit out.

"I'm standing in front of you, so I don't know how you think that's impossible," Zayne responded. "But to make a long story short, I was restored, given back my Glory. They let me Fall and keep my *grace* to help fight Gabriel."

"They let you?" Disbelief filled Roth's tone. "A restored angel Fall and keep the *grace* when the only other being that equals that monumental bad life choice is—"

An intense burst of white light streaked across the sky, startling me. I looked up, flinching as another bolt of light ripped through the darkness, slamming down to the ground not too far from where we stood. A boom of thunder rattled my very bones and then the sky erupted in lightning. I jerked back, heart leaping.

"We're going to have to finish this conversation later," Roth said.

Dozens of lightning strikes hit the ground, the impact a continuous roar of thunder. Static charged the air, raising the tiny hairs all over my body.

Zayne was suddenly beside me as another thick crack of lightning hit a nearby tree. The oak split straight down the middle and then went up in flames.

Thunder roared through the skies, and the ground...the ground *rolled*, knocking me off balance. Zayne caught me by the waist, holding me as steady as he could while the earth seemed to quake to its very core. There wasn't even time to really feel fear or to wonder if standing in a field surrounded by trees was a good place to be in the middle of an earthquake. Everything stopped as quickly as it started. The lightning. The thunder. The earthquake.

Heart thumping, I glanced up at Zayne. "Um..."

Twin bright lights appeared behind us, funneling through the darkness. A creepy, crawling sensation shimmied over my skin as Zayne and I turned to where his Impala was parked. The headlights were now on. So was the interior light.

"That's odd," Zayne commented.

A second later, the radio kicked on, volume near eardrum-bursting levels as it rapidly changed channels like someone was in there spinning the dials.

Except no one, not even a really bored ghost, was in that car. It was empty of the living and the dead.

"That's *really* odd," I said.

"What in the Hell?" Zayne murmured.

The radio stopped spinning channels, and the sound…the sound of a guitar riff drifted out from inside the Impala. It was a song. A vaguely familiar one. A scratchy male voice sang, "'*I'm on my way to the promised land…*'"

My brows knitted as I started mouthing the words. The chorus picked up in a very recognizable lyric. "Is that…?"

"'Highway to Hell'?" Zayne finished for me as he looked over his shoulder. "Please tell me *he* doesn't have his own entrance song?"

Before Zayne's question could be answered, the ground by the burning tree erupted. A geyser of dirt and flames spewed hundreds of feet into the air.

I turned slowly, head tilting to the side as I stared into the mass of churning flames and dirt. There were shadows in there, a darkness that took shape, and even with my poor vision I could make out massive wings and horns—wings the length of two Impalas and horns the size of a person.

"He's heeeeeerrrre," Cayman's voice echoed eerily through the phone Zayne held as AC/DC sang "Highway to Hell."

My mouth dried.

The thing inside the fire stretched toward us. It was a monster made of rippling flames—a type of demon I'd never seen before. Its mouth gaped open in a deafening roar, spitting fire into the sky and across the ground. The heat blew back our clothing and hair.

Dear God, was Lucifer a giant?

Probably shouldn't be asking God that question, but how

in the Hell were we supposed to work with and hide something like that?

Man, this was a bad idea.

The fire monster stretched its arms as it tossed its head back in a fiery laugh.

A very bad idea.

The flames flared brightly and then evaporated. A small breath parted my lips as the fire monster thing shrank down until it was just under seven feet tall.

Definitely a more manageable fire monster size, but still, fire monster.

The grass sparked and then smoldered with each step the creature took as it stalked forward.

"Um," I repeated, forcing myself to stand still and keep my *grace* locked down.

"It's okay," Roth assured us. "He just likes to make an entrance."

"Understatement of the year," Zayne murmured.

Just when I was about to ask if the fire thing was permanent, the flames faded, revealing skin—skin that surprisingly carried the same kind of glow Zayne's did, but brighter. It did the same thing my father's did, an ever-changing kaleidoscope of pinks and browns before settling on a tawny hue that seemed neither white nor brown. As the glow receded, the first thing I noticed was that his features were clear to me—well, as clear as they could be in the moonlight, but definitely more visible than Roth's or Layla's. The second thing I noticed was how much he looked like my father, even his eyes. They were a vibrant, unnatural shade of blue, and the wings were the same—something else that surprised me even though I knew that Lucifer had retained his wings after his Fall and his *grace*. I just hadn't expected them to be so white and pristine, because he was, after all, freaking Lucifer. They were as large as my father's, stretching at least ten feet. The sculpted jaw and cheekbones were the same. The prominent brow and straight nose nearly identical. The fair, shoulder-length hair also similar. They could be brothers, and it struck me then that Michael and Lucifer *were* brothers, as were Raphael, Gabriel and all the rest.

Oh, man, wasn't that a dysfunctional as Hell family.

That I was a part of.

Wait. Did that mean Lucifer was…was my uncle? My nose wrinkled. We had to have some really messed up DNA relatives on 23andMe.

But family genealogy was so not important right now, because finally, the third thing I noticed, unfortunately, was that he was naked.

Why were they always naked?

Keeping my eyes northward wasn't a problem, though. I didn't want to see any of what he did or did not have going on down below.

He came to a stop a few feet from Roth and Layla, his wings moving soundlessly behind him. A coldness drenched my skin and my bones as those ultrabright eyes drifted over us, and when he spoke, ice encased my soul. His voice…it was like a melody—a hymn. The kind of voice that could convince you to take part in any unimaginable sin.

"Bow," Lucifer ordered. "Bow before your true Lord and Savior."

None of us moved.

Or bowed.

We all stared at him, which probably meant we were

seconds away from being brutally murdered in really horrific ways.

Lucifer clapped his hands together, causing me to give a little jump. "I'm just kidding." He chuckled, and the sound was like dark chocolate, smooth and sinful. "So, I'm told I'm needed to save the world."

"Yeah," I said hoarsely.

Lucifer smiled, and I'd never seen anything so beautiful and so equally frightening before. Goose bumps broke out over my flesh. "Then let's raise some Hell."

26

"Can you put some clothes on first?" Roth asked.

I so seconded that request.

"Does my nakedness make you uncomfortable, Prince?"

"Yes," Roth replied. "It does."

"What about you two...?" Lucifer looked at Zayne and I again. His head tilted to the side. "What in the forbidden fruit do we have here?"

I wasn't exactly sure which one of us he was referring to.

"A child of an angel..." He tipped his head back, inhaling deeply. "Not just any angel, though." His chin snapped back down, and those eyes were no longer blue. They burned a deep crimson. "Michael," he sneered. "You reek of Michael. I've been looking for you."

Zayne was in front of me in a heartbeat, the sound of his shirt tearing as his wings unfurled from his back, bright white and streaked with pulsing *grace*. I thought I heard Layla gasp.

"And a Fallen? A Fallen with his *grace*? What has come of this world that the first thing I see is a nephilim and a Fallen still in possession of *grace*?" Lucifer's laugh sounded like icicles falling, and I kept my mouth shut about the whole nephilim thing. "You think you can take me, Fallen? I've stripped larger wings than yours. Want to learn how that feels?" The scent of brimstone burned my nostrils. "I'll be happy to oblige you."

"I'd rather not, but if you make one move toward her, I'm more than willing to find out when I tear your wings off," Zayne warned.

My eyes widened.

Lucifer let out another dark chuckle. "Cocky. I kind of like it."

"That's not really a good thing," Roth commented from the sidelines. "He likes to collect things he likes."

"And put them in cages," Lucifer confirmed, and what the Hell was up with the whole putting things in cages obsession? "You didn't tell me there was a Fallen involved, Prince."

"I didn't know there was one," he replied as I peeked around one of Zayne's wings. Lucifer was still eyeballing Zayne like he wanted to have him for dinner. "This is the Warden we were telling you about. The one Gabriel killed."

"Aha, so you were given back your Glory. Restored to righteousness, but you Fell. For her." Lucifer's head snapped to his left, and those glowing red eyes met mine. "Peek-a-boo, I see you."

I shivered. "Hi?"

He dipped his chin, smiling. "How is your dear old father? Haven't seen him in a spell."

"I really don't know." I stepped to the side and under Zayne's wing. He cursed, but I ignored it. "He's kind of an absentee father."

"Well, don't we have that in common?" Lucifer's gaze shifted to Zayne. "And don't you and I have things in common? But I still have my Glory, Fallen. Step to me, and I'll have you in chains fashioned from your own bones, and your nephilim at my side and in my bed."

Zayne tensed beside me as *grace* surged, overriding my already limited common sense. I took a step forward as the corners of my vision turned white. "If you touch a hair on his head, I'll cut off what you think you're going to use in that bed and force-feed it to you."

Lucifer's brows shot up as his smile grew. "Now, you shouldn't flirt with me so obviously in front of your boy. That may hurt his feelings."

"Boy?" The growl that came from Zayne reminded me of something a very large, very predatory animal would make.

"Guys," Roth sighed. "Can we not do this? You both have big wings and all three of you have a whole lot of *grace*. Zayne isn't going to step to you. Lucifer isn't going to hurt Zayne, and, Trinity, you're not cutting off any unmentionable pieces," he said. "And can I also not be the voice of reason? I don't like it. At all."

"I kind of like it," Layla said. "It's a nice change."

"I so wish I was there to see this," Cayman's voice came through the phone. "All of this sounds really hot, but it's me time."

"What in the Hell are you still doing on the phone?" I snapped.

"Living my life," Cayman shot back. "Don't judge me—"

Zayne disconnected the call, and I felt his wings lower behind me. "I wasn't a part of this decision that brought you here. I'm sure we're all going to regret it."

"Probably." Lucifer smirked.

"But Roth seems to think you can help us defeat Gabriel," Zayne continued, his voice as thin as his patience. "If you're here to do that, I don't have a problem with you, but you come at her—"

"You're going to hurt me?" Lucifer pouted. "Real bad? Make me go ouchie?"

"*She's* going to hurt you real bad," Zayne warned. "And I'm going to stand by and laugh as she does."

"Just so you know, Zayne," I said. "If we were alone and possibly not about to throw down with a naked Lucifer, I would so be all over you right now."

"There's always later," Zayne told me. "And there will be a later."

I smiled.

Lucifer eyed both of us for several moments, and then I swore he rolled his eyes. "Love," he spat, the blue returning to his eyes. "How quaint. I hope you all are at least somewhat less sickening than these two."

Sensing that the immediate threat of Lucifer stripping the skin from our bones had eased, I reined in my *grace*. Zayne's wings were still out, though, spread wide behind me. "Did you send demons after me?"

"What?" Roth demanded.

"Ghouls and an Upper Level demon came for Trinity," Zayne answered. "They're dead now."

"That's a shame," Lucifer murmured in possibly the most disingenuous tone imaginable. "I learned of what Gabriel planned before my latest and greatest disappointment showed up."

"Wow," Roth muttered.

"Bael was acting sketchy for a while now," Lucifer explained, and my brows lifted. Sketchy? "So, I got curious and put some feelers out. Didn't take long to learn what the whiniest of all my brothers planned. I knew I had to do something to stop him."

Surprise flickered through me. "You already wanted to stop Gabriel?" I glanced at Roth and Layla. "Before they even spoke to you."

"You're surprised?" Lucifer glanced back at them. "She thinks I wanted to help mankind, doesn't she?"

"She doesn't know you like I do," Roth replied.

"How cute." Lucifer laughed as he refocused on me. "Make no mistake, I don't give a flying shit about mankind or Heaven, but there are rules. Agreements. Ones that even I follow. What Gabriel plans to do upsets the balance, and that is one of two things I cannot allow."

"What is the other thing?" I asked even though I knew I probably shouldn't have.

"Bael or Gabriel upstaging him," Layla supplied.

"True," Lucifer confirmed, and my eyebrows rose. "I'm the biggest badass, something Gabriel needs to be reminded of apparently. He is not who others should fear and pray for protection against. That's me. My job. And just like the greatest television show of all time, *Highlander*, there can only be one."

I blinked once and then twice. "You know of the show *Highlander*?"

Lucifer looked at me like I was half-stupid as Roth said,

JENNIFER L. ARMENTROUT

"Every so often, a stray iPad makes it to Hell and has some movie or TV shows downloaded on it. One of them had *Highlander*."

"Have you seen the movie?" I asked.

"There's a movie?" Lucifer's eyes widened with interest.

"A couple actually. Six or seven, I think?" I answered.

"I don't think now is the time to talk about *Highlander*," Zayne said, and the look Lucifer shot him would've sent most running. Zayne simply cocked an eyebrow. "Why did you send those demons after Trinity?"

"Because logic? Duh?"

The devil did not just say the word *duh*. I refused to accept that I had heard that.

"I figured that I'd be helpful and save Heaven from its own creations and ignorance by removing the key component of what Gabriel needs to complete his rather clever plan."

"Unfortunately, I'm that key component," I stated.

"Unfortunately for *you*, that is." Lucifer tilted his head again. "Removing you from the equation seemed like the easiest and quickest method of solving this issue. You can't disagree with that. Everyone should be thanking me."

"I can one hundred percent disagree," Zayne bit out.

Lucifer's eyes narrowed. "With you out of the picture, problem solved. It's nothing personal."

"Sorry but it feels sort of personal." I kept my gaze fixed on Lucifer.

"Wasn't like I was going to kill you," Lucifer said. "They were only going to bring you to me."

"What he's failing to mention is that without demonic

blood, you wouldn't have survived very long in Hell," Roth clarified.

I crossed my arms as I stared at Lucifer.

Lucifer rolled his eyes. "Way to throw me under the bus and back up, *son*."

"Wait. He's your father?" I asked. Did that mean I was also related to Roth?

"Not in the sense you're thinking," Roth said. "He created me."

"Does that not make me your father? As it makes God mine?" Lucifer challenged. "I'm just a more hands-on parent. Unlike You-Know-Who."

Roth shook his head. "Not this conversation again. Please."

"Now that you're here, have your plans to remove Trinity from the equation changed?" Zayne pulled us all back on track. Again. And man, it was nice to have him around to do that. "Because the last thing we need to be worried about is demons trying to retrieve her for you."

"I won't send any more after her." Lucifer turned to me. "Unless we somehow fail in stopping Gabriel. Then all bets are off."

Zayne opened his mouth, but I held up my hand. "Agreed."

His head shot toward me. "We do not agree with that."

"I just did." I spared him a brief glance. "Look, if all of us combined can't stop Gabriel, then there is no other option. It's as simple as that. We can't allow him to open the portal. Let's just hope it doesn't come to that."

Zayne's jaw hardened in a way that told me there would be nothing simple about that.

"She's smart. I like her," Lucifer commented, and I resisted the urge to take a step back. "Anyway, I'm here to help now, so me trying to kidnap you is water under the bridge. No harm. No foul."

"I wouldn't go that far," I muttered under my breath. "But yeah, whatever."

One side of Lucifer's lips curled up as he stepped back, taking in our group. "Don't worry, my newfound friends. I'll save the day. I'll even save Heaven," he said. "Now, the problem is the problem we're going to create when we kill Gabriel, but that's not going to be my problem."

"Wait," I said. "What problem?"

"Cross that bridge later." Lucifer waved my question off. "There's something I need to do real quick."

Lucifer vanished.

Like there one moment and straight-up gone the next.

Slowly, I turned in a full circle, finding no sign of him. My heart started thumping.

"Please tell me," Zayne began, "that he just likes to make himself invisible to mess with people and that he didn't just disappear."

Roth sighed as his head fell back. "I was afraid this was going to happen."

Standing in the kitchen of Roth and Layla's place, I mentally prepped myself for the last thing I wanted to do. And that was saying something since there were a whole lot of things I didn't want to do at the moment.

But calling Nicolai and letting him know that Lucifer was MIA topped the list of *I don't wanna.*

I glanced over my shoulder, spotting Zayne and Layla.

They were in a darkened sunroom off the kitchen, talking to one another. I squinted, trying to see their expressions, but it was no use. At least it no longer looked like Layla was crying, so I hoped that was a good sign. My gaze lowered to the thick, dark mass coiled around Zayne's leg.

Bambi.

The moment we walked into the McMansion, Bambi had peeled herself off Roth's arm and all but attached herself to Zayne's side. When I left the sunroom to give Zayne and Layla some privacy, the familiar had her diamond-shaped head resting on Zayne's knee and was staring up at him with a look of pure adoration.

I guessed I was no longer her snuggle buddy.

A moment later, a small reddish blur scampered across the kitchen and into the sunroom. A fox. Layla's familiar, to be exact. His name was Robin, and he was a hyper little thing, running from one corner of the house to the other. According to Roth, it was a baby…familiar.

I wanted to pet it. Just once. On the top of its furry little head.

Sighing, I returned to staring at the blurry contact on my phone.

"You can do it." Roth bent at the waist and leaned against the counter. "I believe in you."

"Shut up."

His golden eyes glimmered with amusement as he looked up at me. "Rude."

"If you knew there was a chance that Lucifer would up and disappear, that should've been the first thing out of your mouth," I shot back.

"Not like it would change anything. No one would've

been able to stop him. Stop procrastinating and give them a much needed heads-up."

Swallowing a mouthful of curses, I called Nicolai. He answered on the third ring.

"Trinity? Was just getting ready to call you."

"You were?" I winced, hoping it wasn't because Lucifer had already done something to catch their attention.

"Yeah, got good news. We're able to get the stones from Yellowstone."

"Stones?" Roth murmured.

"Really?" That was great news. "So that just leaves...?"

"The onyx and tourmaline. Hopefully we'll hear something soon about them," he said. "So, what's up?"

"Well," I said, drawing the word out. "You got a moment?"

"I'm on the phone with you, so yes."

"I just wanted to make sure you weren't busy," I said, and Roth raised an eyebrow at me. Flipping him off, I turned away from him. "So, I'm just going to say it." I cleared my throat. "Roth and Layla were successful—well, I guess successful would be considered subjective and would depend on whether or not you were on board with the idea of bringing Lucifer into the fold."

"I still haven't made my mind up when it comes to that," he replied flatly.

I doubted what I was about to tell him was going to push him toward Team On Board. "So, Lucifer did come topside, and good news is he did agree to help. Was actually pretty enthusiastic about it."

There was a pause and then Nicolai said, "Okay?"

"But we, uh…" My entire body and brain cringed. "We sort of lost Lucifer."

"What?"

"Don't freak out—"

"Don't freak out? Are you kidding me? You lost Lucifer, and you're telling me not to freak out?" Nicolai shouted from the phone. "How in the world do you even lose Lucifer?"

"Well, it's easier than you'd think. He did that really annoying demon thing and popped out of existence."

"Don't be a hater," said Roth.

Nicolai sounded like he was trying to take several deep breaths. "Are you legitimately telling me that Lucifer—*the* Lucifer—is out there, roaming around because you all lost him?"

"I wouldn't say we lost him—"

"You just said you lost him!"

"Okay. Bad word choice. We just *misplaced* him, but we're going to find him." I hoped we found him. "And he seemed pretty calm for, you know, being Lucifer, and all, so I don't think he's going to cause much trouble."

"You seriously think Lucifer, who hasn't walked Earth in how many years, isn't going to cause trouble?" Nicolai asked. "Are you high? Am I high?"

The corners of my lips turned down. "I'm not high, and hey, at least I'm not calling to tell you that we've jump-started the biblical end times."

"Yet," he growled. "You're not calling to tell me that *yet*."

He kind of had a point there. "Look, we're going to find him. I just wanted to give you all a heads-up in case you happen to run into a hopefully fully clothed Lucifer to not engage. Okay? So, I've got to go and find him now."

"Trinity—"

"Got to go. Going to be very busy," I rushed on. "Stay safe!" I hung up, barely resisting the urge to throw the phone across the room. Instead, I silenced it and placed it facedown on the counter before Nicolai could call back, because if I couldn't see that he was calling me, then I could pretend that he wasn't.

"That went well," Roth commented.

I turned to him. "How long would it take for us to know if we jump-started the apocalypse?"

His brows rose as he scrunched his hand through his hair. "Hard to say. I doubt there's an exact time limit, but we'll know if it happens."

"Do I even want to know how we'll know?"

He snorted. "You know you do."

I sighed. I did.

"If we've kicked off the big end times, you'll know because they'll show up."

A shiver tiptoed down my spine. "And who exactly is 'they'?"

"The Horsemen." Roth smiled tightly. "They'll ride. That's how you know."

"Oh." I almost sat down on the floor. "Okay. I'll keep an eye out for some dude on a white horse."

"Actually, what you'll be keeping an eye out for is the opening of the Seven Seals. War isn't riding the white horse. He comes with the second Seal. Then Famine with the third. The fourth Seal is the real fun one," he explained. "That brings out Pestilence and Death. A two-for-one special. Then things really get fun."

I stared at him.

"We're talking judgments, mark of the beast, tribulations, fiery pits and general chaos."

I blinked slowly.

"Then, you know, God will be like 'Daddy's home,' and kick ass or something." Roth shrugged. "Or so they say."

"Well, this has made me feel so much better about things. Thanks for that."

"You're welcome." Roth looked over his shoulder, into the sunroom. "I'm glad they're talking."

"So am I," I agreed softly. "For a moment there, when you first showed up, I thought you would go at Zayne."

"I didn't know what he'd become. He didn't feel right." Roth faced me. "Now I know."

"Now I know why you made your snarky little comments about Wardens," I said.

A quick grin appeared. "I haven't seen an angel Fall. Ever. And the only ones I ever knew were the ones who'd already been stripped of their wings, and sure as Hell didn't have their *grace*." A certain sense of knowing filled his amber gaze. "How was he when he first came back?"

I exhaled raggedly as my attention returned to the darkened sunroom. "Not particularly good."

"Sounds like there's a story there."

"There is. Maybe I'll tell you about it once we find Lucifer," I told him. "What do you think he's doing out there?"

Roth bent, picking up what look like a dog toy shaped like a fudge bar. "Knowing Lucifer? He's probably looking for the oldest nearby church and currently terrifying hapless priests while simultaneously causing the One up there to lose His mind."

I considered that. "Well, I guess he could be up to worse things, right?"

"Right." Roth pushed on the center of the bar, and the toy squeaked.

"We need to get out there and find him." I dragged a hand over my face. "Especially before he decides to get more creative with his time."

Without any warning, Layla's fox shot across the counter, snatching the toy out of Roth's hands. Robin jumped to the floor and took off, the toy in his mouth, squeaking away as he rushed into the living room.

"I really want to pet him," I said.

"I wouldn't recommend it. He's a bit nippy. What were you—?"

Focused on Roth, I didn't see Layla coming until she plowed into me. I squeaked, sounding like Robin's toy as she wrapped her arms around me, pinning my arms to my sides.

"Thank you," she said. "Thank you."

"For what?" My wide-eyed gaze swept through the room, meeting Zayne's.

He smiled.

"You know what." She squeezed harder.

"I don't," Roth observed.

"Trinity brought Zayne back after he Fell. She used the Sword of Michael on him, and brought him back," Layla said, pulling back. She clasped my arms. "I'm sorry for being so standoffish when we first met. I was being a bitch, but Zayne's important to me. He's always been, even when he didn't want anything to do with me, and I didn't know you and—"

"It's okay. I wasn't exactly friendly myself," I admitted.

"And you really don't need to thank me. Zayne did the hard work with the whole getting his Glory back and then Falling thing."

"I know what you did couldn't be easy." Layla shook me. "I can't even think about what I would've done if it had been me who had to do that. You had to be terrified, and the fact you still did it says a lot about you." Her pretty face started to crumple again, and the next second, she had her arms around me. "Thank you."

Zayne started forward, catching Roth's gaze. The demon prince grinned as he came around the counter. "Come on, shortie." Placing his hands on her shoulders, he tugged her back. "I think she knows how grateful you are without you squeezing out her insides."

Zayne came to my side, curling his arm around my shoulders. He dipped his head and kissed my cheek. "You look so comfortable with hugs," he murmured.

"Shut up."

He chuckled, kissing my temple. "Sounded like you called Nic. How'd he take the news?"

"Oh, you know, amazingly well. Very level response—"

A knock from the front of the house interrupted me. I glanced to Roth. "Could we get lucky and that's Lucifer?"

Roth snorted. "Doubtful."

"I'll get it!" Cayman's voice carried from somewhere in the house.

"He's been here the whole time?" I asked.

"He's been upstairs, soaking in the tub," Layla said, leaning into Roth. "It's Tuesday. 'Me time' always happens on Tuesday evening."

I shook my head. "You'd think he'd make an exception."

Cayman appeared in the doorway, a greenish-blue clay mask slathered across his face. "Someone is here to see you—all of you," he said. "Not me, because I have nothing to do with you all apparently losing Lucifer. Heads-up, he's not happy."

I stiffened. Who would even know all of us were here and that we'd lost Lucifer? It couldn't be Nicolai. I doubted he knew where Roth lived.

I felt Zayne stiffen beside me at the same time a strange shiver of awareness skated over my skin.

A man entered the kitchen—a man who was nearly as tall as Lucifer. Dark-haired and bearded, he had a glacial gaze that sent a chilled warning down my spine. So did the fact his features were clearer to me—like with Zayne and Lucifer. He wasn't a demon, but power radiated from this man—the final kind of power—and my *grace* kicked at my skin.

Roth stepped forward. "To what do we owe the unexpected and questionable honor of your presence, Grim?"

Grim.

Grim.

My eyes nearly popped out of my head as I realized I was staring at *the* Grim Reaper.

The Angel of Death.

27

If a year ago, anyone told me that I would meet both Lucifer and the Angel of Death in one day, I would've laughed straight in their face.

But here I was, staring at the Grim Reaper, otherwise known as Azreal.

And I wasn't laughing. Not at all. This angel didn't answer to Heaven or Hell. Or maybe he answered to both. I had no idea, but he could end any of our lives with just the snap of his finger, and I was talking the final kind of death that ended with the destruction of the soul.

"Cute," Grim replied to Roth. "Do you think I want to be here?"

"I'm going to go with a no." Roth idly crossed his arms.

My brows knitted. Was it just me or did Grim have a... British accent?

The Angel of Death's head tilted in Layla's direction. "Nice to see you again."

Layla gave a short, awkward wave that I felt in every part of my being.

"What in God's green Earth have you all done?" he demanded as I saw Cayman slink from the room. "You brought Lucifer topside?"

"You have to know why," Roth stated. "And you're not going to ask where he is?"

I really didn't think it was wise to bring up his absence, but what did I know?

His lips thinned behind his trimmed beard. "I know he's not here, which is what you should have expected the moment he got topside."

"We'll find him," Roth replied.

"Damn straight you will," Grim fired back. "Because everyone who is anyone knows Lucifer is on the field, and you know what that means?"

"End of the world, Bible-study-style. Ironically, I was just having that conversation. We're hoping that God realizes what we're doing and doesn't go end times on everyone," Roth told him. "And by the way, finding Lucifer was what we were about to do before you interrupted." Roth smirked even as Grim's eyes narrowed. "Just saying, but since you're here, I'm sure you could just tell us where he is."

"I know exactly where that prima donna is and you also know that I cannot say anything."

"Why not?" I blurted out, and those cold, cold glittering eyes swung toward Zayne and I. Yikes. I resisted the urge to take a step back. "I mean, that would be really helpful, uh, Mr. Grim—er, Mr. Azreal."

"Mr. Grim?" Zayne whispered under his breath.

"You can just call me Grim," he stated. "And to answer

your question, the moment Lucifer reached this realm, the potential for the good old end times became a possibility. Meaning, I cannot interfere even if his presence has nothing to do with what will come to pass."

That…sounded as stupid as any other angelic rule, so not entirely shocking. Something else did occur to me, though. "So does the rule against taking up arms against another angel also apply to you?"

"It does." His gaze shifted to Zayne, and I tensed. "You slipped right through my grasp, didn't you?"

"I did." Zayne didn't sound remotely concerned, considering the Angel of Death could try to take his *grace* and his wings.

"And you won't be the only one, it appears," Grim replied, and I had no idea what he meant by that. "Unnatural things come from unnatural deals." His attention flicked to Layla. "This one can tell you all about that."

I couldn't exactly make out Layla's expression, but she looked a little offended by the statement.

But then his icy focus was once more on me. "Just so you know, I wouldn't have brought him back if it had come down to you summoning me."

Another wave of shivers danced over my skin. "You knew I planned to do that?"

"Of course I did." A tight smile appeared on Grim's face. "I always know. I'm like Santa, but with more death."

"Wow," I murmured. "That comparison just ruined Christmas for me."

"No life is worth being brought back," he said. "Not even his."

His comment sent a bolt of irritation through me. "Not to be rude, but why are you here? Just to lecture us?"

Silence filled the kitchen as Zayne shifted closer to me.

One side of Grim's lips kicked up. "Pretty much." He paused. "And I think you were knowingly being rude."

I crossed my arms. "I was. It's not personal," I said, using Lucifer's own words. "It's just that I'm a little tired of angels doing nothing more than talk and air their grievances while everyone else is having to do the dirty work."

"Hey," Zayne said. "I'm more than talk."

"You're a Fallen. You don't count in my sweeping and mostly accurate generalization," I reasoned. "And by the way, why do you sound like you have a British accent?"

Grim eyed me. "Why would you even ask that?"

"I'm just curious."

"You shouldn't question what you cannot possibly understand."

I rolled my eyes. "That makes no sense."

"Well, at least I don't sound like an American. 'Y'all comin' down to the crick to catch some catfish for a fish-and-fry,'" he mocked. "That's how you sound."

"We do not sound like that."

"Yeah, you kind of do," Roth said.

"What?" Layla demanded. "Even me?"

Roth shrugged. "Yeah, not as bad as Trinity, though. I blame West Virginia for that."

My eyes narrowed. "I'm offended."

"Your accent is cute," Zayne assured me.

"I didn't even realize I had an accent," I said.

"And I didn't realize I was here to talk about accents," Grim replied.

"I also didn't realize there was an actual reason," I muttered.

Grim raised a dark eyebrow in my dire[c] "[?] who you remind me of?"

"Someone you've probably killed at som[e] noying you?" I offered with a yawn.

He smirked. "You remind me of your father."

My lip curled. "I think I'd rather remind you one you murdered."

"You both have a quick mouth and lack of tact," h[e] tinued. "Both you and your father are lucky I find [?] amusing."

I opened my mouth, but Zayne curled his arm around my shoulders as he said, "Was there another reason?"

"Yes. I'm here to drive home the importance of you all finding Lucifer as soon as possible."

"That's the game plan," Zayne said, squeezing my shoulders before I could say that with...well, with less tact.

"He's not going to break any major rules," Roth chimed in. "He won't expose what he is beyond messing with people."

"If you think that's what he's doing, then I overestimated your intelligence," Grim snapped.

Roth's brows lifted. "Ouch."

"Lucifer is most likely out there, right now, trying to procreate a real-life, breathing son who won't be a disappointment to him."

My mouth dropped open.

"You're kidding, right?" Layla asked. "Please tell me he's not out there, trying to create the—"

"Antichrist?" Grim finished for her. "Yes, that is exactly what I'm saying, and he's probably already well on his way to doing it."

ating the Antichrist not breaking a rule?"

t's a part of the big plan." Grim paused as
into the room, the squeaky fudge bar in his
lan that wasn't due to start anytime soon, but
Lucifer wasn't expected to roam freely among
nytime soon. But here we are."

know how we were just talking about the Seals?"
looked at me. "Some theorize that the Antichrist is
e first Seal."

"Yay." I let my head fall back. Were there seriously not
enough messed-up things already going down?

"Wait. Correct me if I'm wrong, but for Lucifer to bring
the worst child known to be possible into the world, he can't
use any form of manipulation, right?" Layla said, and Grim
nodded. "Then how can he already be well on his way to
accomplishing that?"

The corners of Grim's lips turned down. "I'm not going
to explain to you how that's possible."

"What?" Layla threw up her hands. "I think it's a valid
question."

Cayman popped his head in the room, the mask having
been washed from his face. "Have you not seen our darkest of dark lords? He's a good-looking man. And he can be
charming...when he wants to be. All he has to do is hook
up with someone. It's not like he has to tell them, 'Hi, I'm
Lucifer and I'm going to get you all kinds of impregnated
with the Antichrist. Congrats! It's a boy!'"

"That sounds incredibly problematic," Zayne pointed out
as Cayman disappeared back into the living room.

"He is Lucifer." Grim bent down and scratched the top

of Robin's head without getting nipped. "His middle name is problematic."

"God." I dragged a hand over my face. "I really don't want to think of procreation any more than I already have to."

Roth's hazy features formed a frown. "What is that supposed to mean?"

"Just procreation in general," Zayne tacked on, and then quickly steered the conversation back to Lucifer. "Is there a way you could give us a good starting point when it comes to where we might find Lucifer? Technically, giving your best *guess* isn't intervening."

"He has a point." Roth pushed away from the counter.

Grim snorted while Robin trotted toward me, yellow eyes wide. The toy squeaked in his mouth. "All I can say is that if I was Lucifer and looking for a one-night stand that turns into a lifetime of Hell, I would go where people are more inclined to make bad life choices."

"The bars," Zayne and Roth answered at the same time.

"We're going to have to split up." Layla sighed as she glanced down at her dress. "I need to get changed."

"Same. I smell like Hell," Roth said as I started to reach for Robin. "If you value your fingers, I wouldn't do that, Trinity."

I froze. "But Grim petted him."

Robin clamped down on the toy, squeaking it.

"That's because I'm Grim," the Angel of Death replied as Roth followed Layla out of the kitchen.

Robin spit out the toy and sat, swishing his bushy tail.

"You'll bite me if I pet you, but you want me to throw your toy?"

He let out a little yip.

"Doesn't seem fair." I swiped up the toy and gave it a toss toward the living room. I grinned as the fox took off. "He looks so soft. I just want to pet him. Once."

"He is very soft." Grim snagged my attention, having moved closer to Zayne and I. "You should be nicer to me."

"Probably," I admitted. "But it's been a rough couple of days, and I ran out of being nice to scary dude cards roughly around the time Lucifer showed up and opened his mouth."

"He often has that effect on people." Grim gave a faint smile. "I can answer a question that both of you would like answered."

I stilled as my heart turned over heavily.

"I'm not sure if I should be concerned that you know we are in need of answers to any questions," Zayne stated, and I seconded that.

"I'm death. Like I said before, I'm always watching, and there is very little I don't know."

I held up a hand. "Please don't make a Santa reference again. I don't think I can handle two of them in one night."

That faint smile turned into a lopsided grin. "I'm going to do you both a solid and clear something up for you, and I'm only doing this because you both need to focus on the mess you've made—"

"I would like it to go on record that I was not a part of the bringing Lucifer topside discussion," Zayne commented.

I shot him a dark look, and one side of his lips curved up.

"And you both need to focus on the task at hand," Grim continued, ignoring both of our comments. "There's a reason why there's no record of any Trueborn reproducing."

My breath caught as Zayne's arm slid away from my shoulders. He took my hand in his, but my fingers felt strangely numb. I was too caught off guard to really be freaked out about the fact that he was even aware of any of this.

"You know why it is forbidden for Protectors and Trueborns to fall in love. Their love interferes with their duty to protect mankind, weakens them both mentally and physically. Or so they say. I am of the belief that there are few things more empowering than love. Only the already weak would be further weakened by it. But the Alphas were of a different mind. They created that rule. The same sentiment was directed toward offspring. Most Trueborn were made sterile when they reached adulthood. The age of which varied greatly during the years Trueborns fought beside Wardens," he explained. "It was so ingrained in both the Trueborns and the Wardens that the idea of becoming pregnant was considered taboo, nearly sacrilegious. But then a Trueborn who hadn't yet been sterilized fell in love with her Protector, and from their forbidden union, a child was born. This was not received well."

"This is what brought on the end of the Trueborns and Protectors." Zayne's hand tightened around mine. "Isn't it?"

Grim nodded. "The Wardens demanded the pregnancy be ended before the Alphas could become aware. There were some Trueborns who agreed, but there were others who didn't. Those who stood behind the young couple and demanded that their child be able to live. As it was, the Protector was already physically weakened by their love. Divine punishment rendered."

"But that wasn't enough," I whispered, clearing my throat. "Something happened to them—their child, didn't it?"

Those cold, hard eyes met mine. "Their child was never given a chance to breathe its first breath. Both the Protector and the Trueborn were slaughtered in their sleep by those who believed they were carrying out what God wanted."

Horrified, I pressed my other hand to my chest.

"This enraged those who supported the couple—it even enraged many who did not. The Trueborns and their Protectors turned not only on the Wardens but the Alphas who'd finally intervened. It was a bloody mess wiped from history." Grim dipped his chin. "As most things are by those who do not wish to own up to their dark deeds. This is why Trueborns died off. That is why there is no record of any having reproduced."

My heart started pumping fast as I stared up at the angel.

"As with any being that carries the heavenly fire in their blood, procreation is extremely difficult, volatile and unpredictable," he went on while I felt like I might collapse into a puddle of anxiety. "While some may find it unfair or odd how easily two mortals can reproduce, it's actually not all that easy for them. It's about timing and luck—good or bad, depending on how you look at it—but it would frankly be shocking for a child to have resulted from one heated moment of unplanned passion between a Trueborn and a Fallen."

I repeated those words and I was still unsure if he was saying I was or wasn't pregnant.

Apparently Zayne was just as uncertain. "So, she's not pregnant?"

"You two would have to put a whole lot more effort into it if that was what you were attempting to achieve," Grim answered, his gaze returning to me. "No, you are not pregnant."

"What?" Roth exclaimed from the doorway, startling

me. My gaze swung to him and I saw both him and Layla standing there.

Both of their mouths appeared to be hanging open.

Zayne shifted his stance so that he partially blocked me from their view. "Can we get a little privacy here?"

I saw what I thought was Roth's arm rise as he said, "You know, I actually don't want to be a part of this conversation, anyway."

"But why would that even be a conversation?" Layla protested.

"Come with me, shortie, and I'll explain to you what can happen when two people have sex—better yet, I can show you—"

"I know what happens," Layla snapped, and whatever else she said was lost as Roth dragged her from the room.

I waited until they were gone. "How would you even know if I'm pregnant or not? Can you see inside my uterus?"

Zayne looked over at me. "I can't believe those words just came out of your mouth."

"*I* can't believe those words came out of my mouth, but they did."

"That has to be one of the most disturbing things I've heard, and I've heard a lot." Grim's lip curled behind his beard. "Death and life are two sides of the same coin. I can sense when the youngest life has taken root and know when the process of death has begun long before the body begins to rot."

"I bet you're amazing at dinner parties," I whispered as I exhaled slowly.

I wasn't pregnant.

Thank you baby gargoyles everywhere.

Relief swept through me, leaving me a little dizzy and guilty. Like should I be this relieved to learn I wasn't expecting?

I thought about how I'd just mouthed off at the Angel of Death.

Yeah, I should be this relieved.

But there was this teeny, tiny, seed-size sense of disappointment. While I had serious doubts about my parenting ability, Zayne would've made an amazing father. It would've been kind of awesome to have seen that.

But this was one less thing to worry about—to stress about and worry about having to protect.

"You two can have children," Grim said, dragging my attention back to him. "Maybe one day, if that is what you decide you want. It will be hard but it won't be impossible. What your child would be, well, that would be interesting. A possible whole new class of angelic bloodlines. Evolution. Isn't it grand?"

My head was turning over a whole lot of stuff at the moment. "Wouldn't our child just be a...Trueborn since we both have a lot of *grace* in us? Or like those with way watered-down *grace*?"

"Your child would've been like that—like you," he said. "But that was before."

"Before what?" Zayne asked.

Grim's smile spread. "Find Lucifer. Take care of Gabriel, and then worry about that. In the meantime, I would invest in birth control." His ancient gaze drifted from Zayne to me. "I'll see you again."

And with possibly the most unnerving words the Angel of Death could ever say, Grim vanished from the kitchen.

"He's…" I slowly shook my head. "He's something else."

"That he is." Zayne turned to me.

I looked up at him, mind still reeling. "The actual Angel of Death just popped in to yell at us and to tell me I'm not pregnant. Our lives are so strange."

A smile played over his lips as he placed his hands on my upper arms. "It is definitely strange. How are you feeling about what he told us?"

"I…" There were so many emotions and thoughts rolling through my head, but there was a lessening of tension in my chest. "I feel relieved? Does that make me a bad person?"

"No. It doesn't. I also feel relieved." Curling his arms around my shoulders, he stepped into me. "Don't get me wrong. If you were, we would've been okay. We would've figured things out, but now…"

"Now is so not a good time for any of that." I rested my chin on his chest. "At least we know it can happen."

"He did give good advice about birth control." His lips twitched.

"That was advice I never needed to hear from the Angel of Death," I retorted. "As were his parting words, but I guess all of us—or at least most of us—will see him again one day."

Zayne's jaw hardened. "That's not going to happen."

I smiled as I rested my cheek on his chest. He said that like he could somehow prevent death from taking me. He couldn't. One way or another, I would meet death. Hopefully it was a long time from now.

"But it's good to know that it is possible. You know?" He threaded his fingers through my hair. "If down the road we decide we want to."

"What? Ruin a child?"

He laughed. "Yeah, that."

Another smile curled up my lips. I still felt a little guilty for being so damn relieved, but I was so not ready for that. Not with everything going on. Maybe not ever, but at least that would be a choice we would get to make.

"What do you think he meant about the whole 'before' part?" Zayne asked. "About what our child would be."

"God, that's anyone's guess. We're going to have to obsess over that later." I started to pull back.

Zayne stopped me, dipping his chin so that when he spoke, his lips brushed my cheek. "What happened to the Protector and the Trueborn? That's not us. That will never be us."

"I know." I stretched up as far as I could, and he lowered his head the rest of the way. I kissed him. "Whoever would be stupid enough to try that wouldn't be walking back out of our bedroom."

"Agreed." The kiss he gave me then was longer, deeper, and when it was over, I wished we had more time. "We need to get out there and find Lucifer."

"We do." I stepped out of his embrace. "At least we don't have to go to a drugstore."

"We still need to get you new sunglasses," he reminded me as we left the kitchen.

Since the living room was dark, Zayne had worked his way so he was only a step ahead of me, leading a path around the furniture. God, I had missed that. I reached out, curling my fingers around the edge of his shirt.

Roth was waiting for us in the foyer, alone.

"Where's Layla?" Zayne asked.

"Chasing down Robin. He thinks it's playtime so he ran upstairs."

I stepped around Zayne. "Where's your nope rope?"

"Nope rope?" Roth chuckled. "My danger noodle is on my arm. She's not as ill-behaved as Robin. It'll take her a minute to catch him, so I figured you guys can go ahead and head out. If you guys want Dupont Circle, we'll check H Street."

"Sounds good to me," Zayne said as we started for the door.

I was thinking it was going to be a long night as we stepped out into the muggy July night air.

"By the way," Roth started.

Zayne turned back to him. "I really hope you're not bringing up what you heard Grim talking to us about."

"Nope. Knowledge that you two aren't going to be parents isn't any of my business," Roth said, and I frowned. "There's just something I need to say."

"Can't wait to hear this," Zayne replied.

"I know you can kick my ass up and down the city now." Roth leaned against the threshold of the door. "You're a Fallen with *grace*. I'm demon enough to recognize when I'm outgunned, but if you go toe to toe with Lucifer, you will lose."

"And knowing you wouldn't win against me, that wouldn't stop you from coming at me if you thought Layla was threatened," Zayne replied. "Right?"

"Not for one damn second."

"Then you understand why knowing I'm likely to die won't stop me," he stated, and I rolled my eyes. "But it warms my heart to know that you care."

Roth smirked. "Whatever, Stony."

"You missed me." Zayne grinned. "Admit it."

The grin on Roth's face was brief. "Just be careful. That's all I'm saying. If you find Lucifer first, don't push him. He's impulsive and has a tendency of destroying things before he thinks his actions through. He'd happily cut off his own nose to spite his face. If you irritate him, he'll kill you. He'll kill both of you."

28

Searching for Lucifer was like a game of Clue, if the game of Clue included things like attractive, half-naked Satan found with a shot of vodka in the bathroom of a shady-as-Hell club.

Zayne and I had hoofed it through most of Dupont Circle, stopping at every bar and club we came across, and God only knew why there were so many bars.

Strangely, no one asked for our IDs. I had a feeling that was Zayne's doing. Again and again, a bouncer or waiter would say that our description sounded familiar, reporting that a man who looked a lot like who we were looking for did come in, shirtless. This was often told to us right next to the no-shoes, no-shirt policy on a window or door. Then they'd direct us to a bartender who would swear that a man matching our description had come in and ordered top-shelf vodka, watched the crowd like a total creeper and then asked for recommendations on other bars he should check out. The first club we'd stopped at seemed more like an exotic dance club to me, since there'd been a whole lot of half-naked people on the dance floor, but then, I didn't think there were unisex exotic clubs. By the third establishment that would've fit right in with Sodom and Gomorrah, we quickly began to realize that wherever Lucifer went, his presence was felt, leaving behind an aura of temptation that thickened the air with sin.

This happened over and over. I stopped counting at ten.

"Do you think he's just going to get superdrunk and pass out somewhere?" I'd asked. "Because how many shots of vodka can he take?"

"Demons don't respond the same way to alcohol as humans do. I imagine angels are the same way," he'd told me, being all smart and stuff.

Hours later, I'd seen a whole lot of people engaging in various degrees of public intoxication, more skin and body parts than I ever needed to see in my entire life and some really brutal hangovers in the making.

But we didn't find Lucifer.

Neither did Layla or Roth. Cayman had also sacrificed his "me time" and joined the search, but he, too, was coming up empty-handed. Apparently Lucifer was picky, and I could appreciate the fact that he had standards and all, but I was tired and I was hungry. Like bordering on hangry kind of hungry.

So that was how we ended up on the roof of a nearby building. I sat on the edge, my feet dangling off into nothing as I happily munched away on a cheeseburger and fries. Zayne had gotten a grilled chicken sandwich—ew—of which he immediately disposed of the bun and just ate the chicken breast before we even reached our hidey-hole on the roof.

"Is there a reason you feel the need to eat on the actual edge of a roof?" Zayne asked as he hopped up on the ledge.

I popped a fry into my mouth. "A bird's-eye view of the city."

He knelt beside me, wings hidden away. "And what do you see of the city from up here?"

I squinted as I picked up my drink. "Numerous...identifiable blobs." I took a drink as I looked over at him. Moonlight shone across his face. He'd pulled his hair back in a smooth knot earlier. "But I bet you see everything perfectly."

He grinned, shaking his head. "I'm thinking you wanted to come up here just so I can live on the verge of a heart attack every time you move around."

I smirked. "Maybe. Want a fry?"

"No."

"Come on. It's just a thinly sliced carb stick."

"No, thank you."

I offered the fry, anyway, squinting as I aimed for his mouth. "It's tasty, salty goodness." I poked the corner of his lip. "It wants to be eaten by you."

"I doubt that fry is the only thing that wants to be eaten by me."

My face flushed hot. "What a naughty thing to suggest."

"Uh-huh." Zayne caught my wrist, turning his head just the slightest. He took the fry, chewing slowly. "Happy?"

I nodded.

His eyes met mine, a vibrant blue luminous in the moonlight as his tongue flicked over the tips of my fingers, sweeping away the crystals of salt. "Tasty."

"Yeah," I whispered, stomach tightening deliciously low.

He kissed the pad of my finger, those burning eyes still holding mine. "I love you, Trinity."

There was a catch in my breath and in my chest. I could never grow tired of hearing him say that. Ever. Each time he said it, it was like hearing it for the first time, as was the realization of how utterly wondrous it was to feel that deep and to know that kind of love was returned. And I knew I would do *anything* to protect that.

"I love you," I whispered.

He tipped his head back, and I thought I saw a smile as he stared up at the sky. I followed his gaze as I chowed down on a handful of fries. All I saw was the glare of the moon and different shades of black.

"Are the stars out?" I asked, hoping that he would say no, but sort of already knowing what the answer would be.

"There's a few of them. They're bright." Lowering his chin, he looked over at me. "You don't see any of them?"

Shaking my head, I shoveled the remaining fries into my mouth.

"Have you seen them since that night?" Zayne fished a napkin out of the fast-food bag as I finished off the fries. "Switch?"

"Thank you." I handed over the empty carton and took the napkin. "No. I haven't."

He was quiet for a moment and then took the balled napkin from me. "How's your vision otherwise?"

"Pretty much the same, I guess." Clasping the edge of the warm stone, I swung my feet. "I mean, I don't ever notice exactly when my vision worsens. It's usually so slow you can't really pinpoint the change."

"But it was getting harder to see the stars before then?"

"It was." I stared down. Other than the streetlamps and the headlights of passing cars, there was nothing but a void of darkness. "It was strange, though—how I saw all the stars so perfectly clearly. If it was real, it makes me wonder if... I don't know, like if my father had something to do with that?" As soon as the words left my mouth, I felt foolish, so I slurped half of my drink. "I know that sounds stupid—"

"No, it doesn't." He touched my arm first and then my cheek. "I think it's possible. Your father knows about your vision. Like I said before, I think your father finds ways to show that he cares—ways that aren't always obvious."

I smiled faintly, lowering my drink. "It felt like a...like a gift."

"It sounds like it was." His thumb swept over the curve of my jaw. "I wish you could see them now."

"So do I." I looked over at him. "But I have the Constellation of Zayne."

He smiled, and it amazed me how clear his features were now despite the lack of lighting and my eyes. Granted, someone with functional eyeballs could probably see him even better, but normally, his face would've just been an unfocused blur to me.

"We should get going," he said. "We need—"

I knew he felt the presence of demons at the same moment I felt the pressure on the nape of my neck. I sat my drink on the ledge. "You see them?"

"Looking." He took ahold of my hand, helping me stand as he turned to look over his shoulder. "Incoming."

I pivoted on the ledge, squinting. Several man-shaped blurs passed under the moonlight, their skin a shiny onyx.

There were four pairs of deep red eyes. That's all I needed to see to know what I was dealing with.

"Hellions," I groaned, hopping down on the thankfully flat roof. Forbidden topside, Hellions were created by pain and misery, and somehow, Gabriel had swayed way too many of them to his cause. "Let me guess, they're naked."

"Unfortunately."

"Why are they always naked?" I asked, summoning my *grace*. With the lack of light, I wasn't going to mess around with the daggers. The corners of my vision brightened as white light powered down my arm. My fingers curled around the handle as the sword flamed to life, cracking with fire and energy.

"Try to keep one alive," Zayne reminded me.

I nodded as the faint glow of Zayne's skin pulsed. Static charged the air. The back of his shirt ripped as his wings tore free.

"You should check out the shirt the Warden Jordan was wearing," I told him. "He'd cut two slits in the back for his wings. You'd go through less shirts if you do that."

He shrugged the ruined shirt aside. "But then you wouldn't get to see me shirtless."

I grinned. "Good point."

"Just looking out for you," he replied as golden fire spiraled down both his arms, forming those wicked sickle blades.

If any of the Hellions hesitated at the sight of Zayne going full Fallen, I couldn't tell. They rushed us, and that was when I realized there were more than four.

I'd never seen so many in one place. Good God, there had to be a dozen.

Zayne shot forward, slicing one blade through the chest of a Hellion as his wings lifted him in the air. He landed behind it as it burst into flames, his blades sweeping in a wide arc around him.

The Hellion in front of me disappeared. Cursing, I spun around and jabbed the flaming sword through its belly as it appeared behind me. It roared as I danced back, spinning. "Do you guys really not have clothing in Hell?"

"Would you like to find out?" one of the Hellions snarled, darting to my left and shooting forward, trying to come into my field of restricted vision.

Someone had been talking.

Oh Hell to the no, we were not going to play that game.

Growling under my breath, I shot back into the moonlight, lowering the sword. I stilled, centering myself just as Zayne had taught me. The Hellion's rasping chuckle came from my right. I heard his steps, and I turned sharply. The Sword of Michael caught the Hellion in the chest.

"Nice try," I muttered as the Hellion burst into flames. The stench of sulfur filled the rooftop.

"The Harbinger will reward me well." Hot, fetid breath touched my cheek.

My heart stuttered as I tensed to jump back. A flash of white filled my vision. Zayne came down in front of me, his fiery sickle blade cleaving through the neck of a Hellion.

"Why are you so fascinated by their lack of clothing?" Zayne asked.

Exhaling roughly, I turned. "I'm not fascinated per se." I lurched forward, thrusting my sword into the midsection of another Hellion. "I'm just curious to why they are always freaking naked."

"Just don't think about it." Zayne's wings stirred the loose hairs by my face as he moved with dizzying speeds.

"Don't think about it?" I dipped under the arm of a Hellion, mindful of its stupid mouth. Their bite was venomous, killing a human within seconds and paralyzing a Warden for days. I had no idea what their bite would do to anyone with angelic blood in them. I didn't plan to find out. "That's hard to do when they're naked."

"Can you see anything traumatizing, Trin?" Zayne asked.

Feinting to my right, I turned to my left. "No, but I know their junk is out." I aimed for said junk. The howl of pain and then ripple of flames told me I'd hit my target. "That is all I need to know."

A Hellion rushed out into the stream of moonlight, and I groaned. "Now I can see it—I can see all of it."

"I really wish you would stop pointing it out." Zayne landed a few feet from me, slicing through the air with both sickle blades. He took down two Hellions.

I frowned. "I want two swords."

Zayne laughed as he rose. "You can't always get what you want."

"Whatever." I rolled my eyes as a Hellion raced toward me. "This is the last one?"

"It is." Zayne's wings were like two glowing white beacons.

I darted to the left, holding my sword out. The Hellion skidded to a stop. He started to turn, but saw Zayne behind him. The Hellion sunk down onto its haunches, letting out a rumbling growl.

"I wouldn't try it," Zayne warned, his sickle blades sparking golden white embers.

"It's your lucky day," I said, holding the Sword of Michael with both hands. "You get to live. That is, if you're smart, and I hope you're smart. We have a message we want you to deliver to Gabriel."

Red eyes snapped to mine. A moment passed and then the Hellion grunted out a thick, garbled laugh.

I arched a brow as Zayne muttered, "I don't think this one is smart."

"Smarter than you two," the Hellion snarled.

Claws scraped over stone as a wall of dark, bulky shapes poured over the ledge of the roof. There was a glimpse of moonstone-colored skin and tusklike horns.

"Uh," I said. "There is like a horde of Nightcrawlers on the roof."

"How many is a horde?" Zayne asked.

"Um…" I swallowed as I scanned the line that stretched the entire length of the roof. There had to be…dozens. "A metric crap ton, to be exact."

The Hellion laughed again.

"Shut up." Zayne struck down the Hellion and then turned, checking out the newcomers. "I have a feeling Gabriel has learned of my upgrade."

"You think?" I scanned the line of Nightcrawlers as my heart started thumping. None of them were on leashes this time—not like that would've made much difference. I liked to think both Zayne and I were badasses, but that was a whole lot of Nightcrawler.

"Kill the Fallen," one of the Nightcrawlers said. "The nephilim must be alive."

I sighed as I lifted my sword. "I'm so tired of pointing out that *Trueborn* is a more appropriate term."

"That's kind of sad." Zayne's wings rose, *grace* pulsing and throbbing throughout them. "I like those lectures."

I didn't get a chance to response. The Nightcrawlers swarmed forward, the rooftop trembling under their weight. Maybe we'd get lucky and the roof would collapse. I pulled on the *grace*, preparing for the possibility that we may need to cut our losses and run.

There was a sudden sound of whooshing air. A bright orangey-red burst of light shattered the moonlight-drenched rooftop. My eyes widened as flames spilled over the ledge, licking across the concrete. The fire swept forward so fast, so unexpectedly, that I didn't even move as it swallowed the Nightcrawlers. I was frozen as their screams echoed all around us.

Zayne's sickle blades collapsed as he whirled, snagging an arm around my waist. My sword flared intensely and then shattered into a shower of golden embers. Power coiled in Zayne as he prepared to take flight. Heat scorched my cheeks and then the wave of fire retracted, rolling backward.

"What the—?" I squinted as a shape took form in the center of the flames. A man stepped *through* the fire, his wavy golden hair and bare chest untouched. The fire evaporated as the man continued forward, his feet stirring the dust of the fallen Nightcrawlers.

Holy crap.

I knew my mouth was hanging open. I didn't care. That kind of power was unimaginable.

"No need to thank me," he drawled. "I couldn't let any harm come to my new friends."

"Lucifer." Zayne's arm around me didn't slacken. "We've been looking for you."

Stepping into the moonlight, the devil smiled. "I know."

Lucifer sat in Roth's living room, stretched out on the sectional, watching television. Clothed at least. Actually, partially clothed. He'd manifested a pair of black leather pants, and that was about it. We had no idea if he was successful in creating *The Omen*. We'd asked. He gave us a look even I could see that said mind your own business.

And at the moment, that's what we all were doing. Minding our own business.

That and trying to get Lucifer to be somewhat useful and tell us how he could kill Gabriel.

He wasn't being exactly helpful.

First, he was hungry. So Cayman ordered up some late-night Uber eats. While he waited for the food to arrive, he found the television, and I'd never seen someone so enthralled before. He flipped through the channels continuously and then somehow ended up on one of the streaming services. I'd gone to use the bathroom, and when I came back, someone—I was going to blame Cayman for this—had turned on *Supernatural*, to the Lucifer season, and the real one was *invested*. He'd all but forced Layla to pull up some website to give him a blow-by-blow description of season one through whatever. By the time the food arrived, he was completely caught up. Then he ate. Then he watched two more episodes, a box of Pop-Tarts appearing out of thin air it seemed. At this point, it had to be almost four in the morning. Layla had passed out on the end of the couch and woke up, and I was this close to throwing the TV through a wall.

"Lucifer," Roth tried again, at the end of another episode. "You said that if you killed Gabriel, we would create a whole new problem. Can you tell us what that is?"

"If you let me watch one more episode in peace and quiet, I will," Lucifer retorted.

"You said that at the end of the last episode," I said, sitting on the edge of the couch, struggling with my patience.

"But Lucifer is about to start the apocalypse—"

"He doesn't succeed!" I shouted, and yes, it was super-weird to hear Lucifer refer to the fictional version of himself. "He ends up in the cage with Michael, who has possessed the one Winchester brother everyone has forgotten!" I shouted. "It will be, like, seven more seasons until he comes back."

Lucifer stared at me.

I stared back at him.

"You just spoiled the plot," he snarled.

"It came out over ten years ago! There is a time limit. Sorry. You can no longer cry spoiler."

"But there's no cable television in Hell," he shot back.

"He has a point," Zayne murmured from where he stood behind me.

I sent him a glare that should've fried him on the spot. "Look, Lucifer comes back again and again. Okay? There's plenty more seasons for you to watch. I won't tell you what happens if you just answer our questions." I drew in a deep breath. "Please."

"I'm starting to regret saving your life earlier." Lucifer sighed heavily. "Do any of you even know what happens when you kill an angel?"

"No. Sorry," I said. "We don't make a habit of killing angels."

"Well, my familiar ate two of them once," Roth chimed in. "Nothing really happened."

"Nothing that you were aware of. When an angel dies, their Glory will return to its source."

"God?" I guessed.

He nodded. "Just like a kid returning home to Daddy Dearest."

I blinked.

"Okay. So is that a problem?" Zayne asked.

"Is that a problem?" Lucifer chuckled. "Not normally, but what's inside Gabriel is a festering taint. His Glory and his *grace* are corrupted. Probably more so than mine, and it would be like launching napalm at the Heavens. God isn't going to allow that to return home." Lucifer glanced at the TV, and yep, he was sucked right back in. He grinned as he unwrapped yet another Pop-Tart. "I like this portrayal. Though Sam and Dean really need to start communicating better."

I took a deep breath and tried to count to ten.

Roth leaned forward, impatience crowding his features. I half expected him to snap his fingers. "So what does that mean exactly?"

"What does what mean?" Lucifer asked around a mouthful of pastry.

"I think he has that thing you have. You know, being unable to pay attention," Cayman whispered from where he collapsed on the couch beside me, and I nodded in agreement. There wasn't enough amphetamine in the world to treat Lucifer.

Roth briefly closed his eyes. "What will happen if God doesn't let it return home?"

"Oh. That." Lucifer stretched back, sweeping away a dusting of crumbs from his chest as he kicked his feet up on the coffee table. "Knowing God like I do? He's going to punt-kick that shit back down to Earth. All that nastiness is going to explode all over His most treasured creations— How many seasons are there of this?"

"A lot," I answered. "What's that going to do? All that... nastiness?"

"What will it do?" A slow smile crept across his face, and the tiny hairs all over my body rose. He truly was unbelievably beautiful, especially when he smiled, but dear God and baby angels everywhere, he was also unbelievably creepy, especially when he smiled like *that*. His eyes closed and he made a sound that made my cheeks heat. "You won't just have an air quality problem. The taint will reach across the world, until every land, every sea and all the mountains are coated with the corruption. All that anger, that hatred and bitterness and evil, will work its way into everyone." He moaned, the sound rapturous. "Brother will turn against brother, mother against child. It will be an unending orgy of violence and depravity. Only the most pious will be spared and even they will suffer great losses."

Uh.

"That, um, sounds problematic," I murmured.

Lucifer took a bite of the Pop-Tart as he refocused on the screen. "To you? Yes. To me? I'll have an influx of long-term houseguests to occupy my time with."

Roth sat back, dragging his hand through his hair, while Layla gaped at Lucifer.

I glanced over at Zayne, who now looked like *he* was a second away from throwing the TV through the wall. "We can't let that happen," I said. "We're trying to save the world, not destroy it."

"No, you're not trying to save the world." Lucifer's attention snapped to me, and it took everything in me not to shrink back from his full focus. "You're trying to save the world and what awaits beyond this realm. There will be casualties. Untold ones. Souls will be lost. You're going to sacrifice a whole lot to save *everything*."

His words settled heavily on my shoulders, and I could tell they weighed on Zayne, too. He stared at the TV, but I knew he wasn't aware of what was on the screen.

But would God really do that? Watch the world and the Heavens be saved only for it to slowly be ripped apart? That sounded even worse than the Old Testament God.

"So..." Layla cleared her throat. "That's going to be the outcome if we kill Gabriel? A world descending in chaos?"

"Pretty much." Lucifer finished off the Pop-Tart. "Except there is one thing that might happen."

Everyone in the room was on pins and needles while Lucifer slowly crumpled up the silver foil and tossed it. The Pop-Tart wrapper landed in the small hill of empty junk food containers.

Once Lucifer took his sweet time reclining back onto the couch, readjusting his legs and folding his hands behind his head, he said, "God could always intervene."

We all stared at him.

He raised one eyebrow.

Zayne's jaw worked as he bit out, "How could God intervene?"

"That's a very good question, Fallen," Lucifer purred,

and now Zayne looked like he was about to throw Lucifer through a wall with the TV.

The image of Lucifer flying through a wall behind a flat-screen TV brought a rather disturbing smile to my face.

"God could always nullify all that bad stuff." Lucifer wiggled his toes. "Stop it before all that nastiness could infect the little, pure and precious human souls."

"How does God do that?" I asked, almost too afraid to be hopeful.

Lucifer lifted a shoulder. "God could snap His fingers and stop it."

"That's all?" Disbelief filled Roth's tone.

"God is God." Lucifer glanced at the crown prince. "You of all people know exactly what God can do. And you of all people know that just because God can do anything and everything doesn't mean God will do anything other than sit back and let it work itself out. Free will and all."

Roth tipped his head back and sighed after a moment. "Yeah, you have a point there. What is the likelihood of God stepping in?"

"About as likely as me no longer singing 'Barbie Girl' while I make my rounds through the Circles of Hell."

Wait. What?

"Aw, Hell," muttered Roth.

"You're really suggesting that God wouldn't do anything?" Layla asked.

"I'm suggesting what all of you should already know," he responded. "Hate to say it, but Gabriel has a point. A dull one, but one nonetheless. Mankind isn't the greatest. I'm not going to bore myself listing all the obvious reasons why, but I know I get more new arrivals than the Heavens do. Maybe

God has checked out," he said, and there was an unnerving softness to his tone. Each word wrapped in silk. "Maybe God just doesn't care anymore, forsaking the most treasured creations. Look throughout history. There were many times God could've stepped in and ended countless horrific and senseless tragedies but chose not to. God acts like the rules can't be broken when God is the one who created them."

No one in the room spoke. Not even Cayman. Everyone, including Roth, was transfixed.

"Some say I'm the monster, the nightmare in the dark and the evil hiding in plain sight, but when a child dies needlessly, it is not a life I've taken. When a mother takes her last breath due to disease, it is not by my will. When a brother dies senselessly, it is not a part of my plan. Death and war and disease are not my creations. I cannot stop them. I'm not the creator. Right or wrong, at the end of the day, I'm just an opportunist," Lucifer said. "But what is God? Because at the end of the day, God could take all that pain away. So, tell me, who is the real monster?"

"The father of lies," Zayne murmured, and I blinked, as if coming out of a daze. "Yeah, God is to blame for everything—the true wolf hiding among the sheep and the other wolves. Sure. I'm also the tooth fairy and you're not the great manipulator."

A slow smile crept across Lucifer's face. "And just think of how many would have heard my words and believed me? Believed my legions?"

"Based on what I've seen people believe on social media?" Layla whispered. "Millions."

I nodded slowly, suddenly hyperaware once more of who and what sat on the couch, watching *Supernatural*. People needed someone to blame, even if there was no one at fault or if the fault rested solely in their hands.

"People have already believed your words," I said.

"They have." Lucifer's focus shifted once more to the television. "So, my friends, do you really need to wonder why God wouldn't intervene?"

29

Bleary-eyed and still half-asleep, I cradled the cup of coffee like it held the answers to life, while I sat curled up on the small, thickly cushioned sofa in the sunroom of Roth and Layla's place. Zayne's sunglasses shielded the bright rays of sunlight streaming in from the windows and ceiling. Normally, I felt weird wearing sunglasses indoors, but I was too tired to care.

Actually, I just didn't care. Everyone around me knew I had vision problems, but even if they didn't, who cared if they thought I was trying to act cool. That was their problem. Not mine.

Beside me, Zayne stretched out his long legs as he took a drink from the bottled water. Even as a Fallen, he had way healthier eating and drinking habits than me and half the population of the world.

"We still have to try," Layla said, smothering a yawn as she picked up the conversation that had ended when we all had been mere minutes from passing out. Zayne and I had ended up crashing at their place since it had been so late and they had a million rooms in their house. "Even if God punt-kicks Gabriel's essence back down to Earth, we have to try."

"And then what?" Roth scratched a hand through his messy, dark hair.

"Then we take care of whatever mess comes from this," Zayne stated. "That's all we can do."

"We?" Roth snorted, leaning back and crossing his arms.

"Yes. We." Layla smacked his arm. "Because I don't want to spend the next how many hundred years living in a world descending into chaos. I also don't want to watch a whole bunch of innocent people getting hurt or dying because of it."

A twinge of jealousy cut through my chest. Layla and Roth had a real future—one where neither had to worry about the other growing old and dying while the other out-lived them. I at least had the common sense to not blame them for what they had no control over.

"I also don't want to spend the next how many hundred years fighting everyone and everything," Roth replied, and I really couldn't blame him for that.

"We really don't have an option," Zayne said, draping his arm along the back of our couch. "Either we deal with the possible fallout or we allow the Heavens to basically close up shop."

"And that would be worse," I said, my grip tightening on the mug. "Anyone who dies would be stuck here. Every square inch of Earth would turn into the high school. So we'd have that in addition to the demons to deal with, but you know—"

A burst of deep laughter from the living room interrupted me. Rolling my eyes, I took a sip of the coffee. "Do you think he even slept?"

Layla sighed as she shook her head. "I don't think so. He's been watching *Supernatural*."

"I guess I shouldn't complain. At least he's obsessed with a good show." I lowered my mug. "What I don't understand is if Lucifer plays by the rules, why would his demons then swarm Earth if Gabriel is successful?"

"Not all of them would, but a great deal would. There are demons on the fence right now who are tired of being relegated to Hell or only allowed limited visitations topside. They listen to Lucifer, but if Gabriel succeeds, Earth would become one giant playground," Roth explained. "That would be too hard for them to ignore."

"And because they're idiots." Lucifer sauntered past the opening of the sunroom. "And I'll be honest," he said, his voice carrying into the room. "I won't be too upset if it happens. Yeah, it would burn my britches to know that one of my holier-than-thou brothers succeeded where I didn't, but the giant cesspool that Earth would become would be fun."

I glanced at Zayne as we heard the fridge door open and the sound of a tab on a can of soda being popped open. Zayne shook his head.

"At least he's being honest," Layla murmured.

I giggled.

Lucifer appeared in the doorway, a can of Coke in one hand and yet another Pop-Tart in the other. "Do you all even know where Gabriel or Bael are at?"

"We're working on that," I told him.

"In other words, you have no idea where he is and whatever plan you have is pretty much like playing eeny meeny miny moe?"

I frowned. "We're trying to catch one of the demons working for him to send a message—"

"That's all I need to hear." Lucifer held up his hand. "I'll have one of my minions look into it. You're welcome."

I lifted my brows as I stared at him. "And once we find where he is or are able to lead him out, how are you going to kill him?"

"How are *we* going to kill him is what you mean," he corrected. "Two of us could get it done, but it will be a lot easier with the three of us, which is probably why they let you Fall and keep your *grace*."

We already knew that was the case, but I asked, "And how do the three of us do this?"

"All I need to do is remove his heart, and then his head would need to be severed at the same moment the chamber where his heart once was is pierced with *grace*."

I stared at him.

"That's all?" Zayne repeated.

Lucifer nodded. "All three things have to be done as simultaneously as possible. You'll have seconds to remove his head and pierce his chest before his body regenerates his heart. By the way." Lucifer started to turn as he looked at Roth. "You're out of Pop-Tarts. I need more."

Roth glared at his retreating back. "I don't even know where he got those Pop-Tarts. Neither of us bought them."

"Cayman," Layla said, glancing over her shoulder. Lucifer had made his way back to the living room. "His minions?"

"He likes words like that." Roth tapped his fingers off the table. "Well, now we know how to kill Gabriel."

We did, and it sounded a little impossible. And it sounded like completely impossible if we didn't have Lucifer, because how in the world would Zayne and I been able to pull that off? Maybe that was why the biblical end times hadn't kicked off...yet. God knew we needed Lucifer's help.

"Whether any of his contacts will be useful, who knows," Roth went on. "I'd be surprised if he can stop watching *Supernatural* long enough to even contact anyone."

"I wish I had his life right now," I murmured, placing my mug on the table. "I know God hasn't been all that hands-on, but to think that God would allow Earth to just be contaminated?"

"Hard to believe, right?" Roth rubbed his palm along his jaw. "But free will. It's a bitch."

"How is that free will, though?" I reasoned. "If Gabriel's *grace* and his Glory is like an infection that corrupts people, how does free will come into play?"

"Good question." Zayne squeezed my shoulder. "That can't be free will. It sounds like a violation of it."

"That's one way to look at it." Roth leaned forward, resting his arms on the table. "But infections can be beat, right? At least most of them, with medicine. God could take the stance that this infection can be beat by faith."

I rolled my eyes. "That's stupid."

"I don't make the rules," Roth replied.

"Thank God for that," Zayne murmured.

Roth winked at him. "All I'm saying is I wouldn't rely on God, and I'm not saying that because I'm a demon. I'm just relying on statistical, historical evidence."

I exhaled a heavy breath as I tipped my head back against

Zayne's arm. "Either way, it doesn't matter. We have to risk the nuclear-level Gabriel fallout. We don't have a choice."

It was a little after one when Zayne and I made it back to the apartment. As he hopped in the shower, I plugged my phone in to charge and headed for the dryer to retrieve clean clothing. We were going to head out in a little bit, hoping we could draw more of Gabriel's cohorts out. I'd stepped out of the small hall when I thought I saw movement to my right. Turning sharply, I caught sight of Peanut by the TV.

"Peanut!"

He squeaked, flickering out for a moment.

"Don't you dare disappear!" I charged across the room. "You and I need to chat."

He reappeared a few feet from the TV. "How dare you scare me like that. You almost gave me a heart attack."

"You're dead, Peanut. You can't have a heart attack." I folded my arms. "You have a whole lot of explaining to do."

"I was only watching you sleep the other night to make sure you were breathing." He floated through the coffee table. "It wasn't even that long."

I blinked. "Okay. That's not what I was planning to talk to you about, so we're going to have to get back to that."

"Oh. My bad." Half of his legs were obscured by the table. "You can always just forget about that."

"Yeah, that's not going to happen," I told him.

He looked toward the hallway. "I hear the shower running."

"Don't you dare," I warned him.

"Is that Zayne? Did you bring Zayne back?"

"I did. You would know that if you'd been around."

Peanut started bopping up and down, clapping his hands. I supposed he was jumping, but I couldn't see his lower body. "Yay! You did it!" He stopped bouncing. "He's not, like, evil fallen angel anymore, is he?"

"No, he's hot, supernice fallen angel now, and stop distracting me."

"How am I distracting you?" He sank halfway through the coffee table.

I arched a brow. "You've been lying to me."

"About watching you sleep?"

"No. Not about that. About Gena."

His eyes widened in his nearly transparent head. "What do you mean?"

"There's no one who lives here named Gena or any variation of that name. I had the apartment records checked."

He rose from the coffee table. "Have you been checking on me?"

"Yes."

"I feel attacked." He pressed a hand to his chest. "I feel—"

"Why have you been lying to me, Peanut?" I interrupted before he could go drama spiral. "And what have you really been doing?"

"I haven't been lying. Not really, Trinnie." He drifted toward me. "I swear. You see, I just didn't clarify some things."

"I cannot wait to hear what these things are."

"Well, for starters, Gena is…she's not alive. That's why you wouldn't find her listed on anything. I think she died, like, a couple of decades ago."

I wasn't sure if he was telling the truth. "You said that there were some things going on with her parents."

"Not her, like, birth parents. There's this couple I guess

she followed home one day and they're having problems." He shrugged. "Or something like that. I honestly think someone's been stepping out. You know, visiting someone else's bed. Dipping their ink—"

"I get what you're saying." I studied him, still unsure if he was being truthful. Why would he lie now? Then again, why would he have lied before? I heard the shower turn off. "Why didn't you just tell me that? You didn't have to make a story."

He shrugged again. "She's weirded out about the idea of someone seeing her. No one has been able to, and when I told her about you, she freaked out. Thinks you're like a witch or something."

"What?"

He nodded solemnly. "She comes from, like, old puritan times."

"Puritan times? Peanut, that is more than a few decades old."

"How am I supposed to know that?" he fired back. "I'm dead."

"Peanut," I sighed.

"I'm sorry, Trinnie. I didn't mean to upset you—"

"Trin?" Zayne called out. "Who are you talking to?"

"Oh, gee whiz, he's coming in here," Peanut exclaimed. "I cannot be seen like this."

"Seen like this?"

"He's an angel with his *grace*. Fallen or not, he'll be able to see me now!"

"What? Why are you freaking out?" Confused, I watched him spin in a circle. "I thought you wanted people to be able to see you? And I clearly remember you complaining when Zayne couldn't."

"But I'm not ready for that kind of commitment," Peanut cried as he threw himself onto the couch.

And then through it.

My brows flew up. "Peanut?" When there was no answer, I walked to the other side of the couch. He wasn't there. I groaned. "God, you're such a mess."

"Trin?"

I turned, and for a moment, I totally forgot about the bizarreness that was Peanut. Zayne stood in the hallway with just a towel wrapped around his waist. Water dripped from the ends of his hair, forming beads that coursed down his chest and over the tightly coiled muscles of his lower stomach.

I felt like throwing myself on the couch.

"You were just talking to someone, weren't you?"

"Yeah." I found my tongue and made it work. "It was Peanut. Did you know you'd be able to see him now?"

His brows lifted as he looked around. "I don't see him."

"He freaked out and fell through the couch and I guess the floor and whatever else."

Zayne looked at me. "All right, then. And no, I didn't know I would be able to see him."

"He said it's because you're an angel," I explained. "And that does make sense. Angels can see ghosts and spirits."

"At least I'll now know when he's creeping on me."

"I'm not sure that's something you're going to appreciate when he randomly walks through a wall."

"Good point."

I cracked a grin, thoroughly proud of myself for holding a conversation while he was so utterly distracting in the most marvelous way. "I did get to ask him about the whole Gena thing."

"Tell me what he said while I find some clothes." He skimmed a hand through his wet hair, dragging the strands back from his face.

"He claims that Gena is real, but she's a dead girl." I followed him back to the bedroom. "Possibly from the puritan era."

"For real?" He looked over his shoulder at me.

"Knowing Peanut and his remarkable ability to overreact when it comes to everything, it's anyone's guess on that." I made my way over to the bed while he disappeared into the closet. "He said he didn't tell me the truth because the girl is freaked out by the idea of someone being able to see her."

"Do you believe him?"

"Honestly? I can't imagine why he'd lie now." I picked up my phone and tapped the screen. I saw I had a missed call and text from Dez. "And I don't know. Maybe it's a good thing he's hanging out with other ghosts. When he saw Sam, he about had a meltdown."

"Why do I find it so funny that your ghost is in need of socialization?" he asked, and a moment later, I felt his lips press against my cheek.

I turned my head toward his, and his mouth met mine. He kissed me softly, sending a shiver dancing down my spine.

When he pulled back, I saw he'd pulled on a pair of blue jeans. A plain gray shirt dangled from one hand as he sat down next to me.

"I got a text," I said. "From Dez. He asked if we could swing by as soon as possible."

"We can." He pulled the shirt on over his head, and I didn't know if I should be disappointed or grateful. "Did he say what for?"

I shook my head. "I hope it's just Nicolai wanting an update on Lucifer in person so he can lecture us. The last time Dez was this vague, it required a trip to the high school and the chief of police shooting Gabriel."

Zayne stared at me.

I leaned over, giving him a quick kiss. "I just need a few minutes to get ready."

Once I changed clothing, we were back in the Impala. We made a pit stop at a drugstore to pick up a pair of sunglasses for me. The only pair dark enough looked like someone hot-glued rhinestones on the arms, but they'd get the job done.

The trip to the Warden compound wasn't nearly as exciting as the last car ride, but it was quick, and when I hopped out of the car, I managed not to trip like I did nearly every time I came here.

Zayne joined me as we walked up the steps. Dez met us at the door. "Glad you guys could make it on such short notice."

"Let me guess, Nicolai wants an update on Lucifer and to yell at us in person?" I said as I followed him through the empty foyer.

"We found him," Zayne tacked on. "Just want to get that out of the way. He's at Roth's place right now, watching *Supernatural*."

"That has to be the strangest thing I've ever heard," Dez said, and I couldn't see his face, but I could hear the bewilderment in his tone.

"He's a fan of TV," I said. "And apparently, *Highlander*."

"I don't even know what to say."

"Welcome to our world," Zayne replied.

"Yeah, well, you're a part of that world," Dez shot back, and I smirked as Zayne snagged the back of my shirt, tugging me out of the path of a potted plant. "Nicolai does want an update, but that's not why you're here. I figured you'd want your phone and wallet back."

"It's been kind of nice without that thing ringing," Zayne replied. "But yeah, I need it."

"And the angel blades."

"Well, that's one of the reasons why I called you."

Having a really bad feeling about this, I frowned as he stepped around me and opened the door. "What about them?"

"First, there's someone here who wants to see you," he answered, opening the door to Nicolai's office.

All I saw was Nicolai's desk and the empty space behind it, and then someone in a vivid orange tank top stepped in front of it, into the line of my vision.

I skidded to a stop, not believing what I was seeing. Female Wardens didn't travel anywhere alone, especially hours away from their community. I hadn't even seen Danika out by herself. But it had to be *her*. No one pulled off bright orange like she did. "Jada?" I whispered.

Giving me a half wave, she glanced at where Zayne stood behind me. "Hi."

"What are you...?" I stepped forward into the room, realizing she wasn't alone. Her boyfriend, Ty, stood in the corner. He gave me a wave, too. I scanned the rest of the room, expecting to find Thierry or Matthew stowed away in another corner, but no one else was in the room. Even though Ty was with her, it still didn't make sense that either of them were here alone, but at that moment, I didn't care. Jada was here.

I sprang forward, throwing my arms around her. Warden strong, she still stumbled back a good foot.

Jada laughed as she hugged me back, and the sound of bangles jangling was one I hadn't even realized I missed.

"I can't believe you're here."

"We can't, either," Jada said. "But when I heard that Zayne had...well, that he wasn't with us any longer, there was no way I was letting you go through that by yourself." She paused. "But I see he's superalive."

"He is. It's a long story."

"Dez filled us in," Ty chimed in. "We're still a little confused but I think that's just gonna stay that way."

"Why didn't you text and tell me you were coming?"

"I was afraid you wouldn't answer or tell me not to."

I pulled back, stomach churning with guilt. "I'm sorry. I've been a shitty friend and—"

"Girl, it sucked. I wanted to be there for you when everything happened with Misha. I wanted you to be there for me, but you were closer to him than I was. I don't know how I would've reacted." She clasped my cheeks. "Also, I know how your brain works. You internalize everything and basically shut down. I just wasn't going to let you do that this time."

"You're the best." I hugged her again. "But I am sorry. It wasn't just me who was grieving."

"I accept your apology." Jada's voice was thick and muffled. "I already accepted your apology. That's what friends do."

Jada was right. As always. I still felt terrible, but that was the thing about real friends. You could misstep. You could go MIA, but you'd still be there. Both of you would be.

Pulling myself together, I leaned back. "Is Thierry or Matthew here? With Nicolai or something?"

"They're not here."

My mouth dropped open. "Your father let you guys come here?"

"I wouldn't say he let us," Ty said, pushing away from the wall. He came over, tall and broad as any Warden. He gave me a quick hug. "We sort of told him what we were doing after we got here."

Now my eyes were wide.

"And that was after we borrowed a car," Jada said, fighting a grin while Ty looked like he was seconds away from vomiting. "He's not that happy, but I told him I needed to see you. Plus, Ty may end up getting assigned here."

"What?" I blinked. "Really?"

Ty nodded. "Yeah, that's the plan. Or was the plan. Thierry may murder me."

"He's not going to kill you." Jada sighed. "A lot."

I laughed as Ty blanched. "So, he's on his way here now, I guess?"

"God, I hope not," muttered Ty.

"I don't know. He's on the phone with Nicolai right now. I told him that he didn't need to come here. We're with the Wardens and both of us know how to defend ourselves."

They did, but Ty hadn't gone through the Accolade and Jada…well, there were obvious reasons why her father would be losing his mind right now.

Jada glanced to where Zayne lingered just inside the room.

"I'm happy to see that you're still here." Her features pinched. "Did that sound as awkward as it felt saying it?"

Zayne laughed. "It sounded just right."

"I'm sorry," she said, glancing at me. "We're still processing the whole fallen angel thing."

"So am I," Zayne said with a grin. "I'm glad you guys are here, though. Trin's missed you all."

"I know." Jada smiled at me. "That's why we're here."

"I'd hug you again, but I think that'll just make it awkward." My gaze swept over her. "Your hair is growing."

She placed her fingers to the side of her head. Normally she kept her hair cropped close to the skull. "I'm thinking about letting it grow. Haven't made up my mind yet."

I had so many questions—so many things I wanted to talk about—but Dez rejoined us. "I hate to interrupt, but I've got to head out soon."

"The angel blades," I recalled, turning back to him. "What about them?"

"Angel blades?" repeated Ty.

"Basically angelic weapons that can kill literally anything," I explained.

"They're missing," Dez stated, tone hard.

Zayne turned to Dez. "Come again?"

"They're gone." Dez shook his head in disbelief. "Gideon went to grab them from where he had them locked up in the basement, and they were gone."

I couldn't believe what I was hearing. "I'm sure they didn't sprout little angel wings and fly their way out of here."

"I don't understand. Gideon has surveillance cameras everywhere."

"Yeah, but there are blind spots in the basement. You

know that, and with everyone going in and out using the training facilities, anyone could've slipped into a blind spot and broke into the safe."

"But why would a Warden steal the angel blades?" I demanded.

"A Warden wouldn't," Dez said.

Zayne nodded. "I have to agree with that."

"Then we're back to the blades sprouting wings?" I demanded.

"I know I haven't been around," Jada said. "But I'm going to assume the sprouting wings thing is impossible."

"He has wings." I pointed at Zayne. "They're hidden right now."

"What?" Ty turned to Zayne. "I thought Fallen didn't have wings?"

"He's superspecial," I said.

Zayne winked at me. "That I am."

"I know you all always want to believe the best in Wardens, but one of them has to have taken them," I reasoned.

"We're questioning everyone nonetheless," Dez said, unfolding his arms. "If they're still here, we'll find them." He glanced over at Ty. "I'm going to be heading out in about twenty minutes, if you want to tag along."

Ty nodded.

"Hell, I almost forgot." Dez grabbed something from a nearby shelf, handing it to Zayne. "Here's your phone and wallet."

"Thanks, man."

Dez turned to me. "And I have something for you. It's a just in case measure. A tracer. Gideon thought it would be a good idea since there's been attempts to grab you. I just need something of yours that you always have on you."

"My phone?" I glanced over at Zayne. His features were hard, but he nodded. I pulled it out and handed it over to Dez.

He looked over the phone, and then popped off the case. "It'll still work behind the case. Here it won't be so noticeable." His gaze shot to Zayne as a low rumbling sound came out of him. "Hey, man, I know you don't like the idea of someone grabbing her, but this is a good idea."

"I know it is," Zayne bit out. "And you're right. I don't like the idea of someone grabbing her."

"Neither do I." I took my phone back, slipping it in my pocket. "But thank you. This is smart."

"No problem. Hopefully it doesn't become useful."

As Dez walked out, I turned to Zayne. "I can't believe the angel blades are missing."

His jaw was still set in a hard line. "Me, neither, but I also don't see how it could be one of the Wardens."

Rubbing my temples, I cursed under my breath. "Well, at least we still have Lucifer." I dropped my hand, twisting toward Jada. "Uh…"

"We know," Jada responded. "We heard all about you bringing him in."

"And losing him," Ty added.

"I wouldn't say we lost him," I clarified. "We misplaced him for a short period of time, but we found him."

Jada shook her head. "If my father found out about Lucifer, he'd definitely flip."

I was willing to bet Thierry was already flipping out.

My phone dinged from my back pocket. Pulling it out,

I quickly read the message. "Hey." I looked up at Zayne. "Roth says that Lucifer already has someone who may know where Bael is holed up."

His brows lifted. "Damn. He works fast."

"That he does." I shoved my phone back in my pocket. If Lucifer had found someone, we needed to get over there ASAP. I hated to cut and run on Jada and Ty.

"Lucifer," she whispered, shaking her head again. "I can't believe you all are working with *the* Lucifer."

"Yeah," Zayne said. "Neither can we, so when this is all over, we're just going to pretend like it never happened."

I cracked a grin. "Sounds like a good plan."

"What…what is he like?" she asked, and then cringed. "I can't even believe I'm asking that."

"I don't think anyone can blame you for being curious." Zayne smiled at her.

How did one describe Lucifer? "He's, um, he's unique." Zayne snorted.

"Unique?" Ty repeated.

I nodded. "He's not what you'd expect and in a way *totally* what you'd expect from Satan. He's kind of a mess." An idea struck me—a way we could find out who it was that Lucifer had wrangled up and spend time with my friends. "Do you all want to meet him?" I offered, hopeful. "You would be safe. Or should be. I mean, he hasn't seriously threatened us or anything."

"He hasn't *seriously* threatened you guys?" Ty glanced between Zayne and I. "What did he do? Casually threaten you all?"

"We kind of had words," Zayne explained. "But things are fine now." He paused. "Sort of."

"That's reassuring," Ty mumbled.

"So? You guys want to come with us? He's at Roth's house."

"The one who is the actual Crown Prince of Hell?" Jada said.

I nodded. "And Layla will be there. She's part Warden and...yeah, so she's also Lilith's daughter. And yes, *the* Lilith. Also, Cayman may also be there. He's—"

"Let me guess," Ty interrupted. "He's also a demon."

"Middle management level, basically. Man, we have weird friends," I said.

"That we do," Zayne agreed.

I sighed. "Either way, if you guys don't want to, totally understandable. I can catch up with you all afterward."

Ty dragged his hand over his head. "Yeah, no offense, but I'm going to have to pass on that and take Dez up on his offer."

Jada looked over at Ty and then back to me. "This probably has 'bad life choice' written all over it, but yeah, I do want to meet him."

30

Ty wasn't at all happy about Jada's choice. He reminded her that her father would lose his ever-loving mind if he found out, which was true. I couldn't even begin to imagine the rather warranted meltdown Thierry would have, but Jada argued there was no reason for her father to find out. I also agreed with that. Ty tried to put his proverbial foot down, and that didn't end well for him. They argued. It was awkward, but Jada won out in the end, and Ty was going to have a lot of making up to do later.

"I kind of feel bad," I said, looking back at Jada as Zayne guided the Impala down the road leading to Roth's place. "I probably shouldn't have made the offer to bring you here."

Jada waved it off. "Ty will get over it. Besides, he really wanted to scope out the city with Dez. I think he has a friend crush on him."

I started to laugh, but a sudden tingle of awareness forced

me back around. We weren't nearly close enough to Roth's for me to be picking up on him.

"You feel that?" Zayne asked, and I nodded.

Jada leaned between the two seats as Zayne rounded the bend in the road. "Holy crap," she breathed. "How many demons did you say lived here?"

My eyes widened as I took in the front yard of the Mc-Mansion. There were demons everywhere. Sitting on the steps. Sprawled across the lawn. Lining the driveway. Some of them looked human. They could be Fiends, demons like Cayman who were more like middle management or Upper Level demons. Others were definitely not rocking human skin...or human heads, apparently, because some had two or three.

"Oh my God," gasped Jada. "What is *that*?"

I looked out the passenger window, spying a crimson-hued creature no bigger than three feet. I saw horns and a tail. "I have no idea," I whispered. The thing looked like a cartoon demon. "It was so not like this when we left this morning."

Zayne slowed as several of the larger demons started paying attention to us. He glanced in the rearview mirror. I followed his gaze, seeing that several human-looking demons had ended up behind us. "Jada," he said. "It's probably best you stay in the car."

Leaning back, I reached for my daggers to hand them over to her when I heard, "Hey! Get away from that car. Now! Shoo!"

Recognizing Layla's voice, I tipped forward and squinted. I caught a glimpse of platinum blond hair and then the sea of demons parted, shuffling back from the driveway on two and four...and eight legs.

"Is that...a giant spider?" Jada whispered. "If it is, I'm going to catapult myself off Earth right now."

I stared at the thing that looked very much like a spider half the size of the car scurry around the side of the house. "I'm getting in line with you."

Layla started toward us, stopping short when the red-skinned, cartoon-looking demon hopscotched across the driveway. She threw up her hands in obvious frustration.

"Am I hallucinating?" Jada asked.

"Honestly, there is no other explanation for any of this." I shook my head.

Zayne rolled down the window as Layla's face appeared at his side. "What in the world is happening here?"

"The worst block party ever?" she suggested, shoving her hair back from her face. "They started showing up like an hour or so ago. Apparently they sense Lucifer's presence, and everyone who is all like 'Hail Satan' is showing up." She glanced in the back seat and did a double take. "You're a Warden."

"I am," Jada replied tentatively.

"Jada, meet Layla," I jumped in. "She's from the Potomac Highlands community."

"And they let you leave?" Surprise filled Layla's tone.

"Well." Jada drew the word out.

"Are they dangerous?" Zayne cut in. "Causing any problems?"

"Not really." Layla's brows pinched. "But I would definitely pull the car into the garage so one of the demons doesn't end up sitting on it. Or eating it."

Zayne stared at her. "If one of them eats my car, I'm going to kill them."

She grinned. "We're not letting them in the garage or the house, so your precious should be safe. I'll go open it."

Layla turned then and started back to the house. "You need to stay out of the driveway. If not, you're going to get hit and no one will care."

There were some grumbled responses, but the demons scattered as Layla jogged back into the house.

"I have seen a lot of weird things," I said. "But this is superweird. It might even top the list."

"But at least they're all dressed." Zayne shot me a grin.

"Those little red things aren't," I pointed out. "I don't even know what kind of demon they are."

"I think they're sprites?" Zayne said. "I've never seen one before."

I watched the red demon hopscotch along the driveway. "Is the one, like, four years old?"

"I...I kind of think it's cute," Jada admitted. "In a weird, demonic way."

One of the garage doors shuddered opened, and Zayne carefully guided the car forward, eyeballing the demons the whole way. I didn't think he breathed until the Impala was parked inside.

Layla waited for us at the door. "Normally our house is nothing like this," she said the moment we joined her. "I know that may seem hard to believe, but we usually don't have demons everywhere."

Jada nodded. I thought she was handling all of this extremely well, but she'd always been curious. "It's okay,"

Jada said, smiling. "Except for the giant spider thing outside. That's not okay."

"I know, right?" Layla's wide eyes swung between Jada and I. "I asked Roth what that was, and you know how he responded? He said it was just a house spider."

"A house spider?" I exclaimed. "For whose house? Godzilla's?"

"Exactly." She led us through a short, narrow hall. "He then proceeded to tell me that there were even bigger spiders."

"I would literally set myself on fire if I saw a spider bigger than that," Jada said, and I shuddered.

"But what is it doing here?" I asked as Zayne curled his fingers around mine. "Did it come up from Hell?"

Layla glanced back at me. "I don't know if you want to know that answer."

"I kind of do," Zayne said.

"Supposedly it's been living in the subways," she answered. "Eats the LUDs."

"I am never getting on the subway," I told Zayne. "Ever. I don't care. Nope patrol right there."

"Noted." He shot me a grin. "But hey, at least it's eating the LUDs."

"It needs to do a better job at that," I muttered. "So, Lucifer was able to find someone? He stopped watching *Supernatural* long enough for that?"

"Yeah, and that has made him testy." Layla walked us through the kitchen and toward another narrow hall. "Which is why we're in the sitting room. The floor is tile in there."

I didn't have to ask why tile floor was important, because

I saw enough of what was going on in the sitting room. A human male stood in the center of the room, trembling. Thin rivets of blood ran out from the sleeves of his suit jacket, dripping onto the floor. The back of his trousers looked damp, and I had a feeling that wasn't blood.

Lucifer stood in front of him, arms crossed over his bare chest. He seemed unaware of us as we entered the room, wholly focused on the man. I gave a quick glance around the oval-shaped room. Roth and Cayman were standing on the opposite side, the latter chowing down on a slice of pizza.

Jada came to a complete stop, her eyes widening as she stared at Lucifer.

"Now, Johnny-boy, you've been so helpful with just the littlest motivation required," Lucifer said, his voice wrapping around the room like cool silk. "And I really don't want things to get ugly in front of my new friends. Johnny-boy, say hello to my new friends."

The man gave us a shaking glance. "H-hello."

Zayne's hand slipped free from mine. "What are you doing to this man?"

"Ah, don't worry, Fallen. Johnny-boy here was always destined to come face-to-face with me." Lucifer smiled, and there was a catch in my chest at how stunning that smile was. "It's just happening sooner than later. You see, Johnny worked very closely with one Senator Josh Fisher."

My gaze flew to the man. I hadn't seen Fisher's ghost since the night outside the church.

"Johnny-boy has already told us the names of every living person who was working alongside Fisher to aid Gabriel. They are being dealt with." Lucifer lifted a finger, pressing it to the man's cheek. "You don't want to be dealt with, now do you, Johnny-boy."

Smoke wafted out from the skin under Lucifer's finger. The smell of charred flesh filled the air as a slice of skin burned off. The man jerked, letting out a low whine.

"Jesus," Jada whispered, and I bet she was regretting her decision to come here.

I was starting to regret this decision.

"As if," Lucifer replied, falling onto the chair by the window. "I'm nothing like that whiney, all talk and very little action golden Boy."

Jada sat on a couch, I think so she didn't fall down.

I turned to him. "Did you, like, know Jesus?"

Those unfathomable eyes met mine as he hooked a leg over the arm of the chair. "Who do you think was whispering in Judas's ear?"

My eyes widened.

The corners of his lips curved and spread in a slow smile.

"Man," I whispered, sitting down beside Jada. "You are so creepy."

"Thank you."

"That wasn't a compliment," I murmured. "But whatever."

Lucifer refocused on the man. "What I need to know is, where is Gabriel?"

"I don't kn-know."

"You don't?" Lucifer tilted his head to the side. "What about Bael?"

"I d-don't know where either of them are now. They were at that h-hotel. The one the senator was s-staying at," the man said in a rush. "But they're n-not there any longer."

I wisely kept quiet as Lucifer studied the man. "What you're saying, then, is that you're virtually useless to me?"

"N-no! I'm not saying that all," the man was quick to respond. "I don't know where they're at, but I know they're planning something."

"Really?" Lucifer replied dryly.

The man nodded. "Yes. They have this portal——"

"You're boring me." Lucifer snapped his fingers.

The man's skin—it just peeled right off his body, exposing muscle and bone.

"Oh my God!" I jumped up, losing my balance on the cushion. I tumbled over the back of the couch while Jada remained frozen. Zayne moved incredibly fast, catching me as the man went down in a twitching, strangely bloodless heap of raw...raw *meat*.

Layla gagged as she clamped her hands over her mouth.

"Don't!" Cayman pointed at her. "Don't make that sound. I'm a——" His shoulders heaved as she gagged again. The man had stopped moving. "I'm a sympathetic puker."

"Oh my God," she gasped. "The smell——"

"Stop!" Cayman cried.

Layla pivoted, rushing from the room.

"Well, he's superdead." Roth pinned a glare on Lucifer. "Nice work."

"What? He can't...oh, yeah. He wasn't already dead." Lucifer shrugged. "My bad."

"How do you forget he wasn't already dead?" Zayne's chest rose with a deep breath. "I mean, really? I want to know."

"Well, I was kind of lying. I didn't forget." Lucifer picked up the remote. "He was just seriously boring me, and the last episode of *Supernatural* ended on a major cliffy."

I stared at him and then spoke a sentence I never thought I'd ever have to say. "You can't peel the skin off people just because they bore you."

"I can't?"

"No!"

"But I just did." Lucifer looked over at Jada. "Didn't I?"

I snapped out of my stupor. Pulling free from Zayne, I planted myself between Jada and Lucifer. The devil's smile kicked up a notch. "What good is he to us if he's dead?"

"What good was he alive?" Lucifer rose from the chair with the grace of a trained dancer. "He told us all he knew, which was the names of the other humans. They, too, will be questioned."

"By peeling off their skin?" Roth asked.

"If need be."

I shook my head as a demon appeared in the doorway. He gave off major Upper Level vibes as he strode into the room. He didn't even look at us as he picked up what was left of Johnny-Boy and carried him out of the room.

The smell was slow to follow.

"I'm getting some air freshener," Roth grumbled, stalking out the room. "And disinfectant."

"Do you think any of the names he gave you will know where Gabriel or Bael is?"

Lucifer appeared to consider that. "I'm going to be honest with you all. Like I always am," Lucifer said, and I fought to not roll my eyes. "I may have overestimated in my earlier confidence when it comes to rooting out their location. I have serious doubts that anyone knows where those two are. So, whatever plan you have to draw him out better work."

And with that, Lucifer sauntered out of the room.

"What was your plan again?" Cayman asked.

"Draw him out by challenging his ego," Zayne explained.

"There is plan B," I reminded him.

"Plan B is not on the table."

"It's not off the table, either." Dragging my gaze from the spot the man had fallen, I turned to Jada. "You okay?"

She nodded.

"If I'd known he was going to be doing that, I wouldn't have brought you," I told her.

Jada looked up at me. "I mean, you were bringing me to Lucifer. Not like I expected him to be knitting."

"He does like to do that, but with human skin," Cayman decided to share with us. "By the way, I'm Cayman. Your friends suck at introductions."

"Jada," she said.

Roth returned with air freshener. Layla was with him, carrying a WetJet and a tub of disinfectant wipes.

"Heads-up," Zayne said to him as Layla got down to scrubbing the floor. "Those angel blades? They're missing."

Roth stopped midspray. "What?"

As Zayne and Roth went down that road of whether or not a Warden would've taken the blades, Jada finally rose and wandered over to one of the windows. I didn't realize she was even listening to the conversation until she said, "You know, I wouldn't be surprised if a Warden did take them."

Everyone turned to her.

"I don't know you," Roth said. "But I like you."

She looked a little uncomfortable. "What I'm thinking is

that I wouldn't be surprised if a Warden took them and hid them. I mean, most Wardens aren't...friendly with demons, and even though that seems to be, uh, different here... No judgment," she was quick to add. "But I imagine not every Warden here is on board with that."

"They're not," Layla confirmed, looking over at Zayne. "You know that."

He blew out a heavy breath and nodded. "I could see one of them thinking the blades were safer stowed away where Gideon or Nic wouldn't know where they were."

"Or they want to use them against one of us," Roth stated. "Those blades need to be found."

"We'll add that to our ever-growing list of things that need to be done," Zayne commented.

Roth looked around the room, frowning. "Where is Lucifer?"

"I think he's in the living room." I yawned. "Back to watching *Supernatural*, I guess."

"Huh. Kind of like parenting a really annoying toddler, I imagine," Roth replied.

Layla closed her eyes and took a deep breath. "I don't think today can get any weirder."

"Um, guys?" Jada was staring out the window. "I think there is a legion of actual demons out here, playing...badminton? With a..." She took a step back from the window. "They're playing with that dude's head. The dude Lucifer de-skinned." She faced us. "They're actually playing badminton, using that dude's head as a shuttlecock."

We all turned to Layla.

"Sorry," she said, opening her eyes. "I'm never speaking again."

★ ★ ★

It was strange that after what we'd seen Lucifer do, we were able to sit down and eat an early dinner at one of the restaurants in the city.

I didn't know what that said about the three of us, but I was glad that I got to spend more time with Jada. We caught up, chatting about non-Harbinger-related things, and it was nice seeing her and Zayne interact.

It felt so…so normal.

It felt like a future, and even though Zayne's and my future wouldn't be easy considering the whole aging thing, it made me feel good. I held on to that feeling after returning Jada to the compound and while Zayne and I walked the city, hoping to draw out one of Gabriel's goons.

"What were you thinking you'd want for breakfast?" Zayne asked as we walked past several shops closed for the night.

I'd made plans to meet up with Jada and Ty for breakfast. That was if they weren't still fighting. I doubted that they would be. I knew that they'd have to return to the community in the next day or so. I was still expecting Thierry or Matthew to show up.

"I don't know." I scanned the dark trees, having not felt one single demon. All of them had to be congregating around either Lucifer or Gabriel. "I know they're not picky. Neither am I, so if you can think of a good place, I'm sure it will be okay."

"What if I picked a place that only made egg whites and spinach?"

"I'd stop talking to you."

"But you'd keep loving me."

"Reluctantly," I quipped.

Zayne laughed as he swooped down, kissing my cheek. "I'll find us a place with all the fried bacon you can eat."

"And waffles."

"What about pancakes?"

"Ew. No."

"What?" He looked down at me. "How can you like waffles and not pancakes?"

"I just don't."

"You're weird."

"I'm not the one who eats egg whites willingly."

"How is that weird? It's healthy—"

"That's all you need to say to prove my point." We neared an intersection. "You're not going to die of clogged arteries, so live a little and eat the yolk."

Zayne laughed as he placed his hand on my lower back and we crossed the street. He waited till there were several feet between us and anyone who could overhear our conversation. "I've been thinking about how to draw Gabriel out. The last you saw him, he was at that school. Obviously it was a trap, but what if that trap works both ways?"

I immediately picked up on what he was saying. "You're thinking about going to that school—to the portal, to possibly catch Gabriel's attention?"

"He has to have eyes on the place."

"I'm sure he does. I've been thinking of that, too." I paused as he snagged my arm, stopping me as someone cut directly in front of me, rushing into a convenience store. "But the school is still full of ghosts, wraiths and Shadow People. Actually, there are probably more there now than there were before."

"But the difference this time is that I can see them. It won't just be you that has to keep an eye on them," he pointed out.

I thought that over as our steps slowed and we neared several stone, abstract shapes that I was guessing were supposed to be artwork at an entrance to a city park. "That school is the last place I want to visit. It gives even me the creeps," I admitted. "But we may have more luck doing something like that than aimlessly roaming the streets." Stopping near a stone that looked like an oval doughnut, I looked up at Zayne. "Especially when Gabriel has to know that you aren't dead."

"And now a new and improved version," he added.

I cracked a grin. "And if the demons at Roth's place sensed Lucifer, then I imagine the ones who have been working with Gabriel also have sensed his arrival."

"Not to mention his fire display last night."

I nodded, surprised that was last night. It felt like a week ago. "He's probably going to be more careful."

"It's a plan." Zayne crossed his arms. "Better than you being bait and letting yourself get caught."

"That isn't a bad idea and it's still not off the table," I replied, watching Zayne's jaw harden in the glow of the streetlamp. "I know you don't like it, but if we can't get him or Bael to come out by going to the school, we need to try that. I don't want to wait until we're days away from the Transfiguration to try to stop him. That's cutting it too close and that's—" I stopped as a small group of people crossed the intersection. They were too far away and there wasn't enough light for me to see their features, but goose bumps spread across my arms as I watched them.

Three of them were talking and laughing among each other, but there was someone behind them—someone whose shadow didn't look right to me.

Zayne followed my gaze. The group passed under the light spilling out from the park. Three continued on. One didn't.

I squinted as the person walking behind them stopped and looked over at us.

"Holy shit," Zayne whispered.

I took a step forward and then another so I could see better.

And immediately wished I hadn't.

Only half of the man's head looked right. The other side was misshapen, caved in and, from what I could see, a bloody mess.

I recognized him.

Senator Fisher.

31

"I don't know if I want you to confirm or deny what I'm seeing," Zayne said.

"You really are seeing him," I whispered, still a bit shocked that he could.

"Do they always look like that?"

"Some do, unfortunately." I moved around Zayne. "Senator Fisher."

The ghost didn't move, but he did that bad reception on an old TV thing, scrambling in and out. "I've been trying to find you," he said, his voice sounding like he was in a long tunnel, standing at the other end. "But I keep ending up here, over and over."

Zayne twisted at the waist, and let out a low whistle. "The hotel is right across the street. I didn't even realize it."

"Serendipity?" I mused, crossing my arms as I focused on the senator. "You keep ending up here because this is where you died."

The ghost drifted forward. "It's also where I first met him."

"Bael?"

The ghost shook his head, and the sight turned my stomach. "No. Him. The Harbinger."

"I thought you said you only spoke with Bael," Zayne said.

"He said that he came to him," I reminded Zayne.

"I saw the Harbinger only once and then Bael," the senator said, coming even closer. I sort of wished he wouldn't. "I thought he was an angel answering my prayers. He is an angel. I thought he would help me. That he would bring back Natashya."

I'd felt pity for the man before, but there'd been mostly anger. But now? Now that I knew how he felt? There was more pity than anything else. "I'm sorry," I said. "I'm sorry that he lied to you. I'm sorry that you believed him."

One eye focused on me. The other eye…well, I didn't even want to know where that ended up. "She was everything—my strength, my courage. My backbone and the voice of reason. I would've never made it to where I did if she hadn't chosen me—"

A young man walked through the senator, causing the ghost to scatter. I tensed, holding my breath until the senator reappeared.

Zayne was staring at the young man's back. "He didn't even know he walked through him." He looked down at me. "How many times have I walked through ghosts?"

"You probably don't want me to answer that," I told him, and then refocused on Fisher.

"I'm never going to see her again, am I?" he asked, flickering. "I realized that when you all left. I had nothing left."

My heart squeezed. "Did you—?"

"It was the one like you. Sulien. He'd been watching. He was always watching." His voice faded out and came back. "I was going to find you—find you both and tell you what I knew, but Sulien was there...and now there's this thing that keeps following me. It's a light."

"And you don't want to go to it," I surmised, unsure if I was relieved or not to learn that he'd been thrown out of that hotel window. I really couldn't blame him, though, for avoiding the light. The senator knew enough now to know what awaited him, and it was most likely not going to be pretty. I wanted to lie, and not just because it may make him more likely to give us helpful information he'd held back on before, but because Fisher had been played in the worst ways. Maybe if he hadn't been preyed upon, he wouldn't have been in the position to do the damage that he'd done. But it was still a choice he made, and feeling bad for him didn't mean what he did was okay.

And I didn't lie when it came to this. "I don't think you'll see your wife," I told him, exhaling heavily. "The Harbinger preyed upon your grief and used it against you, but you made those choices, even after you began to sense something wasn't right. You'll have to answer for that, because you can't stay here. If you do, you'll end up even worse than you are now."

"But is...is God forgiving?" Fisher lifted half-formed hands. "I always believed that He was. That's what I was taught, but..."

But he met a homicidal archangel, so he was probably questioning everything he knew about God and all of that. I glanced at Zayne, unsure of how to answer.

"We don't know," Zayne spoke up. "And I don't think anyone really knows what can be forgiven and what can't be. Avoiding it, though? Probably not going to do you any favors."

The senator fell quiet as his gaze shifted to the hotel across the street.

I took a deep breath. "You were looking for me—for us? Did you have something to say? If so, you probably want to do it. I know you probably don't have much time until you lose hold—"

"And float," he said. "Sometimes I just float."

"That sounds…disturbing," Zayne murmured.

"I lied. I lied so many times to the people I represented, to families of those kids who were so hopeful," Fisher went on, and I struggled with my patience. "I lied to Natashya. Told her I would go on—that I wouldn't lose myself or lose faith. I lied to both of you." He continued to stare across the street. "It's there. The light."

Zayne turned, and I swore to God, if he was able to see it I may lose my mind. Luckily for him, I didn't think he did, because when he turned back, he was frowning.

"Why were you looking for us? You said you were going to come to us before Sulien showed up." I tried to get him back on track. "If you know something that could help us stop the Harbinger—"

"It won't undo all that I've done. It won't make things right."

"No," I said softly. "I don't think it will, but this is bigger than you—it's bigger than all of us. What the Harbinger plans will destroy this world and parts of Heaven. It will be the end of everything. We need to stop that."

"They're together." Senator Fisher's form scrambled. "The Harbinger and Bael. I lied when I said I didn't know where that was. I was afraid. A coward. I can't be afraid anymore."

I think Zayne and I stopped breathing.

"He's been staying at a farm in Gaithersburg." He rattled off an unfamiliar address. "That's where you should find them." He shuddered again, this time becoming more solid. "I'm sorry for all that I've done and it's time I reap what I sowed."

Senator Fisher took one more step forward and vanished before I could even say thank you.

"He's gone." Zayne turned in a slow circle. "Did he...?"

"He went into the light." Throat thick, I swallowed. "He went to judgment."

We were on the strangest damn conference call known to man. Roth, Layla and Lucifer on one end and Nicolai and several other Wardens on the other.

I was counting all my blessings that it wasn't a video call.

"It's about an hour from here, depending on the traffic," Zayne said, having looked up the address on his phone the moment after Senator Fisher had gone into the light. Now he had his laptop open and resting in his lap as we sat on the couch. We figured it was best to call both at the same time. So far, everyone had been playing nice.

Probably because Lucifer was apparently watching *Supernatural*.

Shocker.

"Turns out, the house was recently up for sale," Zayne said. "The listing is still on one of those realty websites."

"I don't think anyone is looking to buy right now," Roth tossed out there.

"Damn, here I thought you were looking for an upgrade," Zayne retorted, and I grinned as I pushed my glasses up my nose. "The reason why I'm bringing that up is because under property details it lists state-of-the-art video surveillance. Getting onto the property is going to be hard enough without Gabriel being aware, but it should be noted there are apparently cameras everywhere, including the barn."

"And how confident are we that Gabriel is there?" Nicolai asked.

"As confident as we can be," I spoke up. "I believe Senator Fisher was telling the truth. It's the best lead we got."

There were murmurings from the phone from the Warden side, and then I heard Nicolai ask, "So what's the game plan, then?"

Zayne looked over at me.

What? I mouthed.

He raised his brows as his jerked his chin toward the phone, telling me this was my show basically.

Which I appreciated.

But I squirmed a little, unused to, well, to being in control of anything so major. "I think we…" I cleared my throat as I focused on the phone. "We need to move on him fast. Get as much of the element of surprise as we can, especially since he has to be aware of what's happened with Zayne and that Lucifer is topside. The longer we wait, the more time it gives him to gather forces and prepare."

Zayne's gaze met mine when I looked up. He nodded as he said, "Agreed. We need to go at him fast and hard."

"That sounds dirty, Stony," Roth purred.

I shook my head at the phone.

"So, you're thinking...what? We do this tomorrow?" Nicolai asked.

My stomach tumbled a little. Tomorrow. Less than twenty-four hours, and that seemed like nowhere near enough time to prepare myself for coming face-to-face with Gabriel again.

But truth was, I'd been preparing for this all my life.

My thoughts settled, along with my stomach. "Tomorrow," I said, nodding. "Probably close to dusk. It will make it easier for us to get closer to the property instead of broad daylight. There's a lot of trees surrounding it, based on the pictures Zayne found, so that should help."

"Up to a certain point," Zayne tacked on. "I'm sure he has eyes on the area, but based on the listing, it looks like the property is off a private access road in a fairly wooded area."

"Which makes me think we should meet up at the closest but safest point," I said.

"Agreed," Nicolai said. "You have the entire clan backing you up on this."

"And we have all the demons that have come here," Roth said. "Is that going to be a problem? Wardens and demons working together?"

Zayne and I exchanged a look as we waited for Nicolai to speak.

"We got bigger problems than demons at the moment," Nicolai said. "We will not engage any demons who are working toward the same goal as long as they play nice."

"They'll play nice," Roth assured.

"Good," Nicolai clipped out.

I smiled. Demons and Wardens working together to stop

an archangel Hell-bent on ending the world. Who would've ever guessed that?

"I think we let him see only me first," I said. "He's going to know that others are with me, but hopefully not all we have on our side. We need that element of surprise."

When Zayne didn't disagree with that, I went on. "From there, it will be up to us to take care of Gabriel."

The conversation went on for a little bit after that, and then the time was picked, and when we ended the call with everyone, Zayne closed his laptop and looked over at me.

"How are you feeling about this?" he asked.

I thought that over. "Good, I think. Hopeful. In twenty-four hours, this could be all over."

His gaze flickered over my face as he nodded. "It's a good plan. We will stop Gabriel."

"We will." My gaze met his, and there was a catch in my chest.

This would end tomorrow night. Either we succeeded or we failed, but it would end, because there would be no second chances after this.

The reality of that struck me then as I stared at Zayne. If we didn't succeed, we wouldn't be able to launch another attack, because people would be wounded in this. Failure meant Gabriel would capture me, and that I couldn't allow. So either Gabriel died or...

I didn't let that thought finish, but the heaviness was still here. The weight of what I would need to do if we failed had already settled on my shoulders.

Heart kicking around in my chest, I took off my glasses and carefully folded the arms, placing them on the coffee table.

I didn't know what Zayne was thinking when I picked up the laptop, tossing it on the nearby cushion, and took its place. There was a fire in his eyes, though. A golden-white glow behind his pupils that burned bright.

The tips of his fingers brushed over the line of my cheekbone and the curve of my jaw as I skimmed my fingers along his lower lip. "I love you," he whispered.

I dipped my head, my lips replacing my fingers. This kiss started slow and gentle and we took our time, as if we were mapping the layout of our lips and committing the shape to memory. The kiss became fierce, full of soul-burning yearning and a hint of desperation, consuming both of us. Somehow, we made it to the bedroom, and our clothing came off with a speed that was rather impressive and then…then our bodies melded together.

Behind every touch and every kiss there was the knowledge that I didn't want to give life to. So I used my mouth, my hands and my body to say what I couldn't ever say to Zayne.

If we didn't stop Gabriel, I wouldn't be coming home with Zayne. This would be our last time together.

The following day started off like any other normal, good day.

Zayne and I had breakfast with Jada and Ty that lasted till lunch. They wanted to be there tonight, but as trained as Ty was and even though Jada could defend herself, neither were ready for this. They weren't happy, but they understood.

Hugging Jada goodbye as we parted ways was hard, because those words I didn't want to give life to the night before haunted me. It could be the last time I saw her.

Zayne and I spent the rest of the time alone. We watched several episodes of *Fresh Prince*. I got Zayne to drink a can of soda as we shared a bowl of superyummy berry-flavored Italian ice and then we shared ourselves with each other.

And as I dressed an hour before we were supposed to meet with everyone, I kept searching for Peanut. As I strapped on my daggers and then braided my hair, I listened to hear any sign of him. As we walked out the door, I stopped to look for him once more...just in case.

He wasn't there.

The drive to the farmhouse was quiet, as was the walk to where we were supposed to meet the others. We held hands the moment we stepped out of the Impala, both reaching for the other at the same moment. When we neared the group, Zayne stopped us.

He kissed me.

And it was the kind of kiss that held everything we felt for one another. It was a kiss that was deep, claiming and carried a hint of desperation. It was a kiss that promised more—*demanded* more. I was a little shaken when he lifted his mouth from mine, and neither of us moved for a long moment. I think we both wanted to stay there, right there, but we couldn't. We knew that, and we started walking again.

As Zayne and I approached them, I saw only Dez and Nic were there, standing as far away as they could from the other three. I really couldn't blame them since one of them was Lucifer, who... I squinted. Who was apparently watching something on an iPad.

"You guys are here." Nicolai turned to us, and there was no mistaking the relief in his voice.

"Where is everyone else?" I asked.

"We figured it would be better if the others hung back," Nicolai explained, glancing toward the fallen tree Lucifer was perched on. "Less chance for things to go south."

"It's a good call," Layla said. "His legion of unwanted houseguests is also staying back."

"I don't think any of that is really necessary," Roth said. "Like Lucifer is even aware of what is happening right now."

Lucifer didn't even appear to hear us.

"He has earbuds in," Zayne explained. "Let me guess— *Supernatural*?"

Layla nodded.

"I can't believe Lucifer is sitting over there with an iPad," murmured Dez. "This feels like a lucid dream."

"The last several days of my life have felt like a lucid dream," Layla replied.

Grinning at her, Roth then turned to me. "You ready to do this?"

My heart skipped a beat. "Yes. Is he?"

"He is. He knows the plan. Backup is here. Well, almost all backup." Roth dragged a hand over the center of his chest. "Time to play."

Wispy black smoke floated out from underneath Roth's shirt, spilling into the air beside him. The shadows shifted into thousands of little black dots spinning in the air, like minicyclones.

Bambi was the first to come off his skin and take form. The giant snake immediately slithered her way over to Zayne and I.

Three shadows formed from the spinning beads, dropping to the ground—black, white and a mixture of both. Above them, I saw iridescent blue and gold...scales that appeared along the belly and the back of the dragon.

Holy crap, it was the dragon I'd heard about. Excitement filled me, because *dragon*.

My eyes widened as deep red wings sprouted, along with a long, proud snout and clawed hind legs. Its eyes matched Roth's, a bright yellow.

But...but it was, like, the size of a small dog.

I looked down. Three kittens toddled about, one all white, one completely black and a third that was black and white. The white one pounced on the black-and-white kitten, knocking it over and falling over onto its back in the process. The black one jumped, sweeping at the baby dragon's tail.

Slowly, I lifted my head to Roth. I'd never been more disappointed in my life.

"They don't get out much," he said with a shrug.

"Kittens?" I whispered. "And a baby dragon? Seriously? You brought kittens and a baby dragon as backup? Are they a snack for Bambi?"

The black kitten hissed at me.

"Just wait," Layla said as Bambi slid over my foot, lifting her diamond-shaped head. I wasn't sure what I was supposed to be waiting for as Bambi nudged my hand, obviously wanting pets. I patted her head, my hand freezing when the white kitten stretched out its teeny, tiny paws and yawned.

Actually yawned.

"Nitro's just getting warmed up," he said as Dez and Nicolai stared.

"Do you think they can speed this up?" Zayne said under his breath. "Because this is getting awkward."

The little fluff of fur mewled as the fur stood up along the center of its back. It opened its mouth again, and I swore to God, if it yawned once more, I was just going to kick Roth.

In the face.

And then grab the little guys and hide them before they ended up getting trampled to death.

Except what came out of it was a meow that rose and deepened into a guttural growl that raised the hairs all over my body. The black one let out a snarl that didn't match its body, and the black-and-white one hissed like a very large, very angry predator.

And then they *changed*.

The ball of white fur grew and expanded; legs lengthening and shoulders widening. Sleek muscles appeared and fragile claws grew into thick, sharp ones. That cute mewl turned into a roar as Nitro's snout lengthened, mouth opening to bare shark-size fangs.

On four legs, the kittens reached my waist. Totally large enough to eat me.

"Holy crap," I whispered.

Roth stroked a hand down the center of the black-and-white one while the dragon remained pint-size as it sat on Layla's shoulder. "This is Fury. The black one is Thor," Roth said. "And they like to eat things they're normally not supposed to, don't they? Like Wardens?"

"Roth," Layla warned before turning to the Wardens. "He's just kidding."

The way the one named Fury stared at the two Wardens told me not to be so sure about that.

Time to redirect attention. "What about Robin?" I asked. "Does he get bigger?" The image of a giant fox creeped me out.

"He will once he gets older," Layla said, touching her covered arm. "He's still a baby, though. If I let him off, all he would do is chase his tail."

I laughed.

"You all done standing around, thinking I'm not paying attention?" Lucifer asked, startling every single one of us. He stared up at us, iPad cradled to his chest. "The sun is setting. It's time."

The next breath I took snagged in my chest as the shadows continued to grow inside the woods. Lucifer was right.

It was time.

32

The rolling hills of the lush green lawn looked as pictur-esque as a postcard at dusk, but the moment I stepped out from the heavy tree line, my demon spidey senses were going off all over the place.

And that had nothing to do with the fact that Lucifer was standing a few feet behind me, surprisingly enough.

Feeling Zayne's gaze on me as I walked forward, I scanned the blurry house ahead. I saw no movement, but a wave of goose bumps broke out across my arms. I stopped less than half the length of a football field from the sprawling colonial-style farmhouse. I squinted as the last of the sun seeped away and shadows rapidly grew along the front porch of the house, pressing against the white pillars and the walls of the first floor.

Except they weren't normal shadows. They moved too quick, darting from one pillar to the next like Ping-Pong balls.

Shadow People.

"Hey," I called out, the hot tingling at the base of my neck growing.

The shadows stilled.

That was a little unnerving. "Is the Harbinger of Overly Long Monologues home?"

Whispers carried on the breeze reached me, the voices of the SP too low for me to understand. "If he is," I yelled. "Tell him it's rude to keep visitors waiting even if it's a surprise."

"A surprise?" Gabriel's voice echoed all around, but I didn't see him. "Silly nephilim."

I tensed, gaze flickering from the house to the thin trees lining the driveway. He could be anywhere, and with my vision, I'd never know, but I had other eyes with far better vision backing me up.

Without warning, dozens of floodlights from the house and side yards sparked to life. Bright white light funneled through the gathering darkness. Blinded, I didn't resist the urge to shield my eyes. I lifted a hand as my eyes watered and stung from the intense light. Cloudy splotches gathered in my vision as my *grace* stretched at my skin. My eyes would adapt—hopefully—but it would take a couple of minutes.

A shape appeared behind the house, sweeping into the air. I could make out the width of wings. My heart skipped a beat. There he was. I drew in a deep breath and nearly choked on the sickly sweet smell of...of *rot*.

Where was that coming from? I quickly looked around me, and from what I could see, there was nothing nearby. If there were and I was unaware, Zayne would be out here in a nanosecond. Could that smell be coming from Gabriel?

I lowered my hand, wishing I could see him. All I could

tell was that he was hovering above the house like a demented guardian angel.

I ignored the insult as I forced my arms loose at my sides. "You've been looking for me, so I decided to come to you."

"I appreciate that." Gabriel's wings moved silently in the air. "Makes my life so much easier."

"You sure about that?"

His laugh reached me, sending a rush of iciness through me. "Oh, I am sure." He drifted over the home, stopping in front of the porch. "Just as I'm sure you did not come alone."

Warning pricked my skin even though I wasn't surprised he knew. "I would be stupid to come here alone, and I'm not stupid."

"We'll have to agree to disagree on that, child of Michael."

My eyes narrowed. "How're those bullet wounds treating you, Gabriel?"

His wings stilled. "I'll make sure I show you in great detail later."

"I think I'll pass," I told him. "But I did bring you a present. Spoiler alert, it's not me."

"Spoiler alert?" Confusion filled the archangel's tone.

I sighed. "You don't even know what a spoiler alert is? I mean, come on, this is getting ridiculous."

Gabriel flew forward suddenly, and in the next heartbeat, I felt the warmth of Zayne at my back. The golden white glow of his wings washed over me.

Gabriel halted, still several feet away. "Is that who you've brought me?" he asked. "A Fallen in need of his wings and *grace* to be stripped? I'll be more than happy to kill him." He paused. "Again."

Anger flushed my system, but I knew better than to cave to it. I learned that the hard way. "He's a gift," I said, keeping my voice level. "But not for you."

Zayne's right wing brushed over my back as he came to stand by my side. "You're not looking very well, Gabriel," Zayne said, disgust creeping into his voice. He was right. The archangel was close enough for me to see that there was more of an oily sheen to his wings and skin than a luminous glow. "And is it you that smells like decay?"

"You smell that, too?" I asked. "Because I was wondering if Gabriel crapped himself or something."

"My brother didn't crap himself," Lucifer said, and my hands balled into fists. Of course he didn't listen to me. He came to stand to my left. "Yet."

"That's your surprise," I said, feeling like this was so anticlimactic now. "Surprise," I exclaimed, throwing in jazz hands in the process.

"I do not accept this gift," Gabriel snarled.

"Too bad," I said. "No returns or exchanges."

Gabriel focused in on his brother. "I knew I felt the taint of your presence."

"The taint of *my* presence? Have you smelled yourself recently?" Lucifer looked up at Gabriel. "Your essence—your Glory is rotting."

"My Glory is not rotting," the archangel snapped.

"Um." I drew the word out. "Something on you is definitely rotting."

"Even mine never smelled that bad." A twinge of awe filled Lucifer's tone as he continued to stare up at Gabriel. "You know what that means."

"You have no idea what you speak of," Gabriel bit back.

"What does that mean?" I asked, glancing at Lucifer.

The devil smiled. "I have a feeling we're going to find out."

Gabriel drew farther back. "You know what I plan, brother. You of all people should be celebrating what needs to be done. I will end this—end this corruption that has become this realm. I will do what needs to be done. And yet you stand before me instead of behind me?"

"Yeah, well, what you plan is my kind of party," Lucifer said. "But it ain't my party. You feel me?"

"He probably doesn't get your analogy," I told him.

"I understand it fine," snapped Gabriel. "I give you this one chance, Lucifer. More than our Father ever gave you. Join me, and together, we will end this."

Lucifer cocked his head to the side. "Now, you know damn well Father gave me so many chances it was absurd. Even I can admit that, but you? Oh, Gabe, what have you done to yourself?"

The twinge of genuine sadness in Lucifer's voice caught my attention.

He was shaking his head. "You were only ever supposed to be the voice of God. No more. No less. And yet that wasn't enough. You became bitter. Jealous. So full of pride."

"You speak to me about striving for more? Of pride?" Gabriel thundered, and I mean, he kind of had a reason to be dumbstruck. "You? You, who wanted to rule beside God?"

"So? I still see nothing wrong with that. What I wanted was the power due to me and for that I was cast to Earth." A glow began to seep through his skin. "But I was never barred from the Heavens. Tell me, brother, when was the last time you were able to enter the Heavens? When is the last time you spoke to God? Heard the divine Voice? I hear it now. Do you?"

Wait. What?

"Lies," Gabriel hissed. "You do not hear the divine Voice."

"Believe what you will, but I'm going to kill you tonight." Lucifer's eyes briefly closed. "Know that I will mourn you deeply, if only for a few moments."

My brows lifted. Moments? He would mourn him for *moments*? Ouch.

Gabriel drew back as if slapped. "So be it, Satan."

Crimson streaked across Lucifer's eyes. "Oh, no, you did not just call me that."

The archangel flew back, lifting his arms. "I knew you would come to me, child of Michael, this very night."

My head snapped his direction as tension crept into my muscles.

"So, I've prepared my own gift for you," he continued. "It's a shame, though, that you will have to witness so many of those you care for perish."

Movement on the ground drew my gaze to the areas alongside the home. From this distance they were nothing but blobs of different colors and shapes, but I saw enough to know they were demons and there were many.

"How many?" I asked Zayne.

"Hundreds," he answered, looking across to Lucifer. "That's a lot of demons mad at you."

"There will always be demons unhappy with the rules," he replied. The ever-growing mass continued to bulge out from the house. "Gabriel knew you'd have time to prepare if you learned," Lucifer answered. "He really did know we were coming tonight. Someone betrayed you."

Pressure clamped down on my chest. Someone most definitely did.

"I cannot help but think of those angel blades," Zayne commented.

"Same," I whispered, taking a deep breath and exhaling slowly. "How many of your legion were you able to wrangle?"

"Enough," Lucifer answered.

"And when are they going to get here?" Zayne asked.

"Hopefully soon."

"Kill the Fallen," Gabriel ordered. "The nephilim must be alive."

"I'm kind of disappointed." Lucifer pouted. "What about me?"

There was no answer as a wave of demons burst forward, most on the ground but some in the air. A few looked like imps, but others... Their wings gleamed white in the moonlight.

"What about us?" Roth announced, stalking out from the wood line. Layla was beside him, her black feathered wings always a shock to see, but not nearly as distracting as the baby dragon perched on his shoulder. I didn't see the giant kittens.

I hoped they weren't eating the Wardens.

"That's a whole lot of demons," Layla said, iron daggers in hand.

"We got this," Zayne said, looking at me. "Don't we?"

I nodded even as my heart started thumping. "We do."

The line of demons advanced, and I started to draw on my *grace* when Thumper flew off Roth's shoulder, letting out a squeak of warning—a squeak which turned into a roar so loud it felt like my bones rattled.

My breath caught as I watched Thumper grow, sprouting legs the size of tree trunks and claws larger than my own hands.

Zayne grabbed me, hauling me out of the way as those crimson wings unfurled, lengthening to a size triple that of Zayne's. The tail hit the ground, cracking the top layer of grass and soil wide open.

Wide eyed, I watched the dragon the size of two tanks stretch its neck out, mouth open in another roar. Sparks flew from his nostrils as the scent of brimstone filled the air.

Hellions and Nightcrawlers rushed us. They didn't slow when they spotted Thumper. Instead, they split, veering in two directions.

Roth's familiars were having none of that.

Thumper's head whipped to the right, mouth snapping open. Fire poured out, hitting the group of demons, incinerating them.

I stumbled back, bumping into Zayne. "That's a dragon."

Zayne steadied me as Roth chuckled. Thumper caught another demon by its mouth. Bones crunched. "And he's hungry," Zayne commented.

"Very," Roth agreed.

"Heads-up." Layla's wings lifted. "Incoming."

The white kitten that was now the size of a small horse streaked out from the woods, leaping into the air. Landing on a Hellion, Nitro sunk his teeth into the demon's neck, taking the Hellion to the ground. Thumper lifted, snagging a demon up with him.

"The imps," Roth called out as he strode forward, his

skin thinning as wings sprouted from his back and horns protruded from the top of his head. "Eat the yummy imps, Thumper."

I didn't even have time to think about that. Golden white spilled down Zayne's arms and the two sickle blades appeared as a mass of demons reached us.

"Remember the plan," Lucifer said. "We need to weaken Gabriel."

"Understood," Zayne said as I nodded.

Unhooking a dagger, I summoned my *grace*. The weight of the Sword of Michael formed against my palm as Zayne lopped off the head of a Raver.

A Hellion raced past the kittens and dragon, grabbing for me, but I dipped under its arm and spun around, slicing the fiery sword through its back. I whirled around as Lucifer shoved his hand through the chest of the Nightcrawler.

"You done messed up," Lucifer growled, yanking its heart out. Flames erupted from his palm and then the Nightcrawler.

Bambi shot out of the mist gathering among the grass, catching an imp and dragging it back to the ground.

Shooting forward, I kicked out, catching a Raver in the midsection. It stumbled back, mouth open and teeth snapping at air. I shot forward, thrusting the dagger into its hairless chest. Hot blood sprayed my face as I yanked the dagger out. I kept moving forward, getting a little lost in the fight and the pumping adrenaline. Demons fell all around us as Thumper tore through the sky, snatching up imps left and right.

"He's going to have a tummy ache," I said.

Roth ripped through the neck of a Nightcrawler. "That's what Pepto is for."

I snorted. "You're going to need a big bottle—"

Roth lurched for me as fingers tangled in my braid, jerking my head back. I gasped as I suddenly stared up into the young face of some kind of winged demon.

"Gotcha," it grunted, wings sweeping down as he lifted up—

Without warning, the demon's head just fell off. The grip on my hair relaxed as the demon fell.

"Got you," Zayne growled from above.

"That was hot," I whispered as Roth grabbed my arm, pulling me out of the way of the demon slamming into the ground. "Thanks."

Zayne landed beside me. "Thank me later."

I smiled. "Planning on it."

"Gross, guys." Roth launched into the air, joining Layla.

The trees rattled behind us, as if a hundred birds were taking flight. I turned, seeing the dark shapes of Wardens spilling out into the air while Lucifer's legion poured out from between the trees, racing forward.

Zayne grinned, his gaze meeting mine. My smile kicked up a notch as a Warden dropped to the ground.

A wall of flames went up behind, stretching so high I couldn't see the trees behind it. Heat blew back, singeing our skin. At first I thought it was Lucifer, but he was ahead of us.

Then I heard the shouts—the screams—and my heart sank. The Wardens. Dez. Nic. Jordan—

I cut those thoughts off before I let them take hold. I couldn't go down that road right now.

"Bael!" Lucifer shouted, whipping around. "Where are you, you conniving, traitorous—?"

A ball of flames spun from the corner, nearly catching the black kitten's back legs. Another ball of flames rippled across the sky. Thumper dived, but wasn't quick enough. The dragon shrieked as the flames singed his wings.

Roth spun around. "Familiars!" he shouted. "Return to me. Now!"

The familiars turned to shadows as they flew back to Roth, forming beads as they dropped down onto his bare skin. Roaring, Roth turned and shoved his hands through the chest of a nearby demon.

Spinning around, Zayne scanned the yard. "Where is Teller?"

"That was him?" I dipped, springing up behind a Raver. I lopped off its head.

"He was just here." Zayne kept searching. "I don't see him."

"Did the flames get him?" I asked, shoving the dagger into the chest of an imp.

Shaking his head, Zayne turned to me. "Pull your *grace* in," he ordered. "You're starting to weaken." Stalking toward me, he wiped his fingers under my nose. "Pull it in, Trin."

I swiped at my face, but Zayne had gotten the blood. I wanted to deny it, but he was right. Pulling on the *grace* was weakening me. I let it go, cursing as the Sword of Michael collapsed into fiery embers.

Layla dropped on the ground in a crouch, rising slowly. "Dear God," she panted. Oily blood spotted her face and hair. "It's like we haven't even made a dent." She looked over her shoulder. "We needed them." She turned to where Lucifer stood. "We need your backup."

Snarling, he ripped the wings off an imp he caught. "They can't get through."

Heart racing, I peered into the mist and bright light, making out thicker, darker shapes ahead.

This was bad.

So freaking bad.

But that didn't change what we had to do.

Swallowing hard, I turned to Zayne and stretched up, clamping a hand around the back of his neck. I pulled his head down to mine and kissed him. And it was no chaste kiss. Or tender. Our lips bruised together. Our bodies melded into one another. I drank him up in that kiss, as he did me.

When our lips parted, he was breathing raggedly as he pressed his forehead to mine. "We just need to get to Gabriel." He reached down, unhooking my other dagger. "That's all. We get to him and we end this."

I nodded. "Let's do this."

"We'll back you up," Layla said as we pulled away. "We'll keep them off you."

"Thank you." I took the dagger Zayne handed me.

He turned to Layla, touching her cheek softly. "Be safe."

"You, too." She swept into the sky.

Cutting through the demons, we caught up to Lucifer.

Crimson streaked his skin as he looked back at us. "We just need one shot, but we got a Hell of a lot of demons to go through." His wings were out, tucked back and close to his body. "No matter what, Bael is mine."

"You can have him." Zayne swept a blade through the air, severing a Nightcrawler.

I thrust my dagger into the chest of a Hellion, and I let my rage take hold then, feeding me strength as my dagger sliced through the neck of another. I didn't hesitate or pull back when the tips of claws skated down my arms, sending a wave of pain through me. I didn't stop or look back when I heard Roth shout out a mouthful of curses. The three of us kept moving forward. I kicked off the ground, slamming my dagger in the leg of a winged demon as it swept down to grab Zayne. It fell to its back and then under Lucifer's boot. I picked up the pace, jumping over a body as it broke apart and grabbing a fistful of Raver's fur. I yanked his head back as I swung the dagger into the center of its back. The Raver screeched as I let go, his body catching fire.

Another wall of flames went up, too close to Zayne for comfort. The flame hit Lucifer, causing my heart to stop as he bellowed.

He staggered back as the fire swept across his body, exposing muscle and tissue. "Now that really pisses me off," he yelled. His body seemed to already repair itself, but his wings...

Half of them were gone.

Panic bubbled in my throat and I fought it down as the wall of fire continued. I followed its path, knowing what I'd see.

Layla and Roth were now closed off, and it was just the three of us.

"Give up," called Gabriel. "You're not going to win. You lost the first day man sinned. It's already too late. It's always been too late."

I hated it—hated it so much, because Gabriel...he might be right. I looked out, the ground choked with mist and smoke, and I could see a mass of demons coming forward. A practical army of them left, and it was just three of us.

Zayne landed beside me as a horrible, sinking realization hit me. I looked down at my dagger, stomach hollowing. I turned to him, my gaze searching out those beautiful blue eyes.

Zayne's gaze dropped and then lifted back to mine. Understanding skittered across his face. "No."

"I have to." The back of my throat burned.

"No, Trin. Absolutely not—"

My eyes burned. "He can't use me to open the portal, Zayne. He can't. I have to end this and I can. If he can't use me to open the portal—"

"I don't give a fuck about the portal." He shot forward, catching my wrists. "I will not allow you to do this."

A crack started in my chest. "I don't want to, but it's the only way."

"If we leave now—if we run—we aren't going to win the second round," Lucifer warned. "It's either now or never. One way or another."

"Shut up," Zayne snapped, and I was surprised Lucifer said nothing in return. "Forget this. Forget all of this. We run. We keep running and hiding until the whole damn world falls apart."

"Do you hear what you're suggesting?" My eyes widened.

"I don't care," he swore. "I don't care about any of this. All I care about is you."

"You don't mean that—"

"The Hell I don't," Zayne growled.

I twisted, not making it very far as Zayne held on to my wrists. My gaze collided with Lucifer's once more, and the look on his face said it all. It had to be now. There would be no later. Gabriel would capture me. He'd kill Zayne. He'd kill Roth and Layla and anyone else who was still alive. I couldn't let that happen.

"I love you, Zayne. I love you with every fiber of my being," I said, and then nodded at Lucifer.

He charged forward, slamming into Zayne's side as I pulled with all my strength, breaking his hold. Zayne and Lucifer hit the ground, and it was...

It was surreal, like an out-of-body experience. As if it wasn't even me who stood there, right hand steady as Zayne shouted, as Lucifer held him down, turning his head to the side, away from where I stood in a gesture I wouldn't have expected from Satan. I felt nothing as I lifted the dagger. Or maybe I was feeling everything and it was too much, overriding my senses. I lifted my eyes, not wanting to see nothing, but all I saw was gray smoke as I—

A trumpet blared, the sound sudden and loud, seeming to come from all around us. The ground and the very air around us rattled, throwing Lucifer to the side. Zayne popped to his feet, and in a second, his arms swept around me, clamping them to my sides, but I didn't fight him as I stared up at the sky.

At *stars*.

33

"Someone is in trouble," Lucifer sang from where he sat on the ground. "And it's not meee."

Zayne and I looked over at him as he threw his head back, laughing.

Gabriel flew into the air, appearing above the shifting horde of demons and angels. "No! No!" he shouted. "You have got to be kidding me."

The trumpet sounded a third time, and I looked up again. The glimmers of bright lights in the sky were rapidly growing closer.

"Do you see this?" I breathed.

"I do." Zayne held on to me tightly.

Stars fell out of the sky, one after another.

That's what they looked like as they raced toward Earth. Dozens and dozens of them. Angels. Actual battle angels.

I couldn't believe what I was seeing.

Their wings were bright with *grace* and their weapons

fiery, golden flames. The demons started to turn, to run, but it was too late as they swept through the horde between us and Gabriel.

"You have got to be kidding me!" shouted Gabriel once more, rising into the air. "Now? Now You decide to do something?"

"Someone is about to have a fit," Zayne remarked.

Gabriel took out several trees.

"About to?" I asked.

A tree fell onto the roof of the house as the ground ahead was lit with heavenly glow.

"It's not over," Lucifer said. "Not yet."

He was right.

"We need to move fast," Lucifer continued. "I doubt the battle angels are going to hang around. Neither will Gabriel."

The specks of bright light surrounding the angels were already disappearing, launching back into the sky.

"You ready to finish this?" Zayne dipped his head to mine. "The right way?"

"What I was going to do was the right way in that moment," I stated, heart slamming against my ribs. "It's not now."

"We'll talk about this later," he promised, and I rolled my eyes. "I saw that."

"No, you didn't."

"You rolled your eyes." He let go of my arms.

"I did not." I totally did.

"We'll talk about your habitual lying later also."

"When you guys are done with your foreplay, let me know," Lucifer commented, shaking a wing that was slowly repairing itself.

I didn't even bother responding to that as we started forward, picking up speed as we raced across the field.

I didn't even see the demon until Lucifer launched into the air and came down beside a narrow elm. He yanked a tall demon out from behind it.

"Hello, Bael." Lucifer shoved his hand through his—

My steps stumbled. Lucifer's hand had gone straight through Bael's *head*. His actual head. The face. The skull. Oh my God.

The wall of flames collapsed as Lucifer dropped Bael. "Goodbye, Bael."

Zayne threw out his hand, catching me as Gabriel burst out from the smoke, screaming, fiery blade in hand.

"Jesus." I skidded to a stop, summoning my *grace*. It stuttered and then flared hotly. *Grace* pulsed through me. The Sword of Michael exploded in my hand.

"Unbelievable!" Gabriel shouted, swinging at Zayne in pure rage. His blow was blocked by Zayne's sickles. "Do you really think you'll win if you kill me? Mankind is doomed, anyway—"

"Can you not shut up?" I said.

Gabriel drew back, his head shooting toward me. A moment later, a Warden dropped to the ground behind him. It took me a moment to realize who it was.

Teller.

And in his hands was an angel blade.

"Kill them," Gabriel ordered. "Kill them, but leave the nephilim alive."

Two things struck me at once.

That Teller was answering his demand. He shot forward

so fast, swinging out with one angel blade, that none of us immediately responded.

And I remembered the day in the high school—when the Shadow Person had slammed into Teller, knocking him out. It had gone into him, and it had never come back out.

I snapped out of it first, flipping the dagger in my hand. Cocking my arm back, I threw the dagger as hard as I could. It struck true, hitting in the base of the skull. Teller went down before he could even reach Zayne.

There was no time to celebrate that or to find that damn blade in the mist-covered ground. Gabriel came at me.

I ducked as his fiery blade sliced through the air. Shooting forward, I dipped and twisted, kicking out and catching him at the kneecap. He stumbled, swinging out with his fist as I popped up. There wasn't enough time for me to avoid the blow completely. I tried, jumping back, but a flare of pain streaked across my stomach. I sucked in a sharp breath, gritting my teeth. "I think it's time you gave this up. It's over."

"It is?" Gabriel laughed as Lucifer appeared behind the archangel. Gabriel sneered. "You're already dead."

"A bruise," I said, ignoring the burn traveling up my stomach and along my back. "Can't say the same for you, though."

His brows furrowed as Lucifer saw his opening.

And took it.

Lucifer shot forward just as Gabriel spun around. I saw the impact, and almost fell to my knees in relief when Lucifer yanked his bloodied hand back. Even I could see the thumping, fleshy mass in his fist.

"Now!" Lucifer shouted.

Zayne swooped in from above and landed, the twin

sickle-shaped swords flaming as I shot forward. The Sword of Michael felt heavier than before as I lifted it, the weight not as welcomed. Clasping the handle with both hands, I jabbed out with a shout as Zayne whipped his swords through the air.

The Sword of Michael pierced Gabriel's back and cut straight through. The archangel spasmed, arms flinging out. His sword collapsed and he dropped the dagger. A heartbeat later, Zayne's crescent swords sliced through Gabriel's neck, severing his head.

Oh my God.

My next breath punched out of my lungs as I watched the archangel's head fall.

Intense light poured out of the stump that was Gabriel's neck, so bright that I was blinded until I reached up with one hand, shielding my eyes. Even then, they watered as I watched the funnel of light stream upward. The light... chunks of black swirled inside it. That really didn't look right. My *grace* retracted and the Sword of Michael evaporated. Gabriel's body erupted in flames, leaving nothing behind as the light smashed through the sky, stretching up and up, farther than I knew even Zayne could see. Streaks of midnight oil twisted and pulsed inside the stream of light.

It was Gabriel's *grace*, returning to the source. The next breath I took felt too thin.

The heavenly fire slammed into something I didn't think any of us could see. It was like an invisible...force field? That sounded stupid, but it hit something. The whitish-gold fire exploded with a clap of thunder that echoed. The *grace* rippled outward.

There it was.

Unsteady, I staggered back a step. God was doing it. Even though God had sent those angels down to fight off the horde of demons, God had done it. Punted the tainted *grace* back to Earth. Dizzy with horror, I watched it crawl across the sky in an endless wave stretching as far as I could see.

How in the world could anyone explain this sight away?

A hysterical giggle rose up and only by sheer force was I able to stop it as the twisted mass spread. We did it. We stopped Gabriel. We saved Heaven.

And now a different kind of Hell would reign on Earth.

I started to turn to Zayne, my body so incredibly weary. Vaguely aware of others approaching us, I heard Zayne inhale sharply.

"God," he whispered, staring up at the sky.

My head jerked upward, and I blinked, because I wasn't sure if I was seeing what I thought I was or if it was some kind of trick of the imagination.

The *grace* had stopped moving.

"Can you see it?" Zayne asked, moving to my side. "It's like…it's frozen."

"I can see it." I didn't dare take my eyes off it. "What is this, Lucifer?"

He didn't answer.

Or maybe he did and his response was drowned out. The sound reminded me of fireworks sizzling and crackling as they shot into the sky—if there were a thousand of those kinds of fireworks going off at once. It was all I could hear for several moments, and then the mass of tainted *grace* shattered into millions of sparks of light.

I jerked, reaching out and grabbing Zayne's arm. His skin was steady and hot under my hand as my fingers dug in.

"Trin?" Zayne said.

Was this it? The end of the world as we knew it came in a beautiful display of golden light? "What?" I asked as the sparks began to drift downward.

"Your hand." Zayne turned to me, one of his wings brushing across my arm. He folded his hands around mine. "It feels like a chunk of ice."

How my hand felt didn't seem like a huge priority at the moment. Vaguely aware of him rubbing my fingers between his, I struggled to remain standing under the weight of what we were watching. The shining filaments were beautiful, reminding me of fireflies, but the moment they landed— the moment a human was touched by one of them, they'd be corrupted by what was inside Gabriel.

"Your hand isn't warming." Zayne slid his palm over my arm. "Your arm—"

"God did it," Lucifer said, voice ringing with shock. "God actually did it. Look." Lucifer reached out as one of the flakes, mostly white now, drifted toward us. "It's...is this snow?"

I started to ask him how he didn't know what snow looked like, but then realized that he'd been in Hell for...what? Thousands of years? I doubted it snowed in Hell. Or that he could remember what snow looked like.

"It is...snow." Zayne's hands were still on my arm. "Look, Trin. It's snow."

Pulling my gaze from the flurry, I looked down to my arm, to his hands. Little white flakes landed on his skin, evaporating on touch and leaving a glistening speck behind. "Is it contaminated?"

"It doesn't feel evil." Those ultrabright eyes met mine. "Does it feel evil to you?"

I shook my head as the snow continued to land on my arms. "It feels like snow."

"It's not evil," Lucifer said, and I could hear the smile in his voice. "I know evil. It's snow and it's..." He groaned in disgust. "Aw, dammit."

"What?" My heart skipped a beat as I looked over to him.

He stood with his hands on his hips. "It's not contaminated."

"Why do you sound like that's a bad thing?" Zayne demanded.

Better yet, why did Zayne suddenly sound as if he were standing in a tunnel even though he was standing beside me? I looked over at him. His features were fuzzy—well, fuzzier than normal, and I...

"It's full of goodness," Lucifer spat. "It's *pure*, and it's getting all over me. I'm going to need to shower this crap off."

That was good... That was beyond good and beyond what any of us had been too afraid to hope for. God stepped up. He or She or Whatever *stepped up.* Tears filled my eyes, but I...

"I bet you're up there laughing, aren't you?" Lucifer shouted. "Dusting me with the equivalent of a heavenly glitter bomb? Really?"

I stared at the snow as it gathered on my arm. It didn't melt.

"After all I've done for you, this is how You repay me?" Lucifer continued to rage. "I'm going to have to take five showers and I know I won't be able to get the stench of humanity and goodness off me."

Zayne twisted toward me, a laugh in his voice as he said, "We did it, Trin."

We had, but...

I tried to swallow, but my throat felt weird, like it was narrowing. "I don't feel right."

The sound of Zayne's wings snapping back ended in his shout. I didn't know why he yelled my name, but then I was suddenly in his arms and he was above me, his face going in and out focus.

"Trin! What is it?" Zayne wasn't waiting for my answer. His hand swept over my chest and down my stomach. He halted and then yanked up my shirt, swearing. "You're wounded."

"It's just...a punch."

Zayne's hand trembled against my stomach as he cranked his head around. "Lucifer! Stop your bitching and get over here!"

"What?" I asked, or I thought I did. I wasn't sure as I struggled to lift my hand long enough to look down. I saw my stomach, but it looked weird. Like the skin was...like it was turning gray and spreading.

"What is this?" Zayne demanded. "What is happening?"

The blurred face of Lucifer appeared above one of Zayne's wings. His head tilted and then he whipped around, disappearing out of sight.

And my...my head felt too heavy. It fell back, and I was staring beyond Zayne and the tips of his beautiful wings, to the snow that continued to fall. A numbness settled into me. A bone-deep knowing.

"What are you doing?" Zayne yelled at him as he turned me slightly to the side. "Lucifer!"

"I'm looking for—found them." There was a pause. "Damn."

"Damn? Damn what?" Panic crept into Zayne's voice.

Lucifer's voice was closer. "Were you stabbed with this? With one of these angel blades?" he demanded.

A faint golden glow reflected from the spike he held in his hand. "Teller had it," I forced out. "And Gabriel…he only punched me."

"That Warden must've given one to Gabriel, or he always had one," Lucifer said. "He didn't punch you. He nicked you with one of these."

"That…" Zayne trailed off, and then his wings flared out. "*No.* No." He twisted toward me, the arm around me tightening. "Trin. You're going to be fine."

"What happened?" Layla gasped.

"She's fine. I'm going to make sure of it," Zayne said. "You're okay. I just need to find—"

"There's nothing to be found," Lucifer cut him off. "There's nothing to be done."

"There has to be," snapped Roth, and I was glad to hear that the stupid demon prince and Layla were okay.

"It's an angel blade," Lucifer argued. "It's—"

"Don't say it," Zayne growled. "Don't you fucking say it."

Lucifer fell silent, but he didn't need to say what I already knew, what I felt in the sluggish beats of my heart. What had Roth said? Angel blades were deadly. They could kill anything, including another angel.

Including a Trueborn.

We knew this.

"You're going to be okay." Zayne cupped my cheek. I was aware of his hand there, but I couldn't feel it. "You have to be. Okay? I just need you to hang in there. For me. Do you hear me, Trin? I just need you to hold out and I'll figure out a way."

You're already dead.

That's what Gabriel had said after he punched me. Except it hadn't been a punch. He'd known. He'd known then he was going to lose, and he...

And he took me out with him.

That *bastard*.

I'd been willing to die to stop him. That's what I planned before the angels arrived, but now, after winning? I wasn't ready.

But I knew it was too late. Everything in me felt like it was...like it was giving up, shutting down and closing up shop.

I was dying, and I'd always thought dying would be painful, but this was...it was like falling asleep. My eyes fluttered.

"No!" Zayne shook me, startling me. "Don't close your eyes. Don't go to sleep. Look at me. Trinity, please. Look at me. Keep your eyes open. Trin, look at me."

I looked at him. I blinked until his features came into painful focus, and I soaked in every line of his face, every plane and angle. Would I see him again? Panic exploded like a buckshot, but it was too late. "I... I love you." I forced the words out, each one a labor. "I love you."

"I know. I know you do, Trin, and you know that I love you. I'm going to spend eternity telling you that. You'll get tired of hearing it." His voice cracked. "I promise you that. You're not going to leave me. I refuse to let that happen."

But I was, and I couldn't feel his arms around me. A

heartbeat later, I couldn't *see* him. Panic gave way to terror. "Where are you?"

"I'm right here, Trin. I got you. I'm right here. I have you."

He did. He had me. I wasn't alone. Some of the fear eased off. "Don't let...go of me."

"Never," he swore.

"Please."

"Always." He sounded so very far away.

I felt my chest rise, but there was no air. There was no sound. There was no light.

There was just nothing.

And I fell into it.

Gone.

34

"Trinnie, wake up."

I turned my head from the voice, wanting to return to the dream. Or at least I thought I was dreaming, because I'd been in Zayne's arms and he'd been so warm as he held me close to him. And that had to be a dream, because we'd been fighting Gabriel. Lucifer had killed him, and God... God had done something glorious, and I...

"Trinnie," came the voice again. One I realized I recognized. "I'm staring at you. Watching you."

Peanut.

What did I tell him about watching me while I slept?

But that didn't make sense. Peanut hadn't been there, and I couldn't be asleep. Not technically. Maybe figuratively. Semantics didn't really matter right now.

I died.

I freaking died.

Anger pounded through my body. That bastard, psychotic

archangel had actually managed to kill me. I was dead and Zayne was alive—oh my God, *Zayne*. Pressure clamped down on my chest, strangling me. He'd been there, holding me so I wasn't alone, and now he was there and I was... well, I was wherever I was. I was dead.

"Trinity!" Peanut shouted.

My eyes flew open, and a strangled gasp left me. Peanut's freaking transparent face was right *there*, mere inches from mine.

"What the Hell?" I exclaimed, starting to sit up. I pushed my hands down, planting them in...in something soft and dry. Not damp grass.

I blinked several times as Peanut drifted out of the line of my sight. Confusion swirled through me as I realized I was staring up at the muted glow of the Constellation of Zayne.

I was lying in our bed.

The corners of my lips turned down. "Peanut?" I said hoarsely.

"Yes," he answered from wherever he was.

"Am I in our apartment?"

"You are."

What in the what?

Sitting up, I looked around our bedroom. Peanut hovered to the left, in midair, his legs crossed. To the right of me, the bedside lamp was on. The worn, tattered copy of my mother's favorite book sat on the nightstand. I reached over, running my fingers over the soft cover. Was I...was I a ghost? Was that why I was here? That sort of made sense. I sure as Hell wasn't ready to move on, and the recently... departed often returned to places they were comfortable. My heart skipped in my chest—

Wait.

I pressed the same hand against my chest, feeling my heart beat unsteadily. If I died and was now a ghost, would I feel my heartbeat? Would I be able to feel anything?

My head swung toward Peanut.

He waved at me.

"I can feel the bed. I felt the book," I told him, and then thumped my hand off my chest. I winced. That hurt my boob—that actually hurt. Ghosts felt pain? Oh God, if so, how in the Hell did Peanut let himself float through ceiling fans and stuff? "I can feel my heart."

His brows lifted. "I would hope so."

I stared at him. "Can you feel your heart?"

"That's a stupid question."

"How is that a stupid question?" I demanded. "I'm dead. I died, Peanut. I'm superdead, and if I'm a ghost, how can I feel my—"

"You're not a ghost," he cut me off. "You're not dead."

I stared at him.

He stared back at me.

I stared at him some more. Probably for a good full minute before I could even process what he'd just said, and even then, I didn't understand. At all. "How?" I whispered. "How am I not dead?" I looked around the room again, just to make sure it was still the bedroom. It was. "How am I here?"

"Well, it's kind of a convoluted story," he said.

I scrambled to my knees. "Try to make sense of the story, then." Zayne's face suddenly filled my mind, and I started for the edge of the bed. "You know what. It doesn't matter. I need to find Zayne. He has to be—"

"Beside himself?" Peanut suggested. "His heart so broken that he demanded that Lucifer bring you back?"

I froze as my eye shot to where he floated.

"And when Lucifer explained to him that giving life was beyond him, that he is not the keeper of souls, he demanded that Azreal himself answer to him," Peanut continued, but there…there was something a whole lot wrong with his voice, and not just the fact that he'd referred to Grim by his angelic name, which was weird all on its own. It had… strengthened, becoming less *airy*. Gone was the singsongy way he normally spoke.

"Azreal didn't answer, because he knew there was no reason to. There was nothing he could do. You were beyond him."

The tiny hairs all over my body rose. "You're starting to creep me out, Peanut."

His head tilted to the side. "I think you're going to be way more creeped out by the time this conversation is finished."

Skin pimpling, I stood so that the bed separated us. "What's going on?"

It could've just been my wacky eyes, but the window behind him seemed less visible through his head. "You know what people get so wrong about God? That *He* is an absentee father. That He doesn't care for His children, watch over them meticulously, day in and day out. That He doesn't interfere in small ways—ways often and easily overlooked. That random choice to turn left instead of right on the way to work? The unexpected decision to stay home or stay out late? The unplanned trip or phone call, purchase or gift? None of that is random or unknown. That is God, doing what a good parent does. Stepping in when they can and knowing when there is nothing they can do. I never really understood how God could do all of that—be willing to do anything and everything to be near His children and yet be able to walk away." His shoulders seemed to lift in a sigh. "There are always so many rules, Trinity, so many expectations, even for God, and most assuredly for a chief prince."

A shiver skated over my skin. No. There was no way—

Peanut looked over at me, and yep, his face was definitely more *solid*. "You were right, you know? When you said there had to be signs that something had gone terribly wrong with Gabriel. That there had to be signs."

I stepped back, bumping into the wall.

"And there were. You were also right when you said you were a loophole. A weapon that could be snuck past the oath to harm none. At least in the beginning that was all that you were, but then I learned just how and why God could and would do anything for His children." A smile formed. "That sometimes even God bent the rules."

I was completely flattened against the wall, my heart pounding so fast there was no question I was very much alive.

"An archangel cannot remain on Earth and among souls for any real amount of time. There are too many responsibilities and too many consequences. The presence of one would draw too much attention from all manner of things," he said, and the barest white glow started to appear in the center of his chest. "But just like God, I could not walk away from my own creation. My flesh and blood."

The glow from the center of his chest washed across the rest of his body. Heavenly light pulsed an intense white—

the kind of light I knew souls saw before they passed on. It was warm and bearable to look upon, to witness.

Peanut *changed*.

His body lengthened and his shoulders broadened. The mop of brown hair lightened, turning to the color of the sun. His features hardened, shedding the fullness of youth I was familiar with. The old Whitesnake T-shirt turned to a white sleeveless tunic, and the ragged jeans became linen, pearl-hued pants. And his skin...it continuously shifted through the shades of human skin before settling somewhere in between.

"So," he said in that voice that didn't belong to Peanut. "I did what I could to watch over you."

My father, the archangel Michael, stood before me.

"Holy shit," I whispered.

He laughed—he actually laughed, and it was a strange sound, one familiar and yet unknown. It reminded me of Peanut's laugh if that laugh had grown up.

"I am not surprised by that response."

My eyes felt like they were about to pop out of my head. "You... There is..." I shook my head. "Is this real?"

He nodded.

"But where is Peanut?"

Those all-white eyes warmed. I didn't know how that was possible, but it was, because they did. "I am Peanut."

"That's impossible. Peanut was a teenager. He is a teenager, and he died in the '80s—"

"At a Whitesnake concert, after climbing to the top of a speaker tower and then falling to his death?" he finished for me. "Have you ever heard of anything more ridiculous?"

Well, no.

"Let me tell you, humans have found incredibly bizarre ways to die, and there was one who died that way. Except he was older, and the story of his death amused me. It stuck with me for many years."

"The...story of his death...amused you?"

"It did, so I borrowed his death." His head tilted—oh dear God, it tilted in the way it often did when Peanut looked at me. "You should sit down."

I couldn't move. "Peanut wasn't real?"

"Peanut is real," he corrected. "He is, well, a figment of me. A manifestation or projection of me, when I was a... younger, vastly more annoying angel prone to all manner of things."

"Like creeping into the bathroom when Zayne showered?" I screeched like a full-blown pterodactyl.

"When you say it that way, you make it sound perverted."

"Because it is perverted." Oh my God, why would I even have to explain that to anyone, let alone an *archangel*?

"I was curious about the man who I knew would own my daughter's heart. Wasn't like I looked where I shouldn't." He shrugged. "Besides, there is nothing in this world we have not seen a million times before."

"Somehow that makes it all the worse," I murmured.

One side of his lips curled. "It is so human of you to imply that there is a sexual motivation behind literally everything. Newsflash, Trinnie," he said, and every muscle in my body seized. He sounded so much like Peanut. "It's not."

"I think I need to sit down."

"You do."

I didn't. "You would watch me sleep! The way you would talk? The things that came out of your mouth."

"As I said, Peanut is a figment of my youth," he explained. "I was quite obnoxious as a young angel. Ask Lucifer. He can confirm that."

"But all the '80s stuff—"

"The '80s always amused me. The music. The hair." He paused. "The leotards. Very interesting decade that proved, well, you haven't seen it all when you think you have."

Oh God.

Peanut was my father.

My father was Peanut.

I did sit down then, right there, on the floor. "Is it possible that I had, I don't know, a stroke, and that explains all of this?"

"That doesn't even make sense." A moment passed and my *father* peeked around the bed. "Would it be easier for you to see me as Peanut? I can change back into him. I just cannot maintain the projection for very long."

Understanding struck me upside the head. "That's why you were always disappearing! Even back in the community. I just thought you were off doing...ghost things."

"The projection requires my attention. Not a lot, but enough that it can be a distraction. Do you want me to change back to him?"

"No. That would...that would be even weirder, and I don't think I can deal with that."

He nodded and then sat at the foot of the bed. He was silent.

I wasn't. "What about the whole purgatory thing? When you said you were sucked into it?"

"That did happen when Zayne Fell. Not to me, but to those who hadn't moved on." He rested his hands on his knees. "I thought it would be important for you to know the impact of his Fall, even if it was temporary."

Okay. Well, impact known. Not sure what that changed, and for some reason, that seemed like a random, nonsensical thing a parent would try to teach a child.

"You avoided Zayne after he Fell, because he would've known, wouldn't he?"

"He wouldn't have known it was me, but he would've sensed something was not quite as it seemed. That would've been an unnecessary complication."

"And Gena? She isn't a ghost. It was just an excuse for why you couldn't be around." It became clear. "Because of Gabriel being around? Was that why you were...gone more than you were here?"

He nodded.

Another thing struck me. "My mother—"

"She is at peace," he answered quickly. "Happy and comfortable."

My heart was pounding again, and I wasn't even sure if it slowed down. "Do you see her?"

"I do," he said, surprising me. "I like her. She was not chosen at random."

"She wasn't?"

Michael shook his head. "No."

I started to ask more questions about that, and then decided, in that moment, I didn't think I could handle hearing about my mother and father's love affair.

I could only deal with so much.

There was something I needed to ask. "Why has she never visited me?"

"It is the same reason why Zayne's father did not see him

when he was in the Heavens," he said, and I jolted. "Because she knew you would not be able to let her go. You would be stuck, and that pain, that grief and that love and want would've trapped her. She wouldn't do that to you."

A knot formed in my throat. "Does she know how sorry—"

"What happened to her was not your fault. She never thought that. Not for one second, and she would be furious if she knew you believed that."

Tears blurred my eyes. She totally would be furious.

"The actions of others caused her death. You were just a chink in that chain, just like her. It was those who wielded that chain who are at fault. Deep down you know that." His voice softened. "But sometimes no ownership in the end results is worse than the guilt of being the cause."

Ugh.

He sounded so...so wise, and it was weird and wonderful, but mostly weird.

I swiped at the tears. "Why?"

He seemed to know what I was asking. "Because it was the only way I could have any relationship with you. The only way I could know you."

The knot swelled in my throat. "And Zayne?" I asked hoarsely. "You made sure he could Fall so he could be with me."

"It was a small gift I could ensure."

A small gift? A wet laugh left me. "And the stars? That was you."

He nodded.

"And you...you are the reason why I'm alive right now."

"Partly."

I blinked. "Partly?"

"I had help from a certain human with a new lease on life."

"The Crone," I realized.

Michael inclined his head. "The potion she gave you didn't just bring Zayne to you. It bound you to him. Similar to the Protector bond, but stronger. You carry a part of his essence in you. As long as he lives, you live. You are marked."

I pressed tingling fingers to my chest, to where the strange scar had taken shape, right where the light that had come from Zayne had hit me. Suddenly I remembered the look Tony had given the Crone when she told me I needed to draw my own blood.

My wide eyes shot to where Michael sat. "I...I didn't die, then?"

He shook his head. "You were weakened and slipped unconscious while the bond repaired the damage done."

"But I thought an angel blade could kill anything?"

"The bond between you and Zayne supersedes all." He paused. "Well, almost everything. If you were decapitated, then…"

I blinked slowly.

"You have his lifespan, Trinity." Those all-white eyes bore into mine. "You do understand what that means?"

My heart skipped a beat. "I'm… I'm immortal?"

He smiled then, and there was a catch in my chest. There was such familial fondness in the curve of his lips. "You are as immortal as any angelic being is."

"I won't...age?"

He shook his head again. "Most angels stop aging once they reach a certain maturity," he said, which explained why so many of them looked like they were in their late twenties. "But you stopped aging the moment the bond was forged."

All I could do was stare at him, and I did that for probably several minutes as I tried to work my brain through the fact that I would not grow old and break my hips while Zayne remained young and gloriously broken-bone free. Not aging past nineteen meant I would probably be carded for, like, eternity—

Oh my God, like for an actual *eternity*. Or until my head was chopped off, *Highlander*-style, or until Zayne... I wasn't going to even go there. There were far worse things than never looking older than I did now.

Like dying now or by old age, in Zayne's arms— "Wait," I exclaimed, pulling my legs up to my chest to stand. "Do I have two bodies now? The one that was back in that field and this one now?"

A perplexed look settled into Michael's features. "You have the strangest mind. You don't have two bodies."

"Then does Zayne know I'm here?" I asked. "Because I died—or passed out. Whatever. I was with Zayne."

"You were, but I simply willed you here."

"You simply willed me here?" I repeated dumbly. "Like I went poof?"

An eyebrow rose. "Yes."

"Oh my God, Zayne must be really freaking out!"

"Probably." He said this like it was no big deal. That people poofing out of people's arms happened every day.

And the fact that he could just will me from one location to another was another mind-boggling fact. "Is that something all archangels can do?" I asked, thinking if that was the case, then why hadn't Gabriel just willed me to his location?

"You are of my flesh and blood," he said, and I wished he'd stop saying it that way. "That is why."

Made as much sense as any of this did. I scrubbed a hand down my face, over my eyes. *My eyes.* My stomach dropped as I lowered my hand. I was almost afraid to ask, but I had to know. "Will my eyes continue to get worse?"

"Would it change anything if they did?" he asked. "If you'd known that the bond meant an eternity of darkness for you?"

"No." I didn't even need to think about that. "Being blind isn't worse than death. Having this gift of life—of a life longer than I can even comprehend—with Zayne is so much more than being able to see. I can learn to live without my vision." And Zayne would be there to help me. "I can't learn how to come back from the dead."

"Your mind." He shook his head, laughing softly. "The bond stopped your aging. I cannot be a hundred percent sure, as this is not something ever done before, but it may have also stopped the deterioration of your eyes."

"Really?" I whispered, a wave of prickly shock washing over me.

"It's no magic cure. Your vision will not improve, and from what I understand about your particular genetic disorder, there is no guarantee of complete blindness," he said, and he was right. There wasn't. RP often progressed differently for each individual. I was kind of surprised he knew that.

Then it struck me that he did know because Peanut had known everything about my disease.

And he was Peanut.

I might pass out.

"Or it may get worse, Trinity. Your aging has stopped, and

what that does genetically is beyond even me. It is unknown, as are other things, such as your ability to conceive—"

"Let's not talk about that."

He frowned. "Conception is a simple matter of life, Trinity. It's nothing to be embarrassed by. Do you think I'm unaware of your recent scare?"

"Okay. Whoa. Let's just not go there. I don't think my brain could process it." I shuddered, but my brain had already gone there. Grim knew when he spoke to Zayne and I. He'd said that a child between us would be a Trueborn, but that was *before*. I hadn't understood what he meant then, but I did now.

That was before I had taken in a part of Zayne's essence— before the bond. "What am I now?" I asked. "Am I still a Trueborn?"

"You are," he confirmed. "But you are also something else entirely. Something new and without labels. You are, as you've said before, a very unique snowflake."

A shaky laugh left me as I tipped my head back against the wall. I'd said that multiple times to…Peanut. All of this was a lot—a lot of good, but still a mega truck ton of stuff. I looked over at him, throat feeling swollen all over again. "I don't know what to say other than thank you, and that seems inadequate—"

"A thank-you is not necessary. This is not a reward for fulfilling your duty. This was simply the only way I knew how to show you that you are not just a weapon. You are Trinity Marrow. A warrior both mentally and physically, with questionable tastes in food, but spot-on when it comes to television. Except for *Supernatural*. I do not like how they portray me. But you are many things, including my daughter."

Oh God.

Tears crawled up my throat, welling in my eyes. "Don't be like this—like a father."

"I don't understand." Confusion filled his voice.

"It's easier to think of you not caring or just being displeased with everything in general," I blurted out in a rush. "Because then it doesn't seem so unfair that you can't be my father. I'm not missing out. You're not missing out, you know? Because you're going to leave after this, right? You can't stay here. I won't have you."

"No, I cannot stay here."

Tears snuck through, dampening my cheeks. "And Peanut?"

He moved then, kneeling beside me. Carefully, he reached out and brushed the tears away. "I don't think you need Peanut any longer."

But I did.

I'd miss his ridiculous ass, and it didn't matter at the moment that Peanut was Michael.

"That may be hard to accept right now, but deep down, you always knew a day would come when you'd have to say goodbye. You wanted him to go into the light, did you not?"

I nodded.

"This really isn't any different. Peanut did not cease to exist. He will always be there. I will always be here," he said, and my breath caught. "This will not be the last time you see me. I can promise you that."

Swallowing thickly, I nodded again. I got what he was saying. Peanut didn't die. He was Peanut. I understood that. It was just time for me to move on.

"Besides," he said, his warm hand flattening against my

cheek. "You still have a purpose. Both you and Zayne. Sooner than you probably even expect."

I zeroed in on that, sniffling. "W-what do you mean?"

An eyebrow rose. "My brother was very, very bad during his brief sojourn."

"Oh," I whispered, and then stiffened. "Oh, nooo."

Michael nodded.

"Are we going to have to hunt down and kill an Antichrist baby?"

He stilled. "I do not understand how your brain connects point A to point B."

"But—"

"No child, not even the one created by Lucifer, is without hope. He is the child of the people. They will decide what becomes of him."

Hell, that didn't bode well, then.

"There is always hope," he repeated.

"Have you met people?" I asked. "People generally suck."

He smiled. "People are amazing in their ability to change. Some are beyond that, yes, and they will answer for all upon judgment, but most…most can change. Most are already good, but if this child fulfills the destiny of the father, then, well, the great and final war will come."

"Goodie," I murmured.

"Either way, that is a while from now. Decades before the child will have to make a choice. Until then, live your life as bravely and tenaciously as you have so far. Live your life with purpose, my daughter."

35

In a blink of an eye, I was poofed out of the bedroom, but not before my...my father summoned Lucifer to him. Which would've been a really nifty ability when Lucifer had gone missing.

But I wasn't going to be mad about that right now.

Pretty sure my father had his hands full returning Lucifer to his rightful place. I was also sure that was going extraordinarily well considering how the first words out of Lucifer's mouth had been, "So you've come to thank me for saving the Heavens in person. I'm honored."

Lucifer hadn't seemed all that surprised to see me alive. He was all like, "What up?" and then refocused on Michael.

And now I was standing in the middle of the...

"What the Hell?" I whispered, turning around slowly.

I hadn't been sent back to the field, but sent to the... rooftop of the apartment?

My gaze skipped over the softly glowing string lights, the

neatly lined beach chairs and bistro tables. Why had he sent me here? Zayne was nowhere near the apartment rooftop. He was at the field that reeked of sulfur and sickly sweet rot.

I threw up my hands as I turned again, toward the access door. I was going to have to call up a car and have them drop me off...in the middle of nowhere.

Or I could call Zayne. Duh. I reached for my phone and then realized that I hadn't seen my phone since I'd been snatched.

"Dammit." I stomped past a table, barely resisting the urge to pick it up and throw it across the rooftop.

I was superthankful and grateful for everything my father had done, even if some of it was hard to wrap my head around and a wee bit creepy, but seriously? He poofed me to the roof instead of where Zayne was?

I had two options. Either walk my ass back to that field or wait for Zayne in the apartment. Okay. There really weren't two options. Wasn't like I could seriously walk my way back to that field, and Zayne would have to come home eventually. I was just going to go out of my mind waiting for him.

Feeling like I was already going out of my mind with all that was swirling around inside it, I stalked across the rooftop. There was a lot I was going to need to work through, but right now, all I could think about was Zayne. I knew exactly what he had to be going through, because I'd gone through it, and I didn't want him to experience that kind of agony any longer than he needed to. And at least he hadn't vanished in front of me. He had to be in a panic and—

"Trinity?"

I tripped over my feet as my breath caught in my throat. Catching myself, I whipped around.

Across the rooftop, Zayne stood on one of the wide pillars, the wind catching and lifting his hair and the feathers of those glorious wings, revealing the streaks of pulsing, shimmering *grace*. In that moment, I was struck by how much he reminded me of the battle angels that adorned the ceiling of the Great Hall back in the Potomac Highlands. He almost didn't seem real.

"Trinity," he repeated, his voice hoarse but still one of the most beautiful sounds I'd ever heard.

I stumbled forward, my heart thundering. "It's me."

Zayne was so fast I didn't even see him move from the ledge. He was there and then in front of me, and barely a heartbeat later, his arms swept around me. He hauled me to his chest, burying his hand and face in my hair as his wings folded around me.

"It's really you. You're really here." A shudder racked him as I inhaled the wintermint scent of his. "This is real. Not some kind of dream. I'm holding you for real. You're alive."

"I am."

Zayne touched the sides of my face reverently and then slid his fingers down the side of my neck. They stopped at where my pulse beat wildly and then he searched lower, pressing his palm to the center of my chest, over my heart.

Another shudder took him, and he dropped to his knees before me. My heart twisted. The beautiful wings splayed across the tile floor as he grasped my waist and stared up at me.

"You are all I ever wanted, even before I knew what I wanted. It was you. It was always you," he whispered, voice raw. "And I lost you."

"But you didn't." I dropped to my knees in front of him,

cupping his cheeks. His vibrant blue eyes glimmered as they met mine, and my entire chest squeezed when I saw the dampness in them—the panic and grief, the spark of hope, and hardest of all, the fear. I recognized all of that, and I wanted nothing more than to take it all away from him. "This isn't a dream. It's definitely as crazy as one, but it's real. I'm okay. I'm alive. Like really alive apparently, and I love you. I love you so much. I don't say that enough. I know I don't, because I'm weird and awkward, but I love you—"

Zayne's mouth closed over mine in a kiss that washed away all the fear and panic of when I believed I was dying. It swept aside confusion and thoughts alike, leaving no room for anything other than how his lips felt against mine, the taste of him and the depth of what he felt for me. All the fear and grief he'd felt fed that kiss, as did all his love, and that love didn't just overshadow the ugly. It obliterated it, and it amazed me how much a kiss could reveal when it was between two people who loved one another.

And we kissed and kissed, the tears on my cheeks mingling with the ones on his. He ended up sitting back, and somehow I was in his lap, his chest pressed against mine and his wings folded around me. I didn't think we'd ever stop kissing, because there was a joy in it, a sweet relief that we'd both come too close to never experiencing this again too many times. We kissed for an eternity, and it still wouldn't be long enough.

"It's you." The warmth of his breath touched my lips as he rested his forehead against mine, his chest rising and falling heavily. "No one quite gets as many words out in under a few seconds as you do."

"It's a talent," I told him.

His laugh was full of relief. "How is this possible, Trin? You…" His voice roughened. "I was holding you. I could barely feel you breathing, and you couldn't seem to hear me. Then you vanished." His hands slid over my cheeks. "Just gone."

"I'm sorry—"

"God, Trin. Don't apologize. You didn't do anything wrong."

"I know, but I also know what you went through, and I wish you hadn't." I turned my head, kissing the center of his palm. "I would change that if I could."

The bridge of his nose brushed mine. "What happened?"

"My father," I said, touching the curve of his jaw. "It's, uh, it's really out there, but you were right. What he did for you? It was the way he could show he cared, and this…why I didn't die is because of him. The spell the Crone gave me? It did more than bring you to me. It bonded us together. That mark on my chest? It's a bonding mark. Like the Protector bond but in reverse and stronger. Because of it, the angel blade didn't kill me. Just wounded me. I won't age. I won't die unless something happens to you." I pressed a finger to the center of his lower lip. "So, you're kind of stuck with me for, like, eternity? Congrats."

Zayne pulled back enough that our eyes could meet. "Are you…if you're—you wouldn't lie about something like this."

"I wouldn't." I'd never heard Zayne so flustered before.

His eyes were wide. "I… God, Trin. I don't know what to say other than how in the Hell could you even suggest that I was stuck with you?"

I laughed, and the rigidity in my muscles started to lessen.

"Thought my aging wasn't a big deal? You'd love me, broken hips and all?"

"I *would* love you broken hips and all," he said, one hundred percent serious. "I would love you as much as I do now when you were eighty. There was no way I was going to let any of that get in the way of the time I had with you, but there was going to be nothing easy about watching you slowly leave me, day by day, year by year. And when that day came, I would've found my way to you. I would've followed. Nothing would have stopped me."

My throat clogged with emotion. "I know."

His gaze searched mine. "But to not have to worry about that? Dread that day? To know that you will be beside me fifty years from now? A hundred?"

Now was probably not a good time to mention the whole Antichrist thing. Later.

"I almost can't believe this is real. That we're this lucky." His gaze now tracked over my features. "That we have this. A real future where I'm not dreading the day I lose you and you no longer have an obsession with broken hips."

I laughed again, and more tension left me.

He kissed me, quickly and deeply. "I love that sound."

"I can tell," I breathed.

His lips curved into a smile against mine. "I don't even know what to say."

"Well, I haven't told you everything."

"I don't think anything could shock me more." He kissed my cheek.

"Peanut was Michael. Or is my father."

Zayne sat back.

"My father is Peanut," I repeated. "He's been Peanut this

whole time. A figment of his…younger years, or a manifestation. Something extremely bizarre and confusing."

"What?"

I nodded. "You heard me right. It was the only way he could be a part of my life," I told him, exhaling roughly, and then I told him everything my father had told me.

It all sounded just as ridiculous coming out of my mouth.

"Okay. You were right," Zayne said when I finished. "That is… I don't even know what to say."

I snorted.

"But didn't he often walk…in on me while I was showering?" Zayne asked.

I cringed. "He claims it wasn't anything creepy and that he didn't do it half the times he said he did, but yeah, I don't know."

"I'm just not going to think about that."

"Probably for the best."

He smoothed a hand along my cheek, catching the strands of my hair. "What do you think of all of this?" He pressed a small kiss to the corner my lip. "How do you feel?"

"I… God, I don't know. I don't think I've even begun to process any of it," I admitted, toying with the edges of his hair. "Especially how much Michael…my father has done for me. How much I never knew, and here I was, hating on him—hating on him to Peanut. And that makes me feel like a grade-A douche."

"Don't feel like a grade A-douche," he told me, and hearing him say that made me crack a grin. "I think he understands why you felt the way you did. He's your father. He loves you."

"He does," I whispered, blowing out a deep breath as I

lifted my gaze to Zayne. There was a lot going on in my head, but I would have… I would have forever to process through it all. "We defeated Gabriel."

"We did." He kissed the tip of my nose. "We saved the Heavens."

"And God saved mankind."

"I think we also get some credit for that." His lips brushed over my brow. "Lucifer disappeared again."

"That was Michael," I said, wondering if I would ever stop feeling weird calling him my dad or my father. "He's being escorted back to Hell. By the way, how did you know I was here?"

"After Lucifer vanished, Grim showed up." He pressed his lips to my temple. "Told me I would find what I was looking for if I returned home. I knew he had to be talking about you even if I was too afraid to hope."

I rested my forehead to his. "I heard you demanded that Lucifer bring me back and then called for Grim. I hate that you had to go through that."

"What you went through when I died was far worse. Yeah, those minutes felt like an eternity for me, but you had days." He curled his hand around the back of my neck. "But we don't have to worry about that happening again. We're together now."

"Forever."

"Forever," he repeated, kissing me softly.

I smiled. "We need to let the others know I'm okay."

"We will." His hand slid down my spine as his wings opened. "But not right now. I have different priorities that involve you and me, and I do not care how selfish it makes me."

My breath caught as his hand slipped over my hip. "I think I like it when you're selfish."

Zayne stood with me in his arms. "You're going to love it by the time I'm through with you."

And he wasn't wrong.

At all.

In our bedroom, under the glow of the Constellation of Zayne, we didn't just make love to one another. We showed each other as we undressed. It was in every brush of our skin and every teasing, lingering touch. Love shone with each kiss and soft sigh, and it was in full display as our bodies joined together, unable to miss as we moved together, fueled by the knowledge that we had a lifetime—several of them—of this, of love and acceptance, respect and passion. And still, somehow, even that didn't feel like enough time.

It was afterward, while I was sprawled across his chest and one wing was draped over my back, that Zayne asked, "Do you know what will happen with your vision?"

"I don't know. I asked, but he didn't know, either. There's a possibility the death of the cells could've stopped or it will continue. It's a wait and see game."

"Like before."

"Yep."

He continued tracing idle circles along my upper arm. "Either way, you got this."

I grinned. "We got this."

"We do." He stretched his neck and kissed the top of my head. Several moments of silence passed. "Did I ever tell you what Heaven smelled like to me?"

I lifted my head, searching to find his features in the dim light. "No, you didn't."

"Jasmine," he said. "Heaven smelled like jasmine."

It took me a moment—okay, it probably took longer than it should for me to get that, but then I did. "My body wash is jasmine."

"I know," he confirmed. "Heaven smelled like you."

My heart skipped and danced a little jig. "I love you."

We kissed and then we spent the rest of those softly lit hours showing each other once again just how much we loved one another.

"Never did I think I'd be at a cookout with demons," Jada said as she dropped onto the picnic table beside me the next evening. She shook her head. "Hell, I never thought I'd see Wardens and demons hanging out."

We were gathered at Roth and Layla's place, in their backyard by an extravagant pool fitting of a…demonic prince. The thing had a rock waterfall! "And don't forget fallen angel." I knocked my shoulder against hers as my gaze flicked to Zayne. He stood on the patio near the pool, talking with Ty and Roth.

I was shocked to have seen Ty show up and even more surprised when he shook Roth's and then Cayman's hand upon meeting them. And I might've stopped breathing a little when Nicolai arrived with Danika and Dez, who'd brought his wife. The fact that the head of the DC clan would come and bring two females with them was astonishing. Yeah, the two male Wardens didn't indiscriminately hate demons, but that also didn't mean they hung out with them.

And they were doing that now, standing with the others, actually talking and laughing. Jasmine and Danika were sitting on the ledge of the pool, their legs dangling in the water as Cayman enjoyed a volleyball game with Stacey.

Maybe the world did end.

But there was a cause for celebration. Gideon had succeeded in tracking down enough gemstones to disrupt the ley lines. They'd be in our possession by the end of the week.

"It's a new start, it feels like," Jada said. "A new era."

"It really is." I glanced over at Jada. She'd taken everything I had to share with her rather well. Even the Peanut being my dad part. I think she processed all of that better than me, but Jada had always been incredibly pragmatic. "When do you think Ty will be officially assigned to the DC clan? Like are they going to wait till the next Accolade?"

"I wish they wouldn't, but do you really think my father would do anything else?"

I grinned. "Probably not."

"You're going to come visit us, right?"

"Of course. Zayne and I deserve some downtime, and we're going to take it as soon as we deal with the portal." I watched Zayne knock the beach ball back to Cayman.

We were going to see all the places we'd talked about. Rome. Edinburgh. The Hollywood sign. Everywhere. And then we would come back here. As of right now, we planned on staying in the area, especially since the Antichrist was around here, somewhere, but maybe we'd leave. We weren't sure yet, and there was something exciting about having the future so unplanned. It wouldn't always be easy. I knew that. We had to step back in that school and disrupt the portal. There were the ghosts and Shadow People, and we still needed to figure out how to break the angelic wards holding them there. There'd be more demons who didn't want to follow the rules and more stupid humans who would some-how do worse than any demonic force could ever carry out. Then there was the Antichrist to possibly deal with and the fact that I could very well still go blind. Things wouldn't always be safe or fun. There would be risks and nights nothing like this one, but we had each other. We had our friends.

And that was all that mattered.

Sometime later, flames crackled from the firepit. Actual s'mores were being made, and I was in Zayne's arms, the back of my head resting against his chest as I looked up at the dark sky.

There were no stars I could see, but that was okay. I had the Constellation of Zayne to look upon every night. I would always remember how beautiful the sea of dazzling, twinkling lights was. That memory would never fade. It would always be there when I looked up at the sky. I would always see the stars no matter what, because of him.

Peanut.

My father.

Thank you, Dad. I mouthed the words, giving them no sound, but I think he heard them, anyway.

Thank you.

★ ★ ★ ★ ★

Acknowledgments

Coming to the end of a series is always a bittersweet moment, especially this one. Trinity will always hold a special place in my heart and I hope, through her, you've learned a little more about what it's like to live with retinitis pigmentosa (RP).

Thank you to my agent, Kevan Lyon, editors Natashya Wilson and Melissa Frain, to the amazing team at Inkyard Press and to my assistant, Stephanie Brown, for her hard work and support. A big thank-you to Jen Fisher, Malissa Coy, Stacey Morgan, Lesa, Jillan Stein, Liz Berry, JR Ward, Laura Kaye, Andrea Joan, Sarah Maas, Brigid Kemmerer, KA Tucker, Tijan, Vonetta Young, Mona Awad, Kayleigh Gore, Krista and Valerie (for their undying love of Zayne) and many more who have helped keep me sane and laughing. Thank you to the ARC team for your support and honest reviews, and a big thank-you to JLAnders for being the best reader group an author can have.

None of this would be possible without you, the reader. Thank you.